Spinifex and Sand

David Carnegie

Spinifex and Sand

A Narrative of Five Years' Pioneering and Exploration in Western Australia by the Hon. David W. Carnegie (1871–1900)

David W. Carnegie
To my mother

Introduction

"An honest tale speeds best, being plainly told."   The following pages profess to be no more than a faithful narrative of five years spent on the goldfields and in the far interior of Western Australia. Any one looking for stirring adventures, hairbreadth escapes from wild animals and men, will be disappointed. In the Australian Bush the traveller has only Nature to war against—over him hangs always the chance of death from thirst, and sometimes from the attacks of hostile aboriginals; he has no spice of adventure, no record heads of rare game, no exciting escapades with dangerous beasts, to spur him on; no beautiful scenery, broad lakes, or winding rivers to make life pleasant for him. The unbroken monotony of an arid, uninteresting country has to be faced. Nature everywhere demands his toil. Unless he has within him impulses that give him courage to go on, he will soon return; for he will find nothing in his surroundings to act as an incentive to tempt him further.

I trust my readers will be able to glean a little knowledge of the hardships and dangers that beset the paths of Australian pioneers, and will learn something of the trials and difficulties encountered by a prospector, recognising that he is often inspired by some higher feeling than the mere "lust of gold."

Wherever possible, I have endeavoured to add interest to my own experiences by recounting those of other travellers; and, by studying the few books that touch upon such matters to explain any points in connection with the aboriginals that from my own knowledge I am unable to do. I owe several interesting details to the "Report on the Work of the Horn Scientific Expedition to Central Australia," and to "Ethnological Studies among the North-West Central Queensland Aboriginals," by Walter E. Roth. For the identification of the few geological specimens brought in by me, I am indebted to the Government Geologist of the Mines Department, Perth, W.A., and to Mr. W. Botting Hemsley, through the courtesy of the Director of the Royal Gardens, Kew, for the identification of the plants.

I also owe many thanks to my friend Mr. J. F. Cornish, who has taken so much trouble in correcting the proofs of my MSS.

Part I: Early Days in Coolgardie

Chapter I: Early Days in the Colony

In the month of September, 1892, Lord Percy Douglas (now Lord Douglas of Hawick) and I, found ourselves steaming into King George's Sound — that magnificent harbour on the south-west coast of Western Australia — building castles in the air, discussing our prospects, and making rapid and vast imaginary fortunes in the gold-mines of that newly-discovered land of Ophir. Coolgardie, a district then unnamed, had been discovered, and Arthur Bayley, a persevering and lucky prospector, had returned to civilised parts from the "bush," his packhorses loaded with golden specimens from the famous mine which bears his name. I suppose the fortunate find of Bayley and his mate, Ford, has turned the course of events in the lives of many tens of thousands of people, and yet, as he jogged along the track from Gnarlbine Rock to Southern Cross, I daresay his thoughts reverted to his own life, and the good time before him, rather than to moralising on the probable effect of his discovery on others.

We spent as little time as possible at Albany, or, I should say, made our stay as short as was permitted, for in those days the convenience of the passenger was thought little of, in comparison with the encouragement of local industries, so that mails and travellers alike were forced to remain at least one night in Albany by the arrangement of the train service, greatly to the benefit of the hotel-keepers.

We were somewhat surprised to see the landlord's daughters waiting at table. They were such tremendously smart and icy young ladies that at first we were likely to mistake them for guests; and even when sure of their identity we were too nervous to ask for anything so vulgar as a pot of beer, or to expect them to change our plates.

Between Albany and Perth the country is not at all interesting being for the most part flat, scrubby, and sandy, though here and there are rich farming and agricultural districts. Arrived at Perth we found ourselves a source of great interest to the inhabitants, inasmuch as we announced our intention of making our way to the goldfields, while we had neither the means nor apparently the capability of getting there. Though treated with great hospitality, we found it almost impossible to get any information or assistance, all our inquiries being answered by some scoffing remark, such as, "Oh, you'll never get there!"

We attended a rather remarkable dinner — given in honour of the Boot, Shoe, Harness, and Leather trade, at the invitation of a fellow-countryman in the trade, and enjoyed ourselves immensely; speech-making and toast-drinking being carried out in the extensive style so customary in the West. Picture our surprise on receiving a bill for 10s. 6d. next morning! Our friend of the dinner, kindly put at our disposal a hansom cab which he owned, but this luxury we declined with thanks, fearing a repetition of his "bill-by-invitation."

Jarrah forest, Western Australia

Owing to the extreme kindness of Mr. Robert Smith we were at last enabled to get under way for the scene of the "rush." Disregarding the many offers of men willing to guide us along a self-evident track, we started with one riding and one packhorse each. These and the contents of the pack-bags represented all our worldly possessions, but in this we might count ourselves lucky, for many hundreds had to carry their belongings on their backs — "humping their bluey," as the expression is.

Our road lay through Northam and the several small farms and settlements which extend some distance eastward. Very few used this track, the more popular and direct route being through York and thence along the telegraph line to Southern Cross; and indeed we did pass through York, which thriving little town we left at dusk, and, carrying out our directions, rode along the telegraph line. Unfortunately we had not been told that the line split up, one branch going to Northam and the other to Southern Cross; as often happens in such cases, we took the wrong branch and travelled well into the night before finding any habitation at which we could get food and water.

The owner of the house where we finally stopped did not look upon our visit with pleasure, as we had literally to break into the house before we could attract any attention. Finding we were not burglars, and having relieved himself by most vigorous and pictorial language (in the use of which the teamsters and small farmers are almost without rivals) the owner showed us his well, and did what he could to make us comfortable. I shall never forget the great hospitality here along this road, though no doubt as time went on the settlers could not afford to house hungry travellers free of cost, and probably made a fair amount of money by selling provisions and horse-feed to the hundreds of gold-fever patients who were continually passing.

Southern Cross, which came into existence about the year '90, was a pretty busy place, being the last outpost of civilisation at the time of our first acquaintance with it. The now familiar corrugated-iron-built town, with its streets inches deep in dust under a blazing sun, its incessant swarms of flies, the clashing of the "stamps" on the mines, and the general "never-

never" appearance of the place, impressed us with feelings the reverse of pleasant. The building that struck me most was the bank — a small iron shanty with a hession partition dividing it into office and living room, the latter a hopeless chaos of cards, candle ends, whiskey bottles, blankets, safe keys, gold specimens, and cooking utensils. The bank manager had evidently been entertaining a little party of friends the previous night, and though its hours had passed, and a new day had dawned, the party still continued. Since that time it has been my lot to witness more than one such evening of festivity!

On leaving Southern Cross we travelled with another company of adventurers, one of whom, Mr. Davies, an old Queensland squatter, was our partner in several subsequent undertakings.

The monotony of the flat timber-clad country was occasionally relieved by the occurrence of large isolated hills of bare granite. But for these the road, except for camels, could never have been kept open; for they represented our sources of water supply. On the surface of the rocks numerous holes and indentations are found, which after rain, hold water, and besides these, around the foot of the outcrops, "soaks," or shallow wells, are to be found.

What scenes of bitter quarrels these watering-places have witnessed! The selfish striving, each to help himself, the awful sufferings of man and beast, horses and camels mad with thirst, and men cursing the country and themselves, for wasting their lives and strength in it; but they have witnessed many an act of kindness and self-denial too.

Where the now prosperous and busy town of Coolgardie stands, with its stone and brick buildings, banks, hotels, and streets of shops, offices, and dwelling-houses, with a population of some 15,000, at the time of which I write there stood an open forest of eucalyptus dotted here and there with the white tents and camps of diggers. A part of the timber had already been cleared to admit of "dry-blowing" operations — a process adopted for the separation of gold from alluvial soil in the waterless parts of Australia.

Desperate hard work this, with the thermometer at 100 degrees in the shade, with the "dishes" so hot that they had often to be put aside to cool, with clouds of choking dust, a burning throat, and water at a shilling to half a crown a gallon! Right enough for the lucky ones "on gold," and for them not a life of ease! The poor devil with neither money nor luck, who looked into each dishful of dirt for the wherewithal to live, and found it not, was indeed scarcely to be envied.

Water at this time was carted by horse-teams in waggons with large tanks on board, or by camel caravans, from a distance of thirty-six miles, drawn from a well near a large granite rock. The supply was daily failing, and washing was out of the question; enough to drink was all one thought of; two lines of eager men on either side of the track could daily be seen waiting for these water-carts. What a wild rush ensued when they were sighted! In a moment they were surrounded and taken by storm, men swarming on to them like an army of ants. As a rule, eager as we were for water, a sort of order prevailed, and every man got his gallon water-bag filled until the supply was exhausted. And generally the owner of the water received due payment.

About Christmas time the water famine was at its height. Notices were posted by order of the Warden, proclaiming that the road to or from Coolgardie would soon be closed, as all wells were failing, and advising men to go down in small parties, and not to rush the waters in a great crowd. This advice was not taken, and daily scores of men left the "field," and many were hard put to it to reach Southern Cross. It was a cruel sight in those thirsty days to see the poor horses wandering about, mere walking skeletons, deserted by their owners, for strangers were both unable to give them water, and afraid to put them out of their misery lest damages should be claimed against them. How long our own supplies would last was eagerly discussed, as we gathered round the butcher's shop, the great meeting-place, to which, in the evenings, most of the camp would come to talk over the affairs of the day.

Postmaster, as well as butcher and storekeeper, was Mr. Benstead, a kind-hearted, hard-working man, and a good friend to us in our early struggles. What a wonderful post-office it was too! A proper match for the so-called coach that brought the mails. A very dilapidated buckboard-buggy drawn by equally dilapidated horses, used to do the journey from the Southern Cross to the new fields very nearly as quickly as a loaded waggon with eight or ten horses! The mail-coach used to carry not only letters, papers, and gold on the return journey, but passengers, who served the useful purposes of dragging the carriage through the sand and dust when the horses collapsed, of hunting up the team in the mornings, and of lightening the load by walking. For this exceedingly comfortable journey they had the pleasure of paying at least five pounds. It was no uncommon sight at some tank or rock on the road, to see the mail-coach standing alone in its glory, deserted by driver and passengers alike. Of these some would be horse-hunting, and the rest tramping ahead in hope of being caught up by the coach. There would often be on board many hundred pounds' worth of gold, sent down by the diggers to be banked, or forwarded to their families; yet no instance of robbing the mail occurred. The sort of gentry from whom bushrangers and thieves are made, had not yet found their way to the rush.

General store and Post-office, Coolgardie, 1892

Many banks were failing at that time, and men anxiously awaited the arrival of news. The teamsters, with their heavy drays, would be eagerly questioned as to where they had passed Her Majesty's mail, and as to the probability of its arrival within the next week or so! The distribution of letters did not follow this happy event with great rapidity. Volunteers had to be called in to sort the delivery, the papers were thrown into a heap in the road, and all anxious for news were politely requested to help themselves. Several illustrated periodicals were regularly sent me from home, as I learnt afterwards, but I never had the luck to drop across my own paper!

On mail day, the date of which was most uncertain as the coach journeys soon overlapped, there was always a lengthy, well-attended "roll-up" at the Store. Here we first made acquaintance with Messrs. Browne and Lyon, then negotiating for the purchase of Bayley's fabulous mine of gold. No account of the richness of this claim at that time could be too extravagant to be true; for surely such a solid mass of gold was never seen before, as met the eye in the surface workings.

Messrs. Browne and Lyon had at their camp a small black-boy whom they tried in vain to tame. He stood a good deal of misplaced kindness, and even wore clothes without complaint; but he could not bear having his hair cut, and so ran away to the bush. He belonged to the wandering tribe that daily visited the camp — a tribe of wretched famine-stricken "blacks," whose natural hideousness and filthy appearance were intensified by the dirty rags with which they made shift to cover their bodies. I should never have conceived it possible that such living skeletons could exist. Without begging from the diggers I fail to see how they could have lived, for not a living thing was to be found in the bush, save an occasional iguana and "bardies*", and, as I have said, all known waters within available distance of Coolgardie were dry, or nearly so.

Benstead had managed to bring up a few sheep from the coast, which the "gins," or women, used to tend. The native camp was near the slaughter-yard, and it used to be an interesting and charming sight to see these wild children of the wilderness, fighting with their mongrel dogs for the possession of the offal thrown away by the butcher. If successful in gaining this prize they were not long in disposing of it, cooking evidently being considered a waste of time. A famished "black-fellow" after a heavy meal used to remind me of pictures of the boa-constrictor who has swallowed an ox, and is resting in satisfied peace to gorge.

The appeal of "Gib it damper" or "Gib it gabbi" (water), was seldom made in vain, and hardly a day passed but what one was visited by these silent, starving shadows. In appreciation no doubt of the kindness shown them, some of the tribe volunteered to find "gabbi" for the white-fellow in the roots of a certain gum-tree. Their offer was accepted, and soon a band of unhappy-looking miners was seen returning. In their hands they carried short pieces of the root, which they sucked vigorously; some got a little moisture, and some did not, but however unequal their success in this respect they were all alike in another, for every man vomited freely. This means of obtaining a water supply never became popular. No doubt a little moisture can be coaxed from the roots of certain gums, but it would seem that it needs the stomach of a black-fellow to derive any benefit from it.

Though I cannot say that I studied the manners and customs of the aboriginals at that time, the description, none the worse for being old, given to savages of another land would fit them admirably — "Manners none, customs beastly."

* "Bardies" are large white grubs — three or four inches long — which the natives dig out from the roots of a certain shrub. When baked on wood-ashes they are said to be excellent eating. The natives, however, prefer them raw, and, having twisted off the heads, eat them with evident relish.

Part I: Early Days in Coolgardie

Chapter II: "Hard Up"

During that drought-stricken Christmas-time my mate was down at the "Cross," trying to carry through some business by which our coffers might be replenished; for work how we would on alluvial or quartz reefs, no gold could we find. That we worked with a will, the remark made to me by an old fossicker will go to show. After watching me "belting away" at a solid mass of quartz for some time without speaking, "Which," said he, "is the hammer-headed end of your pick?" Then shaking his head, "Ah! I could guess you were a Scotchman — brute force and blind ignorance!" He then proceeded to show me how to do twice the amount of work at half the expenditure of labour. I never remember a real digger who was not ready to help one, both with advice and in practice, and I never experienced that "greening" of new chums which is a prominent feature of most novels that deal with Australian life.

In the absence of Lord Douglas, an old horse-artilleryman, Richardson by name, was my usual comrade. A splendid fellow he was too, and one of the few to be rewarded for his dogged perseverance and work. In a pitiable state the poor man was when first we met, half dead from dysentery, camped all alone under a sheet of coarse calico. Emaciated from sickness, he was unable to follow his horses, which had wandered in search of food and water, though they constituted his only earthly possession. How he, and many another I could mention, survived, I cannot think. But if a man declines to die, and fights for life, he is hard to kill!

Amongst the prospectors it was customary for one mate to look after the horses, and pack water to the others who worked. These men, of course, knew several sources unknown to the general public. It was from one of them that we learnt of the existence of a small soak some thirteen miles from Coolgardie. Seeing no hope of rain, and no prospect of being able to stop longer at Coolgardie, Mr. Davies, who camped near us, and I, decided to make our way to this soak, and wait for better or worse times. Taking the only horse which remained to us, and what few provisions we had, we changed our residence from the dust-swept flats of Coolgardie to the silent bush, where we set up a little hut of boughs, and awaited the course of events. Sheltered from the sun's burning rays by our house, so low that it could only be entered on hands and knees, for we had neither time nor strength to build a spacious structure, and buoyed up by the entrancement of reading "The Adventures of a Lady's Maid," kindly lent by a fellow-digger, we did our best to spend a "Happy Christmas."

Somehow, the climate and surroundings seemed singularly inappropriate; dust could not be transformed, even in imagination, into snow, nor heat into frost, any more easily than we could turn dried apples into roast beef and plum-pudding. Excellent food as dried fruit is, yet it is apt to become monotonous when it must do duty for breakfast, dinner, and tea! Such was our scanty fare; nevertheless we managed to keen up the appearance of being quite festive and happy.

Having spread the table — that is, swept the floor clear of ants and other homely insects — and laid out the feast, I rose to my knees and proposed the health of my old friend and comrade Mr. Davies, wished him the compliments of the season, and expressed a hope that we should never spend a worse Christmas. The toast was received with cheers and honoured in weak tea, brewed from the re-dried leaves of our last night's meal. He suitably replied, and cordially endorsed my last sentiment. After duly honouring the toasts of "The Ladies," "Absent Friends," and others befitting the occasion, we fell to on the frugal feast.

For the benefit of thrifty housewives, as well as those whom poverty has stricken, I respectfully recommend the following recipe. For dried apples: Take a handful, chew slightly, swallow, fill up with warm water and wait. Before long a feeling both grateful and comforting, as having dined not wisely but too heavily, will steal over you. Repeat the dose for luncheon and tea.

One or two other men were camped near us, and I have no doubt would have willingly added to our slender store had they known to what short commons we were reduced. Our discomforts were soon over, however, for Lord Douglas hearing that I was in a starving condition, hastened from the "Cross," not heeding the terrible accounts of the track, bringing with him a supply of the staple food of the country, "Tinned Dog" — as canned provisions are designated.

Wandering on from our little rock of refuge, we landed at the Twenty-five Mile, where lately a rich reef had been found. We pegged out a claim on which we worked, camped under the shade of a "Kurrajong" tree, close above a large granite rock on which we depended for our water; and here we spent several months busy on our reef, during which time Lord Douglas went home to England, with financial schemes in his head, leaving Mr. Davies and myself to hold the property and work as well as we could manage and I fancy that for a couple of amateurs we did a considerable amount of development.

Here we lived almost alone, with the exception of another small party working the adjoining mine, occasionally visited by a prospector with horses to water. Though glad of their company, it was not with unmixed feelings that we viewed their arrival, for it took us all our time to get sufficient water for ourselves. I well remember one occasion on which, after a slight shower of rain, we, having no tank, scooped up the water we could from the shallow holes, even using a sponge, such was our eagerness not to waste a single drop; the water thus collected was emptied into a large rock-hole, which we covered with flat stones. We then went to our daily work on the reef, congratulating ourselves on the nice little "plant" of water. Imagine our disgust, on returning in the evening, at finding a mob of thirsty packhorses being watered from our precious supply! There was nothing to be done but to pretend we liked it. The water being on the rock was of course free to all.

How I used to envy those horsemen, and longed for the time when I could afford horses or camels of my own, to go away back into the bush and just see what was there. Many a day I spent poring over the map of the Colony, longing and longing to push out into the vast blank spaces of the unknown. Even at that time I planned out the expedition which at last I was enabled to undertake, though all was very visionary, and I could hardly conceive how I should ever manage to find the necessary ways and means.

Nearly every week I would ride into Coolgardie for stores, and walk out again leading the loaded packhorse, our faithful little chestnut "brumby," i.e., half-wild pony, of which there are large herds running in the bush near the settled parts of the coast. A splendid little fellow this, a true type of his breed, fit for any amount of work and hardship. As often as not he would do his journey into Coolgardie (twenty-five miles), be tied up all night without a feed or drink — or as long as I had to spend there on business — and return again loaded next morning. Chaff and oats were then almost unprocurable, and however kind-hearted he might be, a poor man could hardly afford a shilling a gallon to water his horse. On these occasions I made my quarters at Bayley's mine, where a good solid meal and the pleasant company of Messrs. Browne and Lyon always awaited me. Several times in their generosity these good fellows spared a gallon or two of precious water for the old pony.

They have a funny custom in the West of naming horses after their owners — thus the chestnut is known to this day as "Little Carnegie." Sometimes they are named after the men from whom they are bought. This practice, when coach-horses are concerned, has its laughable side, and passengers unacquainted with the custom may be astonished to hear all sorts of oaths and curses, or words of entreaty and encouragement, addressed to some well-known name — and they might be excused for thinking the driver's mind was a little unhinged, or that in his troubles and vexations he was calling on some prominent citizen, in the same way that knights of old invoked their saints.

Thus, our peaceful life at the "Twenty-five" passed on, relieved sometimes by the arrival of horsemen and others in search of water. Amongst our occasional visitors was a well-known gentleman, bearing the proud title of "The biggest liar in Australia." How far he deserved the distinction I should hesitate to say, for men prone to exaggerate are not uncommon in the bush. Sometimes, however, they must have the melancholy satisfaction of knowing that they are disbelieved, when they really do happen to tell the truth. A story of my friend's, which was received with incredulous laughter, will exemplify this.

This was one of his experiences in Central Australia. He was perishing from thirst, and, at the last gasp, he came to a clay-pan which, to his despair, was quite dry and baked hard by the sun. He gave up all hope; not so his black-boy, who, after examining the surface of the hard clay, started to dig vigorously, shouting, "No more tumble down, plenty water here!" Struggling to the side of his boy, he found that he had unearthed a large frog blown out with water, with which they relieved their thirst. Subsequent digging disclosed more frogs, from all of which so great a supply of water was squeezed that not only he and his boy, but the horses also were saved from a terrible death!

This story was received with laughter and jeers, and cries of "Next please!" But to show that it had foundations of truth I may quote an extract from *The Horn Scientific Expedition to Central Australia* (part i. p. 21), in which we read the following:—

... The most interesting animal is the Burrowing or Waterholding Frog, (Chiroleptes platycephalus). As the pools dry up it fills itself out with water, which in some way passes through the walls of the alimentary canal, filling up the body cavity, and swelling the animal out until it looks like a small orange. In this condition it occupies a cavity just big enough for the body, and simply goes to sleep. When, with the aid of a native, we cut it out of its hiding-place, the animal at first remained perfectly still, with its lower eyelids completely drawn over the eyes, giving it the appearance of being blind, which indeed the black assured us that it was.... Most travellers cannot fail to have noticed how clay-pans recently filled by rain, even after a prolonged drought, swarm with tadpoles and full-grown frogs and numberless water insects, the presence of which must only be explained by the ability of the frog to store his supply in his own body, and the fact that the eggs of the insects require moisture before they can hatch out.

Many a laugh we had round the camp-fire at night, and many are the yarns that were spun. Few, however, were of sufficient interest to live in my memory, and I fear that most of them would lose their points in becoming fit for publication. "Gold," naturally, was the chief topic of conversation, especially amongst the older diggers, who love to tell one in detail how many ounces they got in one place and how many in another, until one feels that surely they must be either millionaires or liars. New rushes, and supposed new rushes, were eagerly discussed; men were often passing and repassing our rock, looking for somebody who was "on gold" — for the majority of prospectors seldom push out for themselves, but prefer following up some man or party supposed to have "struck it rich."

The rumours of a new find so long bandied about at length came true. Billy Frost had found a thousand! two thousand!! three thousand ounces!!! — who knew or cared? — on the margin of a large salt lake some ninety miles north of Coolgardie. Frost has since told me that about twelve ounces of gold was all he found. And, after all, there is not much difference between twelve and three thousand — that is on a mining field. Before long the solitude of our camp was disturbed by the constant passing of travellers to and from this newly discovered "Ninety Mile" — so named from its distance from Coolgardie.

As a fact, this mining camp (now known as the town of Goongarr) is only sixty odd miles from the capital, measured by survey, but in early days, distances were reckoned by rate of travel, and roads and tracks twisted and turned in a most distressing manner, sometimes deviating for water, but more often because the first maker of the track had been riding along carelessly, every now and then turning sharp back to his proper course. Subsequent horse or camel men, having only a vague knowledge of the direction of their destination, would be bound to follow the first tracks; after these would come light buggies, spring-carts, drays, and heavy waggons, until finally a deeply rutted and well-worn serpentine road through the forest or scrub was formed, to be straightened in course of time, as observant travellers cut off corners, and later by Government surveyors and road-makers.

Prospectors were gradually "poking out," gold being found in all directions in greater or less degree; but it was not until June, 1893, that any find was made of more than passing interest. Curiously, this great goldfield of Hannan's (now called Kalgoorlie) was found by the veriest chance. Patrick Hannan, like many others, had joined in a wild-goose chase to locate a supposed rush at Mount Yule — a mountain the height and importance of which may be judged from the fact that no one was able to find it! On going out one morning to hunt up his horses, he chanced on a nugget of gold. In the course of five years this little nugget has transformed the silent bush into a populous town of 2,000 inhabitants, with its churches, clubs, hotels, and streets of offices and shops, surrounded by rich mines, and reminded of the cause of its existence by the ceaseless crashing of mills and stamps, grinding out gold at the rate of nearly 80,000 oz. per mouth.

Arriving one Sunday morning from our camp at the "Twenty-five," I was astonished to find Coolgardie almost deserted, not even the usual "Sunday School" going on. Now I am sorry to disappoint my readers who are not conversant with miners' slang, but they must not picture rows of good little children sitting in the shade of the gum-trees, to whom some kind-hearted digger is expounding the Scriptures. No indeed! The miners' school is neither more nor less than a largely attended game of pitch-and-toss, at which sometimes hundreds of pounds in gold or notes change hands. I remember one old man who had only one shilling between him and the grave, so he told me. He could not decide whether to invest his last coin in a gallon of water or in the "heading-school." He chose the latter and lost... subsequently I saw him lying peacefully drunk under a tree! I doubt if his intention had been suicide, but had it been he could hardly have chosen a more deadly weapon than the whiskey of those days.

The "rush to Hannan's" had depopulated Coolgardie and the next day saw Davies and myself amongst an eager train of travellers bound for the new site of fortune. "Little Carnegie" was harnessed to a small cart, which carried our provisions and tools. The commissariat department was easily attended to, as nothing was obtainable but biscuits and tinned soup. It was now mid-winter, and nights were often bitterly cold. Without tent or fly, and with hardly a blanket between us, we used to lie shivering at night.

A slight rain had fallen, insufficient to leave much water about, and yet enough to so moisten the soil as to make dry-blowing impossible in the ordinary way. Fires had to be built and kept going all night, piled up on heaps of alluvial soil dug out during the day. In the morning these heaps would be dry enough to treat, and ashes and earth were dry-blown together — the pleasures of the ordinary process being intensified by the addition of clouds of ashes.

A strange appearance these fires had, dotted through the brush, lighting up now a tent, now a water-cart, now a camp of fortunate ones lying cosily under their canvas roof, now a set of poor devils with hardly a rag to their backs. Oh glorious uncertainty of mining! One of these very poor devils that I have in my mind has now a considerable fortune, with rooms in a fashionable quarter of London, and in frock-coat and tall hat "swells" it with the best!

How quickly men change to be sure! A man who at one time would "steal the shirt off a dead black-fellow," in a few short months is complaining of the taste of his wine or the fit of his patent-leather boots. Dame Fortune was good to some, but to us, like many others, she turned a deaf ear, and after many weeks' toil we had to give up the battle, for neither food, money, nor gold had we. All I possessed was the pony, and from that old friend I could not part. The fruits of our labours, or I should say my share in them, I sent home in a letter, and the few pin's-heads of gold so sent did not necessitate any extra postage. Weary and toil-worn we returned to Coolgardie, and the partners of some rather remarkable experiences split company, and went each his own way.

It is several years since I have seen Mr. Davies; but I believe Fortune's wheel turned round for him at length, and that now he enjoys the rest that his years and toils entitle him to. I have many kindly recollections of our camping days together, and of the numerous yarns my mate used to spin of his palmy days as a Queensland squatter.

Part I: Early Days in Coolgardie

Chapter III: A Miner on Bayley's

Returned from the rush, I made my way to Bayley's to seek employment for my pony and his master. Nor did I seek in vain, for I was duly entered on the pay-sheet as "surface hand" at 3 pounds 10 shillings per week, with water at the rate of one gallon per day. Here I first made the acquaintance of Godfrey Massie, a cousin of the Brownes, who, like me, had been forced by want of luck to work for wages, and who, by the way, had carried his "swag" on his back from York to the goldfields, a distance of nearly 300 miles. He and I were the first amateurs to get a job on the great Reward Claim, though subsequently it became a regular harbour of refuge for young men crowded out from the banks and offices of Sydney and Melbourne. Nothing but a fabulously rich mine could have stood the tinkering of so many unprofessional miners. It speaks well for the kindness of heart of those at the head of the management of the mine that they were willing to trust the unearthing of so much treasure to the hands of boys unused to manual work, or to work of any kind in a great many cases.

How rich the mine was, may be judged from the fact that for the first few months the enormous production of gold from it was due to the labours of three of the shareholders, assisted by only two other men. The following letter from Mr. Everard Browne to Lord Douglas gives some idea of what the yield was at the time that I went there to work:—

I am just taking 4,200 oz, over to Melbourne from our reef (Bayley's). This makes 10,000 oz. we have brought down from our reef without a battery, or machinery equal to treating 200 lbs. of stone per day; that is a bit of a record for you! We have got water in our shaft at 137 feet, enough to run a battery, and we shall have one on the ground in three months' time or under, Egan dollied out 1,000 oz, in a little over two months, before I came down, from his reef; and Cashman dollied 700 oz. out of his in about three weeks and had one stone 10 lbs. weight with 9 lbs. of gold in it, so we are not the only successful reefers since you left. I hope you will soon be with us again. If you are speaking about this 10,000 oz. we have taken out of our reef in six months, remember that Bayley and Ford dollied out 2,500 oz. for themselves before they handed it over to us on February 27th last, so that actually 12,500 oz. have been taken out of the claim, without a battery, in under nine months. The shoot of gold is now proved over 100 feet long on the course of the reef, and we were down 52 feet in our shaft on the reef, with as good gold as ever at the bottom. The other shaft, which we have got water in, is in the country (a downright shaft). We expect to meet the reef in it at 170 feet. Besides Massie, myself, and Tom Cue, there were not then many employed, and really we used to have rather an enjoyable time than otherwise. Working regular hours, eight hours on and sixteen off, sometimes on the surface, sometimes below, with hammer and drill, or pick and shovel, always amongst glittering gold, was by no means unpleasant. It would certainly have been better still had we been able to keep what we found, but the next best thing to being successful is to see those one is fond of, pile up their banking account; and I have had few better friends than the resident shareholders on Bayley's Reward.

What good fellows, too, were the professional miners, always ready to help one and make the time pass pleasantly. Big Jim Breen was my mate for some time, and many a pleasant talk and smoke (Smoke, O! is a recognised rest from work at intervals during a miner's shift) we have had at the bottom of a shaft, thirty to fifty feet from the surface! I really think that having to get out of a nice warm bed or tent for night shift, viz., from midnight to 8 a.m., was the most unpleasant part of my life as a miner.

The first hotel at Coolgardie

As recreation we used to play occasional games of cricket on a very hard and uneven pitch, and for social entertainments had frequent sing-songs and "buck dances" — that is, dances in which there were no ladies to take part — at Faahan's Club Hotel in the town, some one and a half miles distant. "Hotel" was rather too high-class a name, for it was by no means an imposing structure, hessian and corrugated iron taking the place of the bricks and slates of a more civilised building. The addition of a weather-board front, which was subsequently erected, greatly enhanced its attractions. Mr. Faahan can boast of having had the first two-storeyed house in the town; though the too critical might hold that the upper one, being merely a sham, could not be counted as dwelling-room. There was no sham, however, about the festive character of those evening entertainments.

Thus time went on, the only change in my circumstances resulting from my promotion to engine-driver — for now the Reward Claim boasted a small crushing plant — and Spring came, and with it in November the disastrous rush to "Siberia." This name, like most others on the goldfields, may be traced to the wit of some disappointed digger.

The rush was a failure or "frost," and so great a one that "Siberia" was the only word adequately to express the chagrin of the men who hoped so much from its discovery. Being one of these myself, I can cordially endorse the appropriateness of the name. What a motley crowd of eager faces throngs the streets and camp on the first news of a new rush — every one anxious to be off and be the first to make his fortune — every man questioning his neighbour, who knows no more than himself, about distances and direction, where the nearest water may be, and all manner of similar queries.

Once clear of the town, what a strange collection of baggage animals, horses, camels, and donkeys! What a mass of carts, drays, buggies, wheelbarrows, handbarrows, and many queer makeshifts for carrying goods — the strangest of all a large barrel set on an axle, and dragged or shoved by means of two long handles, the proud possessor's belongings turning round and round inside until they must surely be churned into a most confusing jumble. Then we see the "Swagman" with his load on his back, perhaps fifty pounds of provisions rolled up in his blankets, with a pick and shovel strapped on them, and in either hand a gallon bag of water. No light work this with the thermometer standing at 100 degrees in the shade, and the track inches deep in fine, powdery dust; and yet men start off with a light heart, with perhaps, a two hundred mile journey before them, replenishing their bundles as they pass through camps on their road.

"Siberia" was said to be seventy miles of a dry stage, and yet off we all started, as happy as kings at the chance of mending our fortunes.

Poor Crossman (since dead), McCulloch, and I were mates, and we were well off, for we had not only "Little Carnegie," and who, like his master, had been earning his living at Bayley's, but a camel, "Bungo" by name, kindly lent by Gordon Lyon. Thus we were able to carry water as well as provisions, and helped to relieve the sufferings of many a poor wretch who had only his feet to serve him.

The story of Siberia may be soon told. Hundreds "rushed" over this dry stage, at the end of which a small and doubtful water supply was obtainable. When this supply gave out fresh arrivals had to do their best without it, the rush perforce had to set back again, privations, disaster, and suffering being the only result. Much was said and written at the time about the scores of dead and dying men and horses who lined the roads — roads because there were two routes to the new field. There may have been deaths on the other track, but I know that we saw none on ours. Men in sore straits, with swollen tongues and bleeding feet, we saw, and, happily, were able to relieve; and I am sure that many would have died but for the prompt aid rendered by the Government Water Supply Department, which despatched drays loaded with tanks of water to succour the suffering miners. So the fortunes, to be made at Siberia, had again to be postponed.

File:Spinifex and Sand Illustration 5.jpg The "Gold Escort" [Missing image]

Shortly after our return to Coolgardie a "gold escort" left Bayley's for the coast, and as a guardian of the precious freight I travelled down to Perth. There was no Government escort at that time, and any lucky possessor of gold had to carry it to the capital as best he could.

With four spanking horses, Gordon Lyon as driver, three men with him on the express-waggon, an outrider behind and in front, all armed with repeating rifles, we rattled down the road, perhaps secretly wishing that someone would be venturesome enough to attempt to "stick us up." No such stirring event occurred, however, and we reached the head of the then partially constructed line, and there took train for Perth, where I eagerly awaited the arrival of my old friend and companion, Percy Douglas. He meanwhile had had his battles to fight in the financial world, and had come out to all appearances on top, having been instrumental in forming an important mining company from which we expected great things.

Part II: First Prospecting Expedition

Chapter I: The rush to Kurnalpi — We Reach Queen Victoria Spring

Shortly after Lord Douglas's return, I took the train to York, where "Little Carnegie," who had formed one of the team to draw the gold-laden express waggon from Bayley's to the head of the railway line, was running in one of Mr. Monger's paddocks. The Mongers are the kings of York, an agricultural town, and own much property thereabouts. York and its surroundings in the winter-time might, except for the corrugated-iron roofs, easily be in England. Many of the houses are built of stone, and enclosed in vineyards and fruit gardens. The Mongers' house was quite after the English style, so also was their hospitality. From York I rode along the old track to Southern Cross, and a lonely ride I had, for the train had superseded the old methods of travel, much to the disgust of some of the "cockies," or small farmers, who expressed the opinion that the country was going to the dogs, "them blooming railways were spoiling everything"; the reason for their complaint being, that formerly, all the carrying had been in the teamsters' hands, as well as a considerable amount of passenger traffic.

I had one or two "sells" on the road, for former stopping-places were now deserted, and wells had been neglected, making it impossible, from their depth, for me to get any water. I was fortunate in falling in with a teamster and his waggon — a typical one of his class; on first sight they are the most uncouth and foul-tongued men that it is possible to imagine. But on further acquaintance one finds that the language is as superficial as the dirt with which they cannot fail to be covered, since they are always walking in a cloud of dust. My friend on this occasion was apostrophising his horses with oaths that made my flesh creep, to help them up a steep hill. The top reached, he petted and soothed his team in most quaint language. At the bottom of the slope he was a demon of cruelty, at its summit a kind-hearted human being! I lunched with him, sitting under his waggon for shade, and found him most entertaining — nor was the old pony neglected, for he was given a fine feed of chaff and oats.

In due time I reached Coolgardie, where Lord Douglas and our new partner, Mr. Driffield (since drowned in a boating accident on the Swan River), joined me. They had engaged the services of one Luck and his camels, and had ridden up from the Cross. The rush to Kurnalpi had just broken out, so Driffield, Luck, and I joined the crowd of fortune-hunters; and a queer-looking crowd they were too, for every third or fourth swagman carried on his shoulder a small portable condenser, the boiler hanging behind him and the cooler in front; every party, whether with horses, carts, or camels, carried condensers of one shape or another; for the month was January, no surface water existed on the track, and only salt water could be obtained, by digging in the salt lakes which the road passed. The nearest water to the scene of the rush was a salt lake seven miles distant, and this at night presented a strange appearance. Condensers of every size and capacity fringed the two shores of a narrow channel; under each was a fire, and round each all night long could be seen figures, stoking the burning wood or drawing water, and in the distance the sound of the axe could be heard, for at whatever time a party arrived they had forthwith to set about "cooking water." The clattering and hammering the incessant talking, and the figures flitting about in the glare, reminded one of a crowded open-air market with flaring lamps and frequent coffee stalls. Kurnalpi was known at first as "Billy-Billy," or as "The Tinker's Rush" — the first name was supposed by some to be of native origin, by others to indicate the amount of tin used in the condensing plants — "Billy," translated for those to whom the bush is unfamiliar, meaning a tin pot for boiling tea in, and other such uses.

Certainly there was plenty of tin at Kurnalpi, and plenty of alluvial gold as well for the lucky ones — amongst which we were not numbered. Poor Driffield was much disgusted; he had looked upon gold-finding as the simplest thing in the world — and so it is if you happen to look in the right place! and when you do so it's a hundred to one that you think your own cleverness and knowledge guided you to it! Chance? Oh dear, no! From that time forth your reputation is made as "a shrewd fellow who knows a thing or two"; and if your find was made in a mine, you are an "expert" at once, and can command a price for your report on other mines commensurate with the richness of your own!

As the gold would not come to us, and my partner disliked the labour of seeking it, we returned to Coolgardie, and set about looking after the mines we already had. Financial schemes or business never had any charms for me; when therefore I heard that the Company had cabled out that a prospecting party should be despatched at once, I eagerly availed myself of the chance of work so much to my taste. As speed was an object, and neither camels nor men procurable owing to the rush, we did not waste any time in trying to form a large expedition, such as the soul of the London director loveth, but contented ourselves with the camels already to hand.

On March 24, 1894, we started; Luck, myself, and three camels — Omerod, Shimsha, and Jenny by name — with rations for three months, and instructions to prospect the Hampton Plains as far as the supply of surface water permitted; failing a long stay in that region I could go where I thought best.

To the east and north-east of Coolgardie lie what are known as the Hampton Plains — so named by Captain Hunt, who in 1864 led an expedition past York, eastward, into the interior. Beyond the Hampton Plains he was forced back by the Desert, and returned to York with but a sorry tale of the country he had seen. "An endless sea of scrub," was his apt description of the greater part of the country. Compared to the rest, the Hampton Plains were splendid pastoral lands. Curiously enough, Hunt passed and repassed close to what is now Coolgardie, and, though reporting quartz and ironstone, failed to hit upon any gold. Nor was he the only one; Coolgardie had several narrow squeaks of being found out.

Giles and Forrest both traversed districts since found to be gold-bearing, and though, like Hunt, reporting, and even bringing back specimens of quartz and ironstone, had the bad luck to miss finding even a "colour."

Alexander Forrest, Goddard, and Lindsay all passed within appreciable distance of Coolgardie without unearthing its treasures, though in Lindsay's journal the geologist to the expedition pronounced the country auriferous. When we come to consider how many prospectors pass over gold, it is not so wonderful that explorers, whose business is to see as much country as they can, in as short a time as possible, should have failed to drop on the hidden wealth.

Bayley and Ford, its first discoverers, were by no means the first prospectors to camp at Coolgardie. In 1888 Anstey and party actually found colours of gold, and pegged out a claim, whose corner posts were standing at the time of the first rush; but nobody heeded them, for the quartz was not rich enough.

In after years George Withers sunk a hole and "dry blew" the wash not very far from Bayley's, yet he discovered no gold. Macpherson, too, poked out beyond Coolgardie, and nearly lost his life in returning, and, indeed, was saved by his black-boy, who held him on the only remaining horse.

Other instances could be given, all of which show that Nature will not be bustled, and will only divulge her secrets when the ordained time has arrived. It has been argued that since Giles, for example, passed the Coolgardie district without finding gold, therefore there is every probability of the rest of the country through which he passed being auriferous. It fails to occur to those holding this view, that a man may recognise possible gold-bearing country without finding gold, or to read the journals of these early travellers, in which they would see that the Desert is plainly demarcated, and the change in the nature of the country, the occurrence of quartz, and so forth, always recorded. These folk who so narrowly missed the gold were not the only unfortunate ones; those responsible for the choosing for their company of the blocks of land on the Hampton Mains were remarkably near securing all the plums.

Bayley's is one and a half miles from their boundary, Kalgoorlie twelve miles, Kurnalpi seven miles, and a number of other places lie just on the wrong side of the survey line to please the shareholders, though had all these rich districts been found on their land, I fancy there would have been a pretty outcry from the general public.

At the time of which I am writing this land was considered likely to be as rich as Ophir. Luck and I were expected to trip up over nuggets, and come back simply impregnated with gold. Unfortunately we not only found no gold, but formed a very poor idea of that part of the property which we were able to traverse, though, given a good supply of water, it should prove valuable stock country. Before we had been very long started on our journey we met numerous parties returning from that region, though legally they had no right to prospect there; each told us the same story — every water was dry; and since every one we had been to was all but dry, we concluded that they were speaking the truth; so when we arrived at Yindi, a large granite rock with a cavity capable of holding some twenty thousand gallons of water, and found Yindi dry, we decided to leave the Hampton Plains and push out into new country.

Queen Victoria Spring, reported permanent by Giles, lay some seventy miles to the eastward, and attracted our attention; for Lindsay had reported quartz country near the Ponton, not far from the Spring, and the country directly between the Spring and Kurnalpi was unknown.

On April 15th we left Yindi, having seen the last water twenty-six miles back near Gundockerta, and passed Mount Quinn, entering a dense thicket of mulga, which lasted for the next twenty miles. It was most awkward country to steer through, and I often overheard Luck muttering to himself that I was going all wrong, for he was a first-rate bushman and I a novice. I had bought a little brumby from a man we met on the Plains, an excellent pony, and most handy in winding his way through the scrub. Luck rode Jenny and led the other two camels. Hereabouts we noticed a large number of old brush fences — curiously I have never once seen a new one — which the natives had set up for catching wallabies. The fences run out in long wings, which meet in a point where a hole is dug. Neither wallabies nor natives were to be seen, though occasionally we noticed where "bardies" had been dug out, and a little further on a native grave, a hole about three feet square by three feet deep, lined at the bottom with gum leaves and strips of bark, evidently ready to receive the deceased. Luck, who knew a good deal about native customs, told me that the grave, though apparently only large enough for a child, was really destined for a grown man. When a man dies his first finger is cut off, because he must not fight in the next world, nor need he throw a spear to slay animals, as game is supplied. The body is then bent double until the knees touch the chin — this to represent a baby before birth; and in this cramped position the late warrior is crammed into his grave, until, according to a semi-civilised boy that I knew, he is called to the happy hunting grounds, where he changes colour! "Black fella tumble down, jump up white fella." A clear proof that this benighted people have some conception of a better state hereafter.

Once through the scrub, we came again into gum-timbered country, and when fifty miles east of Kurnalpi crossed a narrow belt of auriferous country, but, failing to find water, were unable to stop. In a few miles we were in desert country — undulations of sand and spinifex, with frequent clumps of dense mallee, a species of eucalyptus, with several straggling stems growing from one root, and little foliage except at the ends of the branches, an untidy and melancholy-looking tree. There was no change in the country till after noon on the 18th, when we noticed some grass-trees, or black-boys, smaller than those seen near the coast, and presently struck the outskirts of a little oasis, and immediately after an old camel pad (Lindsay's in 1892, formed by a caravan of over fifty animals), which we followed for a few minutes, until the welcome sight of Queen Victoria Spring met our eyes. A most remarkable spot, and one that cannot be better described than by quoting the words of its discoverer, Ernest Giles, in 1875, who, with a party of five companions, fifteen pack, and seven riding camels, happened on this spring just when they most needed water.

Giles says of it:—

It is the most singularly placed water I have ever seen, lying in a small hollow in the centre of a little grassy flat and surrounded by clumps of funereal pines.... The water is no doubt permanent, for it is supplied by the drainage of the sandhills which surround it and it rests on a substratum of impervious clay. It lies exposed to view in a small, open basin, the water being about only one hundred and fifty yards in circumference and from two to three feet deep. Further up the slopes at much higher levels native wells had been sunk in all directions — in each and all of these there was water. Beyond the immediate precincts of this open space the scrubs abound.... Before I leave this spot I had perhaps better remark that it might prove a very difficult, perhaps dangerous, place to any other traveller to attempt to find, because although there are many white sandhills in the neighbourhood, the open space on which the water lies is so small in area and so closely surrounded by scrubs, that it cannot be seen from any conspicuous one, nor can any conspicuous sandhill, distinguishable at any distance, be seen from it. On the top of the banks above the wells was a beaten corroboree path, where the denizens of the desert have often held their feasts and dances. Some grass-trees grew in the vicinity of this spring to a height of over twenty feet....

A charming spot indeed! but we found it to be hardly so cheerful as this description would lead one to expect. For at first sight the Spring was dry. The pool of water was now a dry clay-pan; the numerous native wells were there, but all were dry. The prospect was sufficiently gloomy, for our water was all but done, and poor Tommy, the pony, in spite of an allowance of a billy-full per night, was in a very bad way, for we had travelled nearly one hundred miles from the last water, and if this was dry we knew no other that we could reach. However, we were not going to cry before we were hurt and set to work to dig out the soak, and in a short time were rewarded by the sight of water trickling in on all sides, and, by roughly timbering the sides, soon had a most serviceable well — a state of affairs greatly appreciated by Tommy and the camels. This spring or soakage, whichever it may be, is in black sand, though the sand outside the little basin is yellowish white. From what I have heard and read of them it must be something of the nature of what are called "black soil springs." Giles was right in his description of its remarkable surroundings — unless we had marched right into the oasis, we should perhaps have missed it altogether, for it was unlikely that Lindsay's camel tracks would be visible except where sheltered from the wind by the trees; and our only instruments for navigation were a prismatic and pocket compass, and a watch for rating our travel. I was greatly pleased at such successful steering for a first attempt of any distance, and Luck was as pleased as I was, for to him I owed many useful hints. Yet I was not blind to the fact that it was a wonderful piece of luck to strike exactly a small spot of no more than fifty acres in extent, hidden in the valleys of the sandhills, from whose summits nothing could be seen but similar mounds of white sand. Amongst the white gum trees we found one marked with Lindsay's initials with date. Under this I nailed on a piece of tin, on which I had stamped our names and date. Probably the blacks have long since taken this down and used it as an ornament. Another tree, a pine, was marked W. Blake; who he was I do not know, unless one of Lindsay's party. Not far off was a grave, more like that of a white man than of a native; about its history, too, I am ignorant.

Numerous old native camps surrounded the water, and many weapons, spears, waddies, and coolimans were lying about. The camps had not been occupied for some long time. In the scrub we came on a cleared space, some eighty yards long and ten to twelve feet wide. At each end were heaps of ashes, and down the middle ran a well-beaten path, and a similar one on either side not unlike an old dray track. Evidently a corroboree ground of some kind. From Luck I learnt that north of Eucla, where he had been with a survey party, the natives used such grounds in their initiation ceremonies. A youth on arriving at a certain age may become a warrior, and is then allowed to carry a shield and spear. Before he can attain this honour he must submit to some very horrible rites — which are best left undescribed. Seizing each an arm of the victim, two stalwart "bucks" (as the men are called) run him up and down the cleared space until they are out of breath; then two more take places, and up and down they go until at last the boy is exhausted. This is the aboriginal method of applying anaesthetics. During the operations that follow, the men dance and yell round the fires but the women may not be witnesses of the ceremony. Tribes from all neighbouring districts meet at such times and hold high revel. Evidently Queen Victoria Spring is a favourite meeting-place. I regret that I never had the chance of being present at such a gathering — few white men have. For except in thickly populated districts the ceremonies are rare; the natives are very ready to resent any prying into their mysteries, and Luck only managed it at some risk to himself. Whilst camped at the Spring we made one or two short excursions to the southward, but met with little encouragement. On turning our attention to the opposite direction we found that nearly two hundred miles due north a tract of auriferous country was marked on the map of the Elder Expedition. Between us and that point, the country was unmapped and untrodden except by black-fellows, and it seemed reasonable to suppose that since the belts of country run more or less north and south we had a fair chance of finding gold-bearing country extending southward. We should be getting a long way from Coolgardie, but if a rich company could not afford to open up the country, who could? To the east we knew that desert existed, to the south the country was known, and to return the way we had come would be only a waste of time. So we decided on the northern course, and chose Mount Shenton, near which a soakage was marked, as our objective point. We were not well equipped for a long march in new country, since we had few camels and scanty facilities for carrying water. By setting to work with the needle we soon had two canvas water-bags made; Luck, who had served in the French navy, like all sailors, was a very handy man in a camp, and could of course sew well, and gave me useful lessons in the handling of a sail-needle.

Part II: First Prospecting Expedition

Chapter II: In Unknown Country

On April 22nd we left the spring, steering due north — carrying in all thirty-five gallons of water, though this supply was very perceptibly reduced by evening, owing to the canvas being new; loss by evaporation was lessened by covering the bags with a fly (a sheet of coarse calico). The class of country we encountered the first and second day can stand for the rest of the march. Spinifex plains, undulating sand-plains, rolling sandhills, steep sand-ridges, mallee scrubs, desert-gum forests, and dense thickets of mulga. The last were most unpleasant to travel through; for as we wound our way, one walking ahead to break down the branches, the other leading the camels, and Tommy following behind, every now and again the water-camel banged his precious load against a tree; and we walked with the constant risk of a dead branch ripping the canvas and letting out the water.

On the second evening, in passing through a mallee scrub, we came on a small tract of "kopi country" (powdered gypsum). Here were numerous old native tracks, and we could see where the mallee roots had been dragged up, broken into short pieces, presumably sucked or allowed to drain into some vessel, and stacked in little heaps. Though we knew that the blacks do get water from the mallee roots, and though we were in a spot where it was clear they had done so perhaps a month before, yet our attempts at water-finding were futile. This kopi is peculiar soil to walk over; on the surface there is a hard crust — once through this, one sinks nearly to the knee; the camels of course, from their weight, go much lower.

On the night of the 23rd, we gave Tommy two gallons of water — not much of a drink, but enough to make him tackle the mulga, and spinifex-tops, the only available feed; none but West Australian brumbies could live on such fare, and they will eat anything, like donkeys or goats. On the 24th there was no change, a few quondongs affording a meal for the camels.

The next day we crossed more old native tracks and followed them for some time without any sign of water being near. More tracks the following day, fresher this time; but though doubtless there was water at the end of them, for several reasons we did not follow them far: first, they were leading south-west and we wished to go north; second, the quantity of mallee root heaps, suggested the possibility that the natives could obtain from them sufficient moisture to live upon. I think now that this is most unlikely, and that roots are only resorted to when travelling or in time of great need. However, at that time we were inclined to think it probable, and though we might have sucked roots in place of a drink of tea or water, such a source of supply was absolutely valueless to the camels and pony.

On the 27th we sighted a hill dead ahead, which I named Mount Luck, and on the southern side a nice little plain of saltbush and grass — a pleasant and welcome change. Mount Luck is sheer on its south and east sides and slopes gradually to the north-west; it is of desert sandstone, and from its summit, nearly due east, can be seen an imposing flat-topped hill, which I named Mount Douglas, after my old friend and companion, to the north of this hill two quaint little pinnacles stand up above the scrub to a considerable height.

Poor Tommy was now getting very weak and had to be dragged by the last camel. I had not ridden him since the second day from the Spring; he was famished and worn to a skeleton. His allowance of two gallons a night had continued, which made a considerable hole in our supply, further diminished by the necessity of giving him damper to eat. Poor little pony! It was a cruel sight to see him wandering from pack to pack in camp, poking his nose into every possible opening, and even butting us with his head as if to call attention to his dreadful state, which was only too apparent. "While there's life there's hope," and every day took us nearer to water — that is if we were to get any at all! So long as we could do so, we must take Tommy with us, who might yet be saved. This, however, was not to be, for on the 28th we again encountered sand-ridges, running at right angles to our course, and these proved too hard for the poor brave brumby. About midday he at last gave in, and with glazed eyes and stiff limbs he fell to the ground. Taking off the saddle he carried, I knelt by his head for a few minutes and could see there was no hope. Poor, faithful friend! I felt like a murderer in doing it, but I knew it was the kindest thing — and finished his sufferings with a bullet. There on the ridge, his bones will lie for many a long day. Brave Tommy, whose rough and unkempt exterior covered a heart that any warhorse might have envied, had covered 135 miles, without feed worth mentioning, and with only eleven gallons of water during that distance, a stage of nearly seven days' duration of very hard travelling indeed, with the weather pretty sultry, though the nights were cool. His death, however, was in favour of our water supply, which was not too abundant. So much had been lost by the bags knocking about on the saddle, by their own pressure against the side of the saddle, and by evaporation, that we had to content ourselves with a quart-potful between us morning and evening — by no means a handsome allowance.

File:Spinifex and Sand Illustration 7.jpg Death Of "Tommy" [Missing image]

On the 29th, after travelling eight hours through scrubs, we were just about to camp when the shrill "coo-oo" of a black-fellow met our ears; and on looking round we were startled to see some half-dozen natives gazing at us. Jenny chose at that moment to give forth the howl that only cow-camels can produce; this was too great a shock for the blacks, who stampeded pell-mell, leaving their spears and throwing-sticks behind them. We gave chase, and, after a spirited run, Luck managed to stop a man. A stark-naked savage this, and devoid of all adornment excepting a waist-belt of plaited grass and a "sporran" of similar material. He was in great dread of the camels and not too sure of us. I gave him something to eat, and, by eating some of it myself, put him more at ease. After various futile attempts at conversation, in which Luck displayed great knowledge of the black's tongue, as spoken a few hundred miles away near Eucla, but which unfortunately was quite lost on this native, we at last succeeded in making our wants understood. "Ingup," "Ingup," he kept repeating, pointing with his chin to the North and again to the West. Evidently "Ingup" stood for water; for he presently took us to a small granite rock and pointed out a soak or rock-hole, we could not say which. Whilst we stooped to examine the water-hole, our guide escaped into the scrub and was soon lost to view. Near the rock we found his camp. A few branches leaning against a bush formed his house. In front a fire was burning, and near it a plucked bird lay ready for cooking. Darkness overtook us before we could get to work on the rock-hole, so we turned into the blankets with a more satisfied feeling than we had done for some days past. During the night the blacks came round us. The camels, very tired, had lain down close by, and, quietly creeping to Jenny, I slapped her nose, which awoke her with the desired result, viz., a loud roar. The sound of rapidly retreating feet was heard, and their owners troubled us no more.

So sure were we of the supply in the granite that we gave the camels the few gallons that were left in our bags, and were much disgusted to find the next day that, far from being a soakage, the water was merely contained in a rock-hole, which had been filled in with sand and sticks.

April 30th and May 1st were occupied in digging out the sand and collecting what water we could, a matter of five or six gallons. So bad was this water that the camels would not touch it; however, it made excellent bread, and passable tea. Man, recognising Necessity, is less fastidious than animals who look to their masters to supply them with the best, and cannot realise that in such cases "Whatever is, is best."

From a broken granite rock North-West of the rock-hole, we sighted numerous peaks to the North, and knew that Mount Shenton could not now be far away. To the East of the rock-hole is a very prominent bluff some fifteen miles distant; this I named Mount Fleming, after Colonel Fleming, then Commandant of the West Australian forces.

May 2nd we reached the hills and rejoiced to find ourselves once more in decent country. Numerous small, dry watercourses ran down from the hills, fringed with grass and bushes. In the open mulga, kangaroos' tracks were numerous, and in the hills we saw several small red kangaroos, dingoes, and emus. At first we found great difficulty in identifying any of the hills; but after much consultation and reference to the map we at last picked out Mount Shenton, and on reaching the hill knew that we were right, for we found Wells' cairn of stones and the marks of his camp and camels. The next difficulty was in finding the soakage, as from a bad reproduction of Wells' map it was impossible to determine whether the soak was at the foot of Mount Shenton or near another hill three miles away. It only remained to search both localities. Our trouble was rewarded by the finding of an excellent little soakage, near the foot of a granite rock, visible due East, from the top of Mount Shenton, some two miles distant. Here we had an abundant supply, and not before it was wanted. The camels had had no water with the exception of a mouthful apiece from the night of April 21st until the night of May 3rd, a period of twelve days, during which we had travelled nearly two hundred miles over very trying ground. The cool nights were greatly in their favour, and yet it was a good performance, more especially that at the end of it they were in pretty fair fettle.

What a joy that water was to us! what a luxury a wash was! and clean clothes! Really it's worth while being half famished and wholly filthy for a few days, that one may so thoroughly enjoy such delights afterwards! I know few feelings of satisfaction that approach those which one experiences on such occasions. Our cup of joy was not yet full, for as we sat mending our torn clothes, two over-inquisitive emus approached. Luckily a Winchester was close to hand, and as they were starting to run I managed to bowl one over. Wounded in the thigh he could yet go a great pace, but before long we caught up with him and despatched him with a blow on the head. What a feed we had! I suppose there is hardly a part of that bird, barring bones, feathers, and beak that did not find its way into our mouths during the next day or two! Tinned meat is good, sometimes excellent; but when you find that a cunning storekeeper has palmed off all his minced mutton on you, you are apt to fancy tinned fare monotonous! Such was our case; and no matter what the label, the contents were always the same — though we tried to differentiate in imagination, as we used to call it venison, beef, veal, or salmon, for variety's sake! "Well, old chap, what shall we have for tea — Calf's head? Grouse? Pheasant?" "Hum! what about a little er — *minced mutton* — we've not had any for some time, I think." In this way we added relish to our meal.

Amongst the hills we saw numerous kangaroos, but could never get a shot. This must be a fine camp for natives. Near the soak was a camp of quite a dozen blacks, but recently deserted. In fact we must have scared them away, for their fires were still smouldering. We spent three days in exploring the hills, but failed to see any auriferous indications, excepting in the immediate neighbourhood of Mount Shenton. We had therefore had our long tramp for nothing, and had to be content with knowing that we had tried our best and had at least proved the useless character of a large stretch of country. For this, however, one gets no thanks.

File:Spinifex and Sand Illustration 8.jpg Fresh meat at last! [Missing image]

On the 6th we moved to a rock-hole near Mount Grant, in the same range as Mount Shenton, and spent another day tramping the hills with no result. Here again we were in luck, for a mob of thirteen emus came to drink whilst I was in the rock-hole. Having seen them early that morning and knowing that they had had no drink, I felt sure they would return, and so had patiently waited, crouched in the rock hole, waist deep in water. This, perhaps, did not improve its flavour, but emu meat was worth procuring at the small cost of tainting the water with the taste of clothes. Presently I heard the drumming of the approaching birds, and, cautiously looking up, found them attentively examining the bucket and pannikin, I had left on the rock. They made such a quaint, pretty picture that unless we had really wanted meat, I should not have disturbed them. Had I been so inclined I could have shot several as they were bunched together within a few feet of me; one, however, was sufficient, and as he fell the rest streamed away up the slope with tremendous speed. This bird we cut into strips of meat which we dried in the sun.

To celebrate this addition to our larder, we held a concert that night, and took it in turns to be the audience. Luck had rather a good voice, and treated me to French songs; his favourite started, "J'ai souvent parcouru le monde, les forets et les grandes savannes — — " This was always loudly applauded. My songs were not a great success — in fact an audience of one is all I can manage, that is if I am stronger, or fleeter of foot than he is. Luck was polite enough to say he enjoyed my rendering of "The Scottish Cavalier." Then we used to read aloud to each other by the light of the camp-fire. I did most of the reading, for my mate's English was not as clear as it might have been.

Athletic sports, too, we used to indulge in, feats of strength, and so forth, in most of which Luck was too good for me, but I always beat him at cock-fighting, which was rather a sore point. In fact, considering that we were alone and had been so for many weeks, and were a long way into the interior, "outside the tracks" by a good many score of miles, we managed to be fairly cheerful on the whole. I do not like writing about my companion's crotchets, because it seems unfair, since one's own shortcomings never find the light unless the other man writes a book too. By freely conceding that sometimes I must have been a horrible nuisance to him, I feel absolved in this matter. When Luck used to get sulky fits, he really was most trying; for two or three days he wouldn't speak, and for want of company I used to talk to the camels; at the end of that time, when I saw signs of recovery, I used to address him thus, "Well, Bismarck, what's it all about?" Then he would tell me how I had agreed to bake a damper, and had gone off and done something else, leaving him to do it, or some such trivial complaint. After telling me about it, he would regain his usual cheerfulness. "Bismarck" was a sure draw, and made him so angry that he had to laugh as the only way out of it without fighting someone. Luck, you see, was from Alsace, and did not care about the Germans.

Part II: First Prospecting Expedition

Chapter III: From Mount Shenton to Mount Margaret

But to continue our journey. We left Mount Grant on May 8th, travelling South-West, and once away from the hills came again into sand and spinifex. From absence of feed we tied the camels down two nights running. The second night we had a visit from a native gentleman, and by his tracks in the morning we saw that he had been quite close to our heads at one time.

On the 10th a great change occurred in the country, and on passing through a thicket, we found a great wall of rock (decomposed granite) barring further progress. Following along the wall we came upon a gap, and, entering, reached a nice little plain of saltbush, surrounded by rocks and cliffs. This remarkable gap in the apparently extensive wall of rock we christened the "Desert's Gate," for we hourly expected to see better country. The next day we cut some recent horse tracks, the first signs of prospectors we had seen since April 15th, and following them back, hoping for water, came to an empty rock-hole amongst some rough hills of black slate, and in places, blows of quartz. No colours of gold could be found, nor signs of water, to induce us to stay longer prospecting. On the 12th we crossed a narrow salt lake and bade adieu to the sand and spinifex. To commemorate this longed-for day, we afterwards composed numerous poems(?) illustrating our daily life in the desert. The one considered by us the best, I beg to submit to the indulgent reader.

SPINIFEX AND SAND.I will sing you a lay of W.A. Of a wanderer, travelled and tanned By the sun's fierce ray, through the livelong day In the Spinifex and Sand.At the day's first dawn, in earliest morn, As a soldier obeys a command, From his blanket he's torn, still weary and worn, By the Spinifex and Sand.Unrested still, he must put on the billy, And eat of the meat that is canned, He must take his full fill, he must face willy-nilly The Spinifex and the Sand.Then he gets on the tracks and sights the arched backs Of his camels of true South Aus. brand, And with saddle and sack he must hasten to pack For the Spinifex and Sand.From the start until night, till he's sick of the sight, There seem to dance hand in hand A lady so bright, and a green-armoured knight, The Spinifex and the Sand.He turns to his mate with "It gets a bit late," His mate, he just answers offhand — "It's the same soon or late, we'll camp 't any rate In the Spinifex and Sand."As the night drags along, a weird-looking throng Fills his dreams of a far-off land, And a voice loud and strong chants the same ceaseless song, Of the *Spinifex and the Sand.*   Since this is one of the few attempts at rhyming that I have been guilty of, I hope I may be excused for wishing to see it in print, for at the time I was exceedingly proud of the composition. Ah! well, it served to pass the time and afforded some amusement. Soon we had other matters to think about, for on the 12th we found ourselves on the outskirts of auriferous country and were lucky in reaching plenty of water. Being lightly loaded we had made good marches, covering 103 miles from the last water on May 8th, an average of twenty and a half miles per day.

From the 13th to the 21st we camped surrounded by hills, any one of which might contain gold if only we could find it. Unremitting labours resulted in nothing but a few colours here and there. We were now thirty miles to the North-West of Mount Margaret (discovered and named by Forrest in 1869, who on that journey reached a point some sixty miles further East than that hill), and though we were the first, so far as I know, to prospect this particular part of the district, it was reserved for subsequent fossickers to find anything worth having.

Wandering about, pick in hand, one day I put up several turkeys from the grass surrounding some granite rocks, and shortly after found their watering-place, a nice little pool.

The next day whilst Luck prospected I returned to the pool with a gun, and, building a hide of bushes, waited all day. Towards evening two fine emus came stalking along, and I shot one. By the time I had him skinned and the legs cut off it was dark. A most deceptive bird is an emu, for in reality he has but little meat on his body. The legs, that is the thighs, are the only parts worth taking, so shouldering these I started for camp a couple of miles off. It was pretty late when I got back, and found Luck ringing a camel-bell violently and frequently. He had been a bit anxious at my long absence, and had taken a bell off one of the camels to guide me in case I was "bushed." A party of two is too small for a journey that takes them far from settlements for if anything happens to one, the other has little chance by himself. The man left in camp does not know what to do — if he goes far from home, there is the danger of the camp being robbed by natives, therefore he hesitates to go in search of his mate, who possibly is in sore need of help from an accident, or bushed, or speared — so many things might happen. If one broke a limb, as he easily might, what could his mate do? Nothing. If in waterless country he would have to leave him, or kill him, or die with him.

Though Luck and I were spared any catastrophes, we often thought of such things, and therefore felt anxious when either was away for long.

On the 22nd we were surprised at cutting a freshly made dray-track, along which it was clear that many had passed — and the next day arrived at the Red Flag, an alluvial rush that had "set in" during our sojourn in the sand. This came as a great surprise, as we had no idea that gold had been found so far afield. This camp, some twelve miles North-East of Mount Margaret, consisted then of only forty or fifty men, though others were daily arriving. These were the first white men we had seen for seven weeks, and they were greatly astonished to see us, when they learnt what direction we had come from.

Here were gathered together men from Coolgardie and Murchison, attracted by the tales of wealth brought by the first prospectors of the new rush. Some of them had been longer away from civilisation than we had, and many arguments were held as to the correct date. Of course I knew, because I kept a diary; but the Queen's Birthday was celebrated by us on the wrong day after all, for I had given April thirty-one days! We heard that hundreds had started for the rush, but this camp represented all who had persevered, the rest being scared at the distance.

This reads funnily now when Mount Margaret is as civilised as Coolgardie was then, and is connected by telegraph, and possibly will be soon boasting of a railway. The blacks had been very troublesome, "sticking up" swagmen, robbing camps, spearing horses, and the like. It is popularly supposed that every case of violence on the part of the natives, may be traced to the brutal white man's interference in their family arrangements. No doubt it does happen that by coming between man and wife a white man stirs up the tribe, and violence results, but in the majority of cases that I know of, the poor black-fellow has recklessly speared, wounding and killing, prospectors' horses, because he wanted food or amusement. A man does not travel his packhorses into the bush for the philanthropic purpose of feeding the aboriginals, and naturally resents his losses and prevents their recurrence in a practical way.

As a matter of fact, the black population was so small, that even had every individual of it been shot, the total would not have reached by a long way the indiscriminate slaughter that was supposed to go on in the bush. The people who used to hold their hands up in horror — righteous horror had the tales been true — at the awful cruelties perpetrated by the prospectors, based their opinions on the foolish "gassing" of a certain style of man who thinks to make himself a hero by recounting dark deeds of blood, wholly imaginary. I remember reading a letter to a friend from his mother, in which she begged him to take no part in the "nigger hunting excursions" that she had heard went on in Western Australia. Poor lady! she need not have disturbed herself, for such things never existed, nor had her boy ever seen a black-fellow, except round the slaughter-yards of Coolgardie!

No luck attended our search in the Mount Margaret district, and we shared the opinion of everybody there that it was a "duffer," and after events had proved what that opinion was worth. Travelling and prospecting as we went, we at last succeeded in finding a reef which we thought was worth having.

May 30th. We made camp amongst some auriferous hills in what is now known as the Niagara District, and within a few miles of a spot where, subsequently, a rich find of gold was made. Since the natives were known to be troublesome in this locality, we adopted the plan of one stopping in camp whilst the other prospected. Formerly we had considered it safe for the one at home to be within reasonable distance of camp, but now, when semi-civilised natives were prowling about, it was unwise to leave the camp at all. Luck found gold first, but in so small a vein of quartz that we did not consider it worth working. The next day, however, we "got colours" in a fine big reef, and, moving our belongings to its vicinity, started prospecting the outcrop. Everywhere we tried we found gold sprinkled through the stone like pepper, and by "dollying" obtained good results. Satisfied with the prospect, the next thing to be done was to cross-cut the reef to ascertain its thickness and character below the surface.

Fortunately water was close to hand, that is to say three miles away, in a creek since named "Dingo Creek." From there we packed water back to camp, as often as we required it. Our luck in securing game had now deserted us, and we had again to fall back on our nearly diminished stock of mince.

After a week's hard work we found that with our limited supply of tools, without drills and dynamite, it was impossible to do any farther sinking; besides which the low tide in our provisions necessitated a return to civilisation before many days.

I pegged out, therefore, an area of four hundred yards by four hundred yards, as a "protection area"; that is to say, that the fact of four corner-pegs and a notice having been put up in some prominent place protects the ground from being taken by any one else for a period of thirty days. After that time has elapsed the area must be applied for at the nearest Warden's office, where, unless disputed, it is registered under the name of the applicant, who must at once commence work upon it. When such work proves the existence of "payable gold" the area must be again applied for as a lease, to hold which the sum of 1 pound per acre, per annum, must be paid to the Government. There are other conditions with which it is necessary to conform, and which need not be enumerated here.

Since we had ample time to go and return from Coolgardie within the prescribed period, we decided that in place of travelling direct homewards, we would make a detour and visit the locality of Mount Ida, where we had heard gold had been found. By rapid travelling our "tucker" could be made to last out the time. Winter was now coming on, and the nights were bitterly cold. Our blankets in the morning were soaked with dew and frost, and when the days were cloudy and sometimes drizzly we had no chance of drying them until we built a fire at night. One is so used to reading of the terrible heat in Australia that it may come as a surprise to many to hear that in the short winter in the interior — which, by the way, is 1,500 feet above sea level — the thermometer sometimes sinks for a brief period of time to 17 degrees F.

This low temperature is reached about an hour before daylight, as you know to your cost, if you are ill-provided with blankets. At that time in the morning your head is drawn into the possum rug, and you lie stiff and shivering until you hear the indescribable something — that heralds the coming of the sun. It may be a camel moving, as he shakes the frost from his woolly coat, it may be a bird, or a grasshopper, but always there is some little noise that would tell even a blind man that the night is over. Often you know by the stars how long it will be before daylight, and stir up the fire, put on the billy, and get the saddles and packs in order. Sometimes you fix on the wrong star, and are thanked accordingly by your mate when, with his feet in his cold, clammy boots, he discovers that his watch reads 2 a.m. Sometimes you have the satisfaction of growling at him, and occasionally, if you feel in very nasty humour, you may lie "dog-oh" and watch his early rising, knowing full well the right time; laughter, however, gives you away, and you are justly rewarded by having the blankets torn off you. Such simple pranks as these make bearable a life that would otherwise suffocate you with its monotony.

And yet there is a charm about the bush — the perfect peace in the "free air of God" — that so takes hold of some men that they can never be happy anywhere else. Civilisation is a fine thing in its way, but the petty worries and annoyances, the bustle and excitement, the crowds of people, the "you can't do this," and "you must do that," the necessity for dressing in most uncomfortable garments to be like other people, and a thousand other such matters, so distress a bushman, who, like a caged beast in a menagerie, wanders from corner to corner and cannot find where to rest, that he longs for the day that he will again be on the track, with all his worldly goods with him and the wide world before him. Such a man in the bush and in the town is as different as a fish in and out of water.

Some of the finest fellows "outside the tracks" are the least respectable in civilised places, where before long they can find no better occupation than drinking, which, owing to months of teetotalism in the bush, they are less able to stand than the ordinary individual who takes his beer or spirits daily. And thus it is that bushmen very often get the name of being loafers and drunkards, though on the aggregate they consume far less liquor than our most respected citizens in the towns. The sudden change in surroundings, good food, and the number of fellow-creatures, the noise of traffic, and want of exercise — all these combined are apt to affect a man's head, even when unaided by the constant flow of liquor with which a popular bushman is deluged — a deluge hard to resist in a country where to refuse a drink amounts to an insult. A plan recommended by some is to "please 'em all by one jolly good spree, and then knock off and drink with nobody." A man only gives offence who discriminates in his entertainers.

I fear I have wandered far from the subject of our journey, for Luck and I had some time yet before us until the joys and troubles of civilised life should be ours. The daily routine of travel was varied occasionally by incidents of no great moment; for instance, when riding through the scrub, Omerod, a rather clumsy old camel, tripped and fell, pinning me beneath him, without injury to either of us; for a water bag acted as a buffer between my leg and the saddle, and by the time all the water was squeezed out of it, Luck had the saddle off, and I was extricated. Certainly some camels are hard to put out or fluster; such a one was Omerod, who lay without a kick until relieved of his saddle, when he rose and at once proceeded to feed on the scrub.

Later, we had another instance of his stolidity; that was when crossing a salt lake. Jenny was light and escaped bogging; not so Omerod, who sank as far as his legs would allow, and there waited calmly until we had unpacked the loads, carried them across the lake, and returned to help Shimsha, who struggled violently in the sticky clay. When he was safely taken across to an island on which we sought refuge, Omerod was attended to. There he lay, half buried in salt mud, chewing his cud unconcernedly; either he had perfect confidence in us, or was indifferent as to his fate — he looked rather as if he were saying "Kismet." We had some trouble in digging him out, during which operation Luck fared as I had done before; he was pinned beneath the camel, waist deep in clay, and in that position had to emulate the stolid patience of Omerod until I could dig him out. At last they were both free, and after considerable labour we landed on the island, camels, baggage, and all, just as night fell. We WERE cold too, clothes and arms and faces covered with moist salt clay, and nothing with which to make a fire but sprigs of dead samphire. A cold night means an early start — so we were up betimes and found that the camels, not tied, since we thought them safe on an island, had in search of feed hobbled across the lake, and were standing disconsolate on this sea of mud, afraid to move now that in daylight they could see their surroundings. A repetition of the preceding day's performance, landed us beyond the treacherous lake-bed, and the following day we were fortunate in finding a fine rock-hole of water, which enabled us to reappear as white men.

Mirages are nearly always to be seen on these lakes of the interior, and from their occurrence it is impossible to determine the extent of the flat expanse of mud. On this occasion I witnessed the finest I have ever seen. The hot sun playing upon the damp breeze rising from the lake, transformed this desolate sea of salt and clay, into a charming picture. The horizon and the sky were joined by a mirage of beautiful clear water, from which islands and hills seemed to rise; even their shadows and those of the trees with which they were clothed were reflected in the unruffled surface of the lake. The long stretch of sand between, gave the picture the appearance of a peaceful, natural harbour, which the tide was about to fill.

We were unable to pay more than a flying visit to Mount Ida, but sufficiently long to assure us of the auriferous character of its neighbourhood. It is quite an imposing hill, rough, dark, and rugged, and formed as if layers of black slate had been thrown violently against each other. It rises some five hundred feet above the surrounding country.

We needed all our time to reach Siberia, before our provisions gave out. There we arrived in due course, passing close, on our way, to the hills near which Menzies afterwards made his great "find."

At Siberia a Government survey party, under Messrs. Newman and Brazier, was camped, preparatory to running a line to connect Coolgardie and the Murchison. Bidding them adieu, we took the road to Coolgardie, and arrived there on June 22nd after an absence of exactly ninety days, having travelled 843 miles. The result of the journey to ourselves was nil, for the company considered that the reef we had found was too far off, and took no further steps to develop it. It was afterwards under offer for 13,000 pounds in cash and shares, though whether the deal came off or not, or what the mine was worth, I am not aware.

The company's representative in Coolgardie welcomed us with great hospitality, and invited us to tea at his camp. Here he produced whisky, and what he told us he considered the very best of tinned meats. "So *help* me never, it's *minced mutton*!" shouted poor Luck, as the tin was opened — a little joke that has never been forgotten.

It is a rather novel sensation to find that you are dead; and this was our experience, for the papers had killed us some time since — our bones had been seen bleaching in the sun, and all that sort of thing. Unfortunately our death was not certain enough to warrant any obituary notices, which might have been interesting reading.

On our return to Perth, the manager of the company for which we had worked, who had arrived in our absence, far from thanking us for having tried our best, asked why we went into a d----d desert to look for gold! This we considered a little mean, seeing that a great part of the country we had traversed had been hitherto unexplored. However, one doesn't look for thanks from a mining company. So our journey was finished — a journey that I shall never look back upon with regret, but with pleasure, for Luck was a fine fellow and the best of mates; and at least we had the satisfaction of knowing that if we had been unsuccessful, it was not for the want of trying.

Part III: Second Prospecting Expedition

Chapter I: The Joys of Portable Condensers

November 8, 1894, was a red-letter day in the history of Coolgardie, for on that date the foundation-stone of the first brick building was laid by Mr. James Shaw, the mayor. Under the stone was deposited a specimen of each coin of the realm, and these, by the way, were purloined in the night. This great day was made the occasion for feasting and jubilation, the feasting taking the not uncommon form of a gigantic "Champagne Spree," to which the whole town was invited.

When once a wave of inebriety swept over the settlement, something a little out of the ordinary was likely to occur. Fights and rows would be started with the most bloodthirsty intentions, only to end in peace and harmony after the swearing of eternal friendships. A good fight in Coolgardie in those days would attract as much attention as a cab accident in the streets of London. The well-known cry of "A fight! a fight!" would bring the greater part of the population from their dwellings — from stores, banks, offices, bars, an excited and rushing crowd would hurry to the scene of the fray, all eager to witness a good row; they were not, as a rule, disappointed, for, as one fight usually breeds several, a fair afternoon's or morning's entertainment could be safely counted on. A mining community must have excitement; even a dog-fight would command a considerable amount of interest.

File:Spinifex and Sand Illustration 9.jpg Bayley Street, Coolgardia, 1894 [Missing image]

On the celebrated night of the laying of the foundation stone I had the pleasure of witnessing a rough-and-tumble fight between two of the most powerful men in Coolgardie. The excitement was intense as one seized his antagonist, and, using him as a flail, proceeded to clear the room with him; he retaliated by overpowering the other man, and finally breaking his leg as they fell heavily together out through the door on to the hard street beyond. How much ill-feeling this little incident engendered may be judged from the fact that the maimed man was employed by his late adversary as clerk until his limb mended, and subsequently held the billet for many months.

It was my misfortune to be engaged in organising a prospecting expedition at this time — misfortune, because of the impossibility of getting any one to attend to business. Camels had to be bought, and provisions and equipment attended to. A syndicate had engaged my services and those of my two companions whom I had chosen in Perth: Jim Conley, a fine, sturdy American from Kentucky, the one; and Paddy Egan, an Irish-Victorian, the other. Both had been some time on the fields, and Conley had had previous experience in South Africa and on the Yukon, where he had negotiated the now famous Chilcoot Pass without realising that it was the tremendous feat that present-day travellers represent it to be.

There are few men more entertaining than diggers, when one can get them to talk; there is hardly a corner of the habitable globe to which they have not penetrated. Round a camp-fire one will hear tales of Africa, New Guinea, New Zealand, Australia, America from Alaska to the Horn, Madagascar, and other strange countries that would be a mine of information to a writer of books of adventure — tales told in the main with truth and accuracy, and in the quiet, unostentatious manner of the habitual digger to whom poverty, riches, and hardships come all in their turn as a matter of course.

Having chosen my mates, the next thing to be done was to procure beasts of burden. Of numerous camels submitted for inspection I took three, which were subsequently christened "Czar," "Satan," and "Misery" respectively; the first from his noble and king-like mien, the second from his wild and exceedingly unpleasant habit of kicking and striking — habits due not to vice but to the nervousness of youth — and the third from his plaintive remonstrances and sad-eyed looks of reproach as his saddle and load were placed on his back.

The price of a good pack-camel then varied from 60 pounds to 80 pounds — and such prices as 100 pounds to 130 pounds were given for first-class riding-camels. For South Australian-bred camels, the descendants of stock originally imported from India by Sir Thomas Elder some thirty years ago, a higher price was asked than for those brought into the Colony direct from Kurrachi; and rightly, for there can be no doubt but that in size, strength, and endurance, the camel of Australian birth is far ahead of his old-world cousin. Not only are Indian camels smaller and less fitted for the heavy work of the interior, but their liability, until acclimatised, to mange and other diseases makes them most undesirable acquisitions.

The near approach of midsummer, and the known scarcity of water, had induced me to include in my equipment a portable condenser, by means of which we should convert the brine of the salt lakes into water fit to drink. It seemed an excellent plan and so simple, for lakes abound — on the maps; and wherever a lake is, there, by digging, will water be found, and thus we should be independent of rock-holes and other precarious sources of supply. Plans so simple on paper do not always "pan out" as confidently expected and a more odious job, or one which entailed more hard work, than prospecting with condensers I have not had to undertake. "Prospecting" is generally taken to mean searching for gold. In Western Australia in the hot weather it resolves itself into a continual battle for water, with the very unlikely contingency that, in the hunt for a drink, one may fall up against a nugget of gold or a gold-bearing quartz reef.

On November 10th we made a start from Coolgardie, and, travelling along the Twenty-five Mile road for some fifteen miles, we branched off in an easterly direction, to try some country where I had previously found "colours" of gold, when journeying from Kurnalpi to the Twenty-five Mile. Finding that in the meantime others had been there and pegged out leases and claims, we passed on and set up our condensers on the "Wind and Water" lake, and began to get an inkling that our job was not to be of the pleasantest.

More than one hole six to fifteen feet deep had to be sunk before we struck any water. To lessen the labour we at first dug our shafts near the margin of the lake; this proving unsuccessful we were forced further and further out, until our efforts were rewarded by a plentiful supply, but alas! some three hundred yards from the shore. This necessitated the carrying of wood from the margin of the lake to the condensers. The boilers required constant attention day and night, the fires had to be stoked, and the water stored as it slowly trickled from the cooling tray. Thus the duties of the twenty-four hours consisted in chopping and carrying wood, watching the condensers, attending to the camels, occasionally sleeping and eating, and prospecting for gold in spare time. I think my readers will readily understand that it was hard indeed to find much time to devote to the proper object of the expedition, however willing we were to do so.

There were one or two others engaged on the same job at that lake, and from one party Czar sneaked a cheap drink by thrusting his head through the opening in the lid of a large two-hundred-gallon tank. His peculiar position was specially adapted to the administration of a sound beating, nor did the infuriated owner of the water fail to take advantage of the situation.

With our tanks filled and our camels watered, we set forth from the lake on November 21st, having prospected what country there was in its immediate neighbourhood. The heat was intense, and walking, out of training as we were, was dry work; our iron casks being new, gave a most unpleasant zinc taste to the water, which made us all feel sick. Unpleasant as this was, yet it served the useful purpose of checking the consumption of water. Our route lay past the "Broad Arrow" to a hill that I took to be Mount Yule, and from there almost due east to Giles' Pinnacles. Our camels were most troublesome; young, nervous, and unused to us or to each other, they would wander miles during the night, and give two of us a walk of three or four miles in the morning; before the day's work began. Two were not content with merely wandering, but persisted in going in one direction, the third in another.

One morning Conley and Egan were following their tracks each in a different quarter. I meanwhile climbed a neighbouring hill to spy out the land ahead, hoping to see the white glitter of a salt lake, for we were in likely country, ironstone blows, quartz, and diorite giving evidence of its probable auriferous nature; we were therefore anxious to find water to enable us to test it. On return to camp, after an absence of not more than half an hour, I was astonished to see it surrounded by the tracks of numerous "black-fellows." I guessed they had paid us a visit for no good purpose, and was hardly surprised when I found that they had not only stolen all our flour, but added insult to injury by scattering it about the ground. Not daring to leave the camp, lest in my absence they should return and take all our provisions, I was unable to follow the thieves, and had to wait in patience the return of the camels.

So far had they wandered in their hobbles, that by the time we were ready to start the blacks must have gained too great an advantage in distance to make it worth our while to follow them; nor, since they started off in the direction from which we had come, was it any use tracking them with the hope of getting water. So we pushed on eastwards, through open forest of gums, scrubs, and thickets, broken by occasional small plains of saltbush, seeing no signs of water or lake, when presently we entered a belt of sandy desert — rolling sandhills, spinifex-clad, with occasional thickets of mulga and mallee.

Monotonous work it was, dragging the wretched camels for eight to ten hours at a stretch, inciting them to fresh exertions by curses and beatings, kindness and caresses, in turn. In some respects a camel resembles a bullock; not only does he chew his cud, but he loves to be sworn at; no self-respecting ox will do an ounce of work until his driver has flung over him a cloud of the most lurid and hair-raising language. Now, a camel draws the line at blasphemy, but rejoices in the ordinary oaths and swear-words of every-day life in much the same way as a retriever. There is no animal more susceptible to kindness than a camel; but in a sandy sea of scrub with the blazing sun almost boiling the water, milk-like from zinc, in the tanks, loads dragged this way and that, boilers and pipes of condensers rolling, now forward, now back, eventually to slip clattering down, bearing camel and all to the ground — with these and other trials kindness was not in us.

Soon after sunset on the 27th, from the branches of a high gum tree we sighted the Pinnacles almost dead on our course; and late that night we reached the lake, and found to our joy a condenser already established, by means of which two men earned a precarious livelihood by selling water to travellers — for these lakes were on the direct track from Kurnalpi to the Mount Margaret district. Thus enabled to assuage the seven days' thirst of the camels forthwith, at the cost of a shilling per gallon, we lost no time in setting up our own plant, and were fortunate in finding water and wood easy of access. The next four days were spent in prospecting the surrounding country, but no gold rewarded our efforts, though numerous reefs and blows of quartz were to be seen in the hills which the lake nearly surrounds.

Whilst camped here, I took the opportunity of breaking in Satan as a riding-camel, and found him at first a most untameable customer, trying all sorts of dodges to get the better of me. Twisting round his neck he would grab at my leg; then, rolling, he would unseat and endeavour to roll on me; finally tiring of these tricks he would gallop off at full speed, and run my leg against a tree, or do his best to sweep me off by an overhanging branch, until I felt satisfied that he had been rightly named. At last he realised that I was master, and after that I hardly remember one occasion on which he gave any trouble; for the three years that I afterwards possessed him, we were the best of friends, and he the most gentle and biddable of beasts. Alas! that I should have had to end his days with a bullet, and leave his bones to be picked by the dingoes of the Great Sandy Desert.

Failing to find any gold, and being in need of flour, we made south to Kurnalpi, through country flat and uninteresting, and arrived at that camp just in time to secure the last two bags of flour. The town was almost deserted, and had none of the lively and busy appearance that it presented when I had last seen it. All who saw us praised our equipment and forethought in having portable condensers. I am not quite sure that we agreed with them.

Hearing that some promising country existed near Lake Roe, I decided to make for that place, and more particularly for a small rock-hole named Beri, at the west end of the lake. Very rough, stony hills covered with dense scrub surround Kurnalpi on the south; once across these, flat, open country of saltbush and samphire, rapidly changing into salt-swamp, made travelling easy; passing over another low range of diorite, from which we got an extensive view of Lake Lapage to the west and Lake Roe to the east, we reached Beri, hitting off the rock with so much accuracy that even Paddy Egan was surprised into praise of the compass. For some bushmen, be it known, can neither understand nor appreciate the use of a compass, and, being quite capable of finding their way back, are content to wander forth into the bush with no guide but the sun, taking no notes of the country, no record of their day's march, and making no observations to help either themselves or anybody else; unable to say where they have been, how they got there, or how they got home again. Some men have a natural instinct for direction, and I know some who could start, say from Coolgardie, to ride seventy miles east and return, then perhaps sixty to the north, and from that point ride across to their seventy-mile point with great ease and certainty, having no notion of the distance or point of the compass.

A good many prospectors, depending on their black-boys almost entirely, wander from one range of hills to another, dodge here and there for water, keep no count or reckoning, and only return by the help of their guide when the "tucker-bags" are empty; others make a practice of standing two sticks in the ground on camping at night, to remind them of the course they have travelled during the day and must resume in the morning. To such men as these a map or compass is useless and therefore of no value; and yet they are often spoken of by the ignorant as "best bushmen in Australia."

In my time I have seen and mixed with most prospectors in the West, and as far as my experience goes the best bushmen not only use the compass, but keep a reckoning, rough though it may be, of their day's travel. Such a man is Billy Frost, to quote a well-known name on the goldfields, a man who has had no chance to learn any of the rudiments of surveying, and who started life as a boundary rider on a cattle station. He has shown me a note-book in which he has jotted down directions and distances from water.

In mountainous country where landmarks are numerous the traveller may manage it; but no man could travel for any length of time without keeping some sort of reckoning, in a flat country like the interior of Western Australia, where for days together one sees no hill or rise, without before long becoming hopelessly lost.

Paddy Egan had been content to travel in this haphazard way, and it was long before he would acknowledge the benefits of a compass and map. That he could travel straight there was no gainsaying, for if, as I sometimes did, I pointed out our line and sent him ahead, he would go as straight as a die, with now and then a glance at the sun, and a slight alteration in his course to allow for its altered position, and require but little correction. Indeed, even when using a compass, one instinctively pays as much and more attention to the sun or the stars, as the case may be.

The rock-hole at Beri was dry, so we pushed on for Lake Roe, and, though we worked sinking holes until past midnight, and nearly the whole of the next day, we were unable to find water. It was only salt water we expected, but a stiff pipeclay, continuing to a depth too great for our limited means of sinking, baffled all our efforts. I followed the lake some six miles to the eastward, carrying a shovel and digging trial holes at intervals, but this pipeclay foiled me everywhere.

I do not know how far this lake runs east, and fancy its limits have never been laid down on the map; not that there is anything sufficiently inviting in its appearance — the usual flat expanse of mud, with banks of sand fringed with low straggling mallee and spinifex — to warrant further investigation.

Lake Roe having failed us, we turned on our tracks for the nearest point of Lake Lapage, some nine miles distant. Here we were more fortunate, and obtained a splendid supply of salt water at a depth of only three feet. Timber was not easily got — that would have been too much joy! It had to be carried nearly half a mile on our shoulders, for the camels, having travelled all day, deserved a rest. The condensers worked well, now that we had had some experience, and produced water at the rate of four gallons an hour. With our casks replenished and our camels filled, leaving the condenser standing, we turned south to some hills that were visible; we intended to be absent for four days, at the end of which the camels would again require water, as the weather was exceedingly hot.

Nothing of interest was met with until we came upon a huge wall-like reef, standing some fifteen or twenty feet above the ground, from ten to twenty feet wide, and running almost due north and south for nearly five miles, without a break of appreciable extent, as we subsequently found. Breaking the quartz at intervals, hoping at each blow of the pick to see the longed-for colours, we followed this curious natural wall, and finally camped, sheltered by it from the wind. A violent storm of dust, wind, thunder, and lightning swept over us that night, tearing the "fly" we had pitched, in the vain expectation of rain, into ribbons.

Leaving the others to continue prospecting, I turned my steps, or rather those of Satan, whom I was riding, towards Cowarna, a large granite rock, some fourteen miles distant, and due south from our camp, if I had reckoned our position on the map correctly. Twelve miles of open forest, alternating with scrubby thickets, brought me to the edge of a fine little plain of saltbush and grass, from the centre of which a bare rock of granite stood out. Arrived at the rock, I hunted long and diligently for water. Numerous rock-holes were to be seen, but all were dry, and my hopes of making this our base from which to prospect in various directions were at first short-lived; but before long I was overjoyed to hear the twittering of a little flock of Diamond sparrows — a nearly certain sign that water must be handy; and sure enough I found their supply at the bottom of a narrow, round hole, down which I could just stretch my arm.

Part III: Second Prospecting Expedition

Chapter II: Granite Rocks, "Namma Holes", and "Soaks"

At this point it may not be amiss to give a short description of these peculiar outcrops of granite, without which the track from York to Coolgardie could never have been kept open, nor the place discovered, nor could its early inhabitants have supported life before the condensing plant came into general use.

The interior of the Colony, between the coast and a point some hundred miles east of Coolgardie, is traversed by parallel belts of granite, running in a general direction of north-north-west and south-south-east. This granite crops out above the surface, at intervals of from ten to twenty or thirty miles, sometimes in the form of an isolated barren rock, and sometimes as low ranges and hills several miles in extent. From them small creeks, and sometimes larger watercourses, run down, to find their way into the stony and gravelly debris which usually surrounds the rocks. Much of what little rain does fall is absorbed by the trees and scrub, and much is taken by the sun's heat, so that a very small proportion can sink below the surface soil, and only when there is some underground basin in the rock beneath will water be found by sinking, except immediately after rain.

Round the granite base a belt of grass of no great extent may be found, for the most part dry and yellow, but in places green and fresh. It is in such spots as these that one may hope to tap an underground reservoir in the rock. To these shallow wells has been given the name of "Soaks." They seldom exceed fifteen feet in depth, though similar subterranean basins have been tapped by a well perhaps a hundred feet deep, sunk some distance from the foot of the outcrop. A good soak will stand a heavy drain for perhaps months, but not having its origin in a spring the supply ultimately ceases.

The soil, being alluvial, is in most cases easy to dig, and when the bed rock is reached it becomes an open question whether to go deeper into the decomposed rock or to be content with what supply has been struck. Many a good soak has been ruined by a too ambitious worker, who, after infinite toil, may see his priceless fluid disappear down some hidden crack beneath. Native soaks dug out with sticks and wooden "coolimans" — small troughs used as spades or as a means of carrying seeds, water, or game — are by no means uncommon, and, when holding water, are easily made more serviceable by throwing out a few shovelsful of sticks, stones, and sand, with which they are generally choked. Often the weary traveller has no such lucky help, and must set to work to dig a soak for himself and his thirsty beasts — against time, too, in a blazing sun, without the comforting knowledge that there is any certainty of finding water. I do not know of any case when a party has actually perished at the mouth of a waterless soak, but in many instances water has been struck when all hope had been given up. The skeletons and carcasses of camels and horses tell a tale of suffering that no man who has travelled can look at unmoved, and go to show that many a beast of burden has been less fortunate than his masters.

With what eager anxiety the shovelsful are watched, when the expected "bottom" is nearly reached, by man and beast alike, who, utterly weary and absolutely parched, know that they are soon to learn their fate. The horses snort and plunge in eager and impatient expectation, whilst the patient camel contents himself with grunts and moans, though, as his knees are probably strapped beneath him, he cannot protest more forcibly. At length, perhaps, all are rewarded by the welcome sight of a tiny trickle in one corner, or perhaps the hole turns out a "duffer," and the weary, weary work must be commenced again in a fresh spot.

In many cases these granite rocks have been utilised as a catchment area for tanks, into which the water is led by drains, which encircle the foot of the outcrop. Before the railway was built, such tanks, sunk by Government along the Southern Cross-Coolgardie track, enabled teamsters to bring their horses through with safety, which would otherwise have been impossible at some seasons of the year.

I append a table showing cost and contents of Government tanks excavated at the base of granite rocks between Southern Cross and Coolgardie: —

Name of Reservoir.	Cost	Contents in Gallons	Cost per Million Gallons (pounds).
Reen's Soak	£3,246	900,000	3,607
Kararawalgee	2,947	1,250,000	2,858
Boorabbin	3,025	900,000	3,461
Woolgangee	3,825	1,2501000	3,100
Bullabulling	4,118	1,250,000	3,294
Coolgardie (No, 1)	1,167	800,000	1,454
Coolgardie (No. 2)	2,110	1,400,000	1,503
Halgoorlie (half-way)	1,266	500,000	2,532
Kalgoorlie...	1,554	500,000	3,108
Twenty-five Mile Tank	1,881	500,000	3,762
Forty Mile Tank	1,546	500,000	3,092
Colreavy's Tank	2,193	997,000	2,199

The above table will give some idea of the enormous expense entailed by the opening up of the interior. In addition to these, wells and bores were put down, many of which failed to strike water.

Ever-thoughtful Nature has provided, on the surface of the "granites," small reservoirs which, after rain, may, in some cases, hold many hundred gallons of water. The Rock — or Namma-holes (I presume "Namma" is a native name, but of this I am uncertain) are usually more or less conical in shape, and vary in depth from a few inches to twenty feet, and in diameter from half a foot to several. Their sides are smooth, and slope down to a rounded bottom, where stones are often found which would suggest that they have had something to do with the formation of these peculiar holes. Beneath a hard surface layer the rock becomes decomposed and comparatively soft; and doubtless the rain of countless ages collecting round the stones, once on the surface and now found at the bottom of the holes, has at length weathered away the rock, and so by slow degrees the stone has ground out an ever-increasing hollow. I am neither geologist nor dentist, but I have often likened in my mind the formation of the Namma-holes to the gradual hollow formed by decay in a tooth. Whatever their history, their use is unquestionable — not so the flavour of their contents; for every bird or beast coming to water will leave some traces behind, and the natives, to prevent evaporation, throw in sticks, stones, and grass. Such a collection of rubbish and filth might naturally be supposed to render the water unhealthy, but apparently this is not the case, for we have often been forced to drink water, which, in civilisation would be thought only fit to be used as manure for the garden, without any injury to health or digestion. Patient search over the whole surface of the rock is the usual method for finding rock-holes, though sometimes the pads of wallabies, kangaroos, or emus, may serve as a guide to them, but game is so scarce that a man must usually trust to his own observation. Sometimes their existence may be detected from a distance by the patch of rock round the mouth showing white, owing to its being worn by the feet of birds and animals.

A typical rock was the high, barren "Cowarna," and one that after rain would store in its depressions a plentiful supply of the life-giving water. Thankful for small mercies, I made the best of a bad job, and, having no dish or bucket from which to give Satan a drink, I was obliged to make him lie down close to the narrow hole, whilst into his willing throat I poured the water which at arm's length I scooped up with my quart pot. This tedious process finished, I still had a potful at my disposal, so, taking a long drink myself, I stripped off my clothes and indulged in a shower bath, Not a luxurious bathe certainly, and a larger supply would have been acceptable, but every little helps, and even a few drops of fresh water have a pleasant effect on one's body made sticky by the salt of the water from the lakes, and serve to remind the traveller that he has once been clean.

Condensing water on a salt lake

Leaving the rock at sundown I travelled well into the night, for progress was slow through the scrub and trees in the darkness, but little relieved by the light of a waning moon. Feeling sure that I had gone far enough, I was preparing to rest awhile and find our camp in the morning, when the welcome glow of a fire shot up through the branches. Jim and Paddy, with characteristic thought and resource, had climbed to the top of two tall and dead gum trees and there built fires, fanned by the fierce draught through the hollow trunks, knowing well at what a short distance a fire on the ground is visible in this flat country. During my absence they had found no gold, but, as they liked the look of the country, we decided to return to our condensers for a fresh supply of water. Having obtained this, Egan and I revisited our previous prospecting ground, leaving Jim behind to "cook" water against our return; and a more uninteresting occupation I cannot well picture. Camped alone on a spit of sand, surrounded by a flat expanse of mud, broiled by the sun, half blinded by the glare of the salt, with no shade but a blanket thrown over a rough screen of branches, and nothing to do but to stoke up the fires, change the water in the cooling-trough, and blow off the salt from the bottom of the boilers, he was hardly to be envied. Yet Jim cheerfully undertook the job and greeted us on our return, after four days, with the smiling remark that his work had been varied by the necessity of plugging up the bottom of one of the boilers which had burned through, with a compound (a patent of his own) formed from strips of his shirt soaked in a stiff paste of flour. That night we were astonished by the passage of a flight of ducks over our heads, which Egan saw, and I and Conley heard distinctly.

A detailed account of our wanderings would be as wearying to the reader as they were to ourselves, a mere monotonous repetition of cooking water and hunting for "colours" which we never found. Christmas Eve, 1894, saw us in the vicinity of Mount Monger, where a few men were working on an alluvial patch and getting a little gold. A lucky storm had filled a deep clay-hole on the flat running north-west from the hills, and here we were at last enabled to give the camels a cheap drink; for over six weeks we had not seen a drop of fresh water beyond what, with infinite labour, we had condensed, with the one exception of the small rock-hole I found at Cowarna. My entry in my journal for Christmas Day is short and sweet: "Xmas Day, 1894. Wash clothes. Write diary. Plot course." We had no Christmas fare to make our hearts glad and but for the fortunate arrival of my old friend David Wilson, who gave us a couple of packets of cornflour, would have had a scanty feast indeed.

Even in the remote little mining camp Santa Claus did not forget us, and spread his presents, in the form of a deluge of rain, on all alike. What a pleasant change to get thoroughly wet through! The storm hardly lasted twenty minutes, but such was its violence that every little creek and watercourse was soon running, and water for weeks to come was secured and plentiful in all directions; but so local is a summer storm that five miles from the camp, no water or signs of rain were to be seen. Our provisions being finished, nothing remained but to make all speed for Coolgardie, some fifty miles distant by road. Unencumbered by the condensers, which were abandoned as useless since the bottom of both boilers had burned through, we made fair time, reaching a good camping-ground two miles from the town on the evening of the second day, the 30th of December.

Part III: Second Prospecting Expedition

Chapter III: A Fresh Start

Four days sufficed to make preparations for another trip, to hear and read the news, and write letters. My first, of course, was to my Syndicate, to report our past movements and future plans, and how I intended making northward, hoping that change of direction would change our luck.

January 4th we set out with the same three camels, and rations for three months. My plan was first to revisit some known good country to the south of Hannan's, and, if unsuccessful, to travel from that point in a more or less north-north-west direction, and so follow, instead of crossing, the trend of the various formations; for in travelling from east to west, or *vice verse*, one crosses a succession of parallel belts, first a sand-plain, then a ridge of granite, next a timbered flat, then a stretch of auriferous country, with possibly a belt of flat salt-lake country on either side. Since these parallel belts run nearly north-north-west, it seemed to the mind of the untrained geologist that by starting in a known auriferous zone, and travelling along it in a north-north-west direction, the chances of being all the time in auriferous country would be increased, and the plan worth trying.

Passing the homestead of the Hampton Plains Land Company, where I was given valuable information and a map by the courteous and kind manager, Mr. Anderson (now alas! dead, a victim to the typhoid scourge), we continued on the Lake Lefroy road as far as the Fourteen Mile rock-hole. This contained water, but so foul that the camels would not look at it. Nor were we more successful in our next water-hole, for it contained a dead horse. Leading to this Namma-hole, which was prettily situated on a low rock at the foot of a rough, broken ridge of granite, surrounded by green and shady kurrajongs, we found a curious little avenue of stones. These were piled up into heaps laid in two parallel rows, and at intervals between the heaps would be a large boulder; evidently this was the work of aboriginals, but what meaning to attach to it we could not think. The beginning of our journey promised well for water, for we were again favoured by a local thunderstorm which, in clay-pans and swamps, left a plentiful supply. Mr. Anderson had told me of some hills in which he had found gold in small quantities, and sure enough wherever we tried a "dish of dirt," colours were sure to result. A pleasant camp was this, plenty of water, numberless quartz reefs, every prospect of finding payable gold, and feed of the best kind in profusion — a welcome change for our beasts. They were shedding the last of their winter coats, and, as the weather was hot, I hastened the transformation by pulling off great flakes of wool with which Egan stuffed one of the saddles. Poor Misery had an uncomfortable experience here in consequence of catching the rings of his hobble-chain in the broken stump of a bush, so that he was held captive all night.

The advance of civilisation was marked by the appearance of a small herd of bullocks, evidently stragglers from "Hannan's," and had we been further from that place I do not doubt that our desire for fresh beef might have overcome our conscientious scruples. Virtue, however, was rewarded, for on awakening one morning I saw advancing towards our camp, with slow and solemn curiosity, two emus, peering now this way, now that, examining our packs and other gear with interest and delight. Choosing the younger bird, I took aim with my Winchester, and dropped him; the report of the rifle startled my companions from their sleep with the thought that we were perhaps attacked by the blacks, for emus are even less numerous than they. But their surprise was not greater than that of the surviving bird, as he gazed spellbound at his dead mate, whom we found most excellent eating. Great as the temptation was to have a shot at the remaining bird, I resisted it, as from the one we could get sufficient meat for our requirements, and it seemed a shame to take the life, for mere pleasure, of the only wild creature we had seen for many weeks.

Tiring at length of prospecting reefs, blows, and alluvial with no better result than an occasional pin's-head of gold, we turned our faces to the north, passing again the herd of cattle wallowing in the swamps and pans of rain water.

Clay-pans usually occur in the neighbourhood of salt lakes, and are merely shallow depressions with smooth clay bottoms. Though as a rule not more than a few inches to a foot in depth, I have seen them in places holding four to five feet of water. Immediately after rain all clay-pans are fresh, before long some will turn salt; those containing drinkable water are often distinguishable by the growth of cane grass which covers the bed, a coarse, rush-like grass of no value as food for stock. Dry for three-quarters of the year, these pans, with their impervious bottoms, hold the rain, when it fills them, for a considerable period.

Salt-water pans are pellucid and clear, as the inexperienced may find at his cost. One thirsty day, having tramped many miles horse-hunting, deceived by a crystal-clear sheet of water, I plunged in my head and hands, and, before I realised my mistake, took a deep draught with most unpleasant results. I have been more careful since that catastrophe. An effective method of clearing muddy clay-pan water is by dropping into it a sort of powdery gypsum, called "Kopi" by the natives, which is usually to be found round the margin of the salt lakes — a wonderful provision of Nature, without which the water after a short time would be useless, becoming as it does red and thick, and of the consistency of strong cocoa. Amongst the many industries started on the goldfields is the novel occupation of clearing clay-water for salt. The process was carried out by means of a series of settling tanks, into which the water was led by drains, and into the last tank the kopi was thrown; the cleared water was then bailed into vessels or casks, and carted up to whatever mining camp was being thus supplied.

Whilst on the subject of industries, I may mention that of obtaining solder from meat-tins by piling them into large heaps and lighting a fire over them. The melted lumps of solder thus formed were collected by the ordinary process of dry-blowing, and sold to tinsmiths and others engaged in the manufacture of condensers. Certainly the scarcity of water was not an unmixed curse, for it gave employment to many who would otherwise have been hard put to it to gain a living. Dam-makers, well-sinkers, water-carters, tinsmiths, condenser-fitters, wood-cutters, employees on condensing plants, water-bag makers, caretakers at Government wells, dams, and soaks, engineers, and many more, all found employment either directly or indirectly in connection with water supply.

By sinking in the bed of dry clay-pans water can usually be obtained, but unfortunately it is almost sure to be salt. The difference between clay-pans before and after rain is most marked. First we have the dry, hard bed of red clay, blistered and cracked into all manner of patterns by the sun's heat; around us the stillness of death, nothing astir unless it be the constant shimmering haze of heat which strikes our faces like the blast from a furnace. Rain falls, and within a few hours the air will be filled with the croaking of frogs and the cackling of ducks.* To my mind it is one of the most incomprehensible things in Nature that wildfowl (for not only ducks, but sometimes swans and geese are seen) know when and where rain has fallen.

But, stranger still, how do they know it is going to fall? That they would seem to do so the following will go to show. Whilst we were condensing on Lake Lapage, one moonlight night we saw a flight of ducks fly over us to the northward. No surface water then existed anywhere near us. This was on December 16th. No rain fell in the district until December 25th, but I ascertained afterwards that rain fell at Lake Carey, one hundred miles north of Lake Lapage about the same date that we had seen the ducks. The exact date I am not sure of, but in any case the ducks either foresaw the rain or knew that rain had fallen at least two hundred miles away; for they must have come from water (and at that season there was no surface water within one hundred miles of us) and probably from the coast. In either case, I think it is an extremely interesting fact, and however they arrive the ducks are a welcome addition to the prospector's "tucker-bags."

* Sir John Forrest, in his exploration of 1874, found ducks, geese, and swans on Lake Augusta — a salt lake in the arid interior, five hundred miles from the coast.

Part III: Second Prospecting Expedition

Chapter IV: A Camel Fight

Leaving Hannan's on our left, we continued our northerly course, over flat country timbered with the usual gum-forest, until we reached the auriferous country in which our camp had been robbed by the blacks; nothing of interest occurring until January 17th, when we found ourselves without water. Knowing that we must soon strike the road from Broad Arrow to Mount Margaret, this gave us no anxiety, and, beyond the necessity of travelling without having had a drink for eighteen hours, but little discomfort.

We struck the road as expected, and, following it some five miles, came to a small, dry creek running down from a broken range of granite. Sinking in its bed, we got a plentiful supply. Mosquitoes are very rarely found in the interior, but on this little creek they swarmed, and could only be kept away by fires of sticks and grass, in the smoke of which we slept.

From the granite hills a fine view to the eastward was obtained, across a rich little plain of saltbush and grass, and dotted here and there over it was a native peach tree, or "quondong," a species of sandalwood. We had now left the timber behind us, its place being taken by a low, straggling scrub of acacia, generally known as "Mulga," which continues in almost unbroken monotony for nearly two hundred miles; the only change in the landscape is where low cliffs of sandstone and ranges of granite, slate, or diorite, crop up, from which creeks and watercourses find their way into salt swamps and lakes; and occasional stretches of plain country.

Through these thickets we held on our course, passing various watering-places and rocks on the several roads leading to the then popular field of Mount Margaret.

All such rocks bear names given to them by travellers and diggers, though one can seldom trace the origin or author of the name, "Black Gin Soak," "George Withers' Hole," "The Dead Horse Rocks," and the "Donkey Rocks," are fair samples.

It was at the last named that we had a slight entertainment in the shape of a camel-fight. On arrival we found another camel-man (i.e., a man who prospects with camels instead of horses, not necessarily a camel-driver) in whose train was a large white bull. Misery, with his usual precocity, at once began to show fight. The owner of the white camel, a gentleman much given to "blowing," warned me that his bull was the "strongest in the — — country," and advised me to keep my camels away. Anxious to see how Misery would shape in a genuine bout, I paid no heed, but took the precaution to remove his hobbles, thus placing him on equal terms with his older and stronger adversary.

Before very long they were at it hammer and tongs, roaring and grunting to the music of the bells on their necks; wrestling and struggling, using their great long necks as flails, now one down on his knees and almost turned over, and now the other, taking every opportunity of doing what damage they could with their powerful jaws, they formed a strange picture. Misery was nearly exhausted, and the white bull's master in triumph shouted, "Take 'em off, beat 'em off; your — — camel'll be chewed up!" But no! With a last expiring effort, brave little Misery dived his long neck under the body of his enemy, and grabbed his hind leg by the fetlock, when a powerful twist turned him over as neatly as could be. It was now time for us to interfere before the white bull's head was crushed by his conqueror's knees and breast-bone. With sticks and stones we drove him off, and the white bull retired abashed — but not more so than his master.

Leaving the rocks in possession of our late adversary we once more plunged into the scrub, altering our course to the west with the object of revisiting the country around Mount Ida, where Luck and I had found colours. Our way lay between salt lakes on our left, and a low terrace or tableland of what is locally known as "conglomerate" on our right. At the head of a gully running from this we were fortunate in finding water, sufficient to fill our casks, and give each camel a drink. This was on the morning of January 25th, and until the 31st about noon we saw no further signs of water. Every likely place was dry. Where Luck and I had found water before, not a drop of moisture could be seen; the holes contained nothing but the feathers and skeletons of disappointed birds. Unable to stop at Mount Ida without packing water twenty-five miles, which the prospects of the country did not warrant, we turned northwards across much broken granite country, which we vainly searched for Namma-holes or soaks. Far ahead of us we could see sharp pinnacles, standing up high and solitary above the scrub. These turned out to be huge blows of white quartz, and were no doubt connected underground, for we traced them a distance of nearly thirty miles. Interesting as these were, our thoughts were turned to water-hunting, for the weather — the season being midsummer — was scorching; the poor camels, sore-footed from the stony granite, parched with thirst, and forced to carry their loads, eight to twelve hours a day, showed signs of distress. Weary and footsore ourselves, tramping at full speed all day over the burning rocks, one with the camels, the others on either hand, scouting, our casks all but empty, our position was not enviable.

The night of the 30th our water was finished. The nearest known to us was thirty-five miles off, and a a salt lake was between — a sufficient bar to our hopes in that direction. Matters were by no means desperate, however, for thirty miles north we were bound to cut the Cue-Mount Margaret road, and having done so it would be merely a question of time, with a certainty of arriving at a watering place eventually, if we and our camels could hold out. A dry stage, however long, with the certainty of relief at the end of it, gives little cause for anxiety when compared with one on which neither the position nor even the existence of water can be known.

Next morning we followed up a small creek, and on crossing saw the tracks of several kangaroos and emus making towards two peaks of quartz. Here was our chance. It was my place of course to go, but I yielded to the persuasion of Paddy and Jim, who insisted that I had denied myself water to eke out our scanty supply (though I doubt if I had done so more than they), and must rest. So, putting the camels down in the welcome shade of a kurrajong, I lay down beside them and was presently relieved by the sound of a revolver-shot, our signal that water was found.

What a beautiful sight it was! Nestling in the hollow between two great white blows of quartz, this little pool of crystal-clear water, filled evidently by a little gully falling over a steep ledge of quartz beyond, presented no doubt a pretty picture after the rains. A soakage it must be, for no open rock-hole could hold water in such terrible heat; and its clearness would suggest the possibility of an underlying spring. A popular drinking-place this, frequented by birds of all kinds, crows, hawks, pigeons, galahs, wee-jugglers, and the ubiquitous diamond-sparrows. During the night we could hear wallabies hopping along, but were too worn out to sit up to shoot them. Though our sufferings had not been great, we had had a "bit of a doing."

One day's rest, occupied in various mendings of clothes, boots, and saddles, and we were off again to the north, cutting the track as expected, and presently found ourselves at the newly established mining camp of Lawlers, prettily situated on the banks of a gum-creek, with a copious supply of water in wells sunk in its bed. A great advantage that the northern fields have over those further south is the occurrence of numerous creeks, sometimes traceable for over thirty miles, in all of which an abundance of fresh water can be obtained by sinking at depths varying from fifteen to fifty feet.

Towards the end of their course the well-defined channels, with banks sometimes ten feet high, disappear, giving place to a grassy avenue through the scrub, lightly timbered with cork-bark, and other small trees. It is on such flats as these that the wells are sunk. All creeks find their way into the lakes, though seldom by a discernible channel, breaking and making, as the expression is, until a narrow arm of the lake stretches to meet them. At the most these creeks run "a banker" three times during the year, the water flowing for perhaps three days; after which pools of various sizes remain, to be in their turn dried up by evaporation and soakage. In the dry weather the creeks afford a weird spectacle. Stately white gums (the only timber of any size in these districts), with their silvery bark hanging in dishevelled shreds around the branchless stems, bend ghost-like over an undulating bed of gravel; gravel made up of ironstone pebbles, quartz fragments, and other water-worn debris washed down from the hills at the head of the creeks.

What a marvellous transformation the winter rains cause! It is then that the expert, or journalist, takes his walks abroad; it is then that we read such glowing accounts of rich grass lands, watered by countless creeks, only awaiting the coming of an agriculturist to be turned into smiling farms and fertile fields.

Numerous parties were camped at Lawlers, with some two hundred horses turned out in the bush, waiting until rain should fall. Though with no better feed than grass, dry and withered, the freedom from work had made them skittish. What a pretty sight it is to see a mob of horses trooping in for water at night; the young colts kicking up their heels with delight; the solemn old packhorse looking with scorn on the gambols of his juvenile brethren, with a shake of his hardy old head, as much as to say, "Ah! wait till you've done the dry stages that I have; wait till you make your evening feed off mulga scrub and bark — that'll take the buck out of you! Why can't you have your drink soberly, instead of dancing about all over the place?"

Then bringing up the rear, far behind, just emerging from the scrub, are seen those who, from their wandering habits, must wear the bracelets, hurrying and shuffling along with a rattle of chains, tripping up in their eagerness to be even with their mates in the scramble for water: presently they pause to look about and neigh — a delay resented by those behind by a friendly bite, answered by a kick; which starts them all off at full gallop, in the approved rocking-horse style, with a tremendous clatter of hobbles and bells. Suddenly they halt, snorting, and as suddenly start aside, wheel round, and dash away, as they catch sight of our long-necked beasts. They have seen them often enough, and know them well, but they must keep up an appearance of panic, if only to please their masters, who never cease to jeer at the ungainly shape of the camel, until they possess one themselves. These unemotional animals watch the horses' play with lips turned up in derision, and hardly deign to move their heads from the bush or branch on which they are feeding. Many of the prospectors, though openly sneering at the camels as slow and unmanageable beasts, secretly envied us our ability to travel in hot weather, whilst they had nothing to do but to kick their heels and be thankful they had feed and water for their ponies. And they envied us all the more on account of the vague rumour that rich gold had been found in the neighbourhood of Lake Darlot, towards which some had pushed out only to be driven back by thirst. Seeing our evident advantage, should the rumour prove correct, in being able to get there before the crowd, I decided to steer for the lake, with the hope of picking up the tracks of the supposed lucky diggers.

A large creek, the Erlistoun, was given on the chart as running into the lake, and on it was marked by the discoverer Mr. Wells, of the Elder Exploring Expedition, 1892, a permanent pool. To cut this creek was my object, and, by following its course, to find the pool, and there make a base from which to investigate the truth of the rumour.

Leaving Lawlers February 7th we struck an arm of the lake on the 10th the country traversed being mostly sand plain, timbered with desert-gum. To reach the creek it was necessary to cross the lake; and what a job we had, twisting and turning to avoid one arm, only to be checked by another; carrying packs and saddles across what we supposed to be the main lake, only to find ourselves on an island. All things have an end, even the ramifications of a salt lake, and eventually we and our mud-plastered camels found ourselves on the northern shore; and travelling east, expected confidently to cut the Erlistoun creek. By its position on the map we should have already crossed it but to make sure we went on five miles more, when our passage was barred by another salt lake not marked on the chart. It was clear that the creek did not reach Lake Darlot. Where could it be? Was it worth while to look for it further? It was evident how it came to be so shown on the map. Mr. Wells had cut the creek near its source and seeing only one lake to the south, naturally supposed that it was joined by the creek, and so had marked its probable course by a dotted line. His work, copied on to other maps had been carelessly drawn, and the creek shown running in a defined channel into Lake Darlot. That this was the case I found afterwards on studying his original chart.

Now to decide our best course! Again our supply was all but done, but we knew of no water save Lawlers, sixty miles away, and to attempt to return to that, recrossing the lake was manifestly absurd. To the south-west we could see some hills which might or might not be granite. We were inclined to think that they were, as in the setting sun of a few nights before they had taken a ruddy glow. These rocks appeared to be our only chance.

It has always seemed to me better in such cases to make people follow one's own wishes by seeming to consult theirs, rather than by a direct order. Acting on this plan, though with my own mind made up, I consulted with my two mates. I felt sure that Jim would agree with me, from a remark he had made to a mutual friend to the effect that "he would follow me to h — l." Of paddy I was not so sure; nor was I mistaken. He strongly advised turning back, but, having agreed to abide by the majority, said no more, and so to the hills we turned our steps.

Our hopes that the two lakes were separate were soon shattered, for before us lay a narrow neck connecting the two. There was nothing for it but to go straight ahead. The lightest-packed camel crossed without mischance, but not so the other two; down they went, too weak to struggle, and again the toil of digging them out, and driving and hauling them foot by foot, had to be gone through. Then the packs had to be carried piece by piece, for we sank too deep in the sticky mud with a heavy load, and our weary legs had to be dragged step after step from the bog. Hungry and thirsty, blistered by the glare of the salt in the pitiless sun, we struggled on, with a wondering thought of what the end would be.

Think of us, picture us, ye city magnates, toiling and struggling that your capacious pockets may be filled by the fruits of our labour: think of us, I say, and remember that our experiences are but as those of many more, and that hardly a mine, out of which you have made all the profit, has been found without similar hardships and battles for life! Not a penny would you have made from the wealth of West Australia but for us prospectors — and what do we get for our pains? A share in the bare sale of the mine if lucky; if not, God help us! for nothing but curses and complaints will be our portion. The natural rejoinder to this is, "Why, then, do you go?" To which I can only answer that one must make a living somehow, and that some like to make money hard, and some to make it easily. Perhaps I belong to the former class.

Whatever the reason, the fact remains that in the heat of the summer we were ploughing our way through salt-bogs, without water or any immediate prospect of getting any, and realised, not for the first time, that the prospector's life in West Australia is not "all beer and skittles."

The lake negotiated, we decided to rest under the scanty shade of a mulga tree, and regaled ourselves on oatmeal washed down with a mouthful of water, the last, hot from the iron casks. At a time when water is plentiful it can be carried and kept cool in canvas bags; but it owes this coolness to evaporation, and consequent waste of water. During the hot weather, when water is scarce, I never allowed canvas bags to be used, and so saved water, not only by avoiding evaporation, but from the fact that water carried in galvanised-iron casks becomes so hot and unpalatable that one is not tempted to take a big draught, and thus the supply is eked out.

That night we camped in the thick mulga, and from one of the larger trees I could see the hills, dead on our course, and not more than two miles off. But we were too tired to go further that night, and in any case could have done but little good in the dark. The poor camels were too dry to eat the mulga we cut for them, too dry even to chew the cud; and lay silent, tied down beside us — the stillness of the night being unbroken by the rhythmical "crunch" of their jaws.

Before sunrise we were packed and away, and shortly reached the hills which we found to be, as we had hoped, bare granite rocks. Leaving the camels, we spread out, and searched every hole and corner without success. Every rock-hole was dry. One native soak we found, from which we scraped about half gallon of water none too clear, and the less tempting from the close proximity of the dead body of a gin, a young native woman, fortunately not long dead. The ashes of a native camp but lately deserted, could be seen close by; no doubt they had moved off as the supply of water was so nearly done. Whether they had left the body to become a skeleton, before making a bundle of the bones (a practice common to some Australian tribes), or whether it is their usual custom to leave the dead where they die, I do not know. I know, however, that this body was subsequently moved, not by the blacks, but by those snarling scavengers, the dingoes.

This finding of a corpse at the mouth of the only soak we had seen was hardly encouraging; but still there was a large extent of rocks that we had not yet visited. Shortly before sunset, as I stood on the summit of the highest rock, I was astonished by the sight of some horses grazing in a little valley beneath. I could hardly believe that I saw aright; it seemed incredible that horsemen should have reached this drought-begirt spot. Little time was wasted in idle speculation, and the appearance of our camels soon proved the horses to be flesh and blood, and not mere phantoms of the brain, unless indeed phantoms can snort and plunge!

The owner of the horses soon made his appearance, and, with reluctant resignation, showed us the soak from which his horses were watered. He and his mates, he said, were sinking for water in a likely spot some half-mile away; in the meantime they used the soak, though it was evident it would not last much longer. We must have water for our camels, and must use the soak, I said, until their thirst was somewhat relieved, then in our turn we would dig for soaks round the rocks. In the hottest time of the year our poor patient beasts had been eight days without food, except of the driest description, and eight days without water, struggling and kicking in the salt-bogs. It was indeed a delight to quench their thirst at last. All that night we worked without a minute's rest, digging, scraping, and bailing, and secured enough to keep the camels going. For the next two days we were engaged in sinking trial holes for soakages; no water, however, rewarded our labours until the night of the second day, when we struck a splendid supply, and for the time being our troubles were over. Pitching a "fly" to keep off the sun's rays in the daytime, we were content to do nothing but rest for the whole of the next day. Here again I was fortunate in shooting an emu, a welcome addition to our provisions.

McIlwraith and his mates (the owners of the horses) had also struck a good supply. From them we got the news which we already suspected that a new find of gold had been made not five miles from the rocks. An apparently rich find too! How strangely things turn out. Our ill-fortune in failing to find the Erlistoun had forced us into a most unpleasant experience, and yet that ill-fortune was turning into good. For here we were on the scene of newly-discovered reefs and nuggets, at the new rush, the existence of which we had gravely doubted. We were the third party on the field, and from Messrs. Rogers and friends I heard the history of its discovery.

Part III: Second Prospecting Expedition

Chapter V: Gold at Lake Darlot

About the month of October, 1894, Rogers and party, with their camels, were camped at Cutmore's (or Doyle's) Well, and, on studying the map of the Elder Exploring Expedition, they saw that Mr. Wells had marked the country north of Lake Darlot as "probably auriferous." This they determined to visit, and, more fortunate than ourselves, were not caught in the intricacies of the salt lake.

Returning in disgust, having found no signs of gold, they passed the granites, where they got water, and camped on a promising piece of country, where they soon found gold in the the reefs. Here they worked for some time with but little encouragement, until after Christmas, when alluvial gold was found on the surface by a member of another party who came upon the original discoverers in a somewhat startling manner.

Cable, Janet, and Pickering had pushed out also from Cutmore's Well, and by finding water on a granite between the two, had reached the rocks near Lake Darlot. Here they found camped a tribe of aboriginals, to whom they showed kindness — too much kindness it appears, for the treacherous thieves, having tasted the white man's food, conceived the bold idea of raiding the camp, killing its occupants, and annexing their provisions. At midnight the prospectors were attacked, Cable and Janet being speared as they lay in their blankets, Cable through the stomach and Janet in the arm, Pickering escaping, for he had laid down his blanket under a tree, away from the packs, to get shade from the moon. He is, too, a man of exceptionally small stature, and so eluded the quick sight of the black-fellow.

In spite of the disadvantage under which they were placed by the sudden attack and wounds, the white men overpowered and dispersed their treacherous foes. In what a terrible position they were now placed, fifty-five miles from Cutmore's Well, the nearest certain water, for the chances that the water found between would be dried up, were great! Only one man unwounded and one suffering the most awful tortures of pain; and nobody with the smallest medical skill, within God knows how many miles! Death seemed certain, but while life remained they were not the men to give in, and they thought of a plan whereby the life of their mate might be saved if only their horses held out. They travelled five miles, then camped, and the available man returned to the rocks to water the horses at the risk of being again attacked by the niggers. And thus dot and go one, they hoped to reach Cutmore's.

So much endurance could not remain unrewarded and the two wounded men were overjoyed by the report of a shot (a dynamite shot as it afterwards transpired, fired by Rogers, Parks, and Lockhart as they worked on their reef), and as soon as the horses returned, the little band set forth in the direction from which the welcome sound had come, and before long saw the camp of the lucky prospectors.

Fortunately Mr. Parks had some knowledge of surgery, picked up in the African bush, where he had been a trader, and so could doctor the wounded men. Here they camped until one morning, Janet, recovered of his hurt, picked up a nugget of gold, strangely enough, close to the track from Roger's camp to the reef he was working. This nugget was the first-fruit of a plentiful harvest, and presently they went down to the coast where poor Cable could be properly attended to in hospital. Pickering and Janet returned as soon as possible, but not before some inkling of their find had leaked out; consequently when they returned, just at the time of our arrival on the scene, their tracks were followed, and a "rush" set in.

We were not long in making our camp at the new diggings, or in getting to work to hunt for gold. Being out for a syndicate, who naturally wanted something big in the way of a reef, we were precluded from the alluring search for alluvial, "specking," as it is termed.

It seems the simplest thing in the world to find a good mine — that is, as I said before, after you have found it! On Sunday, February 17th, Paddy and I took a walk, and stepped right on to an outcrop of quartz showing beautiful gold. Quite simple! Any fool can prospect; all he wants is a little luck, and the strange inner urgings that make him examine a certain quartz reef or blow that others have passed, perhaps dozens of times, without happening to look in the right place! Roughly marking out an area, to establish our prior claim to the ground amongst those already on the field, we returned to camp and gave Jim, who had been packing water from the granites, the joyful news.

On Monday before daylight we were out, and soon had eighteen acres marked off by a post at each corner, and our notices posted on a conspicuous tree, which we had been unable to do the day before, Sunday-pegging being illegal.

Fresh parties were now arriving daily, and the consequent demand for water made it necessary for Jim to camp at the rocks, and bring us a supply whenever he was able.

This was not accomplished without some trouble, for not only were the soaks we had dug with so much labour, made use of by the new-comers, which we did not object to, but our right to the water was often disputed by some who, with small regard for the truth, said that it was they who had sunk the wells! Jim, however, was not the man to be bluffed, and, in spite of lameness from sciatica in the loins and hip, managed to keep us well supplied. Short-handed already, we were further handicapped by Paddy smashing his thumb, and thus, for a time, I was the only sound workman of the party.

Part III: Second Prospecting Expedition

Chapter VI: Alone in the Bush

By March 4th we were satisfied that the appearance of the mine was good enough to warrant our applying for a lease of the area already marked out. So leaving Czar behind, to enable Paddy and Jim to pack water, I, riding Satan and leading Misery, loaded with specimens from the reef, set forth for Coolgardie, to apply for the lease, and get a fresh supply of provisions, of which we were sadly in need. My departure for Coolgardie was taken advantage of by several who wished to bank their gold, and thus I became an escort.

Coolgardie lay almost due south, 220 miles on the chart, but nearly 300 miles by the track, which deviated from water to water. Speed being an object, I decided to strike through the bush to George Withers' hole. Here, by the way, poor Alec Kellis had just been murdered by the blacks — not the pleasantest of news to hear, as I started on my solitary journey. I followed a horse pad for fifty-five miles, mostly through thick scrub, to Cutmore's Well, where several parties were camped, who eagerly questioned me as to the richness of the new field.

Leaving Cutmore's, I struck through the bush, and before long the sickness I had had on me for some time past, developed into a raging fever. Every bone in my body ached and shot with pain. I could neither ride nor walk for more than a few minutes at a stretch; I was unable to eat, nor cared to drink the hot water in my canteen. I struggled on, now riding, now walking, and now resting under a bush, travelling in this fashion as long as daylight lasted, from five in the morning until six at night. Afraid to let the camels go at night lest they should wander too far, or, while I was following them in the morning, my packs should be raided by the blacks, I tied them down, one on either side of my blankets; and thus I had not only a protection against the wind, but the pleasure of their companionship — no slight blessing in that solitude.

How lonely I felt, in that vast uninhabited bush! Racked by pain, I tossed from side to side, until sheer weariness kept me still; so still that the silence of death seemed to have fallen upon us; there was not a sound in all that sea of scrub, save the occasional sleepy grunt of one of the camels, until the quiet night re-echoed with the hoarse call of the "Mopoke," which seemed to be vainly trying to imitate the cheerful notes of the cuckoo. How could any note be true in such a spot! or how could a dry-throated bird he anything but hoarse! At last morning came, heralded by the restless shuffling of the camels, and another day's journey began.

Fever stricken and alone

Tying the camels down at nights necessitated the cutting of scrub and bushes for them to feed upon, and I doubt they got little enough to eat. Before long I was too weak to lift the saddles off, and could only with difficulty load and unload the bags of quartz, and, weakened as I was by illness, my labours were not light. Yet further trouble was in store for me, for presently a salt lake barred my way. Then I began to understand the meaning of the word despair. Neither kindness or cruelty would induce my camels to cross; I was therefore forced to follow the banks of the lake, hoping to get round it, as I could see what I supposed was its end. Here I was again baffled by a narrow channel not ten yards wide. It might as well have been half a mile, for all the chance I had of crossing it. The trend of the lake was north-west by south-east, and I was now at the north-west end, but stopped, as I say, by a narrow channel connecting evidently with another lake further to the north-west.

There was nothing for it but to retrace my steps, and follow along the margin of the lake to the south-east, and eventually I got round, having been forced some ten miles out of my course.

I was fortunate in finding water without difficulty, in a small rock-hole amongst some granite hills in which "Granite Creek" takes its rise. From these I had still eighty miles to travel before I could reach a settlement, Coongarrie (the 90 mile) being the nearest point. Could I do it? I had to succeed or perish miserably, and a man fights hard for his life. So I struggled on day and night, stopping at frequent intervals from sheer exhaustion, cursing the pitiless sun, and praying for it to sink below the horizon. Some twenty miles from Coongarrie I was relieved by striking a track, which did away with the necessity of thinking where I was going.

A few miles more, and — joy unspeakable — I found a condenser and a camp. The hospitable proprietor, whose name I never learned, did all he could to make me comfortable, and I felt inclined to stay, but despatch was imperative, for not only must the lease be applied for forthwith, but Conley and Egan must be provisioned. At Coongarrie I gave a swagman a lift, and he helped me with the camels and loads, until at last Coolgardie was reached.

Giving my camels in charge of the first man I could find willing to look after them, an Afghan, Neel Bas by name, I finished my business at the Warden's office. Then, yielding to the persuasion of my friends in Asken and Nicolson's store, I retired to the hospital, for indeed I could fight against my sickness no longer. Here I remained some three weeks under the kind care of Miss O'Brien (now Mrs. Castieau) and Miss Millar, the pioneer nurses on the goldfields. No words can express the admiration I, and all of us, felt for the pluck and goodness of these two gently nurtured ladies, who had braved the discomforts and hardships of the road from York to Coolgardie — discomforts that many of the so-called stronger sex had found too much for them — to set up their hospital tent, and soothe the sufferings of poor fever-stricken fellows.

The services of these kind ladies, and of many that subsequently followed their example, were badly needed, for the typhoid fiend was rampant — carrying off the young, and apparently strong, men at a rate too tremendous to be credible. Funerals were too common to call for even passing notice. "Unwept, unhonoured, and unsung," they went to a nameless grave.

My chief anxiety was for my mates. How could I send them relief, incapacitated as I was? Fortunately, my friend David Wilson offered to go for me, in consideration of a certain interest in the mine we had found. This was a great help, and now I could rest contented; not altogether though, for Neel Bas had some hesitation in giving up the camels, and had a violent row with Dave Wilson, all of which he would insist on explaining to me in broken English, as he sat cross-legs on the floor of my tent. The doctor happily arrived and kicked him out, and I was left in peace. In less than three weeks I was able to go by coach to Southern Cross, and thence by train to Perth, where, under the kind roof of Colonel Fleming, the Commandant, I soon regained my health.

When I mention that my syndicate never even offered to defray the cost of my illness, my readers will understand that my statements as to the ingratitude of those who benefit by the prospectors' toil are not unfounded. Unfortunately for me, my old mate, Lord Douglas, was absent in England, and, in consequence, much misunderstanding resulted between the syndicate and myself.

Part III: Second Prospecting Expedition

Chapter VII: Sale of Mine

During my convalescence in Perth, I occupied my time by drawing in the Government offices, a map, compiled from the various notes and journals I had kept during the prospecting expeditions in which I had been engaged. I also took the opportunity of getting some knowledge of astronomical subjects, likely to be of service in the more extended expedition I had in my mind. My thanks are due to Mr. Barlee, chief draughtsman, and Mr. Higgins, of the Mines Department, for the kindness they showed in helping me in this work.

It was not very long before I felt it was necessary to return to my duties at Lake Darlot. Timing my arrival in Coolgardie to coincide with that of Mr. Wilson from the mine, we met; and from him I was pleased to hear how well the claim was turning out.

Since it was not necessary for both of us to be on the spot, I took one of the camels, of which we now had five, and made all speed to a reported "new rush" near Lake Lefroy, that was causing much excitement. Knots of men could be seen in every corner of the town eagerly discussing the news; gold, to the tune of 30,000 ounces, was being brought in; was in the town; was actually in one of the banks! Many had seen it (or said so). Where was this Eldorado? Every man knew; every man had directions how to get there, from quite unimpeachable sources. It was actually in the local papers; indeed, there could be no doubt about it. I knew of course that all this must be discounted, but the matter was worth looking into, and I was fortunate to get *the* very latest information from one who was an old mate of the supposed lucky digger. I found my travelling companion had equally well authenticated information. On comparing notes we soon discovered that our directions were entirely at variance.

To make a long story short, we at length found that, like hundreds of others, we had been fooled, and that the whole thing was bogus. The diggers' indignation was righteously intense, the office of the offending newspaper was attacked, and much damage narrowly averted. One unfortunate man, on whom fell the wrath of the crowd, returning from the supposed rush, lied profusely when "in drink," said that he had found the spot, that hundreds of men were gleaning rich gold in fabulous quantities, that the world had never seen so wonderful a find, that gold would soon be as cheap as lead in the market — in fact told a thousand and one similar fairy tales, engendered by whisky and excitement. When sober he foolishly stuck to what he had said; and, in consequence, was sent by the diggers, under escort, to point out the spot, which of course he could not find. His reception in Coolgardie may be imagined! Doubtless on the Western goldfields of America, "lynching" would have been his portion. Even in order-loving Australia he might have had an unpleasant time, had not Mr. Finnerty, the popular Warden, quelled the turmoil, and placed the offender under Police protection. For want of the real article, a well-attended procession burnt this idiot's effigy, and thus the great rush ended.

It was supposed by some, if I remember rightly, that the fire which gutted nearly half the town had its origin in this effigy-burning. What a blaze that was to be sure! Tents, shanties, houses of hessian, shops of corrugated iron and wood, offices, hotels, and banks, consumed in one sheet of flame in a matter of half an hour or so, the blaze accompanied by explosions of dynamite caps, kerosene, and cartridges. Nothing could be done to stay its fury. To save the town, houses were demolished, to form wide gaps across which the flames could not reach. It was the general impression that corrugated iron was more or less fireproof. However, it burnt like cardboard. Ruinous to some as the early fires were, they benefited the general community, as more substantial buildings were erected, and hessian shanties forbidden.

After a good deal of unpleasant business over the mine at Lake Darlot, which the syndicate wished to abandon, for reasons best known to themselves, I was at length on the road for that district, with the agreeable news that our mine was for sale, and would soon be off our hands.

I had a rather more enjoyable journey than my previous one, for not only was I free from fever, and the mine in a fair way to being sold, but winter had changed the face of the bush from dull dead yellow to bright smiling green, dotted here and there with patches of white and pink everlastings. One could hardly believe it was the same country. Instead of the intense heat a bright warm sun dissipated the keen and frosty air of early morning, while the hoar-frost at night made one glad of a good possum rug to coil oneself up in. I did not envy the cyclists, for sometimes, failing to hit off a camp on the road, they had perforce to make the best of a fire as a substitute for a blanket, and to be content with a hungry stomach, in place of having a meal.

Before the erection of telegraph wires, which now connect all the more important mining towns, cyclists made good money by carrying special messages from Coolgardie to the outlying districts. Except where the sand was deep they had a good track, well-beaten by the flat pads of camels, and could do their hundred miles a day at a push. Travelling at express rate, they were unable to carry blankets or provisions except of the scantiest description, and took their chance of hitting off the camp of some wayfarer, who would always be ready to show what hospitality he could, to messengers of so much importance. To have to part with one of your blankets on a cold night for the benefit of another traveller, is one of the severest exercises of self denial.

These little kindly services are always rendered, for a man in the bush who would not show courtesy and hospitality to a fellow-wayfarer is rightly considered a cur. No matter what time one strikes a man's camp, his first thought, whether for stranger or friend, is to put on the "billy" and make a pot of tea.

Arrived at Lake Darlot, I found work being carried on well and with energy, as could not fail to be the case where Dave Wilson was concerned. Poor Jim and Paddy had had hard times, before Wilson arrived, to make the provisions last out. Nevertheless they had worked away on the reef without complaint, while others around them were waxing rich on the alluvial.

The population had increased to some two thousand men during my absence: two thousand men working and living in order and peace, with no police or officials of any kind within two hundred miles — a state of affairs of which we may justly be proud.

Evil-doing, however, was not entirely absent, and occasional cases of robbery of gold, or pilfering of tents occurred; the offenders in such cases were usually caught and summarily dealt with.

A "roll up" would be called, and those who cared to put themselves forward, would form judge, jury, police, and all. The general verdict was notice to quit within so many hours — an order that few would dare to neglect. A case in which this did happen occurred at Kurnalpi when a man was caught passing bad notes in the "Sunday School." He refused to budge, and, seeing that he was a great giant with the reputation of being the roughest and hardest fighter in the country, the question arose who should "bell the cat." The man who had been swindled was a stranger, and unwilling to fight his own battle; who, therefore, would volunteer to get a sound hammering from one of the toughest blackguards in Australia.

The "roll up" slowly dispersed, every man muttering that it was not his business, and that, after all, passing a "stiff 'un" on to a new chum was no great crime as compared to stealing gold or robbing a camp. In this I think they showed sound judgment. The prize-fighting gent, however, became too bumptious, and was eventually hustled out of the place.

Our camp at Lake Darlot was rather pleasantly situated on rising ground by the side of the blow; behind us, sheer cliffs of conglomerate, worn and weathered into queer little caves, the floors of which were covered inches deep by the droppings of bats and small wallabies; and, stretching away to the South, an open plain enclosed in an endless sea of scrub. Every morning we witnessed the strange phenomenon of a lake appearing in the sky to the South, miles away, above the scrub, a lake surrounded by steep white cliffs. This mirage would last perhaps half an hour, and was, I suppose, a reflection of Lake Darlot, which lay at the back of us, some five miles distant to the North.

Our camp consisted of the usual tents and bough-shades and for the first, and probably the only, time in our lives we cooked our pots on a golden fireplace. To protect the fire from the wind, so that a good pile of ashes should collect for baking purposes, we had made a semicircular wall of stones. The nearest available stones, quartz boulders from the blow, were used, and so it came about that we had a gold-studded fireplace! We used to have a curious visitor from the caves — a small black cat, which was tame enough to wander between our legs as we sat round the fire, but too wary to be caught. I can hardly imagine a prospector carrying a cat as companion, and yet how else did it get there? Its shyness inclined us to think it had strayed from civilisation. Jim tried to catch it one evening, and not only got scratched and bitten for his trouble, but so startled the beast that it never returned. Our party was now increased to five; for an extra hand, Alfred Morris, had been engaged. Between us the duties of the day's work were divided.

Our daily labours included hunting up the camels, lest they strayed or were stolen, cutting timber for mining or firewood, packing water from the rocks five miles away, and working on the mine.

I had occasion to make a journey to Lawlers, where a Warden, Mr. Clifton, had lately been established, and I mention here an illustration of one of the many intelligent traits in the character of camels.

Not wishing to follow the road in its many turns from water to water, I cut through the bush for some fifty miles. The first part was over hard, stony ground, then came sand, then more stones, and then I struck the road again about two miles from Lawlers. I stayed there two or three days, intending to return on my tracks. Wishing to test the intelligence of my camel Satan I allowed him a free rein, either to keep on the track or turn off for a short cut. As soon as we came to the spot where we had first struck the road, he turned into the bush without hesitation with his nose for home. After some eight miles of stones, on which I could distinguish no trail, we came to the sand, and at once I could see our former tracks right ahead, which little Satan had followed with the precision of a black-fellow.

In repassing old camping-places on the road, camels will often stop, and look surprised if made to go further. They have, too, an excellent idea of time, and know very well when the day's march should come to an end. With what sad reproof they look at one with their great, brown eyes, that say, as plainly as eyes can speak, "What! going on? I am SO tired." I fancy the reason that camels are so often described as stupid and vicious, and so forth, is that they are seen, as a rule, in large mobs under the care of Indian or other black drivers, whose carelessness and cruelty (so far as my experience goes) are unspeakable. For that reason I never have had an Afghan driver in my employ, nor can I see any advantage in employing one, unless it be on the score of cheapness. Camels are infinitely better managed and treated by white men — of course, I speak within my own knowledge of Australia — and in consequence their characters develop, and they are properly appreciated.

In due course the expected inspecting engineer came to see our mine, and, as he had several reports to make, we had the pleasure of his company at our camp, and very glad we were to do what we could for such a fine specimen of an expert and gentleman as Mr. Edward Hooper. He was satisfied with what he saw — indeed, he could hardly have been otherwise at that period of the mine's existence; and on our arrival in Cue, wither we had travelled part of the way together, a bargain was struck, and before many days Jim and I returned with the glad tidings that the mine was sold, and would be taken over forthwith.

The road from Cue was as uninteresting as all others on the goldfields — miles of flat, sandy soil covered with dense scrub, an occasional open plain of grass and saltbush round the foot of the breakaways, and cliffs that are pretty frequently met with. Travellers on this road had been kept lively by a band of marauding black-fellows, most of whom had "done time" at Rotnest Jail for cattle-spearing, probably, on the coast stations. Having learnt the value of white-fellows' food, they took to the road, and were continually bailing up lonely swagmen, who were forced to give up their provisions or be knocked on the head, since hardly any carried firearms. The finest prize that they captured was a loaded camel, which in some extraordinary way had got adrift from the end of a large caravan, and wandered into the scrub. The Afghans, when they had perceived their loss, tracked up the camel, only to find it dying in agony, with its knees chopped nearly two. This was Jacky-Jacky's way of putting the poor beast down to be unloaded. Happily, after a Warden was appointed at Lawlers, a trooper was sent out, who broke up the gang and captured most of them, at the expense of the life of one black tracker.

One of these thieves paid our camp a visit, but the sight of a rifle, combined with a smart blow on the shins with a stick, quite satisfied him that he had come to the wrong place.

Returned to Lake Darlot, we impatiently awaited the arrival of those who were to take over the mine from us. At last they came, and it only remained to pack up our traps, take the road to Coolgardie, and finish up all business connected with the syndicate. There we parted, Conley and Egan leaving with their shares; and with regret on both sides I think, that our ways no longer lay together: for months of close companionship in the bush, facing hardships and sometimes mutual dangers, make a close tie of friendship between men, that is not easily broken.

File:Spinifex and Sand Illustration 12.jpg Miner's Right [Missing image]

Wishing to pay a visit to the old country, and yet not caring to part with the camels which had been my property for some months past, and of which I was very fond, we formed a syndicate, composed of Dave Wilson, Charles Stansmore, and Alfred Morris, who found the money, and myself, who found the camels, the profits of the venture, if any arose, to be divided in a proportion agreed upon. I could depart, therefore, with the satisfactory feeling of knowing that my faithful animal-friends would be well cared for.

Shares were rising, the mine was sold, and the work done, and it was with a light heart that I booked passage for London in October, 1895.

Part IV: Mining

Chapter I: Quartz Reefing and Dry-Blowing

I would not, even if I had the requisite knowledge, wish to bore the reader by giving a scientific account of gold-mining, but Western Australia presents so many appearances differing from those in other gold-producing countries, and so varied are some of the methods of obtaining gold, that I hope a short account of the usual ways of winning the precious metal, purely from a prospector's point of view, will be of interest.

The area over which the goldfields extend, may be described as very gently undulating country, from which rise, at intervals, low ranges or isolated hills.* These ranges, in reality seldom over 200 feet above the plain, have in the distance a far more important appearance. It is a common experience to steer for a range, sighted from perhaps a distance of fifteen miles, and find on closer inspection that it is no more than a low line of rocks. It is equally common for a hill to appear as quite a respectable mountain when seen from one point, but entirely to disappear from view when seen from the opposite direction, so gentle is the slope.

These ranges, such as they are, occur at intervals of a few miles up to thirty or more, and between them scrub-covered plains, sand-plains, or flat stretches of open forest are found. In the deeper undulations, long chains of dry salt-lakes and samphire-flats are met with, occupying a narrow belt, perhaps one hundred miles in length. Doubtless were the rainfall greater, these lakes would be connected, and take the place of rivers, which would eventually find their way into the Australian Bight. Unfortunately for the comfort of travellers, this is not the case, and their water supply must depend upon one or other of the various sources already described.

The first aim of a party of Western Australian prospectors is to find not gold, but water. Having found this they make camp, and from it start short excursions in all directions towards any hill that may be in sight. Arrived at the hills, which, though bare of undergrowth, are usually covered with low scrub, they can soon determine from the nature the rock whether further search is likely to have good results. Should they see hills of ironstone and diorite, or blows and outcrops of quartz, they will certainly revisit the locality. In what manner, will depend upon the distance from water. They may be able to form camp in the desired spot, with water close at hand; or the party may have to divide, some camping in the likely country, engaged in prospecting solely, while the others "tail" the horses or camels at the watering-place and pack water to their mates. In cases where "good gold is getting," water has sometimes been packed distances of twenty to forty miles; or it may happen that good country must be passed over, from the want of water within reasonable distance.

From his limited appliances and means, a prospector's object is to find a vein or reef of gold-bearing ore, not by sinking, but from surface indications.

Veins or reefs may be described as layers, which have been deposited in fissures and cracks in the rock surrounding them. The enclosing rock is known as the "country rock." "Lodes" are veins composed of a mixture of quartz, ironstone, and other material, and usually exceed in width the "reefs," which sometimes, as at Southern Cross, attain thirty feet, but are rarely more than one to four feet in thickness. The part of a reef showing above the surface is the "outcrop," which may appear either as a mass or "blow" of quartz, sometimes sixty feet in height, or as a solid wall or dyke which can be followed for perhaps five miles without a break; the direction in which it runs is known as its "strike."

Reefs may go down vertically, or on a sloping "dip" or "underlay." The country rock lying immediately above the reef is the "hanging wall," and that immediately below, the "foot wall."

In prospecting a reef, a miner walks along the strike of the outcrop, "napping" as he goes, i.e., breaking off with a hammer or pick, pieces of the quartz or ironstone outcrop. Each fragment is carefully examined for the presence of gold, which is nearly always found, if on the surface, in a free state, that is to say, uncombined with any other mineral. If any gold is present, it may occur in small specks as fine as flour, or in large solid lumps as big as one's fist, as in Bayley's Reward Claim, Londonderry, and one or two other mines. In the latter case the rich find would immediately be pegged out as a claim, or lease, and work commenced, the coarse gold being won by the simple process of "dollying" the ore; or pounding it in an iron mortar with an iron pestle, and passing it when crushed, through a series of sieves in which the gold, too large to fall through, is held.

To estimate roughly the worth of a reef in which only fine gold is visible it is necessary to take several samples along the outcrop, "dolly" them, and wash the powdered quartz by means of two iron dishes, from which the light material is floated off, leaving the gold behind. From a series of experiments an idea can be formed as to whether the reef is worth further work.

It will be found on napping a reef, that the gold occurs at more or less regular intervals. This deposit of gold in the surface outcrop is the top of a "shoot" of gold, which may be followed down on the underlay for many feet. And this peculiarity in the distribution of the metal has been the cause of much disappointment and misunderstanding.

Having determined that your reef is good enough on the surface, the next thing to be done is to ascertain, by means of cuts and shafts, its nature below the surface. This may be done either by an underlay shaft, which follows the reef down from the surface, or by a vertical shaft, sunk some distance away from the outcrop, to cut the reef perhaps one hundred feet below.

By a series of shafts with drives, or galleries, connecting them when they cut the vein, a more accurate estimate of the value of the reef can be made.

Now in the case of a reef which has rich shoots a prospector, naturally anxious to make his "show" as alluring as possible to any possible buyer, sinks his trial shaft, on the underlay, through the shoots. And so it might happen, that by carefully selecting the sites of his shafts, he might have a dazzling show of gold in each one, and merely blank quartz between them. A mining expert, usually only too ready to give a glowing report, makes his estimates on the assumption that the quartz intervening between the shafts is as rich as that visible in them, and the purchase price increases accordingly.

Not only do shoots occur to puzzle the expert, gladden the heart of the prospector, and madden the shareholder, but the eccentricity of gold is further exemplified by the way in which it has been been deposited in "pockets."

No better example of this could be given than the Londonderry Mine, where gold to the value of many thousand pounds was won from quite a small hole in the outcrop. At the bottom of this hole lumps of solid gold could be seen, and inasmuch as other pockets, equally rich, had been found, it was assumed by nearly all concerned that the reef was a solid mass of gold, and the whole community was mad with excitement. However, when the purchasers started work, it was soon discovered that the golden floor to the golden hole only continued golden to the depth of three or four inches, to the despair of the promoters and unlucky shareholders, as well as of the numberless adjoining leaseholders, through whose property this rich reef had been traced.

It seems incredible that a vein should run in more than one direction, and yet it is made to do so, and to go North, East, South, or West, or to any intermediate point of the compass, at the discretion of those responsible for the prospectus! An unmistakable surface outcrop is not popular amongst experts (it leaves no scope for the exercise of an elastic imagination), whereas they cannot be expected to see under ground, and can then make their reef run in the most suitable direction.

I do not think the much-abused expert is any more dishonest than other folk, though he has more temptation. His bread and butter depends on his fee, his fee depends, not on the accuracy of his report, but on the fact, whether or no that report suits his employers. If, as often is the case, he has to report on a "lease" whose only value is derived from its close proximity to a rich show, and if that rich show only appears above the surface in an isolated mass, and its direction of strike can only be guessed at, and, above all, if he knows that his fee or future employment depends on guessing that direction into the property under report, I think he has been led into temptations from which most of us are exempt, and which a good many would find it hard to resist. The term "expert" refers only to the numerous army of "captains" and "mining experts" of mushroom growth, for which the soil of the goldfields is so suitable, and is not applied to the mining engineer of high standing, whose honourable and straight dealing is unimpeachable.

Having brought the mine to such a state that it is ready to be purchased, in which unsatisfactory position it sometimes remains for many long months, I will now leave it, and will not touch upon "mills" and "batteries," which are the same, or nearly so, in all countries, and are outside the province of a prospector, who, from his limited capital, is unable to erect the costly machinery necessary for the extraction of gold from quartz on a large scale. Therefore the prospector parts with his mine as soon as he can find a purchaser, usually an agent, who sells at a profit to some company, which in its turn sells at a greater profit to the British or Australian public.

The humbler prospector confines his attention to alluvial gold, that is to say the gold which has been shed from the outcrop of the reef, by weathering and disintegration. The present small rainfall, and the evidence from the non-existence of river-beds, that the past rainfall was no greater, go to show that this weathering is due to the sudden change in temperature between night and day, the extreme dryness of the atmosphere, and strong winds. Without any rush of water it is not possible for any great depth of alluvial soil to have been formed, nor can the gold have been carried far from the reef, or reefs, in which it has its origin. For this reason, though exceptionally rich in places, the alluvial diggings have never been either of great extent, or depth, or of general richness.

In many places the alluvial soil is not more than a few inches in depth. It is in such places that "specking" may be carried on, which consists in walking slowly about with eyes to the ground, and picking up any nuggets that may be seen. Many thousand ounces of gold have been found in this simple manner. Where, however, the alluvium is deeper, a considerable amount of labour must be expended before gold can be won. In countries blessed with abundant rainfall the nuggets can be separated from the dirt by a comparatively simple arrangement of sluices and cradles. In the drought-stricken west of Australia other means must be adopted, which I will endeavour to describe.

Having picked and dug out a certain amount of the alluvial ground which, it is hoped, contains nuggets of various sizes, the digger then breaks up any lumps of clay or earth by means of a heavy billet of wood, or like implement, and this prepared dirt, as it is called, he treats in one of the following ways:—

By means of two iron dishes, in diameter 15 to 18 inches, and in depth 4 to 5 inches. :

One dish is placed empty on the ground, the other, filled with the prepared dirt, is held up at arm's length above the head, with the mouth of the dish turned to the wind; the earth is then allowed to fall gradually into the dish beneath, all light particles and dust being blown away by the wind. Exchange of dishes having been made, the same process is repeated again and again. When there is only a small amount of dust left, the full dish is held in both hands, and given a circular movement, which causes the larger stones or pebbles to come to the surface; these are cleared away with the left hand, and a sharp look out is kept for nuggets or quartz specimens. This is repeated until nothing is left in the dish but a small quantity of dust, ironstone-gravel, and possibly fine gold, or small nuggets. The dish is then held up at an angle, and shaken from side to side until a compact little heap remains, to the bottom of which the gold will have sunk. The next and final operation is to hold the dish up to the mouth nearly horizontally, and blow the little heap across the dish. Any fine gold will then be seen lying on the bottom just under the nose of the operator.

Given a good hot summer's day, flies as numerous as the supply of water is scanty, clouds of dust, little or no breeze, and the same quantity of gold, and a few score of men working within an area of nine or ten acres, one is sometimes tempted to think that gold may be bought too dear. But the very lowest depths of despair, cannot compare with the heights of satisfaction, attained after a successful day's "dry-blowing."

By means of two dishes, and a tripod stand and polley.

A tripod, twelve or fifteen feet high, is set up over a hard and smooth piece of ground. By a rope and pulley the full dish is hauled up as far as required; the rope is then made fast and a string, fixed to the edge of the dish, is pulled, and the dish tipped up allowing the dirt to fall on to the prepared surface below, where it is swept up and treated as in the first method described. With a fair breeze this is a very effectual way of getting rid of the fine dirt.

By means of a sieve.

This method is only suitable when the soil is wet and sticky, or where the nuggets are fairly large and not too rare.

On the first rush to Kurnalpi, where more alluvial gold was found in a short time than on any other field, sieves were almost the only implements used.

A sieve is very useful for prospecting the surface soil, being more portable and more rapidly worked than the dishes.

A combination of these three methods is found in the *dry blowing machine*.

It has always been a hotly debated question, whether what is known as the "Cement" comes under the heading of "reefs" or "alluvial." This cement is composed of angular quartz-fragments, broken from the reefs or veins, and fragments of diorite and hornblende schists, cemented together by lime; it is very hard and solid and, in places, continues to a depth of over twenty feet. The gold is extracted from these depths by crushing and dry-blowing. I have mentioned this peculiar composition last, as I am not at all clear to which class of formation it belongs.

At first this cement, which the shallow alluvial ground overlies, was supposed to be "bottom," that is to say, that there was considered no likelihood of gold being found at a greater depth. Later developments, however, have proved this theory to be wrong, and with regard to this I cannot do better than quote extracts from a report made by Mr. E. P. Pittman, Government Geologist of New South Wales, in which he says:—

He had considered the question of deep-leads of alluvial, and after visiting Coolgardie, Kalgoorlie, and Kanowna, he thought it probable that there would shortly be a large output of alluvial gold from this source. In Coolgardie the dry-blowing had been confined to a very shallow depth, and yet close to Coolgardie — in Rollo's Bore — there was evidence of the existence of a very deep valley. He produced a specimen, taken by him from an alluvial working near the Boulder Mine, showing what the dry-blowers had all through regarded as the natural floor of the alluvial. Below this floor they had never penetrated until the enterprising prospector at Kanowna recently did so, and followed the lead down to fifty feet.... He was satisfied that the alluvial went down to a depth at Kalgoorlie just as it did at Kanowna. All the conditions were favourable to deep-leads of alluvial.... Rollo's Bore at Coolgardie had proved the existence of alluvial gold at great depths.... So far the alluvial men had been working on a false bottom.

At the time of writing, some two thousand men have found profitable employment in working this newly discovered deposit; and doubtless conditions similar to those found at Coolgardie, Kalgoorlie, and Kanowna, will be proved to hold on other alluvial fields, formerly supposed to be worked out.

How hotly debated this "cement question" has been may be judged from the fact that, at the time of writing, riots are reported from Kalgoorlie, during which the Premier was hooted and stoned. This cowardly act could hardly be the work of genuine diggers, and could doubtless be traced to the army of blackguards and riffraff who have, of late years, found their way to the goldfields.

It would be idle to discuss here the questions of "who is right" and "who is wrong." A great deal can be said on both sides. Let us hope the controversy will be settled to the satisfaction of both parties; that the diggers will not be turned off what is justly theirs, to benefit leaseholding companies, nor leaseholders deprived of their rights.

* Mount Burgess, the highest hill around Coolgardie, is about 500 feet above surrounding country.

Part V: The Outward Journey

Chapter I: Previous Explorers in the Interior of Western Australia

I had not been enjoying the comforts of civilised life for long before I had a letter from Dave Wilson telling me how he and our mates had pegged out, and applied for, a lease which gave every promise of doing well.

In April, 1896, I returned to Australia, and made speed to our new property, which I found to be in every respect as satisfactory as Wilson had told me. To be in the possession of a good mine, and to find someone anxious to change places on terms mutually agreeable, are two very different things. We were fortunate, however, in finding a purchaser, but not fortunate enough to bring him up to the scratch with any promptitude. I had hoped to have had all preparations for the projected expedition complete by the beginning of May, in order that by the time the hot weather came on we should be well on our way, if not at the end of our journey. The Fates ordered things differently, and it was not until the middle of June that I was free to turn my attention to the thousand and one details connected with the composition and equipment of my party.

With what keenness I entered into the preparations may be well imagined, for now at last I was in a position to undertake the expedition I had so long in my mind. In order to explain what my object was, and what my plan of procedure was to be, it will be necessary to give a short sketch of the history of exploration and advance of settlement in Western Australia. The Colony, occupying one third of the continent, has an extreme length of 1,500 miles and a breadth of one thousand miles. The length of coast-line exceeds three thousand miles. A most noticeable feature of the coast-line on the South is the entire absence of rivers — for nearly seven hundred miles no rivers or even watercourses are met with. Along the Western coast rivers are fairly frequent, the largest being the Swan, Murchison, Gascoyne, Ashburton, the Fortescue, and De Grey. The Swan, on which the capital is situated, is the most important — the rivers North of this are not always running, the seasons in the country where they rise being very unreliable. Further North again, where Warburton's Desert abuts on the sea, we find an inhospitable sandy beach (the Eighty-mile Beach), along which no river mouths are seen. In the far North, the Kimberley Division, the coast-line is considerably indented by bays, gulfs, and the mouths of rivers of fair size, which run for the greater part of the year; of these the most important are the Fitzroy, Lennard, Prince Regent, and Ord. The Colony can boast of no great mountain ranges, the highest, the Darling Range, being something over 2,000 feet. The Leopold range in the north is of about the same altitude. No mountain chain breaks the monotony of the central portions of the Colony. In the interior hills are called mountains, and a line of hills, ranges, for want of a better name.

The first settlement was formed on the Swan River in 1826, and gradually spread to the South and North, until to-day we find the occupied portion of the Colony extending along the western seaboard for about 1,200 miles, with an average breadth of perhaps two hundred miles. In the North the occupied country is confined to the watersheds of the two main rivers, the Fitzroy and the Ord.

To the Eastward of Perth the populous mining towns and many scattered mining camps and settlements extend some five hundred miles towards the interior. In spite of the discovery of gold and the advance of the Colony in every way, there still remains more than half the province unoccupied.

How scattered the population of the settled country is may be judged from the fact that the average population is one individual to every six square miles. The vast, almost unknown, interior well merits its designation of "Desert," and I suppose that in few parts of the world have travellers had greater difficulties to overcome than in the arid, sun-dried wilderness of interior Australia. The many attempts to penetrate beyond the head-waters of the coastal rivers date from the earliest days of the Swan River Settlement. But in every case travellers, bold and enduring, were forced back by the impassable nature of the sandy deserts — impassable to all except camels. Roe, Hunt, Austin, and the Gregorys made more than one effort to solve the mysteries of the interior. Numerous attempts were made to cross the Colony from West to East or VICE VERSA, with the double object of ascertaining whether the nature of the country rendered it suitable for settlement, and of establishing some means of communication with the sister colonies to the East.

The first who succeeded in travelling overland from South to West Australia was Eyre, afterwards made governor of Jamaica. He started in 1841, and his route hugged the coast-line along the shores of the Great Australian Bight, and is now closely followed by the telegraph line. In spite of almost insurmountable obstacles in the form of waterless regions, almost bare of vegetation, in spite of mutiny in the camp, and the murder of his white companion by one of the black-boys, the loss of his horses, in spite of starvation and thirst, this gallant man battled his way across, finishing his journey on foot with one companion only, a faithful black-boy. Lucky it was that this district is blessed with a plentiful dew in the cool weather, otherwise Eyre's horses could never have lasted as long as they did. This journey was successfully accomplished again in 1879 by Forrest (now Sir John Forrest, Premier of West Australia) who, keeping somewhat to the north of Eyre's track, had comparatively little difficulty in finding water.

Some 150 miles to the northward, the Colony was traversed from East to West by Giles in 1876, who found it to be a flat, sandy wilderness of scrub, alternating with open limestone plains, covered with saltbush and grass.*

Without camels as transport this expedition could not have been carried out, which will be readily understood when we find that a waterless stage of three hundred miles was negotiated. It is of course likely that Giles passed by waters unknowingly, for owing to the number of camels he had (twenty-two) and the supply of water he was enabled to carry, he was able to push on without turning to the right hand or to the left.

In the following year Giles again crossed the Colony from West to East, some 350 miles North of his first route, and encountered considerably worse country, spinifex desert covered with light gravel. Between Giles's two tracks, Forrest, in 1874, made a remarkable journey from West to East, connecting his traverse with that of Gosse, who from the East had penetrated some 150 miles into the Western Colony, and finally reached the Adelaide-Port Darwin telegraph line. This journey was accomplished with horses, and Forrest, like Stuart in Central Australia, happened to strike a belt of country intersected by low ranges and hills in which he found water. On his left hand was the undulating hill-less desert crossed by Giles, on his right a wilderness of rolling sandhills. Not only was Forrest a surveyor but a bushman as well, and accompanied by good men and black-boys, who let not the slightest indications of the existence of water escape them. One has only to notice the numerous twists and turns in his route to understand that no pains were spared to find water, and thus from rock-hole to rock-hole he wound his way across.

It seems certain that Forrest must have had an exceptional season, judging from the difficulties that have beset subsequent travellers, even though they had camels, over the same route. Mills, Hubbe, Carr-Boyd, Macpherson, and Frost have in late years traversed the same country, not following exactly in Forrest's footsteps, but visiting several waters yielding a plentiful supply when found by him, but which were dry when seen by them. Nevertheless if ever an overland route for stock is found from Central Australia to the Coolgardie fields, I feel confident it will closely approximate to Forrest's route of 1874 for a considerable distance. Between Giles's northern track and that of the next explorer, Warburton, there is a gap of some four hundred miles. Colonel Warburton, with a party of four white men, two Afghans, and one black-boy, left Central Australia, in 1873 to cross to the western coast. This he succeeded in doing after fearful hardships and sufferings, entailing the death of sixteen out of seventeen camels, the temporary failure of his eyesight, and the permanent loss of one eye. One of his party lost his reason, which he never properly recovered, and sufferings untold were experienced by the whole expedition, the members of which narrowly escaped with their lives. Indeed they would not have done so but for the faithful courage and endurance of Samuel Lewis, who alone pushed on to the coastal settlements for aid, and, returning, was just in time to rescue the other survivors. So bad was the account given by these travellers of the interior that it was only by the gradual extension of settlement, rather than by the efforts of any one individual, that any part of it became better known. But for the finding of gold it is certain that the interior would have long remained an unknown region of dangers, so boldly faced by the early explorers.

The existence of gold was known to the Dutch as far back as 1680 or thereabouts, and what is now known as the Nor'-West (including Pilbarra and the Ashburton) was called by them "Terra Aurifera." In spite of vague rumours of the existence of gold, and the report of Austin in 1854, who passed close to what is now the town of Cue and noticed auriferous indications, it was not until 1868 that an authenticated find of gold was made — at Mallina, in the Nor'-West. Since that date the precious metal has been found now in one place, now in another, until to-day we see on the map goldfields extending in a comparatively unbroken line from Esperance Bay on the South, along the Western seaboard to Kimberley in the North.

Whilst prospectors were at work, explorers were not idle, and in 1892 a large expedition, equipped by that public-spirited colonist, Sir Thomas Elder — now alas! dead — was fitted out and put under the leadership of David Lindsay. Sir Thomas was determined to finish what he had so well begun, viz., the investigation of the interior, for by him not only had Giles and Warburton been equipped, but several other travellers in South and Central Australia. This expedition, however, though provided with a large caravan of fifty-four camels, accomplished less than its predecessors. Leaving Forrest's route at Mount Squires, Lindsay marched his caravan across the Queen Victoria Desert to Queen Victoria Spring, a distance of some 350 miles, without finding water except in small quantities in rock-holes on the low sandstone cliffs he occasionally met with. From Queen Victoria Spring, he made down to Esperance Bay, and thence by the Hampton Plains, through settled country to the Murchison. Here Lindsay left the expedition and returned to Adelaide; Wells, surveyor to the party, meanwhile making a flying trip to the eastward as far as the centre of the Colony and then back again. During this trip he accomplished much useful work, discovering considerable extents of auriferous country now dotted with mining camps and towns. On reaching the coast, he found orders to return to Adelaide, as the expedition had come to an end. Why, it was never generally known. Thus there still remained a vast unknown expanse right in the heart of the interior covering 150,000 square miles, bounded on the North by Warburton's Great Sandy Desert, on the South by Giles's Desert of Gravel (Gibson's Desert), on the West by the strip of well-watered country between the coast and the highland in which the rivers rise, on the East by nothing but the imaginary boundary-line between West and South Australia, and beyond by the Adelaide to Port Darwin Telegraph Line.

To penetrate into this great unknown it would be necessary first to pass over the inhospitable regions described by Wells, Forrest, and Giles, and the unmapped expanses between their several routes — crossing their tracks almost at right angles, and deriving no benefit from their experiences except a comparison in positions on the chart, should the point of intersection occur at any recognisable feature, such as a noticeable hill or lake.

Should the unexplored part between Giles's and Warburton's routes be successfully crossed, there still would remain an unexplored tract 150 miles broad by 450 long before the settlements in Kimberley could be reached, 1,000 miles in a bee-line from Coolgardie. This was the expedition I had mapped out for my undertaking, and now after four years' hard struggle I had at length amassed sufficient means to carry it through. I do not wish to pose as a hero who risked the perils and dangers of the desert in the cause of science, any more than I would wish it to be thought that I had no more noble idea than the finding of gold. Indeed, one cannot tell one's own motives sometimes; in my case, however, I believe an insatiable curiosity to "know what was there," joined to a desire to be doing something useful to my fellow-men, was my chief incentive. I had an idea that a mountain range similar to, but of course of less extent, than the McDonnell Ranges in Central Australia might be found — an idea based on the fact that the vast swamps or salt-lakes, Lake Amadeus and Lake Macdonald, which apparently have no creeks to feed them from the East, must necessarily be filled from somewhere. Since it was not from the East, why not from the West?

Tietkens, Giles's first officer in nearly all his journeys, who led an expedition from Alice Springs in Central Australia to determine the extent of Lake Amadeus, cut off a considerable portion of that lake's supposed area, and to the North-West of it discovered Lake Macdonald, which he encircled. To the West of this lake he found samphire swamps and clay-pans, which are so often seen at the end of creeks that seldom join the lakes in a definite channel. He might, therefore, have crossed the tail-end of a creek without being aware of it.

Should such a range exist it might be holding undiscovered rich minerals or pasture-lands in its valleys. Anything seemed possible in 150,000 square miles. Then again it seemed to me possible that between Kimberley in the North and Coolgardie in the South auriferous connection might exist. A broken connection with wide intervals perhaps, but possibly belts of "mixed" country, now desert, now lake, now gold-bearing. Such mixed country one finds towards the eastern confines of the goldfields. No better example of what I mean could be given than Lake Darlot, of which one might make an almost complete circuit and be in a desert country all the time. Should we find auriferous country in the "far back," it was not my intention to stop on it (and, indeed, our limited supplies would have made that difficult), but to push on to Hall's Creek, Kimberley, investigating the remaining portion of unknown on the way; then to refit and increase the means of transport, and so return to the auriferous country in a condition to remain there and properly prospect. These were the ideas that possessed me before our journey commenced.

I do not wish to institute comparisons, but it is often said that a prospector, or pioneer, who explores with the hope of gain to himself, cannot be deserving in an equal degree of the credit due to those who have risked their lives in the cause of science. I may point out that these latter have not only been at no expense themselves, but have been paid salaries for their services, and have, in addition, been rewarded by grants of money and land — and deservedly so. Yet a man willing to take the same risks, and venture the fruits of perhaps years of hard work, in equipping and bearing all the expenses of an expedition, is credited with no nobler incentive than the "lust of gold" — because he hopes, with a vague chance of his hope being realised, to be repaid by compelling Nature to part with some of her hidden treasures.

The prospector in his humble way slowly but surely opens up the country, making horse or camel-pads, here, there, and everywhere, from water to water, tracks of the greatest service to the Government road-maker and surveyor who follow after. He toils and labours, suffers, and does heroic deeds, all unknown except to the few. He digs soaks and wells many feet in depth, makes little dams in creeks, protects open water from contamination by animals, and scores of other services, primarily for his own benefit, it is true, but also for the use of those who come after. Very few recognise the immense value of the work carried out by prospectors who are not actuated only by the greed for gold, as I, who know them, can assert. Some wish to satisfy a longing to determine the nature of new country, to penetrate where others have never been; others work for love of adventure and of the free bush life; while many are anxious to win what distinction may fall to the lot of successful travellers, though reward or distinction are seldom accorded to prospectors. But beyond all this, there is the glorious feeling of independence which attracts a prospector. Everything he has is his own, and he has everything that IS his own with him; he is doing the honest work of a man who wins every penny he may possess by the toil of his body and the sweat of his brow. He calls no man master, professes no religion, though he believes in God, as he cannot fail to do, who has taken the chances of death in the uphill battle of life "outside the tracks," though he would perhaps be annoyed if you told him so; and it is only by intimate acquaintance with him that you can know that his God is the same as other men's, though called by another name. For the rest, he lives an honourable life, does many acts of kindness to those in need, never leaves his mate in the lurch, and goes "straight" to the best of his ability. For him, indeed,

 "Two things stand like stone: Kindness in another's trouble, Courage in his own." As to his work, the results remain, even though he keeps no record. Should he find good country or gold, the land is soon occupied — sooner than if some officially recognised expedition had reported it. For in the one case the man is known and trusted by his fellow-prospectors, while in the other there is not only the bushman's dislike of anything official to be overcome, but the curious conviction, which most of them possess, that any one in the position of a geologist, or other scientific calling, must necessarily be an ass! In the same way, if the country met with is useless, the fact soon becomes known amongst the prospectors, who avoid it accordingly — though a few from curiosity may give it a further trial. Slowly but surely the unaided and individual efforts of the prospector, bring nearer to civilisation the unknown parts of Australia. Many are the unrecorded journeys of bushmen, which for pluck and endurance would rank with any of those of recognised explorers.

The distances accomplished by their journeys are certainly of no great length, as, indeed, they hardly could be, seeing their scanty means and inadequate equipment; and yet in the aggregate they do as great an amount of useful work as a man who by a single journey leaves his name on the map of Australia. It has always seemed a shame to me, how little prospectors are encouraged. No inducement is offered them to give information to the Government; they may do so if they like, but they cannot hope to get anything for it in return. My old mate, Luck, not only surveyed, roughly but accurately, a track between Southern Cross and Menzies, a distance of nearly 150 miles, but actually cut the scrub for a part of the way, to allow his camels to pass; shortly after a Government road was to be cut between the two towns, and Luck sent in his map, at the suggestion of the then head official of the Water Supply, with an application for monetary reward for his work. His request was refused, his map never returned, and strangely enough the new road followed his traverse from water to water with startling exactitude. Who was to blame I cannot say; but someone must be in fault when a man, both able and willing to do such useful work is not only neglected, but to all intents and purposes robbed. This is not the only instance of the apathy of the Government in such matters, but is a sufficient example of the lack of encouragement with which prospectors meet.

*These plains, first crossed by Giles, have every appearance of being splendid pasture-lands. Unfortunately no surface water can be obtained. The formation is limestone, in which are found "blowholes" — that is to say, circular holes two to four feet in diameter, which go down vertically to a depth never yet ascertained. They derive their name from the curious booming noise which they emit, probably caused by the wind. Judging from the growth of saltbush and other herbage it would seem likely that the rainfall on these elevated plains is considerable, and apparently runs to waste down blow-holes and cracks in the limestone. No doubt when other parts of the Colony become occupied and civilisation advances, settlers will turn their attention to this part, and possibly, by means of bores, find a plentiful supply of water, as on the Nullarbor Plains across the border. It seems likely that a most undesirable class of colonists will forestall the "back blockers" from the west, for to the northward of Eucla rabbits have been seen slowly advancing to the westward. The Government fortunately realises the importance of checking the incursion. To my mind the safest plan would be to run a fence, at whatever cost, north from Eucla, for some 150 miles, until the desert was reached, and so force the rabbits into a part of the country where, supposing they could live (which is doubtful), they could do no harm, and might come as a welcome addition to the diet of the wandering blacks, or might serve to break the monotony of "tinned dog" for the weary prospector.

Part V: The Outward Journey

Chapter II: Members and Equipment of Expedition

The most important question in the organisation of an expedition of long duration is the choice of one's companions. Many men are excellent fellows in civilisation and exactly the reverse in the bush, and, similarly, some of the best men for bush work are quite unfitted for civilised life. I was therefore grievously disappointed when I heard the decision of my late partners not to accompany me. Dave Wilson thought it unwise to come because his health was poor and his blood completely out of order, as evinced by the painful sores due to what is termed "the Barcoo Rot." This disease is very common in the bush, where no vegetables or change of food can be obtained, and must be something akin to scurvy. It is usually accompanied by retching and vomiting following every attempt to eat. The sufferer invariably has a voracious appetite, but what he eats is of little benefit to him. The skin becomes very tender and soft, and the slightest knock or scratch, even a touch sometimes, causes a wound which gradually spreads in all directions. The back of the hand is the usual spot to be first affected, then the arms, and in a bad case the legs also, which become puffy at the joints, and before long the wretched victim will be covered with sores and abrasions. No external application of ointment or anything of that nature seems to do any good, though the wounds are deep and leave but little scar. After a month or two in the bush one is pretty sure to develop this complaint, which in the dusty, hot weather is further aggravated by the swarms of flies, whose poisonous nature is made evident to any one who has killed them. In my own case I have found fine white wood-ashes, preferably of the mulga, to have a healing and drying effect. Ashes are used by the natives for healing wounds, and I found them very efficacious in cases of sore backs amongst camels. Nothing but an entire change of diet and way of living can cure the "Barcoo"; constant washing, an impossibility "out-back," being essential. Dave, having had his sickness for some long time, was physically unable to form one of the party, to my sorrow, for he was a man in whom I had the greatest confidence, and one whose pluck and endurance were unquestionable.

Alfred Morris joined his brother in a reef the latter had found, and Charlie Stansmore was not at all well. Thus I was for the time stranded. There was no difficulty in getting men — of a sort! but just the right kind of man was not easily found. My old friend Benstead added one more to the many good turns he has done me by recommending Joe Breaden, who had just finished a prospecting journey with Mr. Carr-Boyd and was looking out for a job. Benstead had known him from boyhood, in Central Australia, and gave him the highest character — not higher than he merited, though, as I hope these pages will make clear. Most of us have, I think, an instinct that tells us at once whether to trust another or the reverse. One can say on sight, "I have perfect confidence in that man." As soon as I saw Breaden I felt a voice within me saying, "That's just the man you were looking for." I told him my plans and the salary I could afford to give him; he, in his silent way, turned me and my project over in his mind for some few minutes before he said the one word "Right," which to him was as binding as any agreement.

A fine specimen of Greater Britain was Joe Breaden, weighing fifteen stone and standing over six feet, strong and hard, about thirty-five years of age, though, like most back-blockers, prematurely grey, with the keen eye of the hunter or bushman. His father had been through the Maori War, and then settled in South Australia; Breaden was born and bred in the bush, and had lived his life away up in Central Australia hundreds of miles from a civilised town. And yet a finer gentleman, in the true sense of the word, I have never met with. Such men as he make the backbone of the country, and of them Australia may well be proud. Breaden had with him his black-boy "Warri," an aboriginal from the McDonnell Ranges of Central Australia, a fine, smart-looking lad of about sixteen years, whom Breaden had trained, from the age of six, to ride and track and do the usual odd jobs required of black-boys on cattle stations. I had intended getting a discharged prisoner from the native jail at Rotnest. These make excellent boys very often, though prison-life is apt to develop all their native cunning and treachery. Warri, therefore, was a distinct acquisition.

Having made so successful a start in the choice of mates, I turned my attention to the purchase of camels. My idea had been to have twelve, for it seemed to me that a big number of camels was more a handicap than an advantage in country where the chances of finding a large supply of water were so small. Another excellent reason for cutting down the caravan was the question of expense. Eventually I decided on nine as being the least we could do with. Nine of the very best they must be, so I spared no pains in the choosing of them. Mr. Stoddart, the manager of a large Carrying Company, from whom I bought them, said that he had never come across any one so hard to please! However, I meant to have none but the best, and I got them — five splendid South Australian bulls, three of mature years and two youngsters — all a proper match for my old train of four. The best camels, unfortunately, are not the cheapest! The average value of our caravan was 72 pounds 10 shillings — a tremendous amount whencompared with their cost in other countries. In Somaliland, for instance, for the price I paid for my nine, I could get one hundred and sixty-three camels! But the Somali camel from all accounts is a very poor performer, compared to his kinsman in the Antipodes, his load being about 200 lbs. against the Australian's 6 to 9 cwt.

The new camels were christened Kruger, Prepeh, Mahatma Billy (always known as Billy), Redleap, and Stoddy. These, together with my old friends Czar, Satan, and Shiddi, I put under Breaden's charge; and he and Warri camped with them a few miles from the town whilst I completed preparations. Rain was falling at the time, the wet weather lasting nearly a fortnight; the whole country around Coolgardie was transformed from a sea of dust into a "Slough of Despond," and, seeing that five out of the nine camels were bulling, Breaden had anything but a pleasant time. Amongst camels, it is the male which comes on season, when, for a period of about six weeks annually, he is mad and unmanageable, and in some cases dangerous. Once, however, a camel knows you as his friend, in whatever state of mind he may be, he will not harm you, though a stranger would run considerable risk. The duration of this bulling depends entirely on what work they are doing; camels running in the bush without work will remain perhaps three months on season, and a horrible nuisance they are too, for they fight anything they come across, and will soon turn a peaceful camp of unoffending camels into a pandemonium. When in this state they will neither eat, drink, nor sleep, and unless tied down or carefully watched will wander far away, and sometimes start off full gallop, in the shortest of hobbles, and not stop under five or six miles. The "scotch hobble" prevents this, for by having a chain from a hobble-strap on the foreleg to another on the hind, the least attempt at galloping will bring the beast down on to his knees. I used this arrangement on Satan, but found that the fixing of the chain on the hind leg was a matter of some danger, which could only be accomplished at the expense of being sent flying by a kick in the stomach at least once; for a camel hates anything touching his hind legs, and any attempt to handle them soon affords ample evidence that he can let out with great vigour with any leg in any direction. You have only to watch one flicking flies off his nose with his toe to be convinced of that little point of natural history. Before many weeks "on season" a bull becomes so thin and miserable, that it is hardly credible that he can carry a burden of nearly twice the usual weight; nevertheless it is a fact. I remember a caravan of "season camels" arriving at Lake Darlot, carrying an average load of nine hundred pounds, exclusive of the saddle. The extra load that they carry hardly compensates for the trouble of looking after them, for when in that state they fight like tigers, especially if they have not been long together. Once, however, the bulls become friendly, they only fight in a more or less half-hearted way amongst themselves; but woe betide any alien who finds himself near them — they will then band themselves together and fall upon that stranger until even his master would not recognise him. There is no fun attached to travelling along a much-frequented track, on which mobs of twenty to fifty camels may be met with; and there is no sleep to be got at night, for if, following the practice of most white men, a man ties down his camels at night, he may be certain that they will be attacked, and from their defenceless position, perhaps seriously injured or killed by the loose camels of some Afghan, who has neither the energy nor sense of fair-play to restrain the bulls under his charge.

In this troublesome state were our camels, and poor Breaden, being a stranger to them, was treated with neither politeness nor respect; Kruger, especially, being so exceedingly ill-behaved as not only to knock Breaden down, but to attempt to kneel on his chest and crush him. This disaster was narrowly averted by the prompt action of Warri, who first dragged his master out of danger, and then chastised Kruger with a heavy stick, across the head and neck. Kruger was equally rough to his fellows, for as in a pioneering party, so in a mob of bull camels, there must be only one boss.

This knotty point was fought out with bitter vehemence, Czar, Shiddi, and Misery being vanquished in turn by the redoubtable Kruger. The others knew their places without fighting; for old Billy, the only one of them not too young to compete, was far too good-tempered and easy-going to dispute anything (except the passage of a salt-lake, as we afterwards discovered). I was naturally sorry to see Misery deposed; but for his age he fought a good fight, and it was gratifying to possess the champion who could beat him. What a magnificent fellow was Kruger — a very tower of strength, and (excepting of course when in the state above described) with a nature like that of an old pet sheep.

In the meantime I was under the sheltering roof of my old foster-mother "Bayley's Reward Claim" — the guest of Tom and Gerald Browne.

Gerald had as his henchman a small boy whom he had taken from a tribe away out to the eastward of Lake Darlot — a smart little chap, and very intelligent, kept neat and clean by his master, whose pride in his "boy" knew no bounds. He was wonderfully quick in picking up English and could count up to twelve. No doubt by this time he is still more learned. It is rather strange that so much intelligence and aptitude for learning should be found in these children of the wilderness, who in their wild and wandering habits are not far removed from animals — for neither "Wynyeri," the boy in question, nor any of his tribe, could by any possibility have seen a white man before 1892. And yet this little chap in a few months is as spruce and clever as any white boy of the same size, and, far from showing any fear or respect, evinces a distinct inclination to boss any white children with whom he comes in contact. The Australian aboriginal is indeed a puzzle: he lives like a beast of the field, using neither clothes nor house, and to the casual observer is a savage of the lowest type, without brains, or any senses other than those possessed by animals; yet he has his peculiar laws and customs — laws of which the Mosaic rule of "an eye for an eye and a tooth for a tooth" is the foundation.

In some districts, and probably all over the continent, were inquiry made, marriage laws of the most intricate kind are strictly adhered to; and though his ceremonies and rites are unique in their barbarity, yet when properly handled he is capable of becoming a useful and intelligent member of the community. Great tact is necessary in the education of the aboriginals. Neglect turns them into lazy, besotted brutes who are of no use to anybody; too kind treatment makes them insolent and cunning; too harsh treatment makes them treacherous; and yet without a certain amount of bullying they lose all respect for their master, and when they deserve a beating and do not get it, misconstrue tender-heartedness into fear. The "happy medium" is the great thing; the most useful, contented, and best-behaved boys that I have seen are those that receive treatment similar to that a highly valued sporting dog gets from a just master; "to pet" stands for "to spoil." Like most black races, the native soon develops a love for liquor; but fortunately there exists a stringent law which prohibits the giving of drink to a black-fellow, except at the request of his master.

It is marvellous how soon a tame boy comes to despise his own people, when he far outstrips any white man in his contemptuous manner of speaking about a "---- black fella."

One visitor to Bayley's Reward Claim, brought with him from Victoria, a highly educated aboriginal who had been born in civilisation, and who afterwards married his master's parlourmaid. Jim was a tremendously smart boy, could ride, shoot, box, bowl, or keep wicket against most white men, and any reference to his colour or family was deeply resented. On his first appearance the cook at Bayley's (the wife of one of the miners) proceeded to converse with him in the sort of pigeon-English commonly used, and handed him a plate of scraps for his dinner, calling out, "Hi, Jacky-Jacky, this one your tucker," to which Jim replied with stern dignity, "Who the h---- are you calling Jacky-Jacky? Do you think I'm a ---- black-fellow?" The cook, a quiet and ladylike little woman, who had been a schoolmistress "at home" was not less astounded by the excellent English, than by the delicate way in which his disapprobation was expressed. This story of Jim reminds me of one about his master. He was a man who liked to have everything about him smart and showy, and was quite willing that every one should look upon him as a tremendous swell with the purse of a Croesus. I heard some diggers discussing him: one said he had come to buy up all the mines in the place and must be a man of importance. "Oh," said his mate, "any one could see 'e was a toff — I seed him black 'is boots and brush his teeth." "Yes, and 'e wears a ---- collar too." Thus was exemplified the old adage "Fine feathers make fine birds."

Camped near Bayley's was Godfrey Massie, a cousin of Brownes and brother of the once famous cricketer. He had taken a contract to sink a shaft on the adjoining lease, but, owing to the death of one of his mates and his own incapacity to work, due to a "jarred" hand, he was forced to throw up the job, and quickly agreed to my proposal that he should form one of my party. People get to a very casual way of doing things on the goldfields. There was no formality about my arrangements; Godfrey helping me pack at a store, and during our work I said without preface, "You'd better come too;" "Right," said he, and the matter was settled. Godfrey, a son of one of the leading Sydney families, had started life in an insurance office, but soon finding that he was not cut out for city life, went on to a Queensland cattle-station, where he gained as varied a knowledge of bush life as any could wish for; tiring of breeding and fattening cattle for somebody else's benefit, he joined the rush to the Tasmanian silver-fields and there he had the usual ups and downs — now a man of wealth, and now carrying his load of bacon and oatmeal through the jungle on the steep Tasmanian mountains. While a field continues to boom, the up-and-down business does not so much signify, but when the "slump" comes it is distinctly awkward to be in a state of "down." It is then that the average speculator bemoans his hard fate, can't think how he is to live; and yet manages to do so by borrowing from any more fortunate fellow, and almost invariably omitting to pay him back. A most lively and entertaining class of men when shares are up, but a miserable, chicken-hearted lot when the luck turns.

Some, however, of these wandering speculators, who follow from "boom" to "boom," are of very different mettle and face their luck like men. Such a one was Godfrey, who, when he found himself "broke" in Tasmania, set to work and burned charcoal until he had saved enough money to pay his passage to Perth; and from there he "humped his bluey" to Coolgardie, and took a job as a miner on his uncle's mine until brighter times should come. The Australian can set us a good example in some matters, and I must confess with sorrow that nine out of every ten young Englishmen on the goldfields, of the same class, would not only be too haughty to work, but would more readily take to billiards, cards, and borrowing when they found themselves in low water — and no man sinks lower than an English "gentlemen" who has gone to the bad, and no one despises him more than an Australian miner, or is more ready to help him when he shows signs of trying to help himself by honest work. I had known Godfrey long enough to be sure that, in the bush, he was as good a man as I could get, hard as nails, and willing to work for other people, as energetically as he would for himself, so long as they treated him fairly.

My party was now complete, and included a little fox terrier, "Val" by name, whose parents belong to Tom and Gerald Browne, and come of the best stock in Australia. I had intended to take another man, but, since I could not get one of the right sort, I had no idea of handicapping the party with one of the wrong. At the last minute, however, Charlie Stansmore changed his mind, greatly to my delight, for I knew him to be as sterling a fellow as one could hope to find. Charlie, too, had knocked about from Queensland to West Australia, now on a station, now a miner, and now engine-driver. His people were amongst the earliest settlers on the Swan River, and could well remember the great massacre of whites by the blacks; subsequently they moved to Victoria, where they have farming land at the present time. A very quiet, reserved man was Charlie, who took a great interest in mechanical work and astronomy, a strong man physically and mentally. Thus at last we were ready to tackle whatever the "great unknown" had in store for us.

With hearty wishes for success from the few friends who knew where we were bound for, we shook the mud of Coolgardie from our feet and took the northern road to Menzies on July 9, 1896. Breaden, Stansmore, Massie, Warri, nine heavily laden camels, and a dog made a fine show, and I confess I was near bursting from pride as I watched them.

Who could foresee that one of us was destined never to return?

Acting on the principle of making mention of matters which I have noticed excite an amount of interest in "Home" people, though to us, who are used to them, their importance hardly seems to warrant it, I subjoin a list of the articles and provisions with which we started: —

8 pack-camels. Bulls. South Australian bred. Of ages varying from five to fifteen years.

1 riding-camel. Bull. S.A. bred. Age five years. Average value of camels; 72 pounds 10 shillings each.

8 pack saddles of Afghan make.

1 riding saddle, made to order by Hardwick, Coolgardie, specially light, and stuffed with chaff. A very excellent saddle.

1 camel brand. D.W.C.

1 doz. nose pegs.

6 coils of clothes line.

3 coils of wallaby line (like window-blind cord) for nose lines.

5 hanks of twine.

2 long iron needles for saddle mending (also used as cleaning-rod for guns).

2 iron packers for arranging stuffing of saddle.

Spare canvas.

Spare calico.

Spare collar-check.

Spare leather, for hobbles and neck-straps.

Spare buckles for same.

Spare bells.

Spare hobble-chains.

6 lbs. of sulphur.

2 gallons kerosene, to check vermin in camels.

2 gallons tar and oil, for mange in camels.

2 galvanised-iron water casks (15 gallons each).

2 galvanised-iron water casks (17 gallons each), made with bung on top side, without taps, for these are easily broken off.

1 India-rubber pipe for drawing water from tanks.

1 funnel,

3 three-gallon buckets.

1 tin canteen (2 gallons).

2 canvas water tanks, to be erected on poles to hold water baled from soak, &c.

4 canvas water-bags (10 gallons each.)

4 canvas water-bags (1 1/2 gallons each) slung on camels' necks.

6 Ballarat picks and handles.

3 shovels.

1 axe (7 lbs.).

1 hammer (7 lbs.).

1 engineer's hammer.

3 tomahawks.

1 saw.

1 small flat iron anvil.

1 small pair of bellows.

1 iron windlass-handle and fittings.

1 1-inch chisel.

1 brace and bits.

1 3/4 inch auger bit.

1 emery stone.

4 iron dishes.

1 sieve-dish.

1 iron dolly.

1 soldering iron for mending water casks.

2 sticks solder for mending water casks.

1 bottle spirits of salts for mending water casks.

1 case of tools. Screwdriver, small saw, hammer, chisel, file, gimlet, leather-punch, wire nipper, screw wrench, large scissors, &c.

1 case of tools for canvas work (sewing needles, &c.).

2 lbs. of copper rivets.

Screws.

Bolts.

1 box copper wire.

Strong thread.

1 1/2 lbs. 3-inch nails.

1 lb. 2-inch nails.

50 feet of rope.

1 duck tent, 6 ft. x 8 ft.

4 flies, 10 ft. x 12 ft., for covering packs.

4 mosquito nets.

3 saucepans.

3 quart pots.

6 pannikins.

6 plates, enamelled tin.

6 knives, forks, and spoons.

1 stewpan.

1 frying pan,

1 small medicine case (in tabloid form).

7 lbs. Epsom salts.

6 bottles of Elliman's embrocation.

3 bottles of carbolic oil.

3 bottles of eye lotion.

3 bottles of eucalyptus oil.

2 galvanised-iron concertina-made boxes for perishable goods, e.g., ammunition, journals, &c.

2 twelve-bore shot-guns.

4 colt revolvers, .380 calibre.

4 Winchester repeaters, .44 calibre.

200 twelve-bore cartridges.

300 Winchester do.

200 revolver do.

1 bicycle lamp (for night observations).

1 5-inch theodolite and tripod.

2 prismatic compasses.

2 steering compasses (Gregory's pattern).

1 telescope.

1 pair field-glasses.

1 map case.

1 drawing-board.

Drawing materials, note-books, &c.

1 binocular camera, with films. (N.B. Not good in hot climate.)

1 tape measure.

14 50-lb. bags of flour (700 lbs.).

35 doz. 1-lb. tins of meat (420 lbs.).

5 doz. 1-lb. tins of fish (60 lbs.). (N.B. — Not fit for consumption — thrown away.)

200 lbs. rice.

70 lbs. oatmeal.

6 doz. tins of milk (condensed).

8 doz. tins baking powder.

4 doz. 1-lb tins of jam.

140 lbs. sugar,

40 lbs. salt (for salting down meat — kangaroo, &c.).

30 lbs. tea.

2 doz. tinned fruit.

2 doz. tinned vegetables.

10 lbs. currants.

10 lbs. raisins

40 lbs. dried apricots.

6 doz. 1-lb. tins butter.

4 doz. Liebig's Extract.

1 1/2 doz. pepper (1/4-lb. tins).

1/2 doz. curry-powder (1/4-lb. tins).

9 packets Sunlight soap.

1 box of candles.

6 lbs. cornflour.

28 doz. matches.

50 lbs. tobacco.

100 lbs. preserved potatoes.

4 bottles good brandy.

1 bottle good rum.

1 hair clipper.

Blankets, boots, flannel shirts, trousers (Dungaree and moleskin); &c.

The stores were calculated to last six months with care and longer should we encounter good country where game could be shot. Everything that could be was packed in large leather bags, made to order. Other expeditions have carried wooden brass-bound boxes; I do not approve of these — first on account of their own weight and bulk; second, when empty they are equally bulky and awkward; third, unless articles are of certain shapes and dimensions they cannot be packed in the boxes, which do not "give" like bags. Wooden water casks are generally used — my objections to them are that they weigh more than the iron ones, are harder to mend, and when empty are liable to spring or warp from the hot sun.

It will be seen that a great part of our load consisted of tools which, though weighty, were necessary, should we come on auriferous country, or be forced to sink to any depth for water: a great many of these tools were left in the desert.

The average load with which each camel started, counting the water casks (the four large ones) full, was 531 lbs., exclusive of saddle. Kruger and Shiddi carried over 750 lbs. including top loading and saddle.

These loads, though excessive had the season been summer, were not too great to start with in the cooler weather; and every day made some difference in their weight.

The brandy was for medicinal purposes only. Even had we been able to afford the room I should not have carried more; for I am convinced that in the bush a man can keep his health better, and do more work, when he leaves liquor entirely alone.

Part V: The Outward Journey

Chapter III: The Journey Begins

The week's rain had made the roads in a terrible state, where dust had been there was now a foot or so of soft mud, and the ground, which had been hard and clayey, was now so sticky and slippery, that it was not easy travelling for the camels. We passed several camps of Afghans, squatting miserably under huge tarpaulins, waiting for the roads to dry before starting their caravans, loaded with stores for some distant district. There are one or two things that camels are quite unable to do, according to an Asiatic driver; one is to travel in wet weather. However, Europeans manage to work camels, wet or fine; the wily Afghan says, "Camel no do this," "Camel no do that," because it doesn't suit his book that camel should do so — and a great many people think that he *must* know and is indispensable in the driving of camels; which seems to me to be no more sensible than to say that a chow-dog can only be managed by a Chinaman.

There is, perhaps, a small amount of risk in travelling in wet weather, for when a camel does slip he does so with a vengeance; each foot seems to take a different direction and thus, spread-eagled under a heavy load, he might suffer a severe strain or even break a bone. Redleap fell once, but, happily, neither hurt himself nor the load.

The winter had caused a transformation in the appearance of the bush; everywhere little patches of green grass or saltbush could be seen, and wherever a teamster had stopped to bait his horses, a miniature field of oats had sprung into life. How we hoped that the rainfall had extended towards the interior!

If only we could have started sooner, we should have benefited by the cool weather for a great part of the journey. But though the days were warm enough, there was no doubt about the coldness of the nights. Our blankets were white with frost in the mornings, and our canvas water-bags frozen into a solid mass. My thermometer registered 17 degrees F. just before dawn on the coldest night. Unhobbling the camels and loading them was freezing work, during which our fingers were quite numbed. Shivering, we walked along until the sun was above the trees, then in a little its rays warmed to their work, and we would peal off now a coat, now a jersey or shirt, until in the middle of the day the heat was too great to be pleasant. Poor little Val hated the cold nights, and, as I always sleep away from a fire, she used to crawl into my blankets and lie up against my back, which was quite pleasant for both of us. Most men like to sleep alongside a roaring fire in the winter, but I have always found that after the fire burns out and the night becomes colder, the change of temperature becomes unbearable. If the fire burned all night it would be a different matter; but to do so it must be replenished, and this entails leaving warm blankets to carry wood. It is amusing to see two men camped by a fire which has burned low, both lying awake, and watching to see if the other will get up and attend to it.

The best recipe for avoiding cold is to sleep soundly; and to sleep soundly one must be tired. As a rule night found us in this state, for we all discovered walking rather trying at first, none of us having done any for some time. We were all pleased, I think, when our stage of seven or eight hours was finished — especially Breaden, who had given himself a nasty strain in loading the camels, and who had a deal more weight to carry than we thin people. Australian bushmen do not, as a rule, make good walkers — their home has been the saddle. It was the more necessary, therefore, that we should start on foot at once and carry out a system of training, in which I am a great believer; thus we never ate or drank between breakfast at daylight and tea at night — from nine to eleven hours afterwards. Stopping in the middle of the day wastes time, and entails the unloading of the camels or putting them down with their burdens on, a very bad plan; the time so spent at midday is far more valuable in the evening, when the camels can employ it by feeding. Then again, a meal, really unnecessary, during the day soon makes an appreciable difference in the amount of provisions used. Breaden and Godfrey consoled themselves with tobacco, but Charlie and I were not smokers. I used to be, but gave up the practice because it made me so dry — an effect that it does not have on every one, some finding that a smoke relieves not only hunger but thirst. I have only one objection to a smoker as a travelling companion, and that is, that if by some horrible mishap he runs out of tobacco, he becomes quite unbearable. The same holds with an excessive tea-drinker. I was specially careful, therefore, to have a sufficient supply of these articles. A large amount of tea was not required, since Godfrey was the only confirmed tea-drinker.

On July 15th we reached Menzies, having followed the telegraph line to that point. And a very badly constructed line this is, the poles being timber and not sunk sufficiently deep into the ground — a contract job. The iron poles which are now used in the Government-constructed lines are a vast improvement. Menzies was the last town we called at, and was not so specially inviting that we regretted leaving it. Niagara, the next city, we avoided, and turned up the old Lake Darlot road, some fifteen miles to the west of it. Between Menzies and Sandy Creek, close to where we turned, the open, saltbush plain which fringes the salt lake, Lake Prinsep, was looking quite charming, dotted all over with patches of splendid green and yellow herbage, plants like our clover and dandelion, and thousands of pink and white everlastings. There can be no doubt that with a better rainfall or with some means of irrigation, could artesian water be found, a great part of the goldfields would be excellent pastoral land. As it is, however, a few weeks suffice to again alter the face of the country to useless aridity. We camped a day on Sandy Creek, to allow our beasts to enjoy, while they could, the luscious green feed; I embraced the opportunity of taking theodolite observations for practice. The pool, some eighty yards long, and twenty wide, fringed with overhanging bushes and weeping willow with its orange-red berries, made a pretty picture; turkeys evidently came there to water, but we had not the luck to shoot any.

The northern track from Sandy Creek deviated so much on account of watering-places, thick scrub, and broken rocks, that we left it and cut through the bush to some clay-pans south of Cutmore's Well; and successfully negotiated on our way the lake that had given me so much trouble when I and the fever were travelling together. All through the scrub every open spot was covered with grass, that horrible spear-grass (*Aristidi*), the seeds of which are so troublesome to sheep and horses. I have seen sores in a horse's mouth into which one could put two fingers, the flesh eaten away by these vicious little seeds. When turned out on this kind of grass, horses' mouths should be cleaned every day. Camels do not suffer, as they seldom eat grass unless long, young, and specially succulent. We, however, were rather annoyed by the persistent way in which the seeds worked through our clothes and blankets; and before much walking, our trousers were fringed with a mass of yellow seeds, like those of a carter who has wound wisps of straw round his ankles. Truly rain is a marvellous transformer; not only vegetable but animal life is affected by it; the bush is enlivened by the twittering of small birds, which come from nobody knows where, build their nests, hatch out their young, and disappear! Almost every bush held a nest, usually occupied by a diamond-sparrow. Her nest is round, like a wren's, with one small entrance and is built roughly of grass, lined with soft, small feathers. The eggs, numbering four to five in the few nests we disturbed, are white and of the size and shape of our hedge-sparrow's. I am pretty sure that the nesting season depends entirely on the rain. After rain, the birds nest, however irregular the seasons.

As well as small birds, teal had found their way to the clay-pans, and gave us both sport and food. These water-holes are the tail-end of Wilson's Creek, on which is sunk Cutmore's Well, where splendid water was struck at a depth of about eighty feet. Flood-waters from the creek spread out over these flats, and eventually reach the lake already mentioned, to the South. The caretaker at the Well occupied his spare time by growing vegetables, and our last meal, with white men near us, for many months to come, was accompanied by pumpkins and turnips. Camped here, too, was a mob of cattle, about 130 head. The stockmen told us they had started from the head of the Gascoyne River with 2,000 sheep and 150 bullock's. Leaving the station, some four hundred miles to the N.N.W. of Cutmore's, they travelled by Lake Way, where a fair-sized mining community was then established, and Lawlers, where the advance of civilisation was marked by numerous "pubs." Their stock had not suffered from want of food or water — in fact, a very general rain seemed to have spread from Coolgardie to the Nor'-West. The cattle and our camels seemed quite friendly; the latter were settling down to work, and could now be allowed to go in their hobbles at night, in place of being tied down. Only an occasional fight disturbed our sleep; but at the the clay-pans two strangers, wild and savage, caused a deal of trouble, necessitating one or other of us being up all night. However, we would soon be beyond such annoyances. At this point our journey might be said to begin, for here we left the last outpost of civilisation, and saw the last white face for some time to come.

Part V: The Outward Journey

Chapter IV: We Enter The Desert

Our position was in lat. 28 degrees 35 minutes, long. 120 degrees 57 minutes, and from this point I started to map the country as we went. We left here on July 23rd steering a general N.E. by E. course, my intention being to strike Mount Allott and Mount Worsnop, on Forrest's route of 1874 — two very noticeable hills, 280 miles distant. I chose these for the double reason that by hitting them off correctly, as I hoped to do, I should not only give confidence to my companions, but have the opportunity of comparing my amateur work with that of a trained surveyor. Our course would clear the southern end of Lake Wells with which I had no desire to become entangled; and by so avoiding it I should cross a piece of country hitherto untraversed.
File:Spinifex and Sand Illustration 13.jpg Typical sandstone gorge [Missing image]

Our way lay across a rough range of bare diorite hills, whose stony slopes and steep gullies were not appreciated by the camels. Beyond the hills flat mulga-clad country extended for several days' march, only broken by the occurrence of low cliffs or terraces of sandstone. These are of peculiar formation, running sometimes for five or six miles without a break; abrupt, on one side, and perhaps fifty feet high, with broken boulders strewn about the foot of the cliff from which jut out occasional buttresses. It takes some time to find a break in the cliffs, or a gully, up which one can pass. Once on the top, trouble is over, for the summit is flat though often covered with dense scrub; from it a gradual slope takes one presently down to the same level as the foot of the cliffs. Occasional pines find a footing on the face of the rocks — how they manage to grow or get moisture is hard to tell — showing up fresh and green against the dull grey background of rock. Round the foot of the cliffs a small plain of saltbush is usually found, through which numerous small creeks and watercourses wind their way into the scrub beyond. In any one of these, as we saw them, water could be obtained by sinking in the gravelly bed. From the summit of the cliffs, which is often perforated by caves and holes opening on to the sheer face, square bluffs and walls can be seen, standing up above the sea of scrub, each exactly like its neighbour, and itself when again seen from another point. Doubtless the numberless creeks join and form one larger creek probably running South, as the general trend of the country is in that direction.

We were getting well into the swing of things now, for at first there is always some trouble in the distribution of the loads and in loading up and unloading. On camping at night the camels were always put down in a circle, as near as might be. All top-loading was taken off and placed near the centre; the side loads placed one on either side of the camel, and the saddle by his tail. Thus everything, instead of being scattered about in a long line, was handy, and easily reloaded the next morning. At this time, when the packs were heavy, it took us thirty minutes from the time Breaden and Warri brought the camels in to the time we were ready to start; Breaden, Charlie, Warri, and I loading, whilst Godfrey, who acted as cook, got his pots and pans together and packed the "tucker-bags." There is little of interest in this scrub; an occasional plant perhaps attracts one's attention. Here and there a vine-like creeper (an Asclepiad) trails upon the ground. With the fruits of this, commonly called cotton-pods, the black-fellows vary their diet of grubs and the very rare emu or kangaroo. The skin, the edible part, is soft, thick, and juicy, and has quite a nice sweet taste. The blacks eat them raw or roasted in wood-ashes. The seeds are of a golden yellow, and are joined on to a silky fibrous core. When bruised the pod exudes a white, milky juice.

Numerous large spiders inhabit the scrubs and build their webs from tree to tree; wonderfully strong they are too, and so frequent as to become a nuisance to whoever is walking first. It is quite unpleasant when one's eyes are fixed on the compass, to find, on looking up, that one's hat has swept off a great web, whose owner runs over one, furious at unprovoked assault. Though I got the full benefit of these insects, I was never bitten; they may or may not be poisonous, but look deadly enough, being from one to four inches from toe to toe. The scrubs for the most part are thick and without a break for many miles. Sometimes open country is met with — not always a welcome change.

July 26th the thickets became more and more open until we came across a narrow salt-lake; by leading each camel separately we reached the other side without mishap, and congratulated ourselves on our good fortune, until the next morning when we found that our camp had been on an island; and the lake stretched North and South as far as the eye could reach, until lake and sky became one in a shimmering mirage. I think it probable that this lake joins the Eastern portion of Lake Darlot, which lies to the N.N.W., and connects with the narrow lake seen by Luck and myself in 1894, to the S.S.E. Whatever its extent there was no doubt about its nature; from 8.30 until 1.30 we were occupied in hauling, digging out, and dragging our camels, and in humping on our backs some 5,000 lbs. weight of packs, across a channel not half a mile wide. Camels vary very much in their ability to cross bogs. Those which take small steps succeed best; the majority take steps of ordinary length and, in consequence, their hind feet slide into the hole left by the fore, and in an instant they are pinned by the hind leg up to the haunch. Kruger was splendid, and simply went through by main force, though he eventually sank close to the shore. I had carried over some of the loading, amongst it my camera, and was just in time to take a snapshot as he was sinking. Shiddi, the cunning old rogue, could not be persuaded across; he would try the ground with one foot and then draw back like a timid bather. We left him roaring to his mates and yet afraid to join them, until we were ready to start again. As soon as he saw the caravan disappear over the sandhill which abutted on the lake, he took a desperate plunge and came through with ease.

File:Spinifex and Sand Illustration 14.jpg Crossing a salt lake [Missing image]

The shores of the lake, as usual, were covered with samphire, having something the appearance of heather. At this season the plant is soft and juicy, and, though salt, makes capital feed for camels. In the summer it withers up to dry sticks and has no moisture. Once out of sight of the lake we were disgusted at coming into a belt of flat spinifex country, and were afraid that already we had reached the confines of the desert, more especially since in 1894 I had placed its edge in that longitude. However, we were agreeably disappointed, for after a few miles the spinifex ceased, and on penetrating a dense thicket we debouched on a fine grassy flat. In the centre ran a line of large white gums (Creek gums, *Eucalyptus rostrata*), the sure sign of a creek. We were not mistaken, for down the avenue a watercourse wound its way. The gravelly bed was quite dry. Climbing a tree, from which to follow with my glasses the course of the creek, I could see some hills to the northward; in them the creek evidently rose. Whilst I was climbing, Breaden amused himself by breaking off pieces of the small roots of the gums which the creek had washed here. By breaking these quite an appreciable amount of moisture could be got, enough to save a man's life. But I fancy that these roots only hold water after rain, and that when they are water-bearing, pools also are to be found in the creeks. Numerous emu and turkey tracks led up the watercourse, but, though seeing several emu, we were unable to get a shot. Following the creek upwards, for near the head one is likely to find rocky pools, we soon came on a nice waterhole and made camp. I traced the creek to its source in the evening and found the hills to be granite, and discovered one deep pool in the solid rock under a steep step in the creek bed. Along the banks herbage and green stuff were growing in profusion. Our beasts were content to feed amicably together, and with the exception of a sly bite no longer showed signs of ill-feeling. We were thankful indeed to see them "off season." Here we gave them a good drink and filled our casks and neckbags, carrying in all sixty-two gallons. We had been so well off for water up to this point, that we had hopes that the rain had penetrated inland.

Leaving the creek on July 29th we again entered the scrub, finding it lower and more open, the ground covered with occasional patches of grass and a little squashy plant straggling along the ground — "Pigweed" is the local name; it belongs, I believe, to the "portulacaceae." It is eaten by the blacks, and would make excellent feed for stock were it higher from the ground.

This day we saw the last auriferous country we were to meet with until Kimberley was reached. These hills, of diorite, with occasional blows of ironstone, I take to be a continuation the Neckersgat Range (Wells, 1892). Many traces of prospectors were visible here — the last to be seen for many a day — shallow dry-blowing holes and little heaps of sieved dirt, and the tracks of camels and horses. This was a piece of country worth trying, had we not had other objects in view.

Two rather curious ironstone dykes, standing square and wall-like above the ground, occur in these hills, some seven miles apart, running nearly North and South and parallel; between them a deep but narrow creek, a saltbush flat, and a ridge of diorite. Standing out prominently to the south of the first dyke are two sugar-loaf hills, and, beyond them, distant ranges are visible. Leaving the range the country to the East underwent a distinct change for the worse; and midday of July 31st found us on the borders of an unmistakable desert, the North-West corner of the Great Victoria Desert. We had so far travelled 110 miles from Cutmore's Well, only some 250 in a direct line from Coolgardie and were already in the desert! Wilderness perhaps would be a better name for this part; for the sand now flat, now blown into dunes, is not bare, but overgrown by the hateful spinifex and timbered pretty thickly with desert gums (*Eucalypus eudesmoides*) and low acacia bushes.

I am told that the term "spinifex," though generally employed by those who have the pleasure of the acquaintance of the plant, is wrongly used. I do not know its right name, and have seen it described as "Spinifex," "Porcupine Grass," "*Triodia*," "*Triodia pungens*," and "*Festuca irritans*." Why such a wretched, useless plant should have so many names I cannot say. So often am I bound to refer to it that I might vary the monotony by using each in turn. However, I will stick to the term I have always heard used. "Spinifex" grows in round, isolated hummocks, one to three feet high; these hummocks are a dense mass of needle-like prickles, and from them grow tall blades of very coarse grass to a height of sometimes six feet. Occasionally the hummocks are not round or isolated, but grow in crescent form or almost complete rings, sometimes there is no top growth — however it grows it is most accursed vegetation to walk through, both for men and camels. Whatever form it takes it seems to be so arranged that it cannot be stepped over or circumvented — one must in consequence walk through it and be pricked, unpleasantly. Camels and horses suffer rather severely sometimes, the constant pricking causing sores on their legs. So long, however, as a camel does not drag his hind legs he will be no worse treated than by having all the hair worn off his shins. The side of the foot is an easily affected spot, and a raw there, gives them great pain and is hard to cure.

There are two varieties of spinifex known to bushmen — "spinifex" and "buck" (or "old man") spinifex. The latter is stronger in the prickle and practically impossible to get through, though it may be avoided by twists and turns. There are a few uses for this horrible plant; for example, it forms a shelter and its roots make food for the kangaroo, or spinifex, rat, from its spikes the natives (in the northern districts) make a very serviceable gum, it burns freely, serves in a measure to bind the sand and protect it from being moved by the wind, and makes a good mattress when dug up and turned over. I should advise no one to try and sleep on the plant as it grows, for "He who sitteth on a thistle riseth up quickly." But the thistle has one advantage, viz., that it does not leave its points in its victim's flesh. In Northern Australia spinifex is in seed for three weeks, and when in this state, forms most excellent feed for horses, and fattens almost as quickly as oats; for the rest of the year it is useless.

I can imagine any one, on being suddenly placed on rising ground with a vast plain of waving spinifex spreading before him — a plain relieved occasionally by the stately desert oak, solemn, white, and mysterious — saying, "Ah! what a charming view — how beautiful that rolling plain of grass! its level surface broken by that bold sandhill, fiery-red in the blaze of sun!" But when day after day, week after week, and month after month must be passed always surrounded by the hateful plant, one's sense of the picturesque becomes sadly blunted.

This was our first introduction to the desert and, though a little monotonous, it seemed quite pleasant, and indeed was so, when compared to the heartrending country met with later in our journey.

The sand has been formed (blown, I suppose) into irregular ridges, running more or less parallel, but in no one fixed direction. From the edge of the desert to Mount Worsnop, a distance of nearly two hundred miles in a straight line, the country presented the same appearance. First a belt, eight to ten miles wide, of sand-ridges from thirty to fifty feet high, with a general direction of E. by S. and W. by N.; then a broad sand-flat of equal breadth, either timbered with desert gums, or open and covered with spinifex breast-high, looking in the distance like a field of ripe corn; next another series of ridges with a S.E. and N.W. direction; then, with startling suddenness, a small oasis, enclosed or nearly surrounded by sheer broken cliffs of desert sandstone, from which little creeks run out into the sand, winding their way for a mile or two between the ridges. Dry watercourses these, except immediately after rain; in their beds are found native wells five to ten feet in depth, sometimes holding water; on their banks, round the foot of the cliffs, and on the flat where the creeks merge into the sand, grows long grass — kangaroo-grass — and, in the winter magnificent herbage. Next we find a dense thicket, and, this passed, we come again to open plains. And thus sand-ridges now E. and W., now S.E. and N.W., now S.W. and N.E. (as in the vicinity of Empress Spring), and now sandhills heaped up without regularity, alternate with mulga thickets, open plains of spinifex, and flat, timbered country. The most noticeable vegetation is of course spinifex; as well as that, however, are several shrubs which form good camel feed, such as ACACIA SALICINA, with its pretty, scented flower like a little golden powder-puff; the quondong (*Fusanus acuminatus*), or "native peach tree," a graceful little black-stemmed tree, against whose fresh, green leaves the fruit, about the size of a cherry and of a brilliant red, shows out with appetising clearness. Alas! it is a fraud and delusion, for the stone forms more than three-quarters of the fruit, leaving only a rather tasteless thick skin, which is invariably perforated by small worms.

Dotted over the open plains the native poplar (*Codonocarpus*) stands sentry, its head, top-heavy from the mass of seeds, drooping gracefully to the setting sun; the prevalent wind at the present day would seem to be from the E.N.E. Here, too, an occasional grass tree or "black-boy" may be seen, and at intervals little clumps of what is locally termed "mustard bush," so named from the strong flavour of the leaf; camels eat this with voracity, of which fact one becomes very sensible when they chew their cuds.

This description hardly suits a "desert"; yet, in spite of the trees and shrubs, it is one to all intent. All is sand, and throughout the region no water is to be found, unless immediately after rain in the little creeks, or in some hidden rock-hole. Even a heavy storm of rain would leave no signs in such country; half an hour after the fall no water would be seen, except on the rocky ground, which only occurs at very long intervals. The greedy sand soaks up every drop of water, and from the sand the trees derive their moisture. The winter rain causes such a growth of herbage around the cliffs and on the sandhills — to die, alas! in a few weeks' time — that one is inclined to wonder if by means of bores this wilderness will be made of use to man. What artesian bores have done for parts of Queensland and Algeria they may in the distant future do for this, at present useless, interior, where all is still, and the desert silence unbroken by any animal life, excepting always the ubiquitous spinifex rat. A pretty little fellow this, as he hops along on his long hind legs, bounding over the prickly stools like an animated football with a tail. As he jumps, he hangs one forepaw by his side, while the other is stretched out with the little hand dangling as if the wrist were broken. Everything must be spoken of comparatively in this country; thus the ubiquitous rat may be seen, at the most, a dozen times in a day's march; an oasis may measure no more than thirty yards across; a creek is dry, and may be only half a mile long and a few feet broad; a high range may stand three to four hundred feet above the surrounding country, seldom more; and "good feed" may mean that the camels find something to eat instead of being tied down without a bite.

For instance, to continue our journey, on August 1st we have "...the same miserable country until the evening, when a sudden change brings us into a little oasis enclosed by cliffs, a small creek running through it. Here we made camp, the camels enjoying a great patch of feed — could find no water — saw several small quails — a number of grasshoppers and little bees — flies of course in abundance. Lat. 27 degrees 40 minutes, long. 122 degrees 54 minutes. Cloudy night."

The next day we sighted a big range to the East across a deep valley, and a broken table-top range to the North. Following down the little creek we came on a shallow native well, quite dry; crossing the grassy flat in which it was dug, winding through a thicket, we again reached open sand. Here we saw for the first time since leaving Coolgardie the tracks of wild aboriginals, and the first tracks of blacks, either wild or tame, since leaving Cutmore's Well. Evidently this part of the world is not overpopulated. Since everything pointed to the rain having been general, since the tracks were leading in a direction nearly opposite to our own, and since at the time we had water enough, we did not waste time in following them up.

That night we were forced to camp on a barren spot, and tied the camels down foodless; one night without feed does them no harm — less harm than if they wandered miles in their hobbles looking for it. The weather was now distinctly hot, unpleasant and stuffy, as if about to thunder; but the nights were still cold. At midday we saw two fine quondong trees; how the camels devoured them, leaves, fruit, stones and all! Emus swallow the stones without inconvenience; apparently a camel has an equally convenient interior, but he brings them up again in his cud and drops them out of his mouth as his jaws move from side to side.

Amongst some broken rocks this day, Breaden found a dingo camped in a cave with a litter of pups. Had we been returning instead of only just starting on our travels, I should certainly have secured one — not, I expect, without some trouble, for the mother showed signs of fierce hostility when Breaden looked into her lair. There were no traces of water anywhere near, and I have no doubt that the mother, having found a suitable spot for her expected family, would think nothing of travelling many miles for her daily drink. Near the rocks I noticed a little blue-flowered plant with the leaf and scent of the geranium.

The appearance of the country now soon began to get less fresh, and drier, and all the next two days we were crossing sandhills, the only variety being afforded by Valerie. She had lately made it evident that she would soon follow the example of the lady dingo. Though I had frequently tried to make her ride on one of the packs, she preferred to trot along at the heels of Czar, receiving from him occasional kicks if by chance she touched him, which did not tend to improve the pups so soon to see the light. Tying her on was no better; she only struggled and nearly hanged herself. She had therefore to walk as she desired. Having made camp, and unrolled our blankets ready to turn into them when the time came, Breaden and I experimented on numerous mallee-roots which we dug up, but in every case failed to find any appreciable moisture, On returning to camp we found our party had been increased by one — a large pup which Val had deposited in her master's blankets. It was dead, which was fortunate, as we could hardly have kept it, and would not have liked to destroy the little animal, born in such unusual surroundings.

No change occurred in the country the next day, but the march was saved from its usual monotony by Warri finding two mallee-hens' nests. Unluckily they had no eggs, though the birds' tracks were fresh and numerous. These nests are hollowed out in the sand, to a depth of perhaps two and a half feet, conical shaped, with a mouth some three feet in diameter; the sand from the centre is scraped up into a ring round the mouth. Several birds help in this operation, and when finished lay their eggs on a layer of leaves at the bottom; they then fill in the hole to the surface with small twigs and more leaves. Presumably the eggs are hatched by spontaneous heat, the green twigs and leaves producing a slightly moist warmth, similar to that of the bird's feathers. I have seen numbers of these nests, never with eggs in, but often with the shells from recently hatched birds lying about. How the little ones force their way through the sticks I do not understand, but Warri and many others who have found the eggs assure me that they do so.

Towards evening we neared a prominent bluff that we had sighted the day before, and got a further insight into the habits of the wild dog. A dingo — a female, and possibly our friend with the pups — had followed us persistently all day. Godfrey, who was walking behind the camels, opened the acquaintance by practising his revolver-shooting upon her. His poor aim seemed to give her confidence, and before long she started to play with Val. By nightfall we had petted and fed her out of our hands, and given her a small drop of water from our fast diminishing supply — this at the earnest request of Godfrey, who offered to give her some of his share; and indeed it seemed rather cruel to refuse a poor famished beast that had come to us in her distress. We all agreed how nice it was to have won the affections of a real wild dog. By daybreak our feelings of love had somewhat abated, as our friend prowled about all night, poking her nose into pots and pans, chewing saddles, pack-bags, straps, and even our blankets as we lay in them, and cared no more for blows than for the violent oaths that were wasted upon her. This strange creature accompanied us for two more days, trotting along ahead of the camels, with an occasional look behind to see if she was on the right course, and then falling at full length in the shade of some bush with her head on her paws, waiting for us to pass. Eventually my irritability got the better of my indulgence, and a shrewd whack over the nose put an end to our acquaintanceship.

Near the bluff were many low, stony hills, with the usual small watercourses; in them we hunted high and low for water until darkness overtook us. To the North other similar hills could be seen, by my reckoning a part of the Ernest Giles Range (Wells, 1892). No doubt from the distance these hills would look more imposing. Our camp was in lat. 27 degrees 9 minutes, long.

123 degrees 59 minutes. August 6th.

On August 7th we continued to search the hills, but had to leave them without finding water. We had now been since July 29th without seeing any, and in consequence of the ease with which we had, up to that date, found water had not husbanded our supply as carefully as we might have done, and now had to put ourselves on a very short allowance indeed. The further we advanced the worse the country became, and the greater the increase in temperature. Shortly after leaving the hills we came again on to sandhills. About midday my hopes were high, as I cut the fresh tracks of two black-fellows.

Warri, after a short examination, said, "Yesterday track water that way," pointing in the direction in which they were travelling; not that he could possibly tell which way the water lay, and for all we knew they might have just left it. However, we decided that better success would probably attend us if we followed them forward. Soon several equally fresh tracks joined the first ones, and not one of us doubted but that our present discomforts would shortly be over.

"There must be water at the end of them," was the general opinion, and so on we went gaily; Warri leading, and Charlie, who was an almost equally good tracker, backing him up. After much twisting and turning, crossing and recrossing of our own tracks, the footprints at last took a definite direction, and a pad, beaten by perhaps a dozen feet, led away North-West for two miles and never deviated. Any doubts as to Warri's correct interpretation were now dispelled, and on we hurried, looking forward to at least water for ourselves, and perhaps a drink for the camels. At full speed through mulga scrub, over sand and stones, on which the tracks were hardly visible, we came suddenly to an open patch of rock on the side of a low ridge, and there in the centre of the flat rock lay before us a fair-sized rock-hole — dry as a bone! — and all our visions of luxury for our beasts and ourselves were ended.

Not only were we baulked of our water, but nothing but dead scrub surrounded the rock, affording no feed for the camels, who had therefore to be tied down. Leaving the rest to dig out the hole on the chance of getting a drop, though it was evident that the natives had cleaned it out nearly to the bottom, Warri and I started off to follow the tracks yet further. Taking a handful of dried peaches to chew, which give a little moisture, for we were very dry, we walked until darkness overtook us. The tracks (a man, two women, and a child) led us back towards the West; we could see their camps, one close to the namma-hole, another four miles away, with crushed seed lying about, and a few roots pulled up. Warri said they were "tired fella" from the way they walked. All this made us doubtful if they knew where the next water was. In any case we could make no further search that night, and made our best way back through the scrub, to the camp.

Godfrey had unsuccessfully explored the neighbouring hills, while Breaden and Charlie cleaned out the rockhole with like result. A very hot, cloudy night did not make things any more pleasant; we were all a bit done, and poor Charlie was seized with a violent and painful vomiting — a not unusual accompaniment to want of food and water. It seemed useless to follow the tracks any more, since they led us in exactly the wrong direction; and as we loaded the camels in the morning two turkeys (bustards) flew over us to the North-East. We would have given something to have their knowledge! We started, therefore, in this direction, and soon came on other tracks, which after some time we concluded were only those of natives who had been hunting from the rock-hole before the water was finished.

I called a halt, and, sitting on the sand, expounded my views as to the situation. "We had determined on getting through this country — that was the main point. Turning back, even if wise, was not to be considered. The tracks had fooled us once, and though doubtless by following them we would eventually get some water, where would we be at the end of it? No further forward. Therefore, since we had still a drop or two to go on with, let us continue on our course. None of us have any idea where water is, and by travelling North, East, South, or West, we stood an equally good chance of getting it. We would therefore go on in our proper direction, and trust to God, Providence, Fate, or Chance, as each might think. I should feel more satisfied if I knew their opinions agreed with mine, for, whatever the outcome, the responsibility rested on me."

Breaden answered quietly, "It's a matter of indifference to me; go where you think best." Godfrey's reply was characteristic, "Don't care a d--n; if we are going to peg out we will, whichever way we turn." Charlie was inclined at first to question the wisdom of going on, but soon cheerfully agreed to do as the rest. So on I went, much relieved in mind that I was leading no one against his will. Possibly I could not — so far as I know, no occasion arose.

The day was sweltering, the night worse; in any other country one could with safety have backed heavily the fall of a thunderstorm. We had to be content, where we were, with about three drops of rain; and even this, in spite of tents, flys, and mackintosh-sheets spread for the purpose, we were unable to collect! Towards dawn the thermometer went down to 40 degrees F. This sudden change was greatly to our advantage, though the sun soon after rising showed his power. The ridges were now running almost parallel to our course, about North-East, and gave us in consequence little trouble. Up to this point I had walked all day, partly because one can steer better on foot and I wished to do all the steering, until we picked up the point on Forrest's route, and so give my companions confidence; and partly because I looked upon it as the leader's duty to set an example. To-day I took my turn with the rest, each riding for an hour — a great relief. Sand is weary walking and spinifex unpleasant until one's legs get callous to its spines.

We had not gone far before our hopes were again raised, and again dashed, by coming on rocky ground and presently on another rockhole — quite dry! We began to think that there could be no water anywhere; this hole was well protected and should hold water for months. Thinking did little good, nor served to decrease the horrid sticky feeling of lips and mouth. "Better luck next time," we said, with rather forced cheerfulness, and once more turned our faces to the North-East.

Part V: The Outward Journey

Chapter V: Water at Last

Presently a single track caught my eye, fresh apparently, and unmistakably that of a "buck." We all crowded round to examine it, and as we stooped caught sight of the owner not a hundred yards ahead, engrossed in unearthing an iguana and entirely ignorant of our presence. A hasty consultation; "Catch him," said someone, Breaden I think, and off we started — I first, and Godfrey near behind. He saw us now and fled, so, shouting to Breaden to stay with the camels, and to Charlie, who was mounted, to cut him off in front, I put my best leg foremost. A hummock of spinifex brought me down, and, exhausted from short rations, I lay, unable to run further. Not so Godfrey, who held on manfully for another fifty yards and grabbed the black-fellow as he turned to avoid Charlie on the camel. The poor chap was shaking with fear, but, after relieving his feelings by making a violent though abortive attack on Godfrey, he soon calmed down and examined us with interest.

Whatever the buck thought of us, close observation could find nothing very remarkable about him. A man of about 5 feet 8 inches, thin but muscular, with very large feet and small hands, very black, very dirty, his only garment consisted of a band of string round his forehead, holding his hair back in a ragged, mop-like mass. On his chest, raised sears; through his nose, a hole ready to hold a bone or stick — such was this child of the wilderness. By signs we made him understand our wants, and the strange procession started, the "buck" (the general term for a male aboriginal) leading the way at a pace too fast for us or our camels. Guarded on one side by Breaden, I on the other, we plied our new friend with salt beef, both to cement our friendship, and promote thirst, in order that for his own sake he should not play us false. For five hours we held on our way, curiously enough almost on our proper course, having often to stop awhile to allow the caravan to overtake us. Buoyed up by the certainty of water so long as we had the buck with us we pushed on, until just after sunset the country changed from sand to stony rises and we felt sure a rock-hole was not far off. A little further, and, by the uncertain light, we could see a fair-sized hole with water in it. I ran ahead, and was the first to realise that the native had deceived us; the hole was dry! and must have been so for months.

No sooner did the buck see that I had found him out than he made a sudden bolt and attempt at escape — very neatly done, but not quick enough to pass Breaden. This was indeed a disappointment! I had thought it probable that our guide would lead us anywhere into the sand and try to escape, but I never guessed that he would tantalise us as he had done. In any case, so long as he was with us, we must some time get water — and we had no intention of letting him escape. With a rope we secured him and watched in turn all through the night.

Never were jailers more vigilant, for that black-fellow meant our lives. He tried all means of escape, and never slept the whole night through. He would lie still with closed eyes for a time, and then make a sudden struggle to wrench the rope away from his captor; then stealthily with his foot he tried to push the rope into the fire; then he started rubbing it on the rock on which we lay; and last of all his teeth were brought into use. When my turn came to watch, I pretended to sleep, to see what he would do, and so discovered all his tricks. I confess that I saw with delight the evident feelings of thirst that before long overcame him — the salt beef had done its duty; he had had no water of course, for we had none to give him, and I felt sure that he would be only too eager in the morning. Nor was I mistaken; long before daylight he showed signs of distress, and anxiety to go on, standing up and stretching out his long, thin arm — "Gabbi" (water), he said, pointing in three different directions, putting his head back and pointing with his chin, making a noise something between a grunt and a puff. To the East, to the North-East, and to the South-West from where we had come, he made it clear that water existed. Evidently we had not been far from his camp when we caught him, and we could hardly blame him for leading us away from his own supply, which he rightly judged we and our camels would exhaust.

Standing by the dry rock-hole we could see for many miles, the country to the North-East being considerably lower than where we were; not a cheerful view — sand-ridges always! Not a hill or range to be seen, and yet people have doubted if this really is a desert!

It may happen that in days to come some other party may be stranded in this region and therefore I will leave out no description that could assist them in finding the water that King Billy (for so had we named the buck) eventually took us to. The dry rock-hole (Mulundella) is situated on a surface outcrop of desert sandstone, about fifty yards across surrounded by thick mulga scrub, enclosed between two sand-ridges running North-East and South-West.

On the North and East side of the outcrop the ground suddenly drops, forming what appears from the distance as a line of sheer cliffs. Down this steep slope, which is covered with scrub, we discovered a passage, and, at the foot, found ourselves in an open spinifex plain with a sand-ridge on either hand. We were steering N.E. by N., and in consequence had now and again to cross a ridge, since they ran due North-East. After three miles low outcrops of limestone appeared at intervals, the scrub in the trough of the ridges became more open with an undergrowth of coarse grass, buck-bush or "Roly-Poly" (*Salsola kali*) and low acacia. Hugging the ridge on our left, we followed along this belt for another one and a half miles; when, close to the foot of a sandhill, our guide, secured to my belt by a rope round his waist, stopped and excitedly pointed out what seemed on first sight to be three rock-holes, in a small, bare patch of limestone not more than thirty feet across. Twenty yards to the right or left and we would never have seen it; and to this spot King Billy had brought us full speed, only stopping once to examine some rocks at the foot of one ridge, as if to make sure that we were in the right valley. On further investigation the three holes turned out to be entrances, of which two were large enough for a man to pass through, leading perpendicularly to a cave beneath. With the help of a rope Charlie and I descended twenty-five feet to the floor of the chamber, which we found to be covered with sand to a depth of two feet. In the sand we dug holes but did not succeed in getting even moisture. Plunged as we were so suddenly into darkness, our eyes could distinguish no passage leading from the chamber, and it seemed as if we had been tricked again. Further exploration by the light of candles revealed two passages, one leading west and upwards, the other east and downwards. Charlie chose the latter; before long I came to the end of mine, having failed to find anything but bats, bones of birds and dingoes, and old native camp-fires. Following Charlie, I found him crawling on hands and knees down a steep slope — progress was slow, as the floor was rough and the ceiling jagged; presently the passage dropped again, and at the end, below us, we could see our candles reflected, and knew that at last we had water! Who, except those who have had similar experiences, can picture one's feelings of relief! "Thank God! thank God!" is all one can reiterate in one's mind over and over again. The visible supply of water was small, and we had grave doubts as to any soakage existing! Not wasting valuable time in discussion, we crawled back with all speed to the cave, shouted up the joyful news, and called for buckets and billies to bale with. The King was now allowed to descend, but not unguarded, as we must first ascertain the value of our supply. We could understand now why he had insisted on carrying with him from our last camp a burning branch (a "fire-stick"); for he proceeded to make a fire on the floor of the cave from some dead leaves and branches, and others along the passage, to light him; after some hesitation he took a candle instead, and bolted down the passage like a rat. He must have been very dry, judging from the time he stayed below and from his distended appearance on re-ascending. He drank a great deal more than any of us and yet had been a comparatively short time without water, whilst we had been walking and working on starvation rations for a good number of days.

File:Spinifex and Sand Illustration 15.jpg Entrance to Empress Spring [Missing image]

Breaden and I set to work to unload the camels while the others started preparations for water-getting. By 3 p.m. we were ready. King Billy at the bottom, baling water with a meat tin into a bucket, which he handed to Warri, who passed it to Charlie; thence VIA Godfrey it reached Breaden, who on the floor of the cave hitched it on to a rope, and I from above hauled it through the entrance to the surface. Useful as he was below, I soon had to call Warri up to keep off the poor famished camels, who, in their eagerness, nearly jostled me into the hole. First I filled our tanks, doubtful what supply the cave would yield; but when word was passed that "She was good enough, and making as fast as we baled," I no longer hesitated to give the poor thirsty beasts as much as ever they could drink. What a labour of love that was, and what satisfaction to see them "visibly swelling" before my eyes! Till after sunset we laboured unceasingly, and I fancy none of us felt too strong. The thundery weather still continued; the heat was suffocating — so much so that I took off my hat and shirt, to the evident delight of the flies, whose onslaughts would have driven me mad had I not been too busily engaged to notice them.

Before night all the camels were watered; they drank on an average seventeen gallons apiece, and lay gorged upon the ground too tired or too full of liquid to eat. We had a very different camp that night, and King Billy shared our good spirits. Now that he had his liberty he showed no signs of wishing to leave us, evidently enjoying our food and full of pride in his newly acquired garment, a jersey, which added greatly to his striking appearance. He took great interest in all our belongings, but seemed to value highest the little round piece of metal that is fixed on the inside of a meat-tin! This, hung on a string, made a handsome ornament for him.

That night, in reviewing our affairs, I came to the conclusion that this dry stage at the beginning of our journey had been a good thing for all. We had had a bad time, but had come out of it all right. Although these things always appear worse, when written or read, yet it is no light task to trudge day after day over such horrible country with an empty stomach and dry throat, and with no idea of when the next water will be found, or if any will be found; and through it all to be cheerful and good-tempered, and work away as usual, as if all were right. It had inspired us with complete confidence in the staying powers of the camels, who, in spite of a thirteen and a half days' drought, had shown no signs of giving in. It had afforded each of us an insight into the characters of his companions that otherwise he never would have had. It had given me absolute confidence in Breaden, Godfrey, and Charlie, and I trust had imbued them with a similar faith in me.

August 11th to 15th we rested at the cave, occupying ourselves in the numerous odd jobs that are always to be found, happy in the knowledge that we had an unfailing supply of water beneath us. I have little doubt but that this water is permanent, and do not hesitate to call it a spring. I know well that previous travellers have called places "springs" which in after years have been found dry; but I feel sure that this supply so far, nearly sixty feet, below the surface, must be derived from a permanent source, and even in the hottest season is too well protected to be in any way decreased by evaporation.

At work in the cave, Empress Spring

As a humble tribute to the world-wide rejoicings over the long reign of our Gracious Majesty Queen Victoria, I have honoured this hidden well of water by the name of "The Empress Spring." A more appropriate name it could not have, for is it not in the Great Victoria Desert? and was it not in that region that another party was saved by the happy finding of Queen Victoria Spring?

The "Empress Spring" would be a hard spot to find. What landmarks there are I will now describe. My position for the Spring is lat. 26 degrees 47 minutes 21 seconds S., long. 124 degrees 25 minutes E. Its probable native name (I say probable because one can never be sure of words taken from a wild aboriginal, who, though pointing out a water, may, instead of repeating its name, be perhaps describing its size or shape) is "Murcoolia Ayah Teenyah." The entrance is in a low outcrop of magnesian limestone, surrounded by buckbush, a few low quondongs and a low, broom-like shrub; beyond this, mulga scrub. Immediately to the North of the outcrop runs a high sand-ridge, covered sparsely with acacia and spinifex. On the top of the ridge are three conspicuously tall dead mulga trees. From the ridge looking West, North, North-East, and East nothing is visible but parallel sand-ridges running N.E. To the South-West can be seen the high ground on which is the rock-hole (Mulundella).

To the South-East, across a mulga-covered flat, is a high ridge one mile distant, with the crests of others visible beyond it; above them, about twelve miles distant, a prominent bluff (Breaden Bluff), the North end of a red tableland. From the mulga trees the bluff bears 144 degrees. One and a half miles N.E. by N. from the cave is a valley of open spinifex, breaking through the ridges in a West and Southerly direction, on which are clumps of cork-bark trees; these would incline one to think that water cannot be far below the surface in this spot.

Close to the entrance to the cave is erected a mulga pole, on which we carved our initials and the date. There are also some native signs or ornaments in the form of three small pyramids of stones and grass, about eight feet apart, in a line pointing S.W.

Several old native camps were dotted about in the scrub; old fires and very primitive shelters formed of a few branches. Amongst the ashes many bones could be seen, particularly the lower maxillary of some species of rat-kangaroo. To descend to the cave beneath, the natives had made a rough ladder by leaning mulga poles against the edge of the entrance from the floor. All down the passage to the water little heaps of ashes could be seen where their fires had been placed to light them in their work. Warri found some strange carved planks hidden away in the bushes, which unfortunately we were unable to carry. King Billy saw them with evident awe; he had become very useful, carrying wood and so forth with the greatest pleasure. The morning we left this camp, however, he sneaked away before any of us were up. I fancy that his impressions of a white man's character will be favourable; for never in his life before had he been able to gorge himself without having had the trouble of hunting his food. From him I made out the following words, which I consider reliable:

English **Aboriginal** Smoke, fire Warru or wallu Wood. Taalpa. Arm. Menia. Hand. Murra. Hair. Kuttya. Nose. Wula or Ula. Water. Gabbi. Dog. Pappa.*   * This word "pappa" we found to be used by all natives encountered by us in the interior. Warri uses it, and Breaden tells me that in Central Australia it is universal.

August 15th we again watered the camels, who were none the worse for their dry stage. Breaden was suffering some pain from his strain, and on descending to the cave was unable to climb up again; we had some difficulty in hauling him through the small entrance.

Part V: The Outward Journey

Chapter VI: Woodhouse Lagoon

But for the flies, which never ceased to annoy us, we had enjoyed a real good rest, and were ready to march on the morning of the 16th, no change occurring in the character of the country until the evening of the 18th, when we sighted a low tableland five miles to the North, and to the West of it a table-topped detached hill. Between us and the hills one or two native smokes were rising, which showed us that water must be somewhere in the neighbourhood. From a high sandhill the next morning, we got a better view, and could see behind the table-top another and similar hill. I had no longer any doubt as to their being Mounts Worsnop and Allott (Forrest, 1874), the points for which I had been steering, though at first they appeared so insignificant that I hesitated to believe that these were the right ones. From the West, from which direction Forrest saw them first, they appear much higher, and are visible some twenty miles off. From the North they are not visible a greater distance than three miles, while from the East one can see them a distance of eight miles.

I altered our course, therefore, towards the hills, and we shortly crossed the narrow arm of a salt-lake; on the far side several tracks of emus and natives caught my eye, and I sent Charlie on Satan to scout. Before long he reported a fine sheet of water just ahead. This, as may be imagined, came as a surprise to us; for a more unlikely thing to find, considering the dry state of the rock-holes we had come upon, could not have been suggested. However, there it was; and very glad we were to see it, and lost no time in making camp and hobbling the camels. What a glorious sight in this parched land! — so resting to the eye after days of sand! How the camels wallowed in the fresh water! how they drank! and what a grand feed they had on the herbage (*Trichinium alopecuroideum*) on the banks of the lagoon! Charlie and I spent the afternoon in further exploring our surroundings, and on return to camp found our mates busily engaged in plucking some teal and waterhen which they had shot. The latter were numerous, and Godfrey at one shot bagged nine. They are almost identical in size and appearance with our British waterhen, though they seem to have less power of flight, thus enabling us to drive them from one gun to the other, and so secure a fine lot for the pot. I doubt if in civilisation they would be considered good eating, but after tinned horrors they were a perfect delicacy. The teal were as numerous; but though there were several emu tracks we saw none of those queer birds. Our bag for three days was seventeen teal, twelve waterhen, one pigeon. The natives whose smoke we had seen, disappeared shortly after our arrival. Godfrey, whilst shooting, came across their camp; the occupants, a man, woman, and child, fled as soon as they caught sight of him, leaving a shield behind them, and did not appear again. This small oasis deserves particular attention, for it is bound to play an important part in any scheme of a stock route from the cattle-stations of Central Australia to the Murchison or Coolgardie Goldfields.

There are three lagoons (or deep clay-pans) connected by a shallow, sandy channel. They are entirely surrounded by sandhills, excepting at one spot, where a narrow creek breaks through the sand-ridge. Of the three the largest and most South-Westerly one is nearly circular, and has a diameter of 600 yards with a depth varying from 1 ft. 6 in. to 4 ft. 6 in. It is capable of holding considerably more water than we saw in it. The bottom is of rock, a sort of cement in which ironstone is visible in the middle, and of clay near the edges. From the N.W. a narrow channel enters, traceable for a distance of two miles to a cane-grass swamp; into this, small watercourses, and the tail end of a larger creek lead.

Following up this flat, it will be found to develop into a defined channel running through a grassy flat timbered with bloodwoods (a kind of eucalyptus). This creek rises in the sandstone tablelands to the N. of Mount Allott, and in it at its head, is situated Alexander Spring (Forrest. 1874).

File:Spinifex and Sand Illustration 17.jpg Alexander Spring [Missing image]

Round the foot of these hills, extending to the lagoon, is a fine little plain of grass, saltbush, and numerous low shrubs, all excellent feed for stock. Mounts Allott and Worsnop are certainly remarkable hills, perhaps 200 feet above the surrounding country, quite flat on the top, which is covered with scrub. From the latter the lagoon is visible, one mile distant on bearing 150 degrees. Our camp at the lagoon was in lat. 26 degrees 10 minutes, long. 124 degrees 48 minutes. This reckoning placed Alexander Spring in a position agreeing very closely with that given it by Forrest, which was very gratifying to me. This water was marked by Forrest as "permanent." He says in his journal: "July 13th . . . Fine water at this place. I have no doubt water is always here. I named it Alexander Spring after my brother, who discovered it. Abundance of water also in rock-holes." This was in 1874. Since that date this spot has been revisited, first and not long after Forrest, by W. W. Mills, who was commissioned to bring over a mob of camels from South Australia. He followed Forrest's track from water to water, at first with no difficulty; depending on Alexander Spring, he made a longish dry stage, reached the spring only to find it dry, and had a bad time in consequence. The second party to follow Forrest's route was that of Carr-Boyd in 1896, whom Breaden accompanied, and who was prospecting for an Adelaide syndicate. They passed by this spot, but having plenty of water, as it was raining at the time, did not visit the spring. From Mount Worsnop, Woodhouse, one of the party, sighted the lagoon; but neither he nor any of the party had troubled to see whether it was salt or fresh, or of what extent it was. I have named it after Woodhouse, who first saw it. Breaden had told me of the fact of his having seen it, but I had supposed that, as rain was falling, Woodhouse was only looking on a shallow pool that could by no possibility hold water for long.

Shortly after Carr-Boyd, there followed Hubbe's party. He was sent out by the South Australian Government to follow Forrest's route, to ascertain its suitability or otherwise for a stock route. Hubbe found the spring dry, or practically so, and was much disappointed. He did not happen to find the lagoon, and had a long stage before he found water. His party arrived at Menzies shortly before we started. I was unable to get any information from him beyond the opinion that the country was worthless and a stock route impracticable. I put more faith, however, in Breaden, whose life has been spent amongst stock and travelling cattle. When with Carr-Boyd he came to the conclusion that as far as the Warburton Range cattle could be taken without much trouble; and indeed in 1873, so I have read, Gosse drove some bullocks as far as that point, which was the furthest west he penetrated when attempting to cross the Colony.

From the Warburton Range to Lake Wells the awkward part came in, but now this lagoon and the Empress Spring go far to bridge it over. I have no doubt that a fortnight's work at both these places would be sufficient to make splendid wells, supposing that the lagoon was found dry and the spring too hard to get at. At the expenditure of no great amount I feel confident that a serviceable stock route could be formed, easily negotiated in the winter months and kept open by wells during the rest of the year. The country through which the route would pass is excellent as far as the border. From there it would be necessary to hit off the small oases which are met with near Mount Squires, Warburton Ranges, Blyth Creek, and Alexander Spring. From this point the route could be taken to Empress Spring, thence to Lake Wells (or direct to Lake Wells) and the Bonython Creek, and from there to Lake Darlot there would be no difficulty. The only really bad bit of the route would be between Woodhouse Lagoon and Lake Wells, and this is no great distance. Whether the scheme would be worth the expenditure necessary to equip a really serviceable well-sinking party I am unable to judge; but it seems to me that it would be a tremendous advantage to Central Australian cattle owners to be able to drive their bullocks direct to the West Australian goldfields, even though they could only do so in the winter, at which season alone it is probable that the feed would be sufficiently good. The fact that Forrest with his horses traversed this route is evidence enough that at some seasons certain surface waters exist at no great distances apart — in some cases large supplies. For cattle to follow the route that we had come so far would be manifestly absurd, and these remarks, especially where the country between Woodhouse Lagoon and Lake Wells, and between that lake and Lake Darlot is discussed, are made with the further knowledge of these regions that our return journey gave us.

File:Spinifex and Sand Illustration 18.jpg Woodhouse Lagoon [Missing image]

It seems a remarkable fact that while a spring should be found dry, not five miles from it a fresh-water lagoon with millions of gallons in it should exist. In the first place Alexander Spring is no spring; Sir John Forrest told me himself that at the time of naming it he was very doubtful. Hubbe dug it out to bedrock and proved it to be merely a local soakage in the gravelly bed of a narrow gully. Now a heavy downpour sufficient to run the creek and fill the lagoon must certainly first fill the spring and neighbouring pools. But the water in the spring would soon evaporate, whilst the depth and area of the lagoon would save its contents from diminishing from this cause, for a much longer period. So that after all it is easily understandable that we should find the lagoon full and the so-called spring dry.

Near the foot of Mount Allott we found Hubbe's camp, and in it several straps and hobble-chains; two tin-lined packing cases had been left behind, and from them we took the lids, not quite knowing to what use we could put them, but yet feeling they might be serviceable; and indeed they were.

On the summit of the hill Forrest had raised a cairn of stones; this had been pulled down by the natives and subsequently replaced by Hubbe. The blacks had again started to take it to pieces; I rebuilt what they had removed and placed on the cairn a board on which I wrote directions to the lagoon, in case any other traveller should pass.

By the side of the little creek to the North-West of the hill a bloodwood tree has been marked on one side with the number of Mills's camp, and on the other with a record of the objects of Hubbe's expedition, S.R. standing presumably for "Stock Route."

The flat on which these trees are growing is, in my opinion, a very likely spot for finding water by sinking.

Part V: The Outward Journey

Chapter VII: The Great Undulating Desert of Gravel

On August 22nd we left this kindly little oasis and directed our course to the North. We were now nearly in the centre of the Colony, and had made enough easting, a general northerly course being necessary to take us through the heart of the great unknown. It was my intention to steer due North for as long a period as possible, only deviating from it when forced by the exigencies of water-hunting, and when it became necessary, to bear somewhat to the eastward so as to hit off the vicinity of Hall's Creek. Unless absolutely forced to do so, I did not propose to make any deviation to the Westward — for from our small caravan it was incumbent upon us to waste no time, unless we could do so in country where game was procurable. So far, although our actual line of march had been through unmapped country, we had traversed a region already crossed by another party, whose route ran parallel to ours and some forty miles to the north. Not that that was of the least benefit to us any more than if we had been at sea; but it gave us the feeling that we were not in an absolutely *terra incognita*. From the lagoon, however, our route lay through country untrodden by any white man, with the exception of Ernest Giles, whose track we should cross at right angles, about one hundred miles North of Alexander Spring. But unless we sighted the Alfred and Marie Range, named by him, we should have no guide, excepting our position on the chart, to show us where we crossed the path of a caravan which marched through the wilderness twenty years before.

To give a description of the country that we now encountered, from day to day, would be so deadly monotonous that the kindest reader would hardly forgive me; and even if it could serve any useful purpose I should hesitate to recount the daily scene of solitude. A general account of this country, followed by any incidents or personal adventures worthy of notice, will suffice to give an idea of this dreary region.

From lat. 26 degrees S. to lat. 22 degrees 40 minutes there stretches a vast desert of rolling sand, not formed in ridges like those already described, nor heaped up with the regularity of those met with further north. "Downs" I think is the only term that describes properly the configuration of the country. "The Great Undulating Desert of Gravel" would meet all requirements should it be thought worthy of a name. In this cheerless and waterless region we marched from August 22nd until September 17th seeing no lakes, nor creeks, nor mountains; no hills even prominent enough to deserve a name, excepting on three occasions. Day after day over open, treeless expanses covered only by the never-ending spinifex and strewn everywhere with pebbles and stones of ferruginous sandstone, as if some mighty giant had sown the ground with seed in the hope of raising a rich crop of hills. The spinifex here cannot grow its coarse, tall blades of grass — the top growth is absent and only round stools of spines remain; well was it named Porcupine Grass!

Occasional clumps of mulga break the even line of the horizon, and, in the valleys, thickets or belts of bloodwood are seen. In these hollows one may hope to find feed for the camels, for here may grow a few quondongs, acacia, and fern-tree shrubs, and in rare cases some herbage. The beefwood tree, the leaves of which camels, when hard pressed, will eat, alone commands the summit of the undulations. As for animal life — well, one forgets that life exists, until occasionally reminded of the fact by a bounding spinifex rat, frightened from his nest. Day after day one or other of us used to walk away from the caravan carrying a gun on the chance of getting a shot; never once did we succeed; the rats invariably got up out of range, and after a time we voted it unnecessary labour. Had they been easily shot their small numbers would hardly have made it worth while to burden one's self with a gun; to see a dozen in a day was counted out of the common. Birds were nowhere numerous — an occasional eagle-hawk, or crow, and once or twice a little flock of long-tailed parrots whose species was unknown to any of us. Unfortunately I was unable to procure a specimen. At any waters pigeons, sparrows, crows, and hawks might be seen in fair quantities; and very rarely a turkey.

From the 22nd to the 24th we saw no signs of natives. On the latter day several smokes rose during the march. So far, we had no certain knowledge of the meaning of these smokes. They might be native signals, or from fires for the purpose of burning off the old spinifex to allow young feed to grow and so attract the rats to a known locality; or it might be that the blacks were burning the country to hunt out the rats and lizards. On the 25th a sudden change took place, and we found ourselves in a small, open thicket with a coarse undergrowth of grass, and scattered about were a few boulders of decomposed granite and occasional low outcrops of rock. Several old native camps put us on the alert, and presently we found a well — a shallow hole, 7 feet deep, and 2 feet 6 inches in diameter, entirely surrounded by high spinifex. Why there should ever be water there, or how the blacks got to know of it, was a problem we could only guess at. Everything looked so dry and parched that we were in no way surprised at finding the well waterless. Prempeh had been very unwell lately, refusing to take what little feed there was to be got. A dose of sulphur and butter was administered, poured warm down his throat by me as Breaden held open his month, grasped firmly by either lip. I believe sulphur is an excellent thing for camels, and used often to treat them to the mixture, some — Satan, for example — being very partial to it. The position of this well I found to be lat. 25 degrees 15 minutes, long. 124 degrees 48 minutes; from the edge of the mulga, one hundred yards or so to the North of it, a range of rough looking hills is visible. This I named the Browne Range, after my old friends at Bayley's Reward, and the two conspicuous points I christened Mount Gordon, after Mr. Gordon Lyon, and Mount Everard, after Mr. Everard Browne, respectively.

Mount Gordon is flat-topped; and Mount Everard a double hill, a peak rising from a flat top, bears 82 degrees from the well. This range stood out boldly from the open country and promised well for hilly country ahead. Nor were we disappointed, for after two hours' travel we sighted an imposing-looking range, and altered our course to the highest point, a queer dome-shaped peak, which we called Charlie's Knob, since he had first seen the hills. On nearer approach the hills lost much of their grandeur. By camping-time we were close to their foot amongst rocky rises, very rough to the feet of our animals. They were rewarded for their discomforts by a small patch of herbage which they quickly demolished. That night we heard the dismal howling of two dingoes, who might either be giving expression to their satisfaction at finding water or to their disappointment at not having done so. Three miles more of rugged ground the next morning brought us to Charlie's Knob, and beyond it the range, which on close examination was not imposing, being a series of detached sandstone hills, their summits flat and slightly sloping to the South, capped with a hard reddish-brown rock (baked shale). On the cap, loose fragments of shale and thick scrub; forming its sides sheer cliffs, at most fifteen feet high, perforated by holes and caves, above rough, stony banks. The whole covered with tufts of spinifex, barren, wretched, and uninviting.

On Charlie's Knob a queer little natural pinnacle of rock stands half-way up the side, and from a hill close by, an excellent view of the Browne Range was obtained, Mount Gordon bearing 148 degrees. With the help of my field-glasses I could make out the character of this range to be similar to that of the Young Range on which I was standing. It is of course necessary to name these hills for future reference, and this range got its name from somebody's remark that it was hardly full grown. From the knob the hills run in a crescent, a line joining the two horns being North-East. In the bend of the crescent I could see some very green-looking bloodwoods and made sure we should find a creek. First we hunted the neighbouring hills without success, and then crossed on to the bloodwood flat which had appeared like a creek. Here for the only time our patience in carrying the gun was rewarded, and Charlie shot two fine turkeys. This welcome occurrence, added to Godfrey's having seen a kangaroo in the hills and the dingoes heard the night before, made us confident that water was not far off. That night Godfrey and I took it in turns to baste the turkeys, as they were baking between two prospecting dishes. Godfrey was an excellent cook, and most particular that everything should be done cleanly and properly. I was quite under his orders in the kitchen, for the cook's art is one that I have not the patience to learn, and cordially hate.

Cold turkey and tea for breakfast, and then I divided the party into two, Breaden with the camels being directed to a prominent hill at the end of the range there to await the arrival of Godfrey and myself, who went off to the hills to make further search for water. All day we hunted in different directions and everywhere found the same barren rocks. We had fixed upon a certain gully as a rendezvous; each gully was exactly like its neighbour. Towards the evening I returned to the gully, which I was sure was the one agreed upon, and there awaited Godfrey. He did the same, only chose another gully, equally sure that he was right. And there we sat, each impatiently blaming the other. At last, to pass the time, I fired some shots at an ant-hill; these had the effect of bringing Godfrey over the rise, and we had a good laugh at each other when we discovered that for nearly half an hour we had sat not two hundred yards apart — and each remained firmly convinced that he was right! Godfrey had shot a kangaroo and carried part of the meat and the tail; he had tracked it a long way, but could see no signs of water.

Still following the hills, we made our way towards the point where the camels should be, and presently cut a deep, rocky gorge, which we followed down. The camels had crossed this; and, as it was getting late, I sent Godfrey along their tracks to rejoin the others, telling him that I should continue down the creek, and return to wherever they made camp; to guide me to it they were to light a fire. I followed the creek, or storm channel as I should rather call it, for some four miles; climbing a tree I could see it apparently continuing for some miles, so, feeling that I had already had a fair tramp, I noted the direction of the smoke from the camp and returned to it. As luck would have it, it was the wrong smoke; Breaden on arriving at the end hill had made a fire, and this the evening breeze had rekindled; and the camp-fire happened to die down at the very time it was most needed. In due course I arrived at the hill, named Mount Colin, after poor Colin Gibson, a Coolgardie friend who had lately died from typhoid. From the summit a noticeable flat-topped hill, Mount Cox, named after Ernest Cox, also of Coolgardie, bears 76 degrees about fifteen miles distant, at the end of a fair-sized range running S.S.W. Between this range and that from which I was observing, I noticed several belts of bloodwoods, which might be creeks, but probably are only flats similar to that crossed by us. Picking up the tracks of the main party, I followed them to camp, not sorry to have a rest; for it was ten hours since Godfrey and I had had anything to eat or drink, and the rocks were rough and the spinifex dense. I mention this, not as illustrating our hardships, but to show what training will do; any one of us would have been quite ready to do the day's tramp over again had any necessity arisen.

That night as I was shooting the stars, by which I found we were in lat. 24 degrees 57 minutes, long. 125 degrees 9 minutes (dead reckoning), I noticed several bronzewing pigeons flying down the creek which I had followed, and on which we were camped. In the morning others observed them flying up the watercourse. As a bronzewing drinks just after dark, or just before daylight, this was pretty good evidence that water existed in the direction in which the creek ran — and probably an open pool would be found. No such luck! for we followed the channel until it no longer was one, that is to say its banks became further apart, and lower, until its wash was spread out in all directions over a flat whose limits were defined by bloodwoods and grass. Here we found an old blacks' camp and spent some time examining its neighbourhood. Little heaps of the yellow seed of a low plant, swept together on clear spaces on the ground, and the non-existence of any well, led us to suppose that this was merely a travelling camp of some buck who had been sent to collect seed. It was rather aggravating to be morally certain that water existed and yet be unable to find it; we still had hopes of the creek making again, and so followed the direction of its previous course.

Before long the tracks of a buck and a gin crossed our path, and we at once turned to follow them through all their deviations. We saw where the woman had dug out bardies from the roots of a wattle, where the buck had unearthed a rat,* and where together they had chased a lizard. Finally we reached their camp. Several implements lay about, including two bark coolimans. These, the simplest form of cooliman, are made by peeling the bark off the projecting lumps so common on the stems of bloodwoods. The bark so obtained forms a little trough. In some regions they are gouged out of a solid piece of wood, but this requires a knowledge of carpentry, and probably tools, not possessed by the desert black. Another kind more simple than the first mentioned, is made by bending the two sides of a strip of bark together, so as to form the half of a pipe; then, by stuffing up the two ends with clay and grass, a serviceable little trough is made. In those we saw the clay was moist, and we knew that this was no mere travelling camp. However, search as we would we could find no water, until a flock of diamond-sparrows rose in front of Warri, and he discovered a little well hidden in the spinifex — so perfectly hidden that our own tracks had passed half an hour before its discovery within a few paces of it!

* The rat mentioned here was probably a "Bandicoot," "Boody," or "Bilby," the scientific name of which I do not know; I have never seen one, only their burrows, and these have always shown every appearance of being unoccupied. Most of the burrows that I have seen have been in a low mound, perhaps 30 feet across, of white powdery soil, like gypsum. The only living things I have seen emerge being a cat (near Lake Prinsep) and snakes or lizards.

There is a smaller rat, which the natives in the goldfields districts get in rather an ingenious way. This rat makes a single burrow, with a nest at the end of it close beneath the surface. When it is inside the hole it fills in the entrance and retires to its nest. This is ventilated by a little hole to the surface, the mouth of this hole being hidden with small stones and sticks. The rat, however, with all his cunning has only built a mark by which his home may be discovered by the native. I had often noticed these little heaps of stones in the scrub, and until a tame boy explained it had no notion of their meaning.]

What chance has one of finding water, except by the most diligent search and by making use of every sign and indication written on the surface of the ground? This well was similar to the one already described, excepting in one important respect. This one had water. Turning the camels out we started work, and by sundown had the well in order. Tying the others down we proceeded to water each camel in turn. Picture our surprise and joy when each turned from the bucket without drinking more than two gallons. Billy rolled up like a great balloon, and one would have sworn that he had just had a long drink. What was this miracle? Here were camels, after an eight days' drought, travelling eight to ten hours daily in hot weather, over rough stones and gravel, actually turning away from water!

The answer to this riddle was "Parakeelia." This is a local, presumably native, name in Central Australia for a most wonderful and useful plant. A specimen brought back by me from this locality was identified at Kew as *Calandrinia Balonensis*. This plant grows close to the ground in little bunches; in place of leaves it has long, fleshy projections, like fingers, of a yellowish-green colour. From the centre grows a pretty little lilac flower at the end of a single thin stalk. The fingers are full of watery juice and by no means unpalatable. We tried them raw, and also fried in butter, when they were quite good eating. The plant is greedily devoured by stock of all kinds, and in dry tracts in Central Australia has been the means of saving many head of cattle. As we found it, it was not easily got hold of, for invariably it grew right in the centre of a hummock of spinifex. At first the camels, not knowing its properties, would not risk pricking themselves, but after we had shown them, by clearing away the spinifex, how nice it was, they did not hesitate to plunge their soft noses into the spiny mass, with what good effect I have already described. Indeed, this plant is a wonderful provision of nature, and compensates a little for the hideous sterility of the country. I am not wide of the mark when I say that given "parakeelia" every second night or so a camel would never want to drink at all, though it is not really as serviceable as water — not having the same lasting effect. A similar plant, also found in Central Australia, is "Munyeru." In the centre of this a little bag of black seeds grows; these seeds are crushed and eaten by the natives. Munyeru, Breaden tells me, is quite a good vegetable for human consumption. Why the locality of this well, "Warri Well," should be specially favoured by the growth of parakeelia I cannot guess.

The well itself was sufficiently remarkable. Our work took us some twelve feet from the surface, and in the well we had nearly five feet of water and the probability of a deal more, as we had not reached "bottom." The question that presented itself to my mind was whether the natives had sunk the well on a likely looking spot and been fortunate in finding a supply, or whether, from tradition, they knew that this well, possibly only a rock-hole covered by surface soil, existed. The depression in which the well is situated must after rain receive the drainage, not only from the channel we followed, but from the stony rise to the north of it. After a heavy storm — and from the way in which this creek has been torn through the sand, scouring a channel down to bedrock, it is clear that occasionally violent storms visit this region — a large volume of water would collect in this depression. Some of it would be sucked up by the trees and shrubs, some would evaporate, but the greater part would soak into the ground where, so long as the bed-rock (which in this particular case is a hard sandstone and iron conglomerate) is impervious, it would remain. I should think it likely, therefore, that on this and similar flats, not far from hills or tablelands, water by sinking could be obtained at no great depth. A good guide to this well is a bare patch of rock on Mount Colin, which bears 138 degrees three miles distant.

This hill is visible from ten miles due North of the well, from which point it shows up prominently. Continuing a northerly march from that point we found that the gravel and stones for the next few miles became much rougher, and made walking tiring work. Occasionally mulga thickets free from stones had to be passed through; in these there often occurred very shallow depressions overgrown with grass and floored with clay. From the floors rose high, pinnacled ant-heaps, built by the white ant; these hills, grouped into little colonies, sometimes attained a height of eleven feet, and had in the distance a weird appearance, reminding me in shape, at least, of the picture of Lot's wife turned into a pillar of salt. Around these clay flats large white gum-trees were growing, a different species from the desert gum, having a quite smooth bark.

On September 1st we sighted the Alfred and Marie Range due East of us. I had expected to find this almost on our course; however, my reckoning differs from Giles's by eight miles, my position for the range being to the East of his. As we approached the range the country improved greatly, and had every appearance of having experienced recent rains, for green herbage [*Haloragis*, and *Trichinium alopecuroideum*.] was in places abundant — that is to say, little patches of it, perhaps twenty paces across. These we saw were feeding-grounds for kangaroos and wallabies. Turkey tracks were fairly numerous; of the latter we saw six, and shot one. They are very wary birds and not easily stalked. A very good plan for shooting them is for one man to hide in a bush or behind a tree whilst the other circles round a good way off, and very slowly advances, and so drives the turkey past the hidden sportsman. He, if he is wise, will let the turkey rise before firing, as their wings are easily broken, whilst the thick breast-feathers readily turn shot.

We made camp one mile from the foot of the hills, and Charlie and I walked over to see what was to be seen. This range is of sandstone, and made up of a series of flat-topped hills of peculiar shapes, standing on the usual rough, stony slopes. The hills are traceable in a broken line for a considerable distance, perhaps twenty miles, in a North-Easterly direction. No doubt some good water-hole exists amongst these hills, judging from the tracks of kangaroos, turkeys, and dingoes. I fancy that animals and birds follow up rain-storms from place to place to take advantage of the good feed which springs into life, and it is most probable that for ten months in the year these hills are undisturbed by animal or bird life. Certainly Giles found that to be the case when he crossed them in 1876; so disgusted was he with their appearance that he did not trouble to investigate them at all. Indeed, he could have no other than sad remembrances of this range, for he first sighted it from the East, when attempting to cross the interior from East to West — an attempt that failed, owing to the impossibility of traversing this desert of rolling sand and gravel with horses only as a means of transport. Baffled, he was forced to return, leaving behind him, lost for ever, his companion Gibson. After him this desert is named, and how he lost his life is related in Giles's journals.

In 1874 Giles, Tietkens, Gibson, and Andrews, with twenty-four horses, left the overland Central Australian telegraph line, to push out to the West as far as possible. Keeping to the South of the already discovered Lake Amadeus, they found the Rawlinson and neighbouring ranges just within the Colony of West Australia. Water was plentiful, and a depot camp was formed, Giles and Gibson making a flying trip ahead to the westward. The furthest point was reached on April 23, 1874, from which the Alfred and Marie was visible some twenty-five miles distant. At this point Gibson's horse "knocked up," and shortly afterwards died. Giles thereupon gave up his own horse, the Fair Maid of Perth, and sent his companion back to the depot for relief; for it was clear that only one could ride the horse, and he who did so, by hurrying on, could return and save his companion. With a wave of his hat, he shouted goodbye to his generous leader and rode off. "This was the last ever seen of Gibson." It appears that the poor fellow failed to follow back the outgoing tracks, got lost in the night, became hopelessly "bushed," and perished, alone in the desert. Giles meanwhile struggled on and on, every hour expecting relief, which of course never came. At last he staggered into camp, nearly dead.

No time was lost in saddling fresh horses, and Tietkens and his exhausted companion set out in search of the missing man. Picking up the Fair Maid's tracks, they followed them until they were four days out from camp, and it became clear that to go further meant sacrificing not only their own lives but that of their mate left behind at the depot, as well as that of all the horses. Gibson's tracks when last seen were leading in a direction exactly opposite to that of the camp. Luckily the cold weather (April) stood their horses in good stead; but in spite of this and of the water they packed for them, the horses only managed to crawl into camp. It was manifestly impossible to make further search, for seventy miles of desert intervened between the depot-camp and the tracks when last seen; and the mare was evidently still untired. So, sorrowfully they retraced their steps to the East, and the place of Gibson's death remains a secret still. I have heard that months after Giles's return, Gibson's mare came back to her home, thin and miserable, and showing on her belly and back the marks of a saddle and girth, which as she wasted away had become slack and so turned over. Her tracks were followed back for some distance without result. Poor thing! she had a long journey, and Giles must have spoken truly when he said, "The Fair Maid was the gamest horse I ever rode."

Giles's account of this desert shows that the last twenty years have done little to improve it! He says:—

The flies were still about us in persecuting myriads;... the country was, quite open, rolling along in ceaseless undulations of sand, the only vegetation besides the ever-abounding spinifex was a few bloodwood trees. The region is so desolate that it is horrifying even to describe. The eye of God looking down on the solitary caravan as it presents the only living object around must have contemplated its appearance with pitying admiration, as it forced its way continually onwards without pausing over this vast sandy region, avoiding death only by motion and distance, until some oasis can   be found.

Not a cheerful description certainly! Every day's Northing, however, would take us further in or out of this region, as the case might be, and fervently we hoped for the latter. Whatever country was before us we were firmly determined to push on, and by the grace of God to overcome its difficulties. Again referring to Giles's journal I find that during this part of his journey — viz., near the range where we were now camped — the change of temperature during night and day was very excessive. At night the thermometer registered 18 degrees F., whilst the heat in the daytime was most oppressive. This, in a less degree, was our experience, for the month being September the days were hotter and the nights less cold. No doubt this extreme change in temperature, combined with the dry atmosphere and the tremendous heat of the sun, has caused the hills to be weathered away in the remarkable shapes of which McPherson's Pillar is a good example. The pillar is formed of a huge square block of red rock, planted on the top of a conical mound, perhaps fifty feet in height, whose slopes are covered with broken slabs and boulders. This remarkable landmark, which, from the North, is visible from twenty-four miles distant, I named after Mr. McPherson, a well-known and respected prospector, who, though leaving no record of his journey, crossed the Colony from West to East, visiting the hills and waters on Forrest's route as far East as the Parker Ranges, and thence striking Giles's route at the Alfred and Marie, and so VIA the Rawlinson into Alice Springs, on the overland telegraph line. Though little of his journey was through new country, yet it had the valuable result of proving the non-existence of auriferous country in the belt traversed.

Due West of the Pillar, distant two and a half miles, situated in a scrub-covered rocky gorge, is a fair-sized rockhole. Breaden and Godfrey managed to get about two gallons of filth from it; I have swallowed all kinds of water, but this was really too powerful. Had we been hard pressed it would undoubtedly have been used, but since we had not long left water, we discarded this mixture, after trying it on Czar, whose indignation was great. In the branches of the mulga round the rock-hole I noticed what I have seen in several other places, viz., stones wedged in the forks — dozens of stones of all sizes and shapes. I have no knowledge of their true significance. It may be, and this is merely a guess, that they indicate the presence of poison in the rock-hole; for by means of a certain plant which is bruised and thrown into the hole, the water is given a not actually poisonous but stupefying property. Thus birds or beasts coming to drink fall senseless and an easy prey to the ambushed native. This is a common plan in many parts of Australia, and was described to me by a tame boy from the Murchison. Here, too, were more little pyramids, similar to those at Empress Spring. Some quaint black-fellows' custom, but what it signifies even Warri cannot explain. Breaden has a theory that they point to the next water-hole. This may be, but, unless for a stranger's benefit, quite unnecessary, as every black knows his waters; and if for a stranger it is equally peculiar, for his welcome is usually a bang on the head! It may be that messengers or those who, wishing to trade from tribe to tribe, get the free passage of the district, are thus guided on their way. The number of pyramids may represent so many days' march.

There must have been some open water besides this dirty rock-hole, but having sufficient for present requirements we did not waste time in further search, and on September 2nd turned again to the North. On this course we continued until September 6th, the country showing no change whatever, which constrained me to say of it, so I find in my diary, "Surely the most God-forsaken on the face of the earth"; and yet we had worse to follow!

Our rate of travel over the gravel was a small fraction more than two miles per hour. This I carefully reckoned by timing, taking into account every halt of ever so small a duration in our march in a due North line between two latitudes.

In lat. 23 degrees 34 minutes, long. 125 degrees 16 minutes, there rose before us, visible for several miles, high banks of stones, such as one sees on either side of the old bed of a river which has altered its course. The slopes were covered with spinifex and on the top red and weeping mulga — the latter a graceful little tree, whose bowed head adds little to the gaiety of one's surroundings. I cannot offer any explanation of these curious banks, except that, from the appearance of one or two large flat boulders on the summit, it may be that they were formed by the entire disintegration of a sandstone cliff, to which decay has come sooner than to its neighbours further South. Future experience showed us that further North the gravel becomes small and smaller until it disappears, the rolling sandhills giving place to regular ridges. If this is the case viz., that the hills and ranges are gradually rotting away until they disappear, leaving only gravel behind, which, in its turn, decays and decays until only sand remains, then in the course of ages the whole of this region will be covered with ridge upon ridge of sand formed by the wind, whose powers so far have been checked by the weight of the gravel. For the sake of future generations I hope my reasoning is incorrect.

As I stood on the stony bank, I could see several native smokes to the eastward. Determined to take advantage of any help extended to us by Nature, to spare no pains in the all-important matter of finding water, to let nothing pass that might assist us on our way, so that if it was our fate to go under in the struggle I should not be assailed by the thought that I had neglected opportunities, determined, in fact, always to act for the best, so far as I could see it, I decided to make use of this sign of the presence of natives, and altered our course in consequence. We started due East and held on that course for eight miles, Godfrey and Charlie lighting the spinifex at intervals. Some men have a theory that the blacks signal by smokes, the appearance of which they vary by using different grasses, branches, or leaves. That may be the case in some parts; here, anyway, they are no more than hunting-fires, as we later proved. If the desert blacks do go in for smoke-telegraphy they must on this occasion have thought that the operator at our end of the wire was mad! Perhaps unknowingly we sent up smokes which appeared to them to be rational messages! If such was the case our signals could not have meant "Please stay at home," for when eventually we did find their camp they had left. Taking the bearing of the most northerly smoke we travelled for the rest of the day in its direction. The next morning, though the smoke had long since died down, we continued on our course and in a few miles reached a large area of still smouldering spinifex. Around this we searched for fresh tracks, and, having discovered some, made camp. And now I have to chronicle the only occasion on which any one disputed my orders. And this goes far to show that all I have said in praise of the loyalty and untiring energy of my companions, is not meant in empty compliment, but falls short of what they merit.

It was necessary for one to stay in camp and watch our belongings and the camels, while the rest were engaged in tracking the natives. Our zeal was so great that the camels were hardly, unloaded and hobbled before each one had set out, and it followed that one must be sent back. For no particular reason I fixed on Godfrey, who, instead of hailing with joy the prospective rest, was most mutinous! The mutiny, however, was short-lived, and ended in laughter when I pointed out how ridiculous his objection was.

Charlie and I went in one direction, whilst Breaden and Warri took another. Before long, so complicated were the tracks, we separated. A more annoying job it is hard to imagine: round and round one goes following a track in all its eccentric windings, running off at right angles or turning back when its owner had chased a rat or a lizard; at length there is a long stretch of straight walking and one thinks, "Now, at last, he's done hunting and is making for home"; another disappointment follows as one wheels round and finds one's self close to the starting-point. Such was the experience this day of Breaden, Charlie, and myself, and disgusted we returned to camp at sundown. Warri was so late that I began to think he must have come upon the natives themselves, who had given him too warm a welcome. Presently he appeared, slouching along with an expressionless face, save for a twinkle in his eye (literally eye, for one was wall-eyed). My supposition was more or less correct; he had been fortunate in getting on the home-going tracks of some gins; following these for several miles he came on their camp — so suddenly that they nearly saw him. Luckily, he beat a hasty retreat, doubtful of his reception, and hurried home.

Part V: The Outward Journey

Chapter VIII: A Desert Tribe

The next morning we were up betimes and ready to start as soon as ever the tracks were visible; presently a smoke, their first hunting-smoke of the day, rose close to us. Despatching Charlie on Satan, and Godfrey on foot, with instructions to catch a native if possible, I hastened along the tracks followed by the rest of the party. We reached their camp just in time to see the late inmates disappear into a thicket of mulga close by. Neither Charlie nor Godfrey was able to come up with the lighters of the fire unseen, and these, too, fled into the scrub, where chase was almost impossible. Their camp deserves description, as it was the first (excepting travelling camps) we had seen of the desert black-fellow.

Facing the belt of mulga, was a low wall of uprooted tussocks of spinifex built in a half circle and some two feet high. On the leeward side of this breakwind, inside the semi-circle, half a dozen little hollows were scraped out in the sand. Between each of these nests lay a little heap of ashes, the remains of a fire which burns all night, replenished from time to time from a bundle of sticks kept handy for the purpose. The nest in the sand is the bed, a double one, and not only double but treble, and more; for in it, coiled up snugly, may lie several of the tribe, higgledy-piggledy, like pups in a basket. The fire takes the place of nightshirt, pyjamas, or blanket — a poor substitute on a cold night! Scattered about were several utensils, two wooden coolimans full of water and grass — this showing that the owners contemplated a journey, for the grass floating on the surface is used to prevent the water from spilling. Two more coolimans were filled with seed — a fine yellow seed from a plant like groundsel. Close by these were the flat stones (of granite, evidently traded from tribe to tribe) used for grinding the seed. In the spinifex wall were stuck numerous spears, varying from eight to ten feet in length, straight, thin, and light, hardened by fire, fined down and scraped to a sharp point. Near these was a gin's yam-stick — a stout stick with a sharp, flat point on one end and charred at the other, used for digging up roots, stirring the fire, or chastising a dog or child. They serve, too, as a weapon of defence. Quaintest of all these articles were the native "portmanteaus," that is to say, bundles of treasures rolled up in bark, wound round and round with string — string made from human hair or from that of dingoes and opossums. In these "portmanteaus" are found carved sticks, pieces of quartz, red ochre, feathers, and a number of odds and ends. Of several that were in this camp I took two — my curiosity and desire to further knowledge of human beings, so unknown and so interesting, overcame my honesty, and since the owners had retired so rudely I could not barter with them. Without doubt the meat-tins and odds and ends that we left behind us have more than repaid them. One of these portmanteaus may be seen in the British Museum, the other I have still, unopened.

Between the camp and the well, which we easily found, there ran a well-beaten foot-pad, showing that this had been a favoured spot for some time past. The well itself was situated in a belt of mulga-scrub, and surrounded by a little patch of grass; growing near by, a few good camel bushes, such as acacia and fern-tree (quondongs, by the way, were not seen by us north of Alexander Spring, with the exception of one near McPherson's Pillar); enclosing the scrub two parallel banks of sand and stones, with the well in the valley between. Above the well, to the, North, high anthills and tussocks of coarse grass appeared. The whole oasis covered no more than three acres. The well itself resembled those already described, and appeared to have a good supply, so much so that we started at once to water the camels, which had had no drink since August 21st, a period of seventeen days, with the exception of two gallons apiece at Warri Well, where the parakeelia grew.

By midnight all but three — Satan, Redleap, and Misery — had drunk as much as they could hold. These three had to be content with a small amount, for we could not get more without digging out the well, and this we proceeded to do. The night was hot and cloudy, and constant puffs of wind made work by the light of candles so impossible that we had perforce to bear the extra heat of a blazing fire. The native well, as we found it, had been scooped out with hand and cooliman, just large enough to allow one to descend to a depth of fifteen feet, and the sides of the hole plastered back with mud, which had baked hard. To follow this hole further was not feasible, for going down on a slope as it did, any further deepening would cause the sand to fall in; we had therefore to start a new vertical shaft from the surface. After a considerable amount of digging we reached water level, and were preparing to bail the water, when with a thud the whole thing caved in, and our labour had to be recommenced. At the time the wedge of ground fell in Godfrey was working below and narrowly escaped being buried. A timely rope fortunately saved him. I never saw a man come quicker out of a hole! Now we were a bit puzzled. Our position was this: six camels were watered, three were not, our tanks were empty (my fault, for I should have first filled them and then the camels; but yet if we had water and the camels had none, would we have been better off?); our well, containing X, an unknown quantity of water, had fallen in. Query, whether to recommence digging, or to pack up and follow the blacks? Now, the well might contain a good supply, or yield no more than a gallon or two; and the blacks might or might not have gone on to a good water. It was a puzzle. Finally we compromised, and I sent Breaden and Warri to hunt up the tracks, whilst we started work again. On one side of the well was rock, and by strengthening the other by timber we hoped for success. Luckily plenty of good mulga trees were handy, and we soon had the timber ready for use. This was the second night without rest or food, and no more than a mouthful of water each, for on arrival we had given what our tanks contained to the thirsty camels.

By putting in crosspieces from side to side of the hole, which we soon discovered to be an underground rock-hole, and by backing these with twigs and grass, we managed to make the walls of sand secure, and at last reached water level, and lost no time, as may well be imagined, in raising a billyful and having the very best drink we had encountered for a long time. At the moment almost Breaden and Warri returned, having done their job admirably. They had followed the tracks to the next camp, away to the North — a dry camp this — and, noticing the direction the blacks had taken, returned home. After a feed and a rest we again set to work, and again the well fell in, but with less danger this time. It was clear that we could go no further without some sort of caisson to hold back the fine sand.

Charlie, with his usual ingenuity, constructed a rough but serviceable one out of the wooden guards on the faces of our water-casks and the tin-lined box lids that we had taken from Hubbe's camp at Mount Allott. Instinct had told us right — they were of use!

By this means we reached a depth of thirty feet, first sinking the caisson, then bailing the water, then continuing the timber and backing.

The hole so narrowed at the bottom that the water could only be obtained by stretching out a stick at arm's length, on which was lashed a small saucepan. It soon became clear that, labour as we would, the hole would yield but little, so, leaving the rest to work, I took Warri, and continued the search for the natives from the point where Breaden had left their tracks. After a long, tedious day of tracking, we found ourselves back at our own camp. The natives — two bucks, two gins, and three picaninnies — travelled North to a dry well, and there split, the men going one way and the rest another. We chose the bucks to follow, and presently the rest joined in, and the whole family swung round until close to our camp. We could, by their tracks, see where they had herded together in fear under a beefwood tree not one hundred yards from us. Just before sunset we again set forth, taking Czar and Satan as riding-camels, and were lucky in picking up tracks going in a fresh direction before night fell.

We camped on the tracks, and ran them in the morning, noticing two interesting things on the way: the first, several wooden sticks on which were skewered dried fruits, not unlike gooseberries; these were hidden in a bush, and are remarkable, for they not only show that the natives have some forethought, but that they trade in edible goods as well as in weapons and ornaments. These fruits are from the *Solanum sodomeum*, and were only seen by us near the Sturt Creek (three hundred miles away). The second, little heaps of the roots of a tree (known to me only as pine-mulga [Probably a "Hakea."]) stacked together, which had been sucked for water; we tried some, but without result, and the tree the natives had made use of did not seem to be different from others of its kind. This showed us, too, that they must be dry, and probably had had no water since our arrival at their well. About midday we rode right on to their camp without warning. Again the scrub befriended them, but in spite of this I could have got ahead of them on Satan had his nose-line not snapped. Determined not to be baulked, I jumped down and gave chase, old Czar lumbering along behind, and Warri shouting with glee and excitement, "Chase 'em — we catch em," as if we were going through all this trouble for pleasure. Happy Warri! he never seemed to see gravity in anything. It is almost incredible how quickly and completely a black-fellow can disappear; as if in a moment the whole family was out of sight. One black spot remained visible, and on it I centred my energies. Quickly overhauling, I overtook it, and found it to be an old and hideous gin, who, poor thing! had stopped behind to pick up some dingo puppies.

Sorry as I was to be rude to a lady, I had to make her prisoner, but not without a deal of trouble. "Dah, dah, dah!" she shouted, scratching, biting, spitting, and tearing me with her horrid long nails, and using, I feel sure, the worst language that her tongue could command. I had to carry this unsavoury object back to her camp, she clutching at every bush we passed, when her hands were not engaged in clawing and scratching me. After her anger had somewhat abated she pointed out a rock-hole from which they had got their water. Securing the woman with a light rope, I put her in Warri's charge, who kept watch above, lest the natives should return and surprise us, whilst I descended the rock-hole to see what supply was there. A little water was visible, which I quickly baled into the canvas bags we had brought for the purpose. The bottom of the hole was filled in with dead sticks, leaves, the rotting bodies of birds and lizards, bones of rats and dingoes. Into this ghastly mass of filth I sunk up to my middle, and never shall I forget the awful odour that arose as my feet stirred up the mess. Nevertheless water was there, and thankful I was to find it, even to drink it as it was. After half an hour's work in this stinking pit, sick from the combination of smells — distinguishable above every other being the all-pervading perfume of aboriginals — I was rewarded by some twelve gallons of water, or, more properly speaking, liquid.

I decided to take the gin back with us, as it had been clear to me for some time past that without the aid of natives we could not hope to find water. With our small caravan it was impossible to push on and trust to chance, or hope to reach the settled country still nearly five hundred miles ahead in a bee-line. Even supposing the camels could do this enormous stage, it was beyond our power to carry sufficient water for ourselves. The country might improve or might get worse; in such weather as we now experienced no camel could go for more than a few days without water. I felt myself justified, therefore, in unceremoniously making captives from what wandering tribes we might fall in with. And in light of after events I say unhesitatingly that, without having done so, and without having to a small extent used rough treatment to some natives so caught, we could not by any possibility have succeeded in crossing the desert, and should not only have lost our own lives, but possibly those of others who would have made search for us after. "A man arms himself where his armour is weakest," so I have read; that, however, is not my case. I am not justifying myself to myself, or defending a line of action not yet assailed. I write this in answer to some who have unfavourably criticised my methods, and to those I would say, "Put yourselves in our position, and when sitting in a comfortable armchair at home, in the centre of civilisation, do not, you who have never known want or suffered hardship, be so ready to judge others who, hundreds of miles from their fellow-men, threatened every day with possible death from thirst, were doing their best to lay bare the hidden secrets of an unknown region, as arid and desolate as any the world can show."

On starting back for camp the gin refused to walk or move in any way, so we had to pack her on Czar, making her as comfortable as possible on Warri's blankets, with disastrous results thereto. Arrived at camp, I found that the rock-hole was bottomed, and now quite dry. Straining the putrid water brought by me through a flannel shirt, boiling it, adding ashes and Epsom salts, we concocted a serviceable beverage. This, blended with the few gallons of muddy water from the well, formed our supply, which we looked to augment under the guidance of the gin. After completing our work the well presented the appearance of a large rock-hole, thirty feet deep, conical in shape, of which one-half the contents had been dug out. This confirmed my opinion that the native wells of these regions are nothing more than holes in the bed-rock, which have been covered over and in by the general deposit of sand. I had no time to observe for latitude at this spot, the position of which is fixed merely by dead reckoning. The rock-hole lies eight miles from it to the S.E. by E., and has no guide whatever to its situation. I christened the well "Patience Well," and I think it was well named.

From September 8th, 9 a.m., until September 12th, 12.30 a.m., we had worked almost continuously, only taking in turn what sleep we could snatch when one could be spared; and the result, 140 gallons as sum total, inclusive of mud and other matter.

We left Patience Well on the 12th, at 10 a.m., taking the woman with us. Breaden was the only one in whose charge she would consent to be at all calm; to him therefore was allotted the duty of looking after her. At eleven we reached the dry well to which Warri and I had tracked the natives. The water we were forced to use was so uninviting that I decided to make another effort to find a supply in this locality. The gin was of no use whatever, and would only repeat whatever we said to her — "Gabbi," which King Billy had understood, was wasted on her. "Gabbi, gabbi," she repeated, waving her arm all round the horizon. Leaving the rest to bottom the dry well, which might have water lower down, Warri and I again started off on the tracks of a buck, and these we followed due North on foot for four and a half hours, hoping every moment to come on a well. Soon after starting an apparently old track joined the other, and together they marched still North. Presently the old tracks changed into fresh ones, and close by I found two rough sandals made of strips of bark. One I kept, the other was too nearly worn out. There was no change in the dreary appearance of the country; through scrubs, over stones and sand we held our way, until Warri, who was now a little way behind, called, "No good, no more walk!" I could see the poor boy was knocked up, and felt little better myself; to go on did not guarantee water, and might end in disaster, so after a short rest we retraced our steps. The night was now dark and oppressive, so hatless and shirtless we floundered through the spinifex, nearly exhausted from the walk, following so close on the last few days' work. I believe that but for Warri I should have been "bushed"; my head was muddled, and the stars not too clear. What a joyful sight met our eyes as we crested a rise of sand — a sight almost as reviving as the food and water we so anxiously looked forward to. Tongues of flame shot up in the air, a fire lit by our mates, but showing that, in spite of Warri's instinct, we had not been walking in quite the right direction. No welcome news greeted our arrival — the well was dry, and the native obdurate. We all agreed she was useless, and since she refused all forms of nutriment I feared she would die on our hands, so she regained her liberty, and fled away with a rapidity not expected in one of her years.

My companions had felt some anxiety at our continued absence, and again I had evidence of the cordial friendship existing between us.

With reference to the bark sandals, the use of which is not so far known, I append an extract from *The Horn Scientific Expedition*, Part IV., where we read the following: SANDALS. Arunta Tribe. *KURDAITCHA SHOES.* — When a native for some reason desired to kill a member of another camp or tribe, he consulted the medicine man of his camp, and arrangements were made for a 'Kurdaitcha Luma.'... Both medicine man and Kurdaitcha wore remarkable shoes. These had the form of a long pad made of human hair, with numberless emu feathers intertwined, and with a certain amount of human blood to act as a cementing substance.... Both ends of the shoes were rounded off, and were exactly similar to one another, which has given rise to the erroneous idea that their object was to prevent the wearer being tracked....   But no other explanation is offered.

Breaden says tracks of a man wearing these emu-feather shoes are very indistinct, but has no certain knowledge of their use. Warri, looking at the bark sandals, said, "Black-fella wear 'em 'long a hot sand." Questioned about the emu-feather shoes, he gave the usual answer, "I dunno," and then added, probably to please me, as I had suggested the explanation, "Black-fella no more see 'em track, I think."

It was clear that no good results were likely to follow further search in this locality, for the tracks were so numerous, and crossed and recrossed so often, that nothing could be made out of them. The country to the North being so uninviting, I altered our course to North-East, and again to North, when we sighted a smoke, and, following tracks, camped on them.

"Mud and oatmeal for breakfast," September 14th; truly the sage spoke who remarked, "What does not fatten will fill." Such was our fare, and the only doubt we had was lest the compound should be turned into brick by the sun's heat! However, it was sustaining enough to last us all day, occupied in tracking. Two dry wells, connected by a well-trodden pad half a mile long, rewarded our labours; and here we had the conviction forced upon us that the blacks themselves were hard pressed: we could see where dust and dirt had been recently removed from the bottom of the wells, both of which were over fifteen feet in depth, and one over twenty. Were the natives hard pressed for water, or had they heard of our coming, and were by smokes guiding us to empty wells? Unpleasant speculation, when one's tanks contain nothing but a nasty brown liquid, and the country looks as if it had not known rain for years!

September 15th. Another smoke to the North-East; again we steer for it, as if following a will-o'-the-wisp. The continued semi-starvation, hard work, and heat was beginning to leave its mark. None of our friends or relatives would have recognised us now! Clothed in filthy rags, with unkempt hair and beards, begrimed with mud, and burnt black by the sun wherever its rays could penetrate our armour of dirt, we were indeed a pretty lot. That night we tied the camels down — there was no feed for them; besides, I wished them handy in the morning, for we could not be far from natives now unless the smoke had deceived us. The next day the desolation of the country was increased by vast areas of burnt ground, from which rose clouds of dust and ashes

— no gravel was here to arrest the onslaught of the wind upon the sand. Towards evening we were doomed to experience fresh discouragement, for in front of us, seen from rising ground, there stretched ridge upon ridge of barren sand, black from the charred remains of spinifex. To tackle those ridges in our then plight meant grave risks to be run, and that night the responsibility of my position weighed heavily upon my thoughts. I prayed for strength and determination — for to each one of us must have come the thought of what our fate might be. I feel sure that all were ready to face boldly whatever was in store, and were resolved to do their utmost — and what more can man do?

To go forward was our only course, since we meant to get through. Before sunrise, black and weary we started, having fed on tinned vegetables, the only article amongst our provisions possessing any moisture.

Before long we were amongst the ridges. What a desolate scene! Ridge upon ridge of sand, black from the ashes of burnt spinifex. Not a sound or sign of life, except the grunts of the camels as they strained up the sandy slopes. Presently we sighted a newly lighted hunting smoke, not a mile from us; with my field-glasses I could see the flames of the fiercely burning spinifex lapping the crest of a high sand-ridge. Leaving the tracks I was following I rejoined the main party, and, calling to Charlie to accompany me, and to the others to follow us as fast as they could, I set off for the fire. Having anticipated reaching the scene of the smoke early this morning, we had divided up Czar's load amongst the remainder of the caravan, and for the time transformed him into a riding-camel, and so two of us were mounted. On nearer approach we pulled up to give our steeds a blow, and, unseen ourselves, we watched the natives hunting, all unsuspicious of the near presence of beings and animals so strange in colour and form.

Advancing slowly from opposite directions, we were able to get within a hundred yards of them before our silent approach was noticed. No words can describe the look of terror and amazement on the faces of those wild savages. Spellbound they crouched in the black and smouldering ashes of the spinifex, mouths open and eyes staring, and then with one terrific yell away they ran, dodging and doubling until a somewhat bushy beefwood tree seemed to offer them means of escape. How many there had been I do not know, but the tree harboured three, the man, woman, and child, that we had first singled out. All kept up a ceaseless screaming and gesticulating, reminding me of the monkey-house at the "Zoo"; but above the others could be distinguished the voice of the old gin who, with frantic haste, tried to screen the man with branches broken from their tree of refuge, and who in the intervals between this occupation and that of shaking a stick at us, set a light to the surrounding spinifex either as a signal or with the hope of keeping us at a distance; for with all her fear she had not let drop her firestick. Thinking that they would be completely overawed by the appearance of the rest of the caravan, and so make no further attempt to escape, we sat sentinel on our camels and awaited the arrival of the main party. Presently they appeared, and the trembling fear of the natives was painful to witness — never by any possibility could they have seen camels or white men, though considering the extent to which articles are passed from tribe to tribe, it is probable they had heard of the "white-fella." Even to European eyes a camel is not the canniest of beasts, and since these people had never seen an animal larger than a dingo, and, indeed, no animal save this and the spinifex rat, their surprise may well be imagined on seeing a thing as large as their whole camp marching solemnly along.

Putting down the caravan we approached them, and from a mad, incoherent yelling their protestations gradually died down to an occasional gulp like that of a naughty child. Making soothing sounds and patting their breasts and our own in turn, in sign of friendship, we had plenty of time to inspect them. An old lady, with grizzled hair, toothless and distorted in countenance, with legs and arms mere bones, and skin shrunken and parched; a girl-child, perhaps six years old, by no means an ugly little thing, and a youngish man made up the trio; all stark-naked, and unadorned by artificial means, unless one excepts a powerfully scented mixture of grease and ashes, with which their bodies were smeared. The buck — poor fellow! — was suffering from some horrible skin disease, which spread over his chest and back. He seemed to have but little power in his arms, and a pitiful object he was, as we uncovered him from his screen of branches. Having apparently satisfied them that it was not our intention to eat them, by signs we showed them our pressing need for water — these they readily understood — doubtless because their own daily experience is one constant hunt for food or water. Evidently we had the former with us in the shape of camels, therefore we could only want the latter. The little child very soon showed great confidence, and, taking my hand, led us over a neighbouring sand-ridge. The old lady took a great fancy to Godfrey, and convinced us that flirting is by no means confined to civilisation.

Leading us obliquely across the ridges we had just passed over, some two miles from the scene of their hunting, they halted at their well. To the North of it an almost barren ridge of sand rising to a height of perhaps sixty feet, and running away East and West for possibly ten miles without a break, from the crest of which we could see a limitless sea of ridges as far as the eye could reach to the Northward (a cheerful prospect!), to the South the undulating treeless desert of gravel we had just crossed. Between the foot of the ridge and a stony slope the well was situated — the usual little round hole in the sand — a small patch of roly-poly grass making a slight difference in the appearance of the country immediately surrounding the hole. As well as this roly-poly, we were delighted to see a few scattered plants of parakeelia, and lost no time in unloading and hobbling the camels, who in their turn made all haste to devour this life-giving vegetation.

File:Spinifex and Sand Illustration 19.jpg A Buck and his gins in camp at Family Well [Missing image]

Camp made, we set to work on the well, sinking our boxes as before, our black friends watching us with evident interest. Presently we heard a shrill call, and, looking up, saw the rest of the family hesitating between curiosity and fear. The old gin reassured them and they approached — a man, a young mother with a baby at the breast, and two more children. There were evidently more not far off who were too timid to come on, as we heard calls from beyond the ridge. This buck was a fine, upstanding fellow, very lithe and strong, though thin and small of bone. Dressed in the fashionable desert costume of nothing at all, excepting a band of string round his forehead, and a similar belt round his waist, from which hung all round him the spoils of the chase, with a spear in one hand and throwing-sticks in the other he looked a queer figure in the setting sun — iguanas and lizards dangling head down from his hair and his waist-string — indeed a novel way of carrying game. His lady followed him with a cooliman under her arm, with a further supply of reptiles and rats.

The whole family established themselves close to us. Their camp had been near the crest of the ridge, but, apparently liking our company, they shifted their household goods, and, starting a fire within twenty yards of us, were soon engaged in cooking and eating their supper. The process of preparing a meal is simple in the extreme. The rats are plucked (for they do not skin the animal, but pluck the hair as we do feathers from a chicken), and thrown on to a pile of hot wood-ashes with no further preparation, and are greedily devoured red and bloody, and but barely warm. A lizard or iguana calls for a further exercise of culinary knowledge. First, a crooked twig is forced down the throat and the inside pulled out, which dainty is thrown to any dog or child that happens to be near; the reptile is then placed on hot coals until distended to the utmost limit that the skin will bear without bursting, then it is placed on ashes less hot, and covered with the same, and after a few minutes is pronounced cooked and ready for the table. The old lady did the cooking, and kept up an incessant chattering and swearing the while. We noticed how kind they were to the poor diseased buck, giving him little tit-bits of half-raw rat's flesh, which he greatly preferred to any food we fed him. They were strange, primitive people, and yet kind and grateful. We anointed the sick man's wounds with tar and oil (a mixture used for mange in camels), and were well rewarded for our unsavoury task by his dog-like looks of satisfaction and thanks. We had ample opportunity to watch them at night, as our well-sinking operations kept us up. They seemed afraid to sleep or lie down, and remained crouching together in their little hollows in the sand until morning. To break the force of the wind, which blew rather chilly, they had set up the usual spinifex fence, and between each little hollow a small fire burnt. The stillness of the night was only broken by the occasional cry of the baby, and this was immediately suppressed by the mother in a novel manner, viz., by biting the infant's ear — a remedy followed by almost immediate success. I beg to recommend this exceedingly effective plan to any of my lady readers whose night's rest is troubled by a teething child — doubtless the husband's bite would have an equally good effect, but the poor baby's ears might suffer from a combination of a strong jaw and a ruffled temper.

What a strange sound — that little picaninny's cry; surrounded as we were by a boundless sea of sand, it made one think how small a speck our party was on the face of the earth; it somehow took one's thoughts back to civilisation and crowded cities, and one felt that it was not just very certain if one would see such things again; and how little it would take to wipe us out, like gnats squashed on a vast window-pane! In the morning we sent the able-bodied man away to hunt, but his interest in us soon overcame his desire for game, and he returned, and presently made himself useful by carrying roots of bushes for our fire, for wood was hard to get, and the nearest tree hardly in sight. I presented the buck with an old pyjama jacket, and a great swell he thought himself too, strutting about and showing himself off to the others. In exchange for numerous articles they gave us, we attached coins round their necks, and on a small round plate, which I cut out of a meat-tin, I stamped my initial and the date, C. 1896. This I fixed on a light nickel chain and hung round the neck of the good-looking young gin, to her intense gratification. It will be interesting to know if ever this ornament is seen again. I only hope some envious tribesman will not be tempted to knock the poor thing on the head to possess himself of this shining necklace.

Amongst their treasures which they carried, wrapped up in bundles of bark and hair, one of the most curious was a pearl oyster-shell, which was worn by the buck as a sporran. Now this shell (which I have in my possession) could only have come from the coast, a distance of nearly five hundred miles, and must have been passed from hand to hand, and from tribe to tribe. Other articles they had which I suppose were similarly traded for, viz., an old iron tent-peg, the lid of a tin matchbox, and a part of the ironwork of a saddle on which the stirrup-leathers hang. This piece of iron was stamped A1; this, I fear, is hardly a sufficient clue from which to trace its origin. Their weapons consisted of spears, barbed and plain, brought to a sharp or broad point; woommeras, throwing-sticks, and boomerangs of several shapes, also a bundle of fire-making implements, consisting of two sticks about two feet long, the one hard and pointed, the other softer, and near one end a round hollow, into which the hard point fits. By giving a rapid rotary movement to the hard stick held upright between the palms of the hands, a spark will before long be generated in the hole in the other stick, which is kept in place on the ground by the feet. By blowing on the spark, a little piece of dried grass, stuck in a nick in the edge of the hollow, will be set alight and the fire obtained.

As a matter of fact this method is not often used, since, when travelling from camp to camp, a firestick or burning brand is carried and replaced when nearly consumed. The gins sometimes carry two of these, one in front and one behind, the flames pointing inwards; and with a baby sitting straddle-legs over their neck and a cooliman under their arms make quite a pretty picture.

Amongst the ornaments and decorations were several sporrans of curious manufacture. Some were made up of tassels formed of the tufts of boody's tails; other tassels were made from narrow strips of dog's skin (with the hair left on) wound round short sticks; others were made in a similar way, of what we conjectured to be bullock's hair. All the tassels were hung on string of opossum or human hair, and two neat articles were fashioned by stringing together red beans [Beans of the Erythrina] set in spinifex gum, and other seeds from trees growing in a more Northerly latitude. This again shows their trading habits. Here, too, were portmanteaus, holding carved sticks of various shapes and patterns, emu-plumes, nose-bones and nose-sticks, plaited bands of hair string, and numerous other odds and ends.

In the evening we watered the camels, and lucky it was that the parakeelia existed, and so satisfied them with its watery juice that they were contented with very little, Satan and Misery not swallowing more than two gallons each. Lucky indeed, because even with another night's work we were only just able to get a sufficient supply to carry us on for a few days, and but for the parakeelia either we or the camels would have had to go short.

We did not completely exhaust the water in the well — not, I fear, because we studied the convenience of the natives, but because our makeshift appliances did not enable us to sink deeper. So we bade adieu to our simple black friends, and set our faces to the sand-ridges. On leaving camp in the morning I found a piece of candle lying on the ground. I threw it to the buck, and he, evidently thinking it good to eat, put it in his mouth, holding the wick in his fingers, and, drawing off the tallow with his teeth, swallowed it with evident relish.

Part V: The Outward Journey

Chapter IX: Dr. Leichardt's Lost Expedition

At this point I must ask pardon of the courteous reader for a seeming digression, and interpolate a short account of Dr. Leichardt's lost expedition — as to the fate of which nothing is known; and although no apparent connection exists between it and this narrative, it may be that in our journey we have happened on traces, and that the pieces of iron mentioned in the last chapter may serve as some clue to its fate. On arrival in civilisation I sent these iron relics, with some native curios, to Mr. Panton, Police Magistrate, of Melbourne, Victoria, a gentleman whose knowledge, and ability to speak with authority on matters concerning Australian exploration is recognised as the highest.

When, therefore, Mr. Panton expresses the opinion that the tent-peg was the property of Dr. Leichardt, one may be sure that he has good grounds for his supposition. Whether Leichardt lost his life in the heart of this wilderness or not, the complete mystery hiding his fate makes his history sufficiently remarkable; and though I consider that there is little to show that he ever reached a point so far across the continent, there is no reason that he should not have done so, and I leave it for my readers to form their own opinion.

Ludwig Leichardt, after carrying out successfully several journeys in Queensland and the Northern Territory, undertook the gigantic task of crossing Australia from East to West, viz., from Moreton Bay to the Swan River Settlements.

Towards the end of 1847, accompanied by eight white men, two black-boys, and provisions to last two years, he started, taking with him one hundred and eighty sheep, two hundred and seventy goats, forty bullocks, fifteen horses, and thirty mules. After travelling with little or no progress for seven months, during which time the whole stock of cattle and sheep were lost, the party returned. Not discouraged by this disastrous termination to his scheme, Leichardt resolved on another expedition with the same object in view.

Before many months he, with the same number of companions but with fewer animals, set out again. On the 3rd of April, 1848, he wrote from Fitzroy Downs, expressing hope and confidence as to the ultimate success of the expedition. Since that date, neither tidings nor traces have been found of the lost explorer, nor of any of his men or belongings. Several search-parties were organised and a large reward offered, but all in vain — and the scene of his disaster remains undiscovered to this day. Many and various are the theories propounded with regard to his fate. It is held by some that the whole party were caught in the floods of the Cooper. This creek is now known to spread out, after heavy rains at its source, to a width of between forty and fifty miles. So heavy and sudden is the rain in semi-tropical Australia, that a traveller may be surrounded by flood-waters, while not a drop of local rain may fall. Leichardt, in those early days, would labour under the disadvantage of knowing neither the seasons, nor the rainfall, and in all likelihood would choose the valley of a creek to travel along, since it would afford feed for his stock. It seems reasonable to suppose that a flood alone could make so clean a sweep of men, cattle, and equipment that even keen-eyed aboriginals have failed (so far as is known) to discover any relics.

Another theory, and that held by Mr. Panton, is that the deserts of Central and Western Australia hold the secret of his death. This theory is based, I believe, on the fact that Gregory, in the fifties, found on the Elsey Creek (North Australia) what he supposed to be the camp of a white man. This in conjunction with some vague reports by natives would point to Leichardt having travelled for the first part of his journey considerably further north than was his original intention, with a view to making use of the northern rivers. Supposing that his was the camp seen on the Elsey, a tributary of the Victoria River, it would have been necessary for him to alter his course to nearly due South-West to enable him to reach the Swan River. This course would have taken him through the heart of the desert, through the very country we now were in. For my part I think that trade from tribe to tribe sufficiently accounts for the presence of such articles as tent-pegs and pieces of iron, though strangely enough an iron tent-peg is not commonly used nowadays, stakes of wood being as serviceable, and none but a large expedition would be burdened with the unnecessary weight of iron pegs.

Part V: The Outward Journey

Chapter X: The Desert of Parallel Sand-Ridges

My position for Family Well is lat. 22 degrees 40 minutes, long. 125 degrees 54 minutes. The well, as already stated, is situated at the foot of the southern slope of a high sand-ridge. This ridge is the first of a series of parallel banks of sand which extend, with occasional breaks, from lat. 22 degrees 41 minutes to 19 degrees 20 minutes — a distance of nearly 250 miles in a straight line. From September 16th to November 16th we were never out of sight of a sand ridge, and during that time travelled 420 miles, taking into account all deviations consequent upon steering for smokes and tracking up natives, giving an average of not quite seven miles a day, including stoppages. This ghastly desert is somewhat broken in its northern portion by the occurrence of sandstone tablelands, the Southesk Tablelands; the southern part, however, viz., from lat. 22 degrees 41 minutes to lat. 20 degrees 45 minutes presents nothing to the eye but ridge upon ridge of sand, running with the regularity of the drills in a ploughed field. A vast, howling wilderness of high, spinifex-clad ridges of red sand, so close together that in a day's march we crossed from sixty to eighty ridges, so steep that often the camels had to crest them on their knees, and so barren and destitute of vegetation (saving spinifex) that one marvels how even camels could pick up a living. I estimate their average vertical height from trough to crest at fifty to sixty feet. Some were mere rises, whilst others reached a height of considerably over one hundred feet. Sometimes the ridges would be a quarter of a mile apart, and sometimes ridge succeeded ridge like the waves of the sea. On October 3rd, for instance, I find that we were crossing them at a rate of ten in forty minutes. This gives a result of 105 ridges to be negotiated in a day's march of seven hours. Riding was almost impossible in such country as this, for all our energies were required to urge on the poor camels. All through, we adhered to the same plan as before, viz., doing our day's march without a halt (excepting of course the numerous stoppages entailed by broken nose-lines, the disarrangement of a pack, or the collapse of a camel), having no food or water from daylight until camping-time. This, without our previous training, would have been an almost impossible task, for each ridge had to be climbed — there was no going round them or picking out a low place, no tacking up the slope — straight ahead, up one side, near the top a wrench and a snap, down goes a camel, away go the nose-lines, a blow for the first and a knot for the second, over the crest and down, then a few paces of flat going, then up again and down again, and so on day after day. The heat was excessive — practically there was no shade.

The difficulties of our journey were increased by the necessity of crossing the ridges almost at right angles. With almost heart-breaking regularity they kept their general trend of E. by N. and W. by S., causing us from our Northerly course to travel day after day against the grain of the country. An Easterly or Westerly course would have been infinitely less laborious, as in that case we could have travelled along the bottom of the trough between two ridges for a great distance before having to cross over any. The troughs and waves seem to be corrugations in the surface of greater undulations; for during a day's march or so, on reaching the top of one ridge, our view forwards was limited to the next ridge, until a certain point was reached, from which we could see in either direction; and from this point onwards the ridges sank before us for a nearly equal distance, and then again they rose, each ridge higher than the last. Words can give no conception of the ghastly desolation and hopeless dreariness of the scene which meets one's eyes from the crest of a high ridge. The barren appearance of the sand is only intensified by the few sickly and shrunken gums that are dotted over it. In the troughs occasional clumps of shrubs, or scrubs, [e.g., Mulga (*Acacia anaeura*), grevillea, hakea, ti-tree (*Melaleuca*) and in the northern portion desert oaks (*Casuarina descaineana*)] or small trees are met with, and everywhere are scattered tussocks of spinifex. True it is, though, that even this poverty-stricken plant has its uses, for it serves to bind the sand and keep the ridges, for the most part, compact. Where spinifex does not grow, for instance on the tops of the ridges, one realises how impossible a task it would be to travel for long over banks of loose sand.

 Cresting a sand-ridge

I find that my estimate for the average height of the sand-ridges is considerably lower than that of Colonel Warburton. It is interesting, therefore, to compare his account of these ridges, though it must be remembered that Colonel Warburton was travelling on a westerly course, and we from our northerly direction only traversed country previously seen by him, for the short distance that our sight would command, at the point of intersection of our two tracks. In an editorial note in his book we read:—

They varied considerably both in their size and in their distance from each other, but eighty feet may be regarded as an average in the former respect and three hundred yards in the latter. They ran parallel to each other in an East and West direction, so that while pursuing either of these courses the travellers kept in the valleys, formed by two of them, and got along without much exertion. It was when it became necessary to cross them at a great angle that the strain on the camels proved severe, for on the slopes their feet sank deeply into the sand, and their labours were most distressing to witness.

Part V: The Outward Journey

Chapter XI: From Family Well to Helena Spring

On leaving Family Well it was suggested by Charlie and Godfrey that we should take one of our native friends with us. No doubt this would have been the most sensible plan, and would have saved us much trouble. However, I did not care to take either of the females, the sick man was evidently of no use to us, and it was pretty evident that the sound buck was the chief hunter, and that without him, the little tribe would be hard pressed to find food. As we were not in absolute need of water for a few days to come, I decided to leave the family in quiet enjoyment of their accustomed surroundings. I had now given up all hope of finding any other than desert country ahead of us, and had no longer any other purpose than that of traversing the region that lay between us and "white settlements" with as little harm to ourselves and our camels as care and caution could command. Our course was now North-East, as it was necessary to make more easting to bring us near the longitude of Hall's Creek. We continued for three days on this course, the ridges running due East and West. The usual vegetation was to be seen, relieved by occasional patches of a low, white plant having the scent of lavender. This little plant grew chiefly on the southern slope of the ridges, and was seen by us in no other locality. A specimen brought home by me was identified at Kew Gardens as a new variety of Dicrastylis, and has been named *Dicrastylis carnegiei*.

Large tracts of burnt country had to be crossed from which clouds of dust and ashes were continually rising, blown up by "Willy-Willies" (spiral winds). These were most deceptive, it being very hard to distinguish between them and hunting-smokes. After one or two disappointments we were able to determine, from a distance, the nature of these clouds of black dust. On the 22nd we turned due East towards some smokes and what appeared to be a range of hills beyond them. The smokes, however, turned out to be dust-storms, and the range to be immense sandhills. Here we saw the first desert oak, standing solitary sentinel on the crest of a ridge. Around the burnt ground several old tracks were visible, some of which we followed, but with no better result than two dry rock-holes and a dry native well one mile from them. Near the latter was an old native camp, in which we found several small, pointed sticks, so planed as to leave a bunch of shavings on the end. I have seen similar sticks stuck up on native graves near Coolgardie, but have no idea of their proper significance. Probably they are merely ornaments.

A line of cliffs next met our view, and to them we turned. These were higher rocks or hills than we had seen for some time, and presented rather a remarkable appearance. Formed of a conglomerate of sandstone and round ironstone pebbles, they stood up like a wall on the top of a long slope of easy grade, covered with gravel and loose pebbles. At the foot lay boulders great and small, in detached heaps like so many pieces broken from a giant plum-pudding. In the face of the cliffs were numerous holes and caves, the floors of which gave ample evidence of the presence of bats and wallabies. Of these latter we saw several, but could not get a shot; careful exploration of these caves, on hands and knees, led to the finding of a fair-sized rock-hole, unfortunately quite dry. I have no doubt that these wallabies, like the spinifex rats, are so constituted that water is not to them a necessity, and that the spinifex roots afford sufficient moisture to keep them alive. We saw no traces of spinifex rats at any of the wells we found, nor did we see any water which they could reach or from which, having reached it, they could climb up again to the surface. From the top of the cliffs an extensive view to the South and North was obtained. But such a view! With powerful field-glasses nothing could be seen but ridge succeeding ridge, as if the whole country had been combed with a mammoth comb. From these points of the compass the cliffs must be visible for a considerable distance. Their rather remarkable appearance made me think them worth naming, so they were christened "Wilson's Cliffs," after my old friend and partner.

The entry in my diary for the 25th would stand for many other days. It runs: "Most wretched sand-ridge country, ridges East and West, and timbered with very occasional stunted gums — extensive patches of bare, burnt country with clouds of dust. Absolutely no feed for camels — or for any other animal for that matter."

Such miserable country beggars description. Nothing is more heartrending than to be forced to camp night after night with the knowledge that one's poor animals are wandering vainly in search of feed. To tie them down would have given them some rest, but at the same time it entailed their certain starvation; whilst, wandering about, they stood some chance of picking up a mouthful or two. How anxiously each ridge was scanned when camping-time drew near — no feed — on again another ridge or two, no feed — just one more ridge, and, alas! "no feed" is again the cry. So we camped perforce without it, and often the famished camels would wander two or three miles in the night in search of it, and this meant an extra walk to recover them in the morning.

On the morning of the 27th Warri brought in all the camels but one, with a message from Breaden that Misery was dying. Small wonder if all had been in the same state, for we were now eight days from the last water, and tough as camels are they cannot go waterless and foodless for very many days in such trying country as this. Poor old Misery! This was sad news indeed, but all that could be done to save him should be done.

This morning a smoke rose due West of us. We had seen so few signs of natives lately that we could not afford to neglect this, even though it was so far from our proper course.

By the time we had loaded the camels and distributed his load amongst the rest, Breaden brought Misery into camp, and when we started, followed with him behind us, coaxing him along as best he could. Eight miles brought us into the region of the burning spinifex and fresh tracks; despatching Charlie on Satan, and Godfrey and Warri on foot, to track up and catch a native if possible, I unloaded the camels and awaited Breaden's arrival. Presently he came alone, saying that poor Misery was done for and could move no further, so he had left him. I felt sure that that was the case, since Breaden would not have come without him if there had been any possibility of getting him further. Nevertheless, I could not bear to leave my faithful and favourite camel to die by slow degrees, and returned on Breaden's tracks. I took with me a brandy-bottle full of Epsom salts and water, for from Breaden's account of his way of going on I felt sure that poor Misery had eaten some poisonous plant. Four miles back I found him lying apparently dead in the shade of a tree, or where the shade would have been had there been any foliage; he knew me and looked up when I spoke to and patted him, and rested his head in my lap as I sat down beside him; but no amount of coaxing could get him on his legs. Having administered the salts, which he evidently enjoyed, I proceeded to bleed him by slitting his ear; my knife, however, was not sharp enough, (for everything becomes dulled in this sand) to do the job properly, and he bled but little. I could do nothing but wait, so taking a diminutive edition of Thackeray from my pocket, for I had foreseen this long wait, I read a chapter from "Vanity Fair." Presently I got him on his legs and he walked for about thirty yards, then down he went in a heap on the ground; another wait, and more "Vanity Fair." Then on again, and down again, and so on hour after hour. Soon nothing but brutal treatment would make him stir, so I hardened my heart and used a stick without mercy. What a brute I felt as he turned his great eyes reproachfully upon me! "Never mind, Misery, old chap, it must be done to save your life!" At last I reached a ridge within one hundred yards of the camp, and here Breaden met me, bringing with him four gallons of water and the welcome news that the others had captured two bucks who had shown a well three miles north.

This water saved Misery's life, and was just in time. We reached camp as the camels were reloaded and ready to start for the well under the guidance of the two bucks. Both of these were fair-sized men, and one stood six feet at least, though from the method of doing the hair in a bunch at the top of the head they appear taller than they really are. Godfrey and Warri had tracked them right into their camp and surprised a family of numerous gins, young and old, several picaninnies, and three bucks, one of whom was stone blind. They were preparing their evening meal, and amongst the spoils of the chase there were opossums, whose tracks on one of two large gum-trees not far off we afterwards saw. I had always associated opossums with good country; however, here they were. Of the natives, some fled as soon as Godfrey and Warri approached, whilst the men were uncommonly anxious to dispute this unceremonious visit to their camp. They were on the point of active hostilities when Charlie rode up on Satan, and they then thought better of it. Even so they were not persuaded to accompany the white men back to camp without considerable difficulty. The smaller man managed to escape; the other we afterwards christened Sir John, because he was so anxious to make us dig out old dry wells, so that presumably they should be ready for the next rain. There seemed to us to exist a certain similarity between his views and those of the Government, which is ever ready to make use of the pioneer's labours where it might be justly expected to expend its own.

This fellow was most entertaining, and took a great interest in all our belongings. I, coming last, seemed to excite keen delight, though he was naturally a little shy of his captors; he patted me on the chest, felt my shirt and arms, and was greatly taken by a tattoo on one of them. Grinning like any two Cheshire cats, he showed his approval by "clicking" his tongue with a side shake of the head, at the same time snapping his thumb and finger. Breaden, too, came in for Sir John's approval, and was similarly patted and pulled about.

Godfrey had taken a rather handy-looking tomahawk from the buck, made from the half of a horseshoe, one point of which was ground to a pretty sharp edge — a primitive weapon, but distinctly serviceable. Unlike our friend at Family Well, this man had not even a shell to wear, and beyond an unpleasantly scented mixture of fat and ashes, with which he was smeared, was hampered by no sort of clothing whatever. As usual, he was scarred on the chest and forehead, and wore his hair in a mop, held back by a band of string. His teeth were a picture, not only clean and white, which is usual, but uncommonly small and sharp, as one of us found! Leaving him to the main party to take on to the well, I and Warri remained behind to bring Misery on — and a nice job we had too. I thought of waiting and packing water back to him, but in that case he would have fallen an easy victim to the natives, who were bound to be prowling about, nor could one of us be spared to watch him. So he had to be beaten and hauled and dragged, by stages of twenty yards at a time, over the ridges. After darkness fell we had to follow the tracks with a firestick until we had the fire at camp to guide us. This we reached about 9.30 p.m., fairly tired out, but satisfied that the poor, patient sufferer's life was saved. The others had already started work on the well, but knocked off when I got back, and we had a good feed and a short rest. Sir John was much distressed at his party having taken away all their food when they retreated, and was hardly consoled by what we gave him. Tethered to a ti-tree, with a little fire to cheer him, he was apparently happy enough.

The rest of the night we worked at the well in shifts, and Charlie and I, the first shift, started off soon after daybreak with the buck to find more water, for it was evident that our present supply was insufficient. We felt pretty certain from the way the tribe had left that another well existed close by; the question was, would our captive show it? He started in great glee and at a great pace, carrying behind him, like a "back-board," a light stick. This will be found to open the lungs and make a long walk less fatiguing, except for the strain on the arms. Occasionally he would stop and bind strips of bark round his ankles and below the knee. "Gabbi" was just over the next ridge, he assured us by signs — it was always "the next ridge" — until when nearly ten miles from camp we saw a smoke rise ahead of us, but so far away that we could do no good by going on. However, we had gained something by locating a fresh camp, so started homewards, the buck becoming most obstreperous when he saw our change of plan, for he made it clear by signs that the gins (indicating their breasts by covering his own with his hands) and the blind man (pointing to his own closed eyes and making a crooked track in the sand) and the rest, had circled round and gone to the camp from which we could see the smoke rising. However, he could not escape and soon gave in, and followed reluctantly behind, dragging at the rope.

Walking was bad enough, but this extra exertion was rather too much. Besides, we were sadly in need of sleep; so, taking advantage of what little shade we could find by following round the shadow of a gum tree as the sun moved, Charlie slept whilst I watched our black friend, and then I did the same. On arrival at camp we found that our companions had been so successful in "soak-sucking," i.e., baling and scraping up the miserable trickle of water as it soaks into the "caisson," that by sunset we were able to give the camels eight gallons each, and two gallons extra to Misery, who was showing signs of a rapid recovery. Luckily there was a little patch of dry herbage not far from the well, and a few acacias over the ridge. All the next day we were occupied in "soak-sucking," and Warri went back for Misery's saddle, which had been thrown off. I took the opportunity of writing up my diary — anything but a pleasant job, for shade there was none, except in a reclining position under our solitary ti-tree bush. The native's close proximity and the swarm of flies, made the task quite hateful, for under the most favourable conditions there are few things I dislike more than writing. On September 28th I chronicled a most remarkable fact, viz., that the two camels Satan and Redleap had had no more than thirteen gallons of water in the preceding thirty-eight days — a wonderful exhibition of endurance and pluck in this burning weather and barren country. It came about in this way: —

August 22nd. At Woodhouse Lagoon they had a full drink in the morning.

August 29th. At Warri Well, where the parakeelia grew, two gallons in the evening.

September 8th. At Patience Well they were the last to be watered, eight gallons in the evening.

September 18th. At Family Well, parakeelia again, three gallons at night.

September 28th. Half a drink.

Therefore between the 22nd of August and the 28th of September they had no more than thirteen gallons.

Satan had more travelling, though carrying a less load, than any of the rest, being used for scouting and finding natives.

On the evening of the 29th I left my work down the well to take some observations; unluckily I was just too late for the stars I wanted, and had to wait up for some long time. We had divided the night into five shifts for baling; when my turn came my companions did not wake me, but did my shift for me. I am sure I appreciated their kindly thought, and felt thankful indeed, and not for the first time, that I had managed to choose such excellent mates — for I had long realised that without peace and unanimity in such a party, our chances of getting through the desert would be greatly minimised.

I found our position to be lat. 21 degrees 49 minutes, long. 126 degrees 33 minutes.

By morning we had given the camels another five gallons apiece and had some to go on with in our tanks, having, by working for two days and three nights, scraped together 140 gallons in all. On the 30th we travelled again Westwards, though making some Northerly progress towards the smoke which Charlie and I had located. We had a long talk about our methods of travelling, and Charlie thought that I was inclined to spare the camels at the expense of ourselves. We travelled all day without a break so that they should have the longer to look for feed at night, then we always hunted for tracks and water on foot, and when we found water, gave it to the camels before looking after our own wants, and he thought we might do longer stages straight ahead so long as we had a native. I held, and I think the outcome of the journey proved me correct, that our own well-being was a secondary consideration to that of our animals, for without them we should be lost. "Slow but sure" was my motto.

Though anxious to make as much northing as possible I did not feel justified in passing by almost certain water for the sake of a few hours. I felt always that we might come into an even more waterless region ahead, and perhaps be unable to find any natives. Some twelve miles brought us to the well — the smoke had been beyond it — and a more wretched spot I never saw. Absolutely barren, even of spinifex, were the high ridges of sand between which was the well — merely a small, round hole, with no signs of moisture or plant life about it, not a tree "within cooee." We had to go far to collect enough wood for a fire, and cut two sticks with which to rig up a fly to shade us from the sun — a purely imaginary shade, for light duck is of little use against the power of such a burning sun; but even the shadow cast by the fly gave an appearance of comfort.

At this camp we made two new caissons, as our old tin-lined boxes were no longer strong enough. Amongst our gear were two galvanised-iron boxes, made to order, with lids which completely covered the boxes and were held on by straps. "Concertina-made boxes" they were called by the tinsmith — a name which gave rise to a curious misstatement in a Perth paper which published a letter I wrote to Sir John Forrest. The letter read: "... We made boxes out of concertinas"! I fear any who read this must have thought me fairly good at "romancing." I had them made that shape so that they might be filled to nearly double the capacity of the boxes and still have serviceable lids. I had hoped to have filled them with specimens of plants and birds. Unfortunately we had neither the time to, nor the opportunity of making any such collection, though we might easily have filled them with specimens of the desert house-fly which swarm at every well! By sawing off the ends of these lids we had two useful boxes, with neither top nor bottom, and by screwing them on to a framework of wood we manufactured a most useful caisson, 2 feet deep by 1 1/2 long and 1 foot wide. By forcing this into the sand in the well and digging out the sand contained in it, and then patiently waiting with a pannikin for the small trickle of water creeping in from between the outside of the caisson and the sides of the rock-hole, then again forcing the box lower, and clearing out the sand above, now drained of its moisture, and repeating the baling process, we were enabled to drain the well of almost every drop it contained. On first acquaintance with these wells a novice's impulse would be to dig out the sand until the bottom was reached; but as the sand holds the water he would find himself with a nicely cleared hole, but cleared of sand and water alike. Therefore, without some such makeshift as that already described one would be in the most unsatisfactory position of knowing that water existed, and yet of being unable to obtain any but a very small supply. The natives use comparatively little water, since it is only for drinking purposes, washing being unknown, and as the water sinks in the well the sand is scooped out gradually and carefully and plastered round the sides of the hole, so preventing the inrush of sand. Very often when they require a drink they bend down and suck up the water through a bunch of grass, which prevents the sand from getting into the mouth.

The water from the wells was always bad, and on first being brought to the surface was hardly fit to use; the camels would not, unless really dry, drink it until it had been exposed in our canvas troughs to the air for some time. Lying stagnant perhaps for a year or more, protected by the sand, it is not to be wondered at that its flavour is not of the best. Digging in the sand discloses all sorts of odds and ends that could not fail to contaminate the water. It contains also — derived, I suppose, from the sandstone — a certain amount of iron, which I believe to have acted as a sort of tonic to us. A many-tinted, bluish scum always floated on the surface and tea made with it turned as black as ink — nevertheless it was quite good drinking.

October 1st and 2nd we spent at the well, working as above described, whilst Warri tended the camels a couple of miles away on a patch of weeds he discovered. This weed which I have mentioned is the only available feed in this region — without it the camels must have starved long since. The plant somewhat resembles a thistle, but has a small blue flower, and when fresh forms the best feed. So far, however, we had only seen it dry and shrivelled. It is known to science as *Trichodesma zeylanicum*. This camp was the scene of a vicious onslaught on Charlie, made by the buck, whilst away looking for the plant from which to make a chewing-ball. Taking Charlie unawares he nearly accomplished his escape. Charlie, as it happened, was the very worst to try such tricks on, for he was the strongest of the party, and a very powerful man. During the struggle the black-fellow grabbed Charlie's revolver pouch, and somehow the revolver exploded, the bullet narrowly missing them both. It had the useful effect of attracting our attention, and we were in time to save Charlie some nasty wounds, as the buck was using his powerful jaws to great advantage. Of course we could not blame him for trying to escape — that was only natural — but it made us more cautious in the future. Excepting the inconvenience of being unable to get away, he had nothing to complain of, and had the advantage of plenty to eat and drink without the trouble of looking for it. The manufacture of the "quid" mentioned above is interesting. Cleaning and smoothing a place in the sand, a small branch from a silvery-leafed ti-tree (a grevillea, I think), is set alight and held up; from it as it burns a light, white, very fine ash falls on to the prepared ground. Now the stems of a small plant already chewed are mixed with the ashes. The compound so formed is squeezed and pressed and kneaded into a small, oval-shaped ball, of sticky and stringy consistency. The ball when in use is chewed and sucked but not swallowed, and is passed round from mouth to mouth; when not in use it is placed behind the ear, where it is carried. Nearly every tribe we saw had such "quids." No doubt they derive some sustenance from them. Sir John preferred his "chew" to any food we gave him; though he did not care about tobacco.

For the next two days the sand-ridges seemed to vie with each other in their height and steepness, between them there was hardly any flat ground at all; mile after mile we travelled, up one and down and over the next without ceasing. First came the native and his guard, then in a long, broken line the string of camels. What a labour it was! Often each camel had to be urged in turn over the ridge whilst those behind were continually breaking their nose-lines to lie down or hurry off to the nearest shade, however scanty, and there await the blows and exhortations of their driver; those which remained in their places were continually lifting their feet, for they could not stay still on the burning sand; then their packs were always being jolted about and thrown out of place, necessitating reloading, and when at last we had them again in line the whole performance had to be repeated a few ridges further on.

Sometimes our caravan would cover half a mile or more, the guide and guardian waiting far in advance whilst the broken line was rejoined and the stragglers brought in, and away far behind the last camel would appear alone, with his nose-line dangling and tripping him up. Usually Billy brought up the rear — nothing would induce him to follow close behind; a jerk of his head and away went the nose-line, and Billy was left behind to follow when so inclined. The heat was really tremendous. It can be fairly sultry around Coolgardie, but never before have I experienced such scorching heat; the sun rose like a ball of fire, and in two hours' time had as great power as at any period during the day. How one prayed for it to set, and how thankful one was when in due course it did so, sinking below the horizon as suddenly as it had risen!

I am not sure which felt the heat most, poor little Val or the buck. He, curiously enough, seemed more affected by it than we were. At night he drank more than we did, and then was not satisfied. Sometimes when waiting on ahead he used to squat down and scoop out a hole in the ground to reach the cool sand beneath; with this he would anoint himself. Sometimes he would make a mixture of sand and urine, with which he would smear his head or body. Poor Val was in a pitiable state; the soles of her paws were worn off by the hot sand; it was worse or as bad for her to be knocked about on the top of one of the loads, and although by careful judgment she could often trot along in the shade of one of the camels, she was as near going mad as I imagine it possible for a dog to go. Poor little thing! She used to yell and howl most agonisingly, with her eyes staring and tongue hanging. We had, of course, to pack her on a camel when her feet gave out, and by applying vaseline alleviated her pain.

Our guide took us to two dry wells and watched our disgust with evident satisfaction, and I had to resort to the unfailing argument of allowing him no water at all. He pleaded hard by sounds and gesture and no doubt suffered to some extent, but all was treated as if unnoticed by us. Thirst is a terrible thing; it is also a great quickener of the wits, and the result of this harsh treatment, which reduced the poor buck to tears (a most uncommon thing amongst natives), was that before very long we were enabled to unload and make camp in one of the most charming little spots I have ever seen. A veritable oasis, though diminutive in size; but not so in importance, for without its life-giving aid it is hard to say how things would have gone with us. The weather, as I have said, was scorching, the country destitute of feed, almost waterless, most toilsome to cross, and our camels were worn to skeletons from starvation and incessant work, and had they not been fine specimens of an exceptionally fine breed must have long since succumbed. Surely this is one of the noblest of creatures and most marvellous works of the Creator!

Brave, dumb heroes, with what patience and undaunted courage do they struggle on with their heavy loads, carrying what no other animal could carry in country where no other could live, never complaining or giving in until they drop from sheer exhaustion! I think there are few animals endowed with more good qualities than the much-abused camel — abused not only by the ignorant, which is excusable, but by travellers and writers who should know better. Patience, perseverance, intelligence, docility, and good temper under the most trying conditions, stand out pre-eminently amongst his virtues. Not that all camels are perfect — some are vicious and bad tempered; so far as my experience goes these are the exceptions. Some few are vicious naturally, but the majority of bad-tempered camels are made so by ill-treatment. If a camel is constantly bullied, he will patiently wait his chance and take his revenge — and pick the right man too. "Vice or bad temper," says the indignant victim; "Intelligence," say I. In matters of loading and saddling, ignorance causes great suffering to camels. I can imagine few things more uncomfortable than having to carry 150 pounds on one side of the saddle and perhaps 250 pounds on the other, and yet if the poor beast lies down and complains, in nine cases out of ten his intelligent master will beat him unmercifully as a useless brute! Nearly every sore back amongst a mob of camels is the result of carelessness. It is hard to avoid, I am well aware, but it can be done; and I speak as an authority, for during our journey to Kimberley and the journey back again, over such country as I have endeavoured faithfully to describe, there were only two cases of camels with sore backs — one was Billy, who had an improperly healed wound when we started, which, however, we soon cured; the other Stoddy, on the return journey. This state of affairs was not brought about except by bestowing great care and attention on the saddles, which we were continually altering, as they were worn out of shape, or as the camels became thinner — and thin they were, poor things, tucked up like greyhounds! A few days' rest and feed, fortunately soon puts a camel right, and such they could have at the little oasis we had reached on October 5th. In the centre of it lay a splendid little spring, in many ways the most remarkable feature we had encountered, and therefore I christened it after one whose love and helpful sympathy in all my work, has given me strength and courage — my sister Helena.

Part V: The Outward Journey

Chapter XII: Helena Spring

My native valley hath a thousand springs, but not to one of them shall I attach hereafter, such precious recollections as to this solitary fount, which bestows its liquid treasures where they are not only delightful, but nearly indispensable. So spake Sir Kenneth of Scotland in "The Talisman."

Surely the Christian knight, dragging his way across the sands of Palestine, was not more pleased to reach the "Diamond of the Desert" than we were to light upon this charming little oasis, hidden away in the dreary solitude of the surrounding sandhills; the one spot of green on which one's eyes may rest with pleasure in all this naked wilderness. At the bottom of a hollow enclosed between two sand-ridges is a small surface outcrop of limestone of similar character to that in which Empress Spring is situated. In this is a little basin, nearly circular, about 2 feet 6 inches in diameter and 3 feet deep, with a capacity of about seventy gallons. This is the spring, fed at the bottom of the basin from some subterranean source by a narrow tunnel in the rock, a natural drain, not six inches in diameter. Through this passage, from the West, the water rises, filling the rocky basin, and evidently at some seasons bubbling over and filling the clay-pan which abuts on it on the Western side. On the East side of the spring is an open space of sand; surrounding it and the clay-pan is a luxuriant growth of pig-face — a finger-like plant, soft, squashy, and full of moisture, but salt; it is commonly seen on the margin of salt-lakes. Beyond the pig-face, tussocks of grass and buck-bush, beyond that again a mass of ti-tree scrub extending to the foot of the sandhills. On the inner slopes of these can be seen the crowning glory of the spot viz., an abundance of splendid green thistle (*Trichodesma zeylanicum*), tall and juicy, growing amongst acacia and other bushes. Outside this, beyond this area of perhaps four hundred yards in diameter, stretching away to the horizon, ridge upon ridge of desolate sand, black and begrimed by the ashes of recently burnt spinifex, from which the charred stumps of occasional gum trees point branchless to the sky. What chance of finding such a place without the help of those natives to whom alone its existence was known?

The winds and storms of past years had filled in the basin with sand and leaves, and except for the extraordinary freshness and abundance of vegetation around it, its peculiar situation, and the absence of the usual accompaniments to rock-holes, such as heaps of sticks and stones which, having served their purpose of protecting the water from evaporation, have been removed and thrown aside by the natives, there was nothing at first sight to lead one to suppose that any further supply existed than was visible in this natural reservoir. This small amount soon vanished down the throats of the thirsty camels; it was then that, having cleared out the sand and leaves, we discovered the small passage through which the spring rises. By continual baling until all the camels were satisfied (and of this splendid spring water they drank a more than ordinary amount) we kept the water back to the mouth of the passage. Within an hour or so of the watering of the last camel, the hole was again full to the brim, of the most crystal-clear water. How we revelled in it! What baths we had — the first since we left Woodhouse Lagoon over seven weeks back! What a joy this was, those only can understand who, like us, have been for weeks with no better wash than a mouthful of water squirted into the hands and so rubbed over the face. Whenever possible Godfrey, who made our damper (bread), washed his hands in the corner of a dish, which was used by each in turn afterwards — and at our work in the wells, a certain amount of dirt was washed off. But to splash about with an unlimited number of buckets of water ready to hand, to be got by the simple dipping of a billy-can — this was joy indeed! This luxury we enjoyed from October 5th to October 10th, and every day the camels were brought to water, and with this and the green feed visibly fattened before our eyes.

File:Spinifex and Sand Illustration 21.jpg Helena Spring [Missing image]

So soon as we had proved the supply of our new watering-place, I had intended giving our guide his liberty. However, he forestalled this by cleverly making his escape. For want of a tree, his chain had been secured to the iron ring of a heavy pack-bag. His food and water were given him in empty meat-tins. With the sharp edge of one of these he had worked so industriously during the night that by morning he had a neat little circle of leather cut out of the bag round the ring.

With a blanket on which he had been lying, he covered his cunning trick and awaited his opportunity. It soon came; when our attention was fixed on the building of a shade, and, in broad daylight, he sneaked away from us without a sign or sound, taking with him some three feet of light chain on his ankle. What a hero he must be thought by his fellow-tribesmen! and doubtless that chain, which he could easily break on a stone with an iron tomahawk, will be treasured for many years to come. Had he not been in such a hurry he would have returned to his family laden with presents, for we had set aside several articles designed for him.

Our camp was specially built to protect us from the flies, and consisted of a framework of ti-tree poles and branches, roofed with grass and pig-face; under this we slung our mosquito-nets and enjoyed perfect peace. A few days in camp are by no means idle ones, for numerous are the jobs to be done — washing and mending clothes, patching up boots and hats, hair cutting, diary writing, plotting our course, arranging photograph plates (the majority of which were, alas! spoilt by the heat), mending a camera cracked by the sun, making hobble-straps, mending and stuffing saddles, rearranging packs cleaning firearms, and other like occupations. The heat was extreme; too great for my little thermometer which registered up to 140 (degrees) F., and intensified by hot winds and "Willy-Willies" (sometimes of great violence), which greatly endangered our camp. Godfrey excelled himself in the cooking department, and our usual diet of "tinned dog" was agreeably varied by small pigeons, which came in numbers to drink — pretty little slate-grey birds with tufts on their heads, common enough in Australia. Of these we shot over fifty, and, as well, a few of the larger bronzewing pigeons. The tufted birds come to water just after daylight and just before sundown, and so are more easily shot than the bronzewing. Throughout the day, galahs, wee-jugglers, parakeets, diamond-sparrows, and an occasional hawk or crow, came to the spring, evidently a favourite resort. Curiously enough, but few native camps were to be seen, nor is this the first time that I have noticed that the best waters are least used. The Australian aboriginal is not usually credited with much thought for the morrow. These desert people, however, have some provident habits, for first the small native wells are used, and only when these are exhausted are the more permanent waters resorted to. As an instance of their powers of following a "spoor," it may be mentioned that on several occasions our captive suddenly darted off at a tangent with eyes to ground, and then started digging his heel in the sand to find where a lizard or iguana was that he had tracked to his hole. Warri, amongst his other accomplishments, was most useful as a retriever of any wounded pigeon; he would hunt about until he spotted a fresh track, and before long had captured the bird. Any one who has noticed the number of hen-tracks in a poultry yard will appreciate this delicate performance. Warri, I am sure, would have been invaluable to Sherlock Holmes.

Pleasant as our camp was we could not stay too long, for we still had a considerable tract of unknown country before us. As the result of numerous observations I make the position of

Helena Spring to be lat. 21 degrees, 20 minutes 30 seconds South, and (by dead reckoning) long. 126 degrees 20 minutes East.

From the native I extracted the following words, which I consider reliable:

English. Aboriginal. Eagle Hawk Gunderu Gum tree Waaldi Sand Nuah Spinifex Godadyuda, * Fire or Smoke Warru * Water Gabbi * Dog Pappa   *The same as used by natives at Empress Spring.

Part V: The Outward Journey

Chapter XIII: From Helena Spring to the Southesk Tablelands

On October 11th we reluctantly left the "Diamond of the Desert" behind us, travelling in a N.E. by N. direction over the interminable sand-ridges, crossing a greater extent of burnt country than we had yet seen, and finally camping on the top of a high ridge so as to catch any breeze that the night might favour us with.

We made a long march that day of eighteen miles a very creditable stage in such peculiarly configured country. The camels had so benefited by their rest and feed that it made little difference to them that they had nothing to eat that night; they were well content to lie round the camp all night and chew the cud. I have often noticed how much camels like society; under favourable conditions — that is to say when travelling in good camel-country like the Southern goldfields — they will feed for an hour or so before dark, then slowly make their way with clattering hobble-chains and clanging bells back to the camp-fire, and there, with many grunts of satisfaction, lie peacefully until just before daylight, when they go off for another feed. On moonlight nights they like to roam about and pick choice morsels of bush on and off until daylight. In this waste corner of the earth where now we battled our way, the poor brutes wandered aimlessly about, now trying a mouthful of sharp spinifex and now the leaves of a eucalyptus; turning from these in disgust, a little patch of weed might be discovered by one lucky camel; no sooner would he hurry towards it than the others would notice it, and then a great scramble ensued and the weakest went without — though I have seen the strong help the weak, as in the case of Czar, who, with his powerful jaws, would break down branches for Misery, then quite young and without the requisite teeth. How fine they look with their long necks stretched upwards with the heads thrown back and the sensitive lips extended to catch some extra fresh bunch of leaves! How cunningly they go to work to break a branch that is out of reach; first the lowest leaf is gently taken in the lips and pulled down until the mouth can catch hold of some hanging twig — along this it is worked, and so from twig to branch, a greater strain being exerted as the branches increase in size, until finally the main limb of the branch is seized, and bent and twisted until broken. Often they try for one branch time after time, for having set their minds on a particular morsel, nothing will satisfy them until they have it.

No such scene could be watched from our camp on the ridge. But still we had something out of the common to look upon in the shape of hills ahead, and my hopes were high that we should soon see the last of the desert. Away to the North high points and bold headlands stood out black and clear above the sea of sand, tablelands and square-edged hills with some high peaks rising from them — the most imposing hills we had seen since passing Mount Burgess, near Coolgardie. From this point little could be determined as to their character even with glasses, for they were, as we afterwards found, over thirty miles distant.

Between them and our camp numerous low detached, table-top hills and conical mounds could be seen — none of any size, but remarkable in shape and appearance. These I named the Forebank Hills, after a hill near my home. These hills gave promise of better country, and, choosing a prominent headland, I altered our course towards it the following morning. We had not been travelling long before a smoke rose quite close to us, and we had another opportunity of seeing native hunting operations without being seen ourselves. A fine upstanding buck was dodging about amongst the blazing spinifex and was too engrossed to notice us; presently his occupation led him over the ridge and we saw him no more. From the earliness of the hour — for the smokes as a rule do not rise before 9 a.m. — it was clear that he could not have come far, so, picking up his tracks, we followed them back to his camp. Though we were not in great want of water, I considered it always advisable to let no chance of getting some slip by, since one never can tell how long the next may be in coming.

The tracks led us along the foot of one ridge; along the next, some three hundred yards distant, the ladies of the tribe could be seen marching along, laughing and chattering, and occasionally giving forth the peculiar shrill yell which only the gins can produce. It is impossible to describe a noise in writing, but the sound is not unlike a rather shrill siren, and the word shouted is a long-drawn "Yu-u-u." There is no mistaking the women's voices, the men's cry is somewhat deeper. Both are rather weird sounds, more especially when heard in thick scrub where one can see no natives, though one hears them all round. In the spinifex they were easily seen, and to their cry an answering yell came over the ridge and other women and children appeared. Presently they saw our caravan, and the "Yu-u-u" became fainter and fainter as the group scattered in all directions, and was lost to view. At the end of the tracks we found a camp, and in it the only attempt at a roofed shelter that we saw in the desert, and this merely a few branches leant against a small tree. The camp-fire had spread and burnt the spinifex close by, which gave the spot anything but an inviting appearance.

Under the shelter were huddled together, asleep, two gins and a young man. I have never seen more intense astonishment expressed in any one's face than that shown by these three when we roused them. All in their way were peculiar and deserving of description. The young gin was by no means uncomely; well-shaped and healthy-looking, with a skin black and shining as a well smoked meerschaum, with beautiful teeth which were shown off to advantage by an extensive smile, when she found that we had no murderous intentions. The other gin was the most repulsive object I have ever seen — like a hideous toad with wrinkled, baggy skin, with legs and arms so thin as to be no more than skin stretched tight over very meagre shinbones; and the face of this wretched being was a mass of festering wounds, on which no one could look without pity and horror. The man, too, was remarkable; an exceedingly smart young buck with an air of irresponsibility about him that suggested madness — a suspicion amply confirmed by his subsequent behaviour. His decorations added to his queer appearance; scarred by deep gashes on chest and arms, his body was daubed with red ochre, and his ribs picked out with white; on his head a kind of chignon formed of grass, hair, and string held his matted locks in place, like a bird's nest on his crown; he had neither beard nor whiskers, and was not blessed with any article of clothing whatever.

File:Spinifex and Sand Illustration 22.jpg The only specimen of desert architecture [Missing image]

He showed us their well, which was nearly dry, and then volunteered to lead us to others; and away he went, swaggering along and clicking his tongue in great glee, occasionally breaking out into shrieks of laughter. When we arrived at one dry rock-hole and then another, it dawned upon me what the secret joke had been that so amused our friend; and I determined that he should be of some use to us before we parted company.

Of these dry rock-holes, one would, after rain, hold a fair amount of water, and is situated on the shoulder between two low table-tops. To the South, about two miles distant, are three conspicuous conical hills, close together, and about the same distance to the North-West a hill that at once calls to mind an old fort or castle. On camping, our native friend became a most intolerable nuisance, and proved himself a cunning wrestler, suddenly bending down and diving between Breaden's legs, which he seized at the ankle, nearly succeeding in throwing him to the ground. With a chain formed of spare hobbles held together by wire, we tethered him to a tree, scraped out a nest in the sand for him to sleep in, and lit a fire to cheer him. There he lay quiet until, on making signs that he was thirsty, one of us went to give him his food and water, when he darted at his benefactor and fought most viciously. After that, all through the night, at intervals, he was yelling and dancing, now upright and now on hands and knees circling his tree and barking like a dog, now tearing his headgear and stamping it in the sand, threatening us with hands raised, and finally subsiding into his sandy nest, crying and whining most piteously. It was an act of some danger to unloose him in the morning, but before long he was laughing away as heartily as before. There is no doubt he was as mad as could be. During the day's march he was up to all kinds of pranks, going through all sorts of antics, idiotic, sorrowful, angry, and vulgar in turn. The space between the ridges was greater now, and on them were numerous pointed ant-hills some two or three feet high. One favourite trick of this lunatic was to rush towards one of these, and sit perched on the top with his knees up and feet resting on the side of the heap, a most uncomfortable position. Another dodge he tried with indifferent success was that of throwing himself under a camel as he passed, with the object, I suppose, of diving out on the other side. The camel, however, did not understand the game and kicked him severely. He was a most extraordinary person, and indeed I can understand any one going mad in this dreary region; and to think that these black folk have never known anything different!

I could enumerate a score of strange tricks that our friend exhibited. What surprised me most was to see him make use, in unmistakable pantomime, of a vulgar expression that I thought was only known to English schoolboys!

File:Spinifex and Sand Illustration 23.jpg The Mad Buck [Missing image]

Between the Forebank Hills and the tablelands we were now approaching is an open plain of spinifex some ten miles wide, bounded on North and South by sand-ridges. From these in the morning the long line of broken tablelands could be seen ahead of us, and running for a considerable distance to the eastward. The highest point of those more immediately to our front I named Mount Fothringham, after my cousin. The headland for which we were steering was too far off to be reached that night, so we camped on a ridge, and during the night noticed a small fire in the hills ahead. It could only be a camp-fire of some natives, so, noting its direction, and being unable to see anything further, we retired to rest.

The next morning, with the help of the glasses, we could see several black figures moving about on the sloping foot of the cliffs, and therefore steered in their direction. Our mad friend had to be accommodated on the top of a camel, as he refused to walk or move, and I wished to leave him with friends, or at any rate with fellow-countrymen, though we no longer required his services as guide, in which capacity he had been singularly useless. Five miles brought us to the hills, and close on to the natives' camp whose fire we had seen, before they discovered us; when they did so they fled, seven or eight of them, and hid in caves in the sandstone. We had now been only four days since the last water, but the weather was so hot, feed so scarce, and so much ground burnt and dusty, that it was time we gave the camels another drink if we wished to keep them in any sort of condition. From the native camp a few tracks led round a corner of rock; these I followed, with the camels coming behind, and soon saw two small native wells sunk in the sand and debris, held in a cleft in the rock. Nothing but bare rock rose all round, and on this we made camp, turning the camels out at the foot of the cliffs where a few bushes grew.

Godfrey and Warri meanwhile had followed the blacks into the caves, and now returned with two of the finest men I have seen in the interior. One, a boy, apparently about eighteen years old, splendidly formed and strongly built, standing nearly six feet high; the other a man of mature years, not so tall but very broad and well-made. The boy had no hair on his face, the man a short beard and moustaches, and both had a far better cast of features than any I have seen further south. Their skin, too, instead of being black, was a shining reddish-brown colour; this was perhaps produced by red ochre and grease rubbed in, but in any case it gave them a finer appearance. Both were quite without clothing or ornament, nor did I notice any of the usual scars upon their bodies; their well-fed frames made us hope that a change in the country was close at hand.

      These natives showed no fear or surprise when once in the camp, and, examining our packs and saddles, sat "jabbering" away quite contented, until Breaden struck a match to light his pipe. This so alarmed them that they bolted. We did not attempt to stop the boy, but detained the man, as I wished for further information about waters, and was also anxious to study his habits. He had evidently been in touch with blacks from settled parts, for he knew the words, "white-fella" and "womany," and had certainly heard of a rifle, for on my picking one up and holding it towards him he trembled with fear, and it was some time before his confidence in us was restored. He really was a most intelligent man, both amusing and interesting, and by signs and pantomime, repeated over and over again until he saw that we guessed his meaning, he told us many things. Plenty of women, old and young, were camped in one direction, and were specially worth a visit; he knew of several watering-places, in one of which we could bathe and stand waist-deep. So I made a compact that as soon as he showed us this wonderful "Yowie" (his word for water) he should go free. He seemed perfectly to understand this. Our mad friend he hardly deigned to notice, and pointed at him in a most contemptuous way.

      Now that he, the lunatic, was free to go where he liked, nothing would induce him to leave us — he would start to go, and after a few paces return and take up a crouching position close to the mouth of the well where we were working, and as each bucketful of mud or moist sand was hauled to the surface he eagerly watched it being emptied, and then proceeded to cover himself with its contents, until at last he was hardly distinguishable from a pyramid of mud — and a stranger object I never saw! Towards dusk he slunk off and sat on a rock below the cliffs, where he ate the food we had given him; and for all I know he may be there yet.

      Work was carried on all night, which was divided as usual into shifts, and this I have no doubt saved us from attack. Before sunset we had seen several bucks sneaking about the rocks, and during the night they came round us and held a whispered conversation with their fellow in our camp. Between them a sort of telegraphy seemed to be going on by tapping stones on the rocks. They may have been merely showing their position in the darkness, or it is possible that they have a "Morse code" of their own. I was on shift when they came, and as the well wanted baling only every twenty minutes, I was lying awake and watching the whole performance, and could now and then see a shadowy figure in the darkness. As soon as I rose to work, our buck lay down and snored heavily, and his friends of course were silent. I awoke Breaden on my way, as it would have been far too much in their favour should the blacks have attacked us and found me down the well and the rest of the party asleep. They were quite right in wishing to rescue their friend, since they could not tell what his fate was to be, but we could not risk a wounded companion or possibly worse, and lay watching for the remainder of the night. Evidently they were inclined to take no risks either, for they left us in peace.

      The wells, situated as they are in the bed of a rocky gully, would after rain hold plenty of water, though we extracted no more than thirty-five gallons. Their position is lat. 20 degrees 46 minutes, long. 126 degrees 23 minutes.

From the rocks above the wells the tablelands to the East have quite a grand appearance, running in a curve with an abrupt cliff on the Western side, and many conical and peaked hills rising from their summit. These tablelands, which in a broken line were seen by us to extend Northwards for over forty miles, and certainly extend Eastwards for twenty miles and possibly a great deal further, are of sandstone. Looking Westwards, a few detached blocks may be seen, but we seemed to have struck the Western limit of these hills. I have named them the Southesk Tablelands, after my father. Between the curved line of cliffs and the wells are several isolated blocks. Seven and a half miles to the Westward a remarkable headland (Point Massie) can be seen at the Northern end of a detached tableland. Again to the West, one mile, at the head of a deep little rocky gorge, whose entrance is guarded by a large fig tree, is a very fine rock-hole. This was the promised water, and our native friend was free to return to his family; he was greatly pleased at the bargain being carried out, and had evidently not expected it. Possibly what he has heard of the white-fella is not much to his credit! The fig tree afforded a splendid shade from the burning sun, and in a recess in the rock close by we could sit in comparative coolness. Here the native artist had been at work, his favourite subject being snakes and concentric rings.

A steep gorge, not very easy for camels to pass along, led up to the rock-hole, which lies under a sheltering projection of rock. From the rock above a good view is obtained; sand-ridges to the West, to the North and East tablelands. Most noticeable are Mounts Elgin, Romilly, and Stewart, bearing from here 346 degrees, 4 degrees, 16 degrees respectively. These hills are named after three of my brothers-in-law. They are of the usual form — that is to say, flat-topped with steep sides — Mount Elgin especially appearing like an enormous squared block above the horizon. To the South-East of Mount Stewart are two smaller table-tops close together.

As I walked over the rocks I noticed numerous wallabies, of which Godfrey shot several later; they were excellent eating, not unlike rabbit. Leaving the rock-hole, we steered for Mount Romilly, first following down the little creek from the gorge until it ran out into the sand in a clump of bloodwoods. Then crossing a plain where some grass grew as well as spinifex, we came again into sand-ridges, then another plain, then a large, dry clay-pan West of Mount Stewart, then more ridges up to the foot of Mount Romilly. It was here that we must have crossed the route of Colonel Warburton in 1873, though at the time I could not quite make out the relative positions of our two routes on the map.

Colonel Warburton, travelling from East to West, would be more or less always between two ridges of sand, and his view would therefore be very limited, and this would account for his not having marked hills on his chart, which are as large as any in the far interior of the Colony. In his journal, under date of September 2nd, we read: ". . . There are hills in sight; those towards the North look high and hopeful, but they are quite out of our course. Other detached, broken hills lie to the West, so our intention is to go towards them." Then, on September 3rd: "N.W. by W. to a sandstone hill" (probably Mount Romilly). "North of us there is a rather good-looking range running East and West with a hopeful bluff at its Western end" (probably Twin Head). From the top of Mount Romilly a very prominent headland can be seen bearing 7 degrees, and beyond it two others so exactly similar in shape and size that we called them the Twins. For these we steered over the usual sand-ridges and small plains, on which a tree (*Ventilago viminalis*) new to us was noticed; here, too, was growing the *Hibiscus sturtii*, whose pretty flowers reminded us that there were some things in the country nice to look upon.

Near the foot of the second headland we made camp. Leaving Charlie behind, the rest of us set out in different directions to explore the hills. There are four distinct headlands jutting out from the tableland, which extends for many miles to the Eastward and in a broken line to the

Southward, the face of the cliffs on the Western shore, so to speak, being indented with many bays and gulfs, and, to complete the simile, the waves of sand break upon the cliffs, while in the bays and gulfs there is smooth water — that is to say, flat sand. Grass and other herbage and bushes grow in a narrow belt around the foot of the cliffs, but everywhere else is spinifex.

The hills present a most desolate appearance, though somewhat remarkable; sheer cliffs stand on steep slopes of broken slabs and boulders of sandstone, reminding one of a quarry dump; from the flat summit of the cliffs rise conical peaks and round hills of most peculiar shape. The whole is covered with spinifex, a plant which seems to thrive in any kind of soil; this rock-spinifex, I noticed, contains much more resinous matter than the sand-spinifex, every spine being covered with a sticky juice. From our camp I walked up the valley between the first and second head, and, ascending the latter, which is crowned with cliffs some thirty feet high, sat down and examined the hills with my glasses. Two black objects moving about caught my eye, and as they approached I saw them to be two fine bucks decked out in most extravagant manner. From my point of vantage some three hundred feet above them, I could watch them, myself unseen. Each carried a sheaf of spears, woommera, and shield, and in their girdle of string a number of short throwing-sticks. Round their waists were hanging sporrans formed from tufts of hair, probably similar to those we found at Family Well that were made from the tufts from the ends of bandicoots' tails; their bodies were painted in fantastic patterns with white. Their hair was arranged in a bunch on the top of their heads, and in it were stuck bunches of emu feathers. Seen in those barren, dull-red hills, they looked strange and almost fiendish. They were evidently going to pay a visit to some neighbours either to hold festival or to fight — probably the latter.

When almost directly below they looked up and saw me; I remained quite still, watching all the time through the glasses. After the first surprise they held a hurried consultation and then fled; then another consultation, and back they came again, this time very warlike. With shouts and grunts they danced round in a circle, shaking their spears at me, and digging them into the ground, as much as to say, "That is what we would do to you if we could!" I rose from my hiding place and started to go down towards them, when they again retired, dancing and spear-waving at intervals. At the end of the valley, that is the third valley, there is a sheer cliff to a plateau running back to the foot of some round hills; across this plateau they ran until, on coming to some thick bushes, they hid, hoping, I have no doubt, to take me unawares. However, I was not their prospective victim, for no sooner had they planted themselves than I saw Godfrey, all unconscious, sauntering along towards them.

The whole scene was so clear to me from my lofty position that its laughable side could not help striking me, but this did not prevent my forestalling the blacks' murderous designs by a shot from my rifle, which was sufficiently well aimed to scare the bucks and attract Godfrey's attention. As soon as possible I joined him and explained my seemingly strange action. We tracked up the natives, and found they had been following a regular pad, which before long led us to a fine big rock-hole in the bed of a deep and rocky gully. A great flight of crows circling about a little distance off, made us sure that another pool existed; following down the first gully and turning to the left up another, deeper and broader, we found our surmise had been correct. Before us, at the foot of an overhanging rock, was a beautiful clear pool. What a glorious sight! We wasted no time in admiring it from a distance, and each in turn plunged into the cool water, whilst the other kept watch on the rocks above. Sheltered as it was from the sun, except for a short time during the day, this pool was as ice compared to the blazing, broiling heat overhead, and was indeed a luxury. By the side of the pool, under the overhanging rock, some natives had been camped, probably our friends the warriors; the ashes were still hot, and scattered about were the remains of a meal, feathers and bones of hawks and crows. Above the overhanging rock, in the middle of the gully, is a small rock-hole with most perfectly smooth sides, so situated that rain water running down the gully would first fill the rock-hole, and, overflowing, would fall some twenty feet into the pool below. The rock is of soft, yellowish-white sandstone. Close to the water edge I carved C96 and Godfrey scratched the initials of all of us. The pool, which when full would hold some forty thousand gallons, I named "Godfrey's Tank," as he was the first white man to set eyes upon it.

Having finished our bathe, we set about looking for a path by which to bring the camels for a drink; the gorge was too rocky and full of huge boulders to make its passage practicable, and it seemed as if we should have to make a detour of a good many miles before reaching the water. Fortunately this was unnecessary, for on meeting Breaden he told us he had found a small pool at the head of the first valley which was easy of access. This was good news, so we returned to camp, and, as it was now dark, did not move that night. And what a night it was! — so hot and oppressive that sleep was impossible. It was unpleasant enough to be roasted by day, but to be afterwards baked by night was still more so! A fierce fire, round which perhaps the warriors were dancing, lit up the rocks away beyond the headlands, the glow showing all the more brilliantly from the blackness of the sky.

File:Spinifex and Sand Illustration 24.jpg Southesk Tablelands [Missing image]

The next morning we packed up and moved camp to the pool, passing up the first valley — Breaden Valley — with the first promontory on our left. At the mouth of the valley, on the south side, are three very noticeable points, the centre one being conical with a chimney-like block on one side, and flanking it on either hand table-topped hills.

Down the valley runs a deep but narrow creek which eventually finds its way round the foot of the headlands into a ti-tree-encircled red lagoon enclosed by sand-ridges. Near the head of the valley the creek splits; near the head of the left-hand branch is Godfrey's Tank; in the other, just before it emerges from the cliffs, is the small pool found by Breaden. Several kinds of trees new to me were growing in the valleys, one, a very pretty crimson-blossomed tree, not unlike a kurrajong in size, shape, and character of the wood, but with this difference, in leaf, that its leaves were divided into two points, whilst the kurrajong has three. One of these trees had been recently chopped down with a blunt implement, probably a stone tomahawk, and a half-finished piece of work — I think a shield — was lying close by. The wood is soft, and must be easily shaped. It is rather curious that the natives, of whom, judging from the smoke seen in all directions, there must be a fair number, should not have been camped at such a splendid water as Godfrey's Tank, the reason of their absence being, I suppose, that camping in the barren hills would entail a longish walk every day to any hunting grounds. To the native "enough is as good as a feast," and a wretched little well as serviceable as a large pool. The nights were so cloudy that I was unable to see any stars, but by dead reckoning only the position of the pool is lat. 20 degrees 15 minutes long. 126 degrees 25 minutes.

From the top of the highest headland, which is divided into two nipple-like peaks, an extensive view can be obtained. To the South and the South-East, the Southesk Tablelands; to the East, broken tablelands and sandhills; to the North, the same; to the North-West, nothing but hopeless ridge upon ridge of sand as far as the horizon. To the West, some ten miles distant, a line of cliffs running North and South, with sand-ridges beyond, and a plain of spinifex between; to the North of the cliffs an isolated table-top hill, showing out prominently — this I named Mount Cornish, after my old friend and tutor in days gone by.

Leaving the hills on the 21st, we soon reached a little colony of detached hills of queer shapes, one, as Breaden said, looking "like a clown's cap." From the top of the highest, which I named Mount Ernest, after my brother-in-law, a dismal scene stretched before us, nothing but the interminable sand-ridges, the horizon as level as that of the ocean. What heartbreaking country, monotonous, lifeless, without interest, without excitement save when the stern necessity of finding water forced us to seek out the natives in their primitive camps! Every day, however, might bring forth some change, and, dismal as the country is, one was buoyed up by the thought of difficulties overcome, and that each day's march disclosed so much more of the nature of a region hitherto untraversed. It would have been preferable to have found good country, for not only would that have been of some practical benefit to the world at large, but would have been more pleasant to travel through. So far we had had nothing but hard work, and as the only result the clear proof that a howling wilderness of sand occupies the greater area of the Colony's interior

By going due East from Mount Ernest I could have cut the Sturt Creek in less than one hundred miles' travel, which would have simplified our journey. But taking into consideration that an equal distance would probably take us beyond the northern boundary of the desert, I determined to continue on a Northerly course, as by doing so we should be still traversing unknown country, until we reached the Margaret River or some tributary of it; whereas by cutting and then following up the Sturt, we should merely be going over ground already covered by Gregory's and subsequent parties.

Careful scanning of the horizon from Mount Ernest resulted in sighting some hills or rocks to the North-East. Excepting that higher ground existed, nothing could be seen as to its nature, for it was ever moving this way and that in the shimmering haze of heat and glare of the sun, which, intensified by powerful field-glasses, made one's eyes ache. I find it hard indeed to render this narrative interesting, for every page of my diary shows an entry no less monotonous than the following:—

Same miserable country — roasting sun — no feed for camels — camp on crest of high ridge in hopes of getting a breath of air — thousands of small ants worry us at night — have to shift blankets half a dozen times. Val's feet getting better — she can again walk a little. The high ground seen from Mount Ernest turned out to be bare rocks of black ironstone, from which we sighted a very large smoke rising to the eastward — miles of country must have been burning, a greater extent than we had yet seen actually alight. Probably the hot weather accounted for the spread of the flames. Though apparently at no great distance, it took us all that day and six hours of the next to reach the scene of the fire, where spinifex and trees were still smouldering and occasionally breaking into flames, whirlwinds of dust and ashes rising in every direction. Having camped we set out as usual to find tracks, Breaden and Warri being successful in finding a pad of some dozen blacks going in the same direction. This they followed for a few miles, and returned long after dark, guided by a blazing bank of spinifex; very worn and thirsty they were too, for tramping about in sand and ashes is a most droughty job.

File:Spinifex and Sand Illustration 25.jpg A native hunting party [Missing image]

Having kept the camels in camp, since there was not a scrap of feed, we were able to be well on our way before sunrise. Luckily the tracks led us between two ridges, and we had only one to cross, which was fortunate, for our beasts were famished from hunger, having had no food or water for five days. At every halt, however short, if whoever was leading them stopped, even to pull out a piece of spinifex which had found its way through some hole in his boot, they would take advantage of it and "plump" down on the sand; and whilst one was being goaded up, down would go the rest. Poor Prempeh had to be unloaded and dragged behind.

Less than a mile beyond where Breaden had turned back we came on the biggest camp of natives we had seen — quite a village! Perhaps a dozen little "wurlies" or branch-shelters were dotted about the foot of a sandhill. Camped under them we found one buck, several gins, and numerous picaninnies; it was clear that more were not far off. The first thing that struck us about the man was his complete assurance, and secondly his pronounced Jewish cast of features. With an ulster and a few tall hats on his head he would have made a perfect "old clo'" man. An oldish man this, with grizzled beard brought to a point, and in the end a tuft of a rat's tail was twisted, others similarly adorning the ends of his moustache. His hair was done in a round lump at the back, held in place by a sort of net of string. His hair in front had been either pulled out or shaved off, giving him a very fine forehead. His nose and lips were Jewish to a degree. His womenfolk showed no such characteristics, most of them being remarkably plain, with the exception of one pretty little gin, who, poor thing, was suffering from a similar disease to the man we saw at Family Well. We dressed her wounds with tar and oil, and I think relieved her sufferings somewhat.

Our next patient was a small boy, who, from his swollen appearance, had evidently enjoyed a hearty breakfast. He had sore eyes, literally eaten away at the inner corners into deep holes, prevented from healing by the myriads of flies that hung in clouds round his head. I made an application of some eye-lotion, at which he shrieked horribly, poor boy. I had never used that particular brand before, and did not know its strength. He was quite a small chap, and the old Jew held him in his arms whilst I doctored him, and nodded his head in approval. They showed us their well close by, the usual sort, just at the foot of the sandhill, and we set to work in the customary style, the buck watching us with interest. Feeling that there must be more natives about, and not liking a treacherous look in the old Jew's eyes, we brought a couple of rifles to the mouth of the well.

Before long we heard the "Yu-u-u" of approaching black-fellows, and in a minute fifteen naked savages came bounding down the sandhill towards us. Fortunately for them we saw they had no weapons; even so, it was a dangerous proceeding on their part, for some white men would have shot first and inquired about their weapons afterwards! They were all big men — the finest we saw anywhere excepting the two near Point Massie, and most of them had a marked Jewish look. [This peculiarity has been remarked amongst the natives of the McDonnell Ranges, Central Australia — but nowhere else.] They were very friendly — too much so — for they crowded round us, patting us, and jabbering so that our work on the well was much hindered. Presently more women came on the scene, and with many cries of "white-fella," "womany," their men made it clear that we might take the whole lot with us if we so desired! This was hospitality, indeed; but underlying it, I fear, were treacherous designs, for the game of Samson and Delilah has been played with success more than once by the wily aboriginal.

We took but little notice of the natives, as obtaining water was of greater interest at that moment than the prosecution of ethnological studies. Charlie worked away down the well with perfect unconcern, while the rest of us were occupied in hauling up the sand from below and keeping the blacks at a distance. Wonderfully cunning fellows they were! I was standing close by a Winchester which lay on the ground; one man came up, patting me all over and grinning in the most friendly way, and all the time he worked away with his foot to move the rifle to his mate beside me. However, he did not succeed, nor another who tried the same trick on Godfrey, and after a time they all retired, for reasons best known to themselves, leaving only the old man and the children behind.

Godfrey pressed the old man into our service and made him cut bushes for a shade; it seemed to me that an axe was not just the best thing for a man who would probably sooner have used it against us than not, so he was deposed from his office as woodcutter. As soon as the well was ready for baling I walked off to see if anything of interest could be found, or if another camp was anywhere near. The instant the old Jew saw me sling a rifle over my shoulder he ran like a hare, yelling as he went. He was answered by similar calls not far off. As he ran he picked up his spears from a bush, and I could see the marks of the weapons of the rest of the tribe, which had been planted just over the rise of sand. They evidently knew all about a rifle, yet we were still over a hundred miles in a bee-line from Hall's Creek. I saw their fleeing figures scattering in all directions, and followed up some tracks for some distance without finding anything of interest.

I noticed a considerable change in the country to the East, over which there spread a forest of desert oak, and near the sandhills thickets of ti-tree. The well seems to be at the head of an ill-defined watercourse, which, lower down, runs between an avenue of bloodwoods. Close to the well are several large ant-heaps, and from the sandhill above it little can be seen; but north of the well one mile distant is a high ridge of sand, from which is visible a prominent square hill, bearing 334 degrees distant eighteen miles; this stands at the Eastern end of a tableland, and is named Mount Bannerman, after my sister-in-law. The well had an abundant supply, though a little hard to get at, as it was enclosed by two rocks very close together, necessitating a most cramped position when baling with a saucepan on the end of a stick.

By daylight we had watered all the camels and were glad to rest under the shade we had made with boughs. Our rest lasted three days to allow Prempeh, who was very poorly, to recover. The flies, as usual, worried us unmercifully, but I was so thankful to regain once more my sense of hearing that I rather enjoyed their buzzing. I had for some weeks been so deaf that unless I had my attention fixed on something, I could not hear at all. I must have been a great bore to my companions very often, for frequently they talked for a long time to me, only to find that I had not heard a word!

We were greatly entertained by two small boys, the sole representatives of the tribe, who showed intense delight and interest in all our doings, and were soon tremendous chums with Warri. One was quite a child, very sharp and clever; the other a young warrior, very proud of his spear and shield — a well-built youngster whose appearance was somewhat spoiled by a severe squint in one eye. They showed no fear whatever of us, or of the camels, and were soon on quite friendly terms with the latter, patting and stroking their noses; they lost confidence before long, when the small boy inadvertently patted the wrong end of a camel and was kicked violently.

The position of the Jew Well is lat. 19 degrees 41 minutes, long. 127 degrees 17 minutes; from it we steered to Mount Bannerman, over the usual ridges of sand, now further apart and lower. On some of the flats between we found splendid little patches of feed [Amongst it *Goodenia ramelii*], where the spinifex had been burnt and was just sprouting up again. One plant, new to us, was growing in profusion and resembled nothing so much as bunches of grapes with the fruit pulled off. We camped early, as such feed was not to be passed by. The next morning, we found that our axe had been left behind at the well; so, as it was a most useful article, I sent Warri back for it, whilst Godfrey and I put in the day by following the young warrior, who volunteered to show us a very large water — a ten-mile walk with nothing at the end of it was not at all satisfactory, nor did we feel very kindly disposed to our small friend. I suppose he wanted to find his tribe again, for when we stopped we could see a smoke in the distance.

We saw quite a number of spinifex rats, and though Godfrey carried a gun one way and I carried it coming home, we never bagged one, and only had one shot, which missed. Every rat got up quite 150 yards off in the most annoying way. We started burning a patch of spinifex, but since we were not pressed for food we concluded that the weather was quite hot enough without making fires! I fancy that only by taking a leaf out of the blackfellows' book could one have any success in spinifex-rat hunting. I have read in Giles's book, and Sir John Forrest has told me, that when he was in the bush the rats were easily secured. Possibly they were more numerous in the better country that he passed through, or larger and not so quick. All our efforts were unavailing, the only occasion on which we slaughtered a rat being when Val caught a young one; the full-grown ones were far too fast for her and too quick in turning round the hummocks of spinifex.

Warri returned with the axe in the evening and reported that no natives had visited the well since our departure. The next day as we approached the hills the two boys, sitting aloft on the top of the loaded camels, were much excited and made many signs that water was not far off. The hills we found to be the usual barren, rocky tablelands, scoured into gullies and gorges, which, forming small creeks, disappear before many miles amongst the sandhills.

Mount Bannerman stands at the eastern end of the hills; a little to the west is a deep and narrow gorge, the bed of which is strewn with great boulders and slabs of rock. The hill is capped with a conglomerate of quartz, sandstone and ironstone pebbles, some of the quartz fragments being as large as hen's eggs and polished quite smooth. From its summit an apparently high range can be seen to the North; to the East and South nothing but sand-ridges; to the South-West a prominent square hill, the highest point in a broken table-range, bears 226 degrees. This hill I named Mount Erskine, after the Kennedy-Erskines of Dun.

Travelling West from Mount Bannerman, we had five miles of very rough and jagged rocks to cross, worn away into a regular network of deep little glens, very awkward to get over. The rocks were burning hot, and the walking was not at all to the liking of our small guide. The young warrior led the way, but was continually turning round for instructions to the little chap riding behind, who directed him with a wave of the hand in a most lordly manner. It is a most noticeable thing how much the natives seem to feel the heat, and I am inclined to think that in the hot weather they hunt only in the morning and evening, and camp during the day. I was walking with the youth, and whenever we stopped to allow the camels to catch us up he would crouch right up against me to get the benefit of my shadow; and he was so fearfully thirsty that I took pity on him and got him some water, though WE had all walked since sunrise without a mouthful.

In crossing these small ravines, I noticed again how much easier it is for camels to step down a steep rock than up — in stepping up they hang their front foot out, and paw about for a place to put it down upon in a most silly way.

In the main channel of a number of conjoining glens we came on a nice little pool under a step in the rocky bed. A few gums shaded the pool, growing in the sand by its edge. On arrival we found a large eagle-hawk with a broken wing flapping about; this our two boys soon despatched with sticks, and I looked forward to getting a handsome bird skin. However, the youngsters had it plucked and on a heap of burning sticks before we had done looking for a way, down which to lead the camels.

We made camp just above the pool, and were lucky in finding a patch of camel feed within a couple of miles across the rocks, for around all was barren excepting a few stunted gums. The next morning I went with Breaden for the camels, and noticed what I had suspected before, viz., that Breaden had lately become very thin and weak. This morning he collapsed, and I was thankful I had seen it; for he is a man who would never complain, but just go on until he dropped. He could not conceal his sickness now, and in a very short time was suffering from severe dysentery. Luckily we had plenty of water close at hand, for he could not possibly travel. For three days he lay in the recess of a sheltering rock near the pool, and we nursed him as best we could. Condensed milk and brandy, thin cornflour and chlorodyne, I doctored him with; he was a very obedient patient, whose pangs of hunger were aggravated by watching us feeding daily on bronzewings, wallabies, and galahs. This pool was a favourite resort for hundreds of birds — crows, hawks, galahs, parakeets, pigeons and sparrows — and numerous dingoes. Of the bronzewings, which at sundown and before sunrise lined the rocks literally in hundreds, we shot as many as we wanted. How thick they were can be judged from the result of one barrel, which killed fourteen.

It was a pretty sight to watch the birds drinking, as we sat in Breaden's sick-room, the cave. By keeping quite still we could watch them all. All day long the sparrows, diamond and black, are fluttering about the water, chirping and twittering, until the shadow of a hawk circling above scatters them in all directions. Then morning and evening flocks of little budgerigars, or lovebirds, fly round and round, and at last take a dive through the air and hang in a cloud close over the water; then, spreading out their wings, they drink, floating on the surface. The galahs make the most fuss of any, chattering away on the trees, and sneaking down one by one, as if they hoped by their noise to cover the advance of their mate. The prettiest of all the birds is a little plump, quail-like rock-pigeon or spinifex-pigeon, a dear little shiny, brown fellow with a tuft on his head. They arrive at the water suddenly and unexpectedly from behind rocks and trees, and stand about considering; then one, more venturesome than the rest, runs quickly down to drink, and is followed by a string of others; then they run up again ever so fast, and strut about cooing and spreading their crests — one seldom sees them fly; when they do they rise straight up, and then dart away close to the ground and drop suddenly within a few yards. Of all birds the crow has most sound common sense; there is no dawdling in his methods; down he swoops with beautifully polished feathers glistening in the sun, to the water's edge, stands for a second to look calmly from side to side; then a long drink and away he goes, thoroughly satisfied to mind his own business and nobody else's.

The two boys were splendid marksmen with short sticks, which they threw into the flights of love-birds and sparrows as they passed. Whenever they killed one they squatted down and heated it on the ashes, and ate it straight away; and so small bird after small bird went down their throats all day long, and they never thought to keep them until they had sufficient for a good square meal. No doubt in their family circle they have to take what they can get, and only make sure of keeping what they have, by eating it at once.

Wandering about the hills I saw an emu, the first I had seen since leaving the Coolgardie districts, though we had found their tracks at Woodhouse Lagoon. He was too shy for me, and I failed to get a shot after a lengthy stalk. Godfrey returned late that night with several wallabies, and many bruises and abrasions, for he had had a nasty fall in the dark down one of the many ravines.

The next morning was a sad one, for it disclosed the death from poison-plant of poor old Shiddi, one of the best and noblest of camels — a fine black, handsome old bull. I declare it was like losing an old friend, as indeed he was. Where one camel is poisoned all the rest may be, and since, from Breaden's dysentery, we could not travel, we must find another camp not far off. So we marched South-West down the creek and found another pool. Here we saw the first signs of white men for many a long day, in the shape of old horse-tracks and a marked tree, on which was carved (F.H. 18.8.96). This I found afterwards stood for Frank Hann, who penetrated thus far into the desert from Hall's Creek and returned. On another tree I carved a large C.

Breaden was slowly getting better when poor Charlie went sick, and we had two in hospital. A most unenviable condition, where no sort of comforts can be got. By digging into the bank of the creek we made a sort of couch, and rigged flies over it for a shade. Bad as the days were, the nights were worse; for myriads of ants followed swarms of flies, and black, stifling clouds followed a blazing sun — all of which is bearable to, and passes after a time unnoticed by a man in good health. But poor fellows, worn to skeletons by unending work and the poorest of food, unable to move from sickness, are worried almost past endurance by the insects and heat. Every night we experienced terrific thunderstorms, but alas! unaccompanied by rain. At sunset the clouds banked up black and threatening, the heat was suffocating, making sleep impossible, lightning would rend the sky, and then after all this hope-inspiring prelude, several large drops of rain would fall and no more, the sky would clear and the performance be over, only to be repeated the following evening.

Our change of camp made no difference in the feed, for on the 9th another camel was found dead in the morning — poor Redleap, who had never once shown a sign of giving in, killed in a matter of a few minutes. We examined his body, swollen to a tremendous degree, the usual indication of poison-plant — evidently very virulent and painful, for we could see how, in his death agony, he had torn up the ground with his teeth, and turned and bitten himself most cruelly. It was clear we must move again. As we prepared to load up, Stoddy was suddenly seized with the poison sickness, and careered at full speed round the camp in circles, falling down and rolling in agony at intervals. After a lot of trouble we stopped him, threw him, and roped him down; administered a gallon of very strong Epsom salts and water, then a dose of soapsuds, and bled him by slitting both ears. This unquestionably saved his life, for the first two remedies take too long to act. This scene had a curious effect on the other camels, and for days after Stoddy was avoided, nor would any bear being tied on behind him without snapping their nose-lines or breaking their nose-pegs to get away.

Further down the creek, some six and a half miles from the hills, is a fine flat of grass and herbage surrounded by large white gums — this is practically the end of the creek, and to this spot we shifted camp, packing water from the pool. On the 10th Prempeh died — another victim to the poison — and I began to dread the morning. Fortunately our new camp was free from poison, and no more deaths occurred. It was sad to think of our camels dying thus after so many hundred miles of desert bravely traversed — yesterday a picture of strength and life, to-day food for those scavengers of the bush, the dingoes. What satisfied howls they gave forth all night long; for, like crows or vultures, they seem to collect from far and wide round the body of any dead thing. From our camp Mount Erskine was visible, but not of sufficiently inviting appearance to make a visit worth while.

On the 15th all were off the sick list and ready to march. I felt sorrowful indeed at the loss of the camels, but thankful that no more had died, and more thankful still that we had been able to camp whilst poor Breaden and Charlie regained their health. Such a sickness in the heart of the desert could have had but one ending.

Our way lay over spinifex plains until just north of the hills a sand-ridge was crossed, remarkable from its regular shape and wonderfully straight course, as if it had been built to most careful measurements and alignment.

File:Spinifex and Sand Illustration 26.jpg Plan of sand-ridges [Missing image]

File:Spinifex and Sand Illustration 27.jpg Exaggerated section of the sand-ridges [Missing image]

The 16th of November was a red-letter day, for on it we crossed the *last* sand-ridge— *in lat. 19 degrees 20 minutes — leaving the desert behind us.* A feeling of satisfaction filled us that we had conquered its difficulties not by chance, but by unremitting toil and patience. I am sure that each in his heart thanked his God that He had been pleased to bring us through safely. Once across the range we had seen from Mount Bannerman — a range of quartzite hills which I named Cummins Range, after the Warden at Hall's Creek — and we had reached the watershed of the tributaries of the Margaret and Fitzroy Rivers. From Cummins Range onward until we struck the Margaret, we had very rough hills and rocks to cross — this hard travelling after the yielding sand was most painful to the camels, and their feet were soon sore and cut by the sharp edges of rock. The country may be roughly described as slate bedded on edge, in such a way as to leave sharp corners and points of rock sticking up in all directions. Through the slate run veins of quartz, often rising above the surface in huge blows, hills, and even small ranges. Innumerable gullies crossed our path, and occasionally fair-sized creeks. Such a one is Christmas Creek, which, where we saw it, is made up of three creeks from fifty to eighty yards across, running almost parallel and not more than half a mile apart. These soon meet and form a fine creek which joins the Fitzroy many miles to the Westward. These creeks are fringed with gums, Bauhinia, and Leichardt trees, all affording splendid shade — and following the banks on either side is a belt of high grass and shrubs, from which occasional kangaroos and wallabies bounded, alarmed by the sound of our advancing caravan.

On the north side of Christmas Creek we crossed the first auriferous country we had seen since leaving the Neckersgat Range, close to Lake Darlot. Standing on a high peak of white, sandy-looking quartz, a hill which I named Mount Hawick after my first mate in West Australia, Lord Douglas of Hawick, innumerable jagged ranges rose before me in all directions. To the south could be seen the Cummins Range, bounding the desert; to the north the black, solid outline of the Mueller Range. And now we were in surveyed country, and without much difficulty I could identify such points as Mount Dockrell, the Lubbock Range, McClintock Range, and others, and was pleased to find that after all our wanderings we had come out where I had intended, and in a general way had followed the line I had pencilled on the chart before starting.

Mount Hawick's approximate position is lat. 18 degrees 53 minutes long. 127 degrees 3 minutes; five miles from it, in a N.W. direction, we found a splendid pool in a deep gorge, whose precipitous sides made it hard to find a passage down which the camels could reach the water. For fear of a sudden downpour and consequent flood in the creek, we camped on the flat rock above the pool. Fish, small and bony, but of excellent flavour, abounded in the water, and we were soon at work with needles, bent when redhot into hooks, baited with pieces of cockatoo flesh, and pulled out scores of the fish; Godfrey, whose skill in such matters is very great, accounting for over a hundred in a very short time. These were very welcome, for we had run out of meat for some days past, nor had we been able to shoot any birds or beasts.

Pigeons and other birds came in small quantities to drink, and kangaroo tracks were numerous; in spite, however, of braving the mosquitoes near the water by sitting up all night, we did not even get a shot. Charlie set some snares with equal ill-success, but the following day Godfrey got a fine kangaroo, and a carpet-snake over nine feet in length. What we did not eat of the former at the first sitting, was dried in strips in the sun and kept for future use.

Here we also made acquaintance with the native bee, and would certainly have been counted mad by any stranger who could have seen us sitting in the smoke of a fire in the broiling sun! This was the only way to escape them; not that they sting, on the contrary they are quite harmless, and content themselves by slowly crawling all over one, up one's sleeve, down one's neck, and everywhere in hundreds, sucking up what moisture they may — what an excellent flavour their honey must have!

On a gum-tree near the pool some initials were carved, and near them a neatly executed kangaroo. The second name I recognised as that of Billy Janet, the first to find alluvial gold at Lake Darlot. He was one of the Kimberley prospectors in the old days of the '87 rush. Keeping north from the Janet Creek we crossed stony tablelands timbered with gums, and numerous ravines and small creeks, until, on following down a nicely grassed gorge with a creek running through it, we struck the dry bed of the Mary River on November 25th. Henceforth our path lay through pleasant places; shady trees, long grass, and frequent pools of water in the shingly beds of the creeks made a welcome change after the awful desolation of the desert. Indications of white men were now constantly met with — marked trees, old camps, and horse-tracks. Striking north from the Mary, over plains of spinifex and grass, passing many queer, fort-like hills, we reached the Margaret River, a noble creek, even when dry as we saw it. Nice grass plains extend along its banks, and the timber and bush is alive with the sounds of birds, whose bright plumage was indeed good to look upon. Cockatoos and parrots of the most gorgeous colouring darted here and there amongst the trees, and every now and then a swamp-pheasant would fly shrieking from the branches above.

Part V: The Outward Journey

Chapter XIV: Death of Stansmore

Where the Margaret River forces its way through the Ramsay Range, a fine pool enclosed between two steep rocks has been formed. This is a permanent pool, and abounds in fish of various kinds. Above and below it the river was merely a dry expanse of gravel and shingle; a month later it was a roaring torrent, in places twenty feet deep. Close to the pool we noticed an old dray road, the old road to Mount Dockrell. I asked Warri where he supposed it led to, and he answered "Coolgardie!" Curious that one impossible to bush in a short distance should be so ludicrously out of his reckoning. Time now being no object, since the numerous ducks and fish supplied us with food, we camped for two days at the pool, enjoying its luxuries to the full. Our larder contained a bucketful of cold boiled ducks, a turkey, and numerous catfish and bream — rather a change from the sand-ridges! As to bathing, we felt inclined to sit all day in the water. I think we enjoyed ourselves more at that pool than any of us could remember having done for a long time. The desert was forgotten, and only looked back upon as a hard task finished.

All were as happy and cheerful as could be, speculating as to what sort of place Hall's Creek was, and in what way our sudden appearance would affect the inhabitants. Charlie was sure that they would receive us with open arms and banquet us, the lord mayor and the city band would meet us, and a lot more chaff of the kind. Only eight miles, I reckoned, lay between us and the telegraph line and the Derby-to-Hall's-Creek road; and we made bets in fun whether we should reach the line before or after a certain hour; as we started our march on the 30th there was no happier little band in the wide world. Charlie followed one side of the river, carrying the gun, as we meant to celebrate the arrival at the telegraph line with a pot of kangaroo-tail soup. To pass the ridge of rock, the end of the Ramsay Range, it was necessary for us with the camels to keep wide of the river bank and descend a steep little gorge. As we started to go down we saw some kangaroos jumping off towards Charlie, and presently heard a shot. A shout from us elicited no reply, so we concluded he had missed, and continued on our march.

When we reached the river bank again, I looked out for Charlie, but somebody said he was across the river-bed in the long grass. After about an hour's travel it struck me that he should have rejoined us, or else that he had shot the kangaroo and was delayed by skinning or carrying it. No thought of any mishap entered my head, for a prolonged absence of one or other of us was of common occurrence. However, after another half-hour a nervous feeling came over me, and, stopping the camels, I sent Warri back to see what Charlie was about. Before very long Warri returned, hardly able to speak from fear mixed with sorrow.

"What on earth's come over the boy?" I said. Then he blurted out, "Charlie dead, I think." "Good God! Are you sure? — did you speak to him, or touch him?" I asked, as we ran back together, the rest with the camels following behind. "Him dead, lie 'long a rock — quite still," Warri answered, and he had not spoken or touched him. Panting and anxious — though even then I thought of nothing worse than a sprained ankle, and a faint in consequence — we arrived at the foot of the rocks where Charlie had last been seen, and whence the sound of the gunshot had come. Right above us, caught by a ledge on the face of the rock, fifty feet from the ground, I saw Charlie lying, and clambering up somehow at full speed, reached his side.

Good God! Warri had spoken a true word. There was no spark of life in the poor old fellow. What a blow! What an awful shock! What a calamity! I sat dazed, unable to realise what had happened, until roused by a shout from below: "Is he hurt? — badly? — not DEAD!" "As a stone," I answered; and that was what we felt in our hearts, a dull weight, pressing all sense or strength from us.

How to describe that sad scene? Poor old Charlie! one of the best and truest men that God ever blessed with life; such a fine manly character; so honest and generous — a man whose life might stand as an example for any in the land to follow; from whose mouth I never heard an oath or coarse word, and yet one whose life was spent amongst all classes, in all corners of Australia; such a true mate, and faithful, loyal companion — here his body lay, the figure of strength and power, he who had been most cheerful of us all. It seemed so hard, to die thus, the journey done, his share in the labour so nobly borne and patiently executed; the desert crossed, and now to be cut off on the edge of the land of promise! Ah well, it was better so than a lingering death in the desert, a swift and sudden call instead of perhaps slow tortures of thirst and starvation! Poor Charlie! the call of death is one that none of us may fail to heed; I only pray that when I am summoned to the "great unknown" I may be as fit to meet my Maker as you were.

It was easy to see how the accident had happened; the marks on the rock and the gun were soon deciphered. He was carrying the gun by the muzzle balanced on his shoulder, the stock to the rear; on climbing down a steep place, his heels — his boots had iron heel plates — slipped, he fell with his back to the rock; at the same time the gun was canted forward, fell right over, striking the hammer of one barrel on the rock at his feet — the cartridge exploded, and the charge entered his body just below the heart. Death must have been instantaneous and painless, for on his face was a peaceful smile, and he had never moved, for no blood was showing except near the wound. An accident that might have happened to any one, not through carelessness, for the gun was half-cock, but because his time had come.

We buried him between the rocks and the river at the foot of a large gum tree. No fine tombstone marked his grave, only a rough cross, and above him I carved his initials on the tree:

C. W. S.
30.11.96.

 Charles W. Stansmore

There we laid him to rest in silence, for who was I that I should read holy words over him? "Goodbye, Charlie, old man, God bless you!" we said, as in sorrow we turned away. The tragedy had been so swift, so unexpected, that we were all unmanned; tears would come, and we wept as only men can weep. A few months past I heard that a brass plate sent by Charlie's brothers had arrived, and had been placed on the tree by Warden Cummins, as he had promised me.

In due course we reached the telegraph line, without enthusiasm or interest, and turned along the road to Hall's Creek with hardly a word. Stony hills and grass plains and numerous small creeks followed one another as our march proceeded, and that night, the first in December, we experienced a Kimberley storm. The rain started about 2 a.m., and in twenty minutes the country was a sea of water; our camp was flooded, and blankets and packs soaked through and through. The next morning every creek was running a banker and every plain was a bog. However, the camels behaved well and forded the streams without any fuss. That day we met some half-civilised natives, who gave us much useful information about Hall's Creek. With them we bartered a plug of tobacco for a kangaroo tail, for we wanted meat and they a smoke. They had just killed the animal, and were roasting it whole, *holus-bolus*, unskinned and undressed. We saw several mobs of grey kangaroos feeding in the timber — queer, uncanny beasts, pretty enough when they jump along, but very quaint when feeding, as they tuck their great hind legs up to try and make them match the fore.

On December 4th we arrived at Hall's Creek; the first man we met was Sergeant Brophy, of the Police — the first white face we had seen since July 21st. At Hall's Creek at last, after a somewhat prolonged journey of 1,413 miles, counting all deviations.

Part V: The Outward Journey

Chapter XV: Wells Exploring Expedition

The first news that we heard was of the disaster that the expedition under Mr. L. A. Wells had met with. Two of his party were missing, and it was feared that they had met with some serious mishap. Fortunately Hall's Creek can boast of telegraphic communication with Derby and Wyndham on the coast, and from thence to Perth; so that I lost no time in letting Wells know of our arrival, that we had seen no traces of the lost men, and that we were ready to do whatever he, who knew all particulars of the matter, should think best. When I told Breaden that I had put my camels and party at Wells' disposal, he said at once that he was ready to go, but that in his opinion the camels were not fit to do another week's journey; Godfrey, too, was as ready. Indeed it would have been strange if we, who had so lately come through the desert, and knew its dangers, had not been eager to help the poor fellows in distress, although from the first we were morally certain there could be no hope for them; the only theory compatible with their being still alive, was that they were camped at some water easy of access, and were waiting for relief, keeping themselves from starvation by eating camel-flesh.

For many reasons, that need not be gone into, it was thought best by the promoters of the expedition in Adelaide that we should remain where we were; and, thanking me very heartily for our proffered assistance, they assured me they would be very glad to avail themselves of it should the search-parties already in the field meet with no success. Had we felt any hope whatever of the men being alive we should certainly have started off then and there; since, however, the chances of finding any but dead men were so very infinitesimal, I agreed to wait and to put myself at their command for a given time. It will be as well to give here a short account, as gathered from letters from Wells and others to the newspapers, of the unfortunate expedition.

This expedition, fitted out partly by the Royal Geographical Society, South Australia, and partly by a Mr. Calvert, was under command of L. A. Wells, who was surveyor to the Elder Expedition (1891-92). The party, besides the leader, consisted of his cousin, C. F. Wells, G. A. Keartland, G. L. Jones, another white man as cook, two Afghans, and one black-boy, with twenty-five camels. The objects of this expedition were much the same as those of my own, viz., to ascertain the nature of the country still unexplored in the central portions of West Australia, "hopes being entertained of the possibility of opening up a valuable stock route from the Northern Territory to the West Australian Goldfields, and of discovering much auriferous country" (vide *Adelaide Observer*, June 6, 1896). A collection of the flora and fauna was to be made, as well as a map of the country passed through. The expedition started from Cue, Murchison district, left civilisation at Lake Way, and travelled in a North-Easterly direction from there to Lake Augusta, thence in a Northerly direction past Joanna Springs to the Fitzroy River. Thus their course was almost parallel to our upgoing journey, and some 150 to 200 miles to the westward, nearer the coast. The class of country encountered was similar to that already described by me — that is sand, undulating and in ridges.

A well, since called "Separation Well," was found in long. 123 degrees 53 minutes, lat. 22 degrees 51 minutes. At this point the expedition split up: Charles Wells and G. L. Jones, with three camels, were to make a flying trip ninety miles to the Westward; then, turning North-East, were to cut the tracks of the main party, who were to travel nearly due North.

The rendezvous was fixed at or near Joanna Springs — which place, however, the leader failed to find (until some months afterwards, when he proved them to have been placed on the chart some eighteen miles too far West by Colonel Warburton in 1873, who in his diary doubts the accuracy of the position assigned to the spring by himself, and remarks, "What matter in such country as this?"). When the latitude of the spring was reached, about a day and a half was spent in searching to the east and west without result. A native smoke was seen to the eastward, but the leader failed to reach it.

The camels were on the brink of collapse, many had already collapsed, and the leader considered that by further search for the spring he would be bringing almost certain death on the whole party. Therefore, abandoning all collections, and in fact everything except just enough to keep him and his companions alive, he pushed on for the Fitzroy River — travelling by night and camping in the day — a distance of 170 miles. They arrived at the Fitzroy River after the greatest difficulties, with one bucket of water left, and only two camels fit to carry even the lightest packs.

The flying party were daily expected, for the arrangement had been that, failing a meeting at Joanna Springs, both parties were to push on to the Fitzroy. Days passed, however, and no flying party appeared.

Before long fears as to their safety began to grow, and Mr. Wells made numerous attempts to return on his tracks. The heat, however, was too much for his camels, and he was unable to penetrate to any distance. Mr. Rudall in the meantime, who had been surveying in the Nor'-West, was despatched by the Western Australia Government to make a search from the West. He had a good base in the Oakover River, and pushed out as far as Separation Well. Nothing, however, came of his gallant efforts, for he was misled, not only by lying natives, but by the tracks of camels and men, which subsequently turned out to be those of prospectors. His journey, however, had many useful results, for he discovered a new creek running out into the desert (Rudall River), and the existence of auriferous country north of the Ophthalmia Range, besides confirming Gregory's account of the country East of the Oakover.

It was not until April, 1897, that Mr. Wells found the bodies of his cousin, Charles Wells, and George Jones. From their diaries (so much of them at least as was published) the dreadful tale of suffering can be traced. It appears that on leaving the main party they travelled westward as directed, and started to turn North-East to cut the tracks of the others. Before many miles on the fresh course, however, they for some reason changed their minds and retraced their steps to Separation Well. From this point they started to follow the main party, but before long they seem to have become sick and exhausted, and the camels to show signs of collapse. Later we read that, exhausted from heat, hardship, and thirst, they lay down, each in the scanty shade of a gum tree; that the camels wandered away too far for them to follow; efforts to recover the stragglers only ended in their falling faint to the ground, and so, deserted by their means of transport, without water, without hope, these two poor fellows laid down to die, and added their names to the long roll of brave but unfortunate men whose lives have been claimed by the wild bush of Australia.

What a death! Alone in that vast sea of sand — hundreds of miles from family or friends — alone absolutely! not a sign of life around them — no bird or beast to tell them that life existed for any — no sound to break the stillness of that ghastly wilderness — no green grass or trees to relieve the monotony of the sand — nothing but the eternal spinifex and a few shrunken stems of trees that have been — no shade from the burning sun — above them the clear sky only clouded by death! slow, cruel death, and yet in their stout hearts love and courage! Poor fellows! they died like men, with a message written by dying fingers for those they left to mourn them — a message full of affection, expressing no fear of death, but perfect faith in God. So might all mothers be content to see their sons die — when their time comes.

They had died, it appears, too soon for any aid to have reached them. Even had Mr. Wells been able to turn back on his tracks at once on arrival at the Fitzroy, it is doubtful if he could have been in time to give any help to his suffering comrades.

The bodies were taken to Adelaide, where the whole country joined in doing honour to the dead.

Part V: The Outward Journey

Chapter XVI: Kimberley

Since we were not to retackle the sand forthwith, we laid ourselves out to rest and do nothing to the very best of our ability. This resolve was made easy of execution, for no sooner had the Warden, Mr. Cummins, heard of our arrival, than he invited us to his house, where we remained during our stay in Hall's Creek, and met with so much kindness and hospitality that we felt more than ever pleased that we had arrived at this out-of-the-way spot by a rather novel route.

Since Kimberley (excepting the South African district) must be an unknown name to the majority of English readers, and since it is one of the most valuable portions of West Australia, it deserves more than passing mention.

Hall's Creek, named after the first prospector who found payable gold in the district, is the official centre of the once populous Kimberley goldfields, and the seat of justice, law, and order for the East Kimberley division.

Attention was first drawn to this part of the Colony by the report of Alexander Forrest, who discovered the Fitzroy, Margaret, and other rivers; but it was not the pastoral land described by him that caused any influx of population. Gold was the lure. The existence of gold was discovered by Mr. Hardman, geologist, attached to a Government survey-party under Mr. Johnston (now Surveyor-General), and, though he found no more than colours, it is a remarkable fact that gold has since been discovered in few places that were not mentioned by him. Numerous "overlanders" and prospectors soon followed; indeed some preceded this expedition, for Mr. Johnston has told me that he found marked trees in more than one place. Who marked them was never ascertained, but it was supposed that a party of overlanders from Queensland, who were known to have perished, were responsible for them.

In 1886 payable gold was found, and during that and the following year one of the largest and most unprofitable "rushes" known in Australia set in for the newly discovered alluvial field. The sinking being shallow, what ground there was, was soon worked out, and before long the rush set back again as rapidly as it had come, the goldfield was condemned as a duffer, and left to the few faithful fossickers who have made a living there to this day. The alluvial gold was the great bait; of this but little was found, and to reefing no attention to speak of was given, so that at the present time miles upon miles of quartz reefs, blows, leaders, and veins are untouched and untested as they were before the rush of 1886. No one can say what systematic prospecting might disclose in this neglected corner of the Colony. There are many countries less favoured for cheap mining; Kimberley is blessed with an abundant rainfall, and the district contains some of the finest pasture-lands in Australia.

A scarcity of good mining timber, the remoteness of the district from settled parts, and the bad name that has been bestowed upon it, are the disadvantages under which the goldfield labours. Nevertheless two batteries are working at the present day, and a good find by some old fossicker is not so rare.

Setting aside the question of gold-discoveries, which may or may not be made, this district has a great future before it to be derived from the raising of stock, cattle, sheep, and horses. So far only a limited area of country has been taken up — that is to say, the country in the valleys of the Ord, Margaret, and Fitzroy Rivers and their tributaries. There still remains, however, a large tract lying between those rivers and the most Northerly point of the Colony as yet unoccupied, and some of it even unexplored. One or two prospectors have passed through a portion of it, and they speak well of its pastoral and, possibly, auriferous value.

Cut off, as it is, by the desert, the district has the disadvantage of none but sea communication with the rest of the Colony. This necessitates the double shipment of live stock, once at either port, Derby or Wyndham, after they have been driven so far from the stations, and once again at Fremantle. A coastal stock route is debarred by the poverty of the country between Derby and the De Grey River, and a direct stock route through the desert is manifestly impracticable. It seems to me that too little attention has been given to horse-breeding, and that a remunerative trade might be carried on between Kimberley and India, to which this district is nearer than any other part of Australia.

What horses are bred, though otherwise excellent, are small — a defect that should easily be remedied. The cattle, too, are rather on the small side, and this again, by more careful attention to breeding, could be improved upon.

Hall's Creek is by no means a large town; in fact, it consists of exactly nine buildings — post and telegraph office and Warden's office and court, Warden's house, hospital, gaol, police-station, sergeant's house, butcher's shop and house, store, and hotel.

Besides these there are several nomadic dwellings, such as tents, bush humpies, and drays.

A house is a luxury, and some of the oldest residents have never built one. "Here to-day and gone to-morrow, what's the good of a house?" was the answer I got from one who had only been there for ten years!

Mud-brick walls and corrugated-iron roofs is the style of architecture in general vogue. The inhabitants are not many, as may be supposed, but those there are simply overflow with hospitality and good spirits. One and all were as pleased to see us, and have us live amongst them, as if we had been old friends. The population is very variable; the surrounding district contains some fifty or sixty fossickers, who come into town at intervals to get fresh supplies of flour and salt beef — the one and only diet of the bushmen in these parts, who, though very rarely seeing vegetables, are for the most part strong and healthy. Sometimes cases of scurvy, or a kindred disease, occur; one poor chap was brought in whilst we were there, very ill indeed. I happened to be up at the hospital, and asked the orderly (there was no doctor) what he would do for him in the way of nourishing food. "Well," said he, looking very wise, "I think a little salt beef will meet the case." And such would indeed have been his diet if I had not luckily had some Liebig's Extract; for the town was in a state verging on famine, dependent as it is on the whims of "packers" and teamsters, who bring provisions from the coast, nearly three hundred miles, by road. Twice a year waggons arrive; for the rest everything is brought per horseback, and when the rains are on, and the rivers running, their load is as often as not considerably damaged by immersion in the water.

A monthly mail, however, and the telegraph line places the community much nearer civilised parts than its geographical position would lead one to suppose. The arrival of the mail, or of the packers, is a great event, more especially since no one knows what they may bring. Thus a train of pack-horses arrived at a time when flour was badly needed, but each load consisted of either sugar or lager-beer — both excellent articles but hardly adaptable to bread-making. The climate, situation, surroundings, and want of means of recreation all combine to make the publican's business a lucrative one. When, as sometimes happens, a fossicker comes in with a "shammy" full of gold, and lays himself out to make himself and every one else happy, then indeed the hotel-keeper's harvest is a rich one. And since nobody cares much whether he buys his liquor, or makes it of red-pepper, kerosene, tobacco, methylated spirits, and what not, the publican's outlay in "only the best brands" need not be excessive.

Christmas and New Year's Day were, of course, great days of revel; athletic sports were held, and horse-races. The latter were not quite a success; the entries were very few, and the meeting was nearly resolving itself into a prize-fight when one owner lodged a complaint against the winner. As a rule the race-meetings are better attended; every bush township has its meetings throughout the continent, and, in remote districts, there are men who entirely "live on the game." That is to say, they travel from place to place with a mob of pack-horses, amongst which, more or less disguised by their packs, are some fast ones, with which they surprise the community. These men, though great scoundrels, are considered to be earning a legitimate living, since no man need gamble with them unless he likes; if he is taken in by them he has himself to thank.

Christmas Eve is celebrated by a performance known as "tin-kettling," in which all join. Each arms himself with a dish, or empty tin, which he beats violently with a stick. To the tune of this lovely music the party marches from house to house, and at each demands drink of some kind, which is always forthcoming. Thus the old institution of Christmas-waits is supported, even in this far corner of the world.

Part V: The Outward Journey

Chapter XVII: Aboriginals at Hall's Creek

It may not at first be very clear what the gaol and police force are used for, since the white population numbers so few. However, the aboriginals are pretty numerous throughout Kimberley, and are a constant source of vexation and annoyance to the squatters, whose cattle are frequently killed and driven wild by native depredators. A squatter, far from being allowed to take the law into his own hands, even when he catches the blacks in the act of slaying his cattle — not only for food but as often as not for mere devilment — has to ride into Hall's Creek and report to the police, and so gives time for the offenders to disappear. The troopers, when they do make a capture of the culprits, bring them in on chains, to the police quarters. By the Warden, through a tame boy as interpreter, they are tried, and either acquitted and sent back to their country or sentenced to a turn of imprisonment and handed over to the gaoler. In gaol they have a remarkably good time, fed upon beef, bread, jam, and water, and made to do useful work, such as drawing and carrying water, making roads, &c. They work in small chain-gangs — a necessary precaution since there is only one gaoler to perhaps fifteen prisoners — are clothed in felt hats and short canvas kilts, and except that they are deprived of their freedom have probably as comfortable a time as they ever had during their lives.

From time to time there have been grave accusations of cruelty made by well-meaning busybodies against the squatters of the North and North-West. Occasional cases have been proved beyond all question, cases of the most revolting brutality. But from these exceptional instances it is hardly fair to class the whole squatting population as savage. ruffians. Since I have had the opportunity of seeing what treatment is meted out I feel it is a duty to give every prominence to what has come under my notice. First of all, let us take it for granted that the white men's civilisation must advance; that, I suppose, most will admit. This being the case, what becomes of the aboriginal? He is driven from his hunting-grounds and retaliates by slaughtering the invading cattle. What steps is the white pioneer, who may have no more than one companion, to take to protect his own? If he quietly submits his herd will be wiped out, and he and his mate afterwards. By inspiring fear alone is he able to hold his position. He must therefore either use his rifle and say nothing about it, or send perhaps 150 miles for the troopers. After a time, during which he carries his life in his hands — for a couple of hundred natives, savage and treacherous, are not the pleasantest neighbours — he succeeds in convincing the natives that he intends to stop where he is. What then do they do? Do they move to fresh hunting-grounds? They might, for there is ample room. No, they prefer to live round about the station, a source of constant anxiety and annoyance. Consequently we find to-day a large number of natives permanently camped round every homestead, living on the squatter's bounty. Too lazy to hunt, too idle and useless to work, they loaf about the place, living on the meat that is given them on killing-days, and on figs and seeds, when in season, between times. Thus, though the squatter takes their country he feeds them for ever after. A smart boy may be trained and partially educated, and becomes useful amongst the horses and so forth, and some few are always employed about the station — the rest just lie about and gorge themselves at the slaughter-yards, and then wait until they can again do so.

It has been suggested that reserves should be set apart for the dispossessed natives. This would, in the opinion of those best able to express one, never succeed, for once the white man is established the blacks will collect round him, and though, as I have mentioned, there remains more than half the Kimberley division untouched by whites, forming a reserve ready to hand, yet the natives prefer to live a hand-to-mouth existence where food can be obtained without trouble, rather than retreat into another region where game abounds, and there continue their existence as wandering savages. Round Hall's Creek there is always a camp of blacks, varying from twenty to fifty or one hundred, who live as best they can without hunting.

On Christmas Day a hundred or so rolled up to receive the Aboriginal Board's liberal bounty — a Board fortunately now reconstructed, for it was continually the cause of much friction between the squatters, the Government, and itself, in the days when it was not controlled by the Government, as it now is. Six pounds sterling was set aside for the Warden to provide food and raiment for the natives under his jurisdiction. Six pounds per annum per two thousand aboriginals — for such is their reputed number — seems hardly adequate. Perhaps if the gentlemen responsible for this state of affairs had concerned themselves more about the aboriginals, and less about the supposed barbaric cruelty of the squatters, the objects of their mission would have been better served. However, whilst the black-fellow must remain content with his scanty allowance, it is found expedient to send an inexperienced youth, fresh from England, from place to place to make a report on the treatment of the aboriginals, at a salary of 500 pounds a year. And a fine collection of yarns he produced — for naturally no one could resist "pulling his leg" to the last degree! However, this question has at last been put into the hands of those best calculated to know something about it; for though the Government is neither perfect nor infallible, yet the colonists are likely to understand a purely local matter better than a Board of gentlemen lately from home.

They were a merry lot of people, the blacks round Hall's Creek, and appeared to see the best sides of a deadly dull existence. Their ways and habits are now so mingled with ideas gathered from the whites that they are not worth much attention. Dancing is their great amusement, and though on Christmas Day we made them compete in running, jumping, and spear-throwing, they take but little interest in such recreations. Though known to Australian readers, a description of such a dance may prove of interest to some in the old country.

"A CORROBOREE," OR NATIVE DANCE.

The entertainment begins after sundown, and on special occasions may be kept up for two or three days and nights in succession. A moonlit night is nearly always made the occasion for a corroboree, to which no significance is attached, and which may be simply held for the amusement the actual performance affords.

Descriptions of the great dances attendant on the initiation of a boy into manhood, and its accompanying brutal rites, find a more suitable place in scientific works than in a book intended for the general reader. I will therefore merely describe some of the dances which are performed for entertainment.

The word corroboree is applied equally to the dance, the whole festival, or the actual chant which accompanies the dancing.

Men and women, the men especially, deck themselves out with tufts of emu feathers, fastened in the hair or tied round the arm, or stuck in the waist-belt of plaited hair; paint their bodies with a white paint or wash made from "Kopi" (gypsum similar to that found by the shores of salt lakes), with an occasional dab of red ochre (paint made from a sandstone impregnated with iron), and fix up their hair into a sort of mop bound back by bands of string. Thus bedecked and painted, and carrying their spears and boomerangs, they present a rather weird appearance.

File:Spinifex and Sand Illustration 29.jpg Native preparing for the Emu-Dance [Missing image]

A flat, clear space being chosen, the audience seat themselves, men and women, who, unless the moon is bright, light fires, which they replenish from time to time. The dancers are all men, young warriors and older men, but no greybeards. The orchestra consists of some half-dozen men, who clap together two sticks or boomerangs; in time to this "music" a wailing dirge is chanted over and over again, now rising in spasmodic jerks and yelled forth with fierce vehemence, now falling to a prolonged mumbled plaint. Keeping time to the sticks, the women smack their thighs with great energy. The monotonous chant may have little or no sense, and may be merely the repetition of one sentence, such as "Good fella, white fella, sit down 'longa Hall's Creek," or something with an equally silly meaning. The dancers in the meantime go through all sorts of queer movements and pantomimes. First, we may have the kangaroo corroboree, in which a man hops towards the musicians and back again, to be followed in turn by every other dancer and finally by the whole lot, who advance hopping together, ending up with a wild yell, in which all join.

Then we may have the emu-corroboree, where each in his turn stalks solemnly around with the right arm raised, with elbow bent, wrist and hand horizontal and poked backwards and forwards, to represent the emu's neck and head. The left hand held behind the back, like that of a shy official expecting a tip, stands for the emu's tail. Thus they advance slowly and jerkily with back bent and arm pointing now this way, now that, like an inquisitive emu who is not sure of his ground.

Next the mallee-hen builds her nest, and each dancer comes forward at a mincing trot, in his hands a few twigs and leaves, which he deposits in front of the "orchestra," and, having built his nest, retires. And so they go on mimicking with laughable accuracy the more common beasts and birds.

The most comical dance in which they all joined — that is all the dancers — was one in which they stood on tiptoe, with knees bent and shaking together as if with fear, then giving forth a sort of hissing noise, through fiercely clenched teeth, they quickly advanced in three or four lines and retired trotting backwards. This ended with a prolonged howl and shrieks of laughter. The energy with which they dance is extraordinary — shaking their spears and grunting, they advance with knees raised, like high-stepping horses, until the thigh is almost horizontal, now one leg now the other, with a will, and then one, two, down come the feet together with a thud, the dancers striking their spears in the ground, growling out savagely a sound that I can only express as "woomph, woomph" — with what a smack their flat feet meet the ground, and what a shrieking yell goes up from all throats as they stop!

To enliven the performance they use flat carved sticks, some eight inches long, and of a pointed oval shape. Through a hole in one point they thread a string, with which the stick is rapidly swung round, making a booming noise — "Bull-roarers" is the general white-fellows' name for them. Amongst some native prisoners brought in from the Sturt I saw a primitive wooden horn, on which a sort of blast could be blown. No doubt this, too, has its place in their performances.

I am told they keep up these corroborees as long as three days and nights, though certainly not dancing all the time. Probably the stick clapping is kept up by relays of performers. I have heard the chant go on all one night and well into the next day, with hardly a break.

Hall's Creek is a great place for corroborees, for there are gathered together boys from all parts of Central Australia, Northern Territory, and Queensland, brought by coastal overlanders. These boys all know different chants and dances, and are consequently in great request at the local black-fellows' evening parties. Warri told me he had learnt several new songs; however, they appeared to my evidently untrained ear to be all exactly alike.

We were to have had a very swell festival at Christmas, but it somehow fell through. I fancy the blacks were not given sufficient notice.

The blacks, in addition to these simple festive gatherings, have solemn dances for the purpose of promoting the growth of edible seeds and roots, of increasing the rainfall, or the numbers of the animals and reptiles on which they feed. But more important still are those connected with their barbarous, but sacred, rites and ceremonials.

Part V: The Outward Journey

Chapter XVIII: Preparations for the Return Journey

Had I known how long our stay in the North was to be, I should have taken the opportunity of further studying the natives and their habits, and should certainly have visited them in their wild homes in the unknown portion of Kimberley. As it was I daily expected a message asking me to start in search of the missing men, and held myself in readiness accordingly. Our small caravan, now further reduced by the death of Czar — a sad loss, for he was one of my old friends, and one of the staunchest camels I have known (together we had seen many a tough bit of work); he fell down a steep gully at night, poor old beast, and so injured himself that he died almost immediately — was increased by the purchase of three horses, with which I intended to carry out my plan of search; since, however, it was never instituted, I need not explain its nature. It sufficiently accounts for the presence of horses in the caravan with which the return journey was made.

As time dragged on it became clear that the missing men could no longer be living, and since there were two search parties already in the field, I felt that I was only wasting time by staying longer in idleness. We were too far off to make any search except by a protracted expedition, and, since I was morally sure of the men's death, I did not feel called upon to expose my party to the risks of the desert when no useful object could be accomplished. Had the intervening country been unknown I should have been quite ready to start forth, for in that case, whatever the result of the search, I should have felt rewarded for any losses incurred, by the knowledge that we had been the means of opening up a further tract of an unexplored region. As it was we should only have followed a route previously traversed by Warburton, from which, unless we achieved the melancholy satisfaction of finding the scene of the disaster, no useful results could follow. I determined, therefore, to leave the search to those who could best afford the time and expense, and set about planning our return to Coolgardie. We had four routes open to us — either the road to Derby and thence by steamer: the road to Derby and thence along the coastal telegraph line: the way we had come: and an entirely new route, taking our chances of the desert. The first was dismissed as feeble, the second as useless, and the third as idiotic. Therefore the fourth remained, and though it was natural enough for me to wish to win distinction in the world of travel (and I daresay this was the motive that inspired me), surely it speaks well for them indeed, that Breaden and Massie were willing to accompany me.

Without the slightest hesitation, though knowing full well what lay before us, that we might even encounter worse difficulties than before, without any thought of prospective gain — for their salary was no fortune — they signified their readiness to return by whatever route I proposed. This is a point that I should like to make clear to all who may read this, for it is indicative of a trait often lost sight of by those accustomed to having, in novels and so forth, the more mercenary side of the Australian's character pointed out to them. A common subject of speculation is whether or no Australians would make good soldiers; as to that my belief is, that once they felt confidence in their officers none could make more loyal or willing troops; without that confidence they would be ill to manage, for the Australian is not the man to obey another, merely because he is in authority — first he must prove himself fit to have that authority.

If, therefore, we are deserving of any credit for again tackling the sand, let it be remembered that my companions are more worthy of it than their leader — for they had nothing to gain, whilst I had at least the distinction of leaving my name upon the map — and though I made plans, without good and true men I could not have carried them out. There seemed to me to be a slight chance of finding better country to the eastward of our first route, and, besides the geographical interest, there would result the proof of the practicability or otherwise of a stock route to the southern goldfields — a route which would be such a boon to the Kimberley squatters. I may as well state at once that such a route is quite out of the question, and that I would hesitate to undertake the journey with a mob of more than twenty camels, let alone cattle.

Fortunately I was able to purchase three more camels, the property of the South Australian Government, which Mr. Buchanan had brought from the Northern Territory for the purpose of looking for a stock route. However, a day or two beyond the end of Sturt Creek satisfied him as to the impracticability of the scheme, and he returned to Flora Valley, a cattle station close to Hall's Creek, that is to say, twenty-five miles away. At the time of our arrival Mr. Buchanan was out with Mr. Wells, and did most valuable service in the search for the missing men. After his return he was very glad to get the camels, which he neither liked nor understood, off his hands.

With eight camels and three horses our caravan was brought up to strength. In the matter of provisioning, equipment, and way of travelling, I made some alteration. Everything was considered with a view to lightness, therefore only absolute necessaries were carried. All tools, except those used in "soak-sucking," and so forth, were discarded; the provisions consisted of salt beef (tinned meat being unprocurable), flour, tea, sugar, and a few tins of condensed milk (damaged and unfit for use in the ordinary way). All possible room was given to water-carrying appliances, so that we could carry in all about one hundred gallons. Had it not been for my former plans I should not have taken horses; but they are animals easier to buy than to sell, and would certainly be most useful if only we could find food and water to keep them alive. With sorrow and regret I had to part with Val, for only a few days before our departure she gave birth to a litter of pups, and had of course to be left behind. However, the Warden, to whom I gave her, promised to be kind to her, as indeed I am sure he has been — nevertheless it was a sad wrench. In her place I took a small mongrel which belonged to the Warden, an "Italian greyhound," as some one suggested, though I never saw a like breed! He rejoiced in the name of "Devil-devil," because, I suppose, he was quite black.

I made no attempt to replace poor Charlie Stansmore, since there were no men willing to come whom I should have cared to take. I cannot say enough in gratitude for the hospitality that we met with at Hall's Creek, from the Warden, whose guests we were the whole time, and every member of the small community. I shall look back with pleasure to our stay in that faraway spot.

Part V: The Outward Journey

Appendix to Part V: Some Native Weapons and Ceremonial Implements

[Refer to list of illustrations at the beginning of the text, (illustrations not included in text). Letters (A to O) refer to the illustrations]

1. SPEARS. — A. Of Desert native; B. Of Kimberley native; C. Method of throwing.

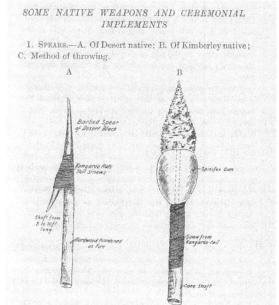

A,B Spears

A. The spear of the desert man is either sharp pointed, spatulate pointed, or barbed. They vary in length from 8 feet to 10 feet, and in diameter, at the head (the thickest portion), from 1/2 inch to 1 inch. As a rule, a man carries a sheaf of half a dozen or more.

B. In the Kimberley District the spears are of superior manufacture and much more deadly. The heads are made of quartz, or glass, or insulators from the telegraph line. Before the advent of the white man quartz only was used, and from it most delicately shaped spear-heads were made, the stone being either chipped or pressed. I fancy the former method is the one employed — so I have been told, though I never saw any spear-heads in process of manufacture.

Since the white man has settled a portion of Kimberley, glass bottles have come into great request amongst the natives, and most deadly weapons are made — spears that, I am told, will penetrate right through a cattle-beast, and which are themselves unimpaired unless they strike on a bone. When first the telegraph line from Derby to Hall's Creek and thence to Wyndham was constructed, constant damage used to be done to it by the natives who climbed the poles and smashed the insulators for spear-head making. So great a nuisance did this become that the Warden actually recommended the Government to place heaps of broken bottles at the foot of each pole, hoping by this means to save the insulators by supplying the natives with glass!

The stone or glass heads are firmly fixed in a lump of spinifex gum, and this is held firm on the shaft by kangaroo tail sinews. The shaft is of cane for half its length, the upper part being of bamboo, which is found on the banks of the northern rivers.

Up to a distance of eighty to one hundred yards the spears can be thrown with fair accuracy and great velocity.

The length of these spears varies from 10 feet to 15 feet. The one shown in sketch is of glass, and is one-half actual size.

In the Nor'-West (that is, the country lying between the Gascoyne and Oakover rivers), wooden spear-heads with enormous barbs are used. Sometimes the barbs are placed back to back, so that on entering a body they can be pulled neither forward nor back.

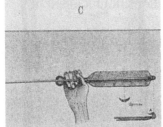
C woomera

C. THE WOOMERA (or Wommera) — the throwing-board — held in the hand as in sketch. The spears rest on the board, and are kept in place by the first finger and thumb and by the bone point A, which fits into a little hollow on the end of the shaft. The action of throwing resembles that of slinging a stone from a handkerchief. As the hand moves forward the spear is released by uplifting the forefinger, and the woomera remains in the hand. These boards vary in size and shape considerably; that shown in the sketch is from the northern portion of the desert. In the central portion the weapons are more crude and unfinished. In the handle end of the woomera a sharp flint is often set, forming a sort of chisel.

In Kimberley the long spears are thrown with narrow and light boards varying from 2 feet 6 inches to 3 feet 6 inches in length.

I believe that the method of holding the spear varies somewhat, some natives placing the handle of the woomera between the first and remaining fingers.

2. TOMAHAWKS. — D. Iron-headed; E. Stone-headed.

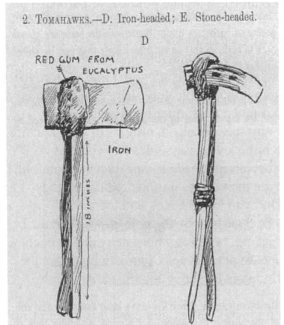
D Iron tomahawks

D. Pieces of iron, such as horseshoes, fragments of the tyres of wheels, and so forth, are traded from tribe to tribe for many hundreds of miles. Those shown in sketch were found about lat. 21 degrees 50 minutes, long. 126 degrees 30 minutes.

E. STONE TOMAHAWK — from Sturt Creek — given to me by Mr. Stretch.

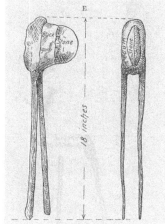

E Stone tomahawks

The head is of a very dark and hard green stone, ground to a fine edge, and is set between the two arms of the handle and held in place with spinifex gum.

The handle is formed by bending round (probably by means of fire) a single strip of wood.

The two arms of the handle are sometimes held together by a band of hair-string.

The iron tomahawks are similarly made.

3. BOOMERANGS. — These weapons are now so well known that a description of the ordinary pattern would be superfluous. However, near Dwarf Well we found one of uncommon shape; and until reading a book on a Queensland tribe I was unaware of its use, nor could I find any one who had seen one of like shape. The weapon in question is the BEAKED or HOOKED boomerang (F).

Mr. W. Roth, in his *"Ethnological Studies Among the North-West Central* Queensland Aborigines*, says:—*

It appears that when warding off a blow from a boomerang of any description the defence consists in holding forwards and vertically any stick or shield that comes to hand, and moving it more or less outwards, right or left as the case may be, thus causing the missile on contact to glance to one or the other side. The hook is intended to counteract the movement of defence by catching on the defending stick around which it swings and, with the increased impetus so produced, making sure of striking the one attacked.

File:Spinifex and Sand Illustration 34.jpg F Boomerangs [Missing Image]

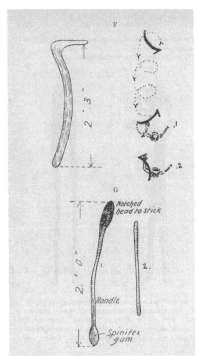

G Clubs and throwing sticks

4. CLUBS AND THROWING-STICKS (G).

1. The uses of these are sufficiently obvious to make a description unnecessary.

2. The throwing-sticks are used chiefly in hunting, and for guarding a blow from a boomerang. Most that I have seen were made of mulga (acacia) hardened by fire.

5. SHIELDS. — H. Of hard wood (Mulga); I. Of soft wood (Cork bark).

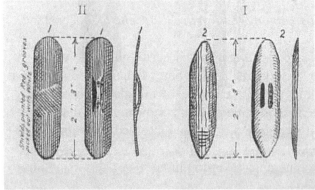

H,I Shields

H. The hard-wood shields are carved from a solid piece of mulga, are grooved to turn spears, and slightly curved for the same purpose. The handles stand out from the back. These were found as far North as lat. 25 degrees S.

I. The soft-wood shields found North of lat. 25 degrees are of about the same size, but are not grooved. Their faces are rounded; the handles are gouged out. It is interesting to notice how in each example the most serviceable shield has been made in the easiest way. The mulga splits into boards, and so cannot be obtained of any thickness, so flat shields are made; whereas the cork wood is a soft and very readily worked tree and can be carved and hacked into shape with the rudest implements, such as that shown in sketch (J).

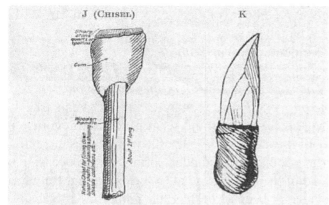

J,K Quartz knife

6. QUARTZ KNIFE (K).

With this exceedingly rough implement self-inflicted gashes on the chest and arms (presumably for ornamentation) are made. The rites of circumcision, and other initiatory operations, for the proper performance of which one would suppose the skill of a trained surgeon necessary, are carried out by means of this crude blade.

7. CEREMONIAL STICKS (L).

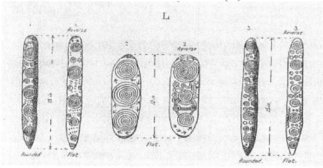

L Ceremonial sticks

In almost every camp flat sticks of various sizes, shapes, and carvings, similar to those shown above, were found. They were always carefully wrapped up in bark secured by hair-string. They are said to be used by the blacks in their several initiation ceremonies, but what their use or significance is, is not known. No tame boy (i.e., native who can speak English) will divulge their mysterious meaning. I have repeatedly asked about them, but have never succeeded in getting any answer beyond "I dunno, gin (or lubra) no more see 'em; gin see 'em, she tumble down quick fella." There must be some very queer superstition connected with them, since the ladies die on seeing them. Indeed, the black fellow has a somewhat arbitrary method of dealing with his gins, and should they be ill-advised enough to attempt to argue with him, does not wait to produce a flat stick, but silences them with a club.

8. RAIN-MAKING BOARDS.

M. Three of similar pattern found at Alexander Spring.

N. Found at Empress Spring hidden away with two similar to M.

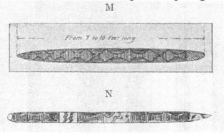

M,N Rain-making boards

With reference to these queer and rudely carved boards I received a letter from Mr. W. H. Cusack, of Roebourne, North-West Australia, in which he says:

... The implement you allude to is used by the Mopongullera, *or Rain-doctor, at their ceremony which they hold annually when they are making the rain. They are very rare, as there is only one every two hundred miles or so in the country. They are generally left at the rain ground, where you found yours, or placed in a cave, where the only one I have seen* in twenty-five years *was found. They are the most sacred implements they possess....* It would seem from the foregoing that we were specially lucky in seeing so many of these boards — viz., six within a distance of fifty miles — though it is possible that of the three found at Alexander Spring (on the occasion of our second visit) two might be identical with two of the three found at Empress Spring. Between our two visits to Alexander Spring there had evidently been a considerable gathering of blacks, and, considering the droughty appearance of the country, it seems feasible that on this occasion every available rain-making board was brought into use.

We were unfortunately unable to carry the Empress Spring boards, owing to their bulk and unwieldy shape.

From the other spot, however, seeing that we were nearing our journey's end, I brought one board — the only one unbroken — into civilisation. This I gave to Sir John Forrest, who in his journey across the Colony in 1874 found a similar board at the same place. In his journal he writes:

... I named it Alexander Spring, after my brother.... We also found about a dozen pieces of wood, some 6 feet long and 3 to 7 inches wide, and carved and trimmed up. All around were stones put up in forked trees. I believe it is the place where the right of circumcision is performed. Mr. Cusack's statement as to their extreme rarity in the Nor'-West, taken in conjunction with Sir John's experience and ours, would point to the strong reliance the natives must place on their Rain-doctor's abilities, for where the rainfall is comparatively great these boards are rare, while in the almost waterless interior, at a spot almost exactly in the centre of the Colony, nearly a dozen have been found. I would respectfully point out to the black-fellows how little their efforts have been successful, and would suggest the importation of several gross of boards, for the climate at present falls a long way short of perfection!

In the McDonnell Ranges (Central Australia) performers in the rain-dance wear on their heads a *long, erect, and ornamented structure of wood* (*Horn Scientific Expedition*, part iv.). This structure is not carved, but picked out with down made to adhere by blood, and is apparently some 3 to 4 feet long. From the length of the boards we found (one being 10 feet), I should say that some other method of using them must be in vogue amongst the desert tribes.

9. MESSAGE STICKS (O).

O Message sticks

These little sticks, rounded, carved, and painted with grease and red ochre, are known as either letter sticks or message sticks, and are common all over the continent. The carvings are supposed by some to represent the actual words of the message; by others it is held — and to this view I am inclined — that the sticks are tokens carried by a messenger to show that his words are authentic, and each stick belongs to one tribe or individual whose identity is shown by the carvings. They vary in length from 2 1/2 to 8 inches.

The sketch (O) shows the same stick turned three times.

Part VI: The Journey Home

Chapter I: Return Journey Begins

We left Hall's Creek, on our return journey, on March 22, 1897. Taking the road to Flora Valley we passed Brockman — where, by the way, lives a famous person, known by the unique title of "Mother Deadfinish." This good lady is the most curious of her sex that I have ever seen; now a little dried-up, wizened old woman of Heaven knows what age, she was in her younger days a lady of wonderful energy. She came overland from Queensland, accompanying her husband who, in the early days of the rush, sought to turn an honest penny by the sale of "sly grog." However, he died on the road, so his mourning widow carried through the job without him, and successfully withstood the trials of the journey, including heat, fever, and blacks. The latter were very numerous, and gave great trouble to the early diggers, spearing their horses and very often the men themselves. Many skirmishes ensued, and, so it is said, "Mother Deadfinish" handled her Winchester with the best of them! Eventually she arrived at the diggings, and has been there ever since, making a living by the sale of goat's milk, fowls, eggs, and a few vegetables. She is quite a character and worth talking to, but not always worth listening to; for her language is notorious; indeed, it is a recognised form of amusement for the diggers to bring into their conversation certain topics, such as the Warden, or the Police, who are so especially distasteful to her that ordinary language cannot express her feelings. In the same way that a boy delights to stir up a monkey and hear him chatter, the fossicker bent on recreation rouses the old lady to feats of swearing far beyond the scope of most people. No man has yet been found who could withstand her onslaught. I saw her angry once! She positively alarmed me; the three witches in Macbeth thrown into one would be of no account in comparison. Had she lived a century or two ago she would infallibly have been burnt.

Group of explorers

A few miles past the Brockman the auriferous country is cut off by what is locally known as the "Sandstone" — a sheer, wall-like range named the Albert Edward.

Just below the gorge where the Elvire River (a tributary of the Ord River) breaks through the range is situated Flora Valley Cattle Station, the property of the brothers Gordon. A charming little place, after the rains; the homestead stands on a high bank above the river, here fringed with high, shady trees. Beyond the homestead and the yards, a fine plain of grass stretches out, surrounded by rough and rocky hills. As charming as their little place were the owners, the most kind-hearted and hospitable folk it is possible to imagine. Here we stayed a few days to get some meat salted for our journey; nothing would satisfy the two brothers but that they must find the finest bullock on their run, kill it, and give it to us. Flora Valley is a great place for the blacks, who live there in scores, camped by the river, and fed by the kind-hearted squatters. Leaving the station and travelling South-East, our route lay through a few low hills, and then we came out upon the Denison Downs, most magnificent plains of grass.

The first few days of a journey are most unsettled, saddles do not fit, packs will not ride, the animals will not agree, and dozens of like annoyances. Our three new camels, Bluey, Hughie, and Wattie, were almost unmanageable; for not only had they been running loose for some time, but had never been well behaved or well looked after. Bluey was a dreadfully wild brute, and all but brought Warri, who was riding him, to grief; after bucking and plunging and trying all manner of tricks, he stampeded at his fullest speed, with his head towards some overhanging branches, under which he might have passed with impunity, but they must have crushed Warri *en route*.

Luckily I was just in time to get Highlander between the tree and the camel, and so saved a nasty accident. Besides these small troubles, Breaden and Godfrey were suffering agonies from "sandy blight," a sort of ophthalmia, which is made almost unbearable by the clouds of flies, the heat, the glare, and the dust. Breaden luckily was able to rest in a dark room at Flora Valley and recovered, or at least sufficiently so to be able to travel; Godfrey was very bad indeed, quite blind and helpless. At night we pitched his mosquito-net for him — for these insects are simply ravenous, and would eat one alive or send one mad in this part of the country — and made him as comfortable as possible; in the morning, until I had bathed his eyes with warm water he was blinded by the matter running from them: then during the day he sat blindfolded on The Monk, one of the horses — a most unpleasant condition for travelling.

File:Spinifex and Sand Illustration 42.jpg Just in time [Missing image]

Fortunately it was not for long, for soon we cut the Sturt Creek, and, following it, reached the Denison Downs Homestead — the last settlement to the southward, and I should say the most out-of-the-way habitation in Australia of to-day. The nearest neighbours are nearly one hundred miles by road, at Flora Valley; in every other direction there is a blank, hundreds of miles in extent. A solitary enough spot in all conscience! Yet for the last ten years two men have lived here, taking their chances of sickness, drought, floods, and natives; raising cattle in peace and contentment. Terribly rough, uncouth chaps, of course? Not a bit of it! — two men, gentlemen by birth and education, one the brother of a bishop, the other a man who started life as an artist in Paris. A rough life does not necessarily make a rough man, and here we have the proof, for Messrs. Stretch and Weekes are as fine a pair of gentlemen as need be. How they came to migrate to such a spot is soon told; they brought cattle over during the rush, hoping to make a large fortune; however, the rush "petered out," half their cattle died, and with the remainder they formed their station, and have remained there ever since, year by year increasing their herd, now numbering some four thousand head, and looking forward to the time when they hope to be well repaid for their labours. A large, single-roomed iron shed, on the bank of a fine big pool, is their home, and there with their flocks and herds they live, like the patriarchs of old, happy and contented. In fact, the only people I have ever come across, who seemed really satisfied with life are some of these far-away squatters.

Numerous natives were collected round the station, and about them Mr. Stretch told me many interesting things. Their marriage laws were expounded to me over and over again, but without pencil and paper nothing can be learned, so confusing are they.

It was not until my return that I worked out the following relationships, but I feel confident of their accuracy: —

MARRIAGE LAWS.

The aboriginals of Northern and Central Australia are governed in their social life by marriage laws and class systems of the most intricate kind. It is generally supposed that these laws have for their object prevention of consanguinity and incest. The laws are strictly adhered to, any offender against them being punished by death. I owe the information on this subject to Mr. Stretch, who took great pains to make clear to me the fundamental principles, from which I have worked out the various combinations. I have tried to arrange these laws and the relationships resulting from them in an intelligible form, and have been greatly aided by a paper by Mr. Gillen, published in the "Horn Scientific Expedition," on the McDonnell Range tribes. I was unable to get the tribal names, but this, for the purposes of explanation only, is unnecessary.

The aboriginals in question belong to the Eastern district of Kimberley generally, and more particularly to the Sturt Creek. These natives are descended from eight original couples, who have given their names to the eight classes into which the tribe is now divided.

For simplicity's sake I will assume that in place of eight there were four original classes. This will illustrate the principle equally well, and be far less involved.

Let A, B, C, and D represent the names of the four classes — to one of which every native belongs.

1. The first law is that — Natives belonging to class A may only intermarry with class B, and natives belonging to C may only intermarry with class D.

2. The progeny of a man and woman of intermarrying classes is of a different class from either father or mother.

Thus a man of class B marries a woman of class A, but their offspring (male or female) is of class D.

Let Am represent a male of class A.

Let Af represent a female of class A, and similarly Bm, Bf, &c.

Let Ap represent progeny who belong to class A, and similarly Bp, Cp, Dp.

Law 2 may now be set down as under —

$$Af + Bm \quad Am + Bf \quad Cf + Dm \quad Cm + Df$$
$$\text{------- ------- ------- -------}$$
$$Dp \quad Cp \quad Bp \quad Ap$$

3. The first law holds good with the progeny of these combinations, i.e., Dp can only marry one of class C — though neither the father nor mother of Dp could marry into class C; similarly for Cp, &c.

4. Dp recognises as father or mother all members of classes A and B; similarly Cp, &c.

This explains the seeming absurdity of the answer one receives from natives to questions concerning their relationships to others. An old man, for instance, may point out a young girl and say, "That one my mother," for the girl belongs to the same class as his actual father or mother.

5. All the progeny of classes A and B are brothers and sisters; similarly C and D.

Thus taking Dp2 to represent the progeny of an Ap and a Bp

$$Af + Bm \quad Ap + Bp$$
$$\text{--------- --------}$$
$$Dp \quad Dp2$$

All of class Dp recognise class Dp2 (though of another generation) as brothers and sisters. For this reason there is no absurdity in a small boy pointing out a very aged woman as his sister.

6. A man may have as many wives as he can get, so long as these laws are adhered to.

Let us now see what degrees of kindred are prohibited by these laws.

Let us take the case of a man of class A. He can only marry a woman of class B, whose parents must therefore have belonged to classes C and D her mother being a C and her father a D.

Therefore his wife's mother and father belong to classes with which he may not intermarry.

Therefore a man may not marry —

His mother-in-law.

The sister of his wife's mother.

The sister of his wife's father.

Nor the sister of any one of the three.

Nor can he marry his sister.

But he may marry —

His wife's sisters (sisters by blood or tribal class).

And as far as I can see, no law prevents a man from marrying his grandmother should he so desire.

Part VI: The Journey Home

Chapter II: Sturt Creek and "Gregory's Salt See"

The Sturt Creek presents many points of interest. It rises in the Northern Territory, runs for nearly three hundred miles in a South-Westerly direction, and comes to an end in a large salt-lake, across the border, in the desert. It runs throughout its entire length once in every three or four years, though each yearly rainy season floods it in certain parts. In the dry season one might in many places ride right across its course without being aware of it. In the wet season such parts of it are swamps and marshes, over which its waters spread to a width of five and six miles. Permanent pools are numerous, and occur wherever a ridge of sandstone rock runs across the course of the creek. On either side of the creek fine grass-plains spread East and West. The further South the creek goes, the less good is the country on the East side; presently there is no grass country except on the West side. Not far below the station the creek is joined by the Wolf, which, like all Kimberley creeks, is fringed with gums, Bauhinia, and Leichardt-trees. From the confluence downwards a war between the grass-lands and the desert is waged for the supremacy of the river-banks. For miles the sandy channel, cut out like a large drain through the country, less than one chain wide in places, is hemmed in on either side by desert gums and spinifex, and once out of sight of the creek the surrounding land receives no benefit from the water.

But lower down again, about the latitude of Mount Mueller, the grass plains gain the day; and a very pretty bit of country they form too, especially when the creek is running, as it was when we were there. In many places its waters had overflowed the banks, expanding into clay-pans and lagoons of beautiful clear water where teal and whistling duck disported themselves.

The Wolf rises on the opposite slope of the watershed to Christmas Creek and the Mary River, and floods twice or thrice a year. Below its junction with the Sturt the combined creek takes on itself the character of the Wolf, and at the point of confluence the Sturt may be said to end. Seeing how seldom the Sturt runs its entire length and how small its channel is at this point, smaller than that of the Wolf, I think that it is to the latter that the lakes (Gregory's "Salt Sea") chiefly owe their existence. However that may be, the combined waters fill but an insignificant channel and one can hardly credit that this creek has a length of nearly three hundred miles.

On nearing the lakes the creek assumes so dismal an appearance, and so funereal is the aspect of the dead scrub and dark tops of the "boree" (a kind of mulga), that one wonders that Gregory did not choose the name of "Dead" instead of merely "Salt Sea." A curious point about this lower part of the creek is, that stretches of fresh and salt water alternate. The stream, as we saw it, was only just running in the lower reaches; in places it ran under the sandy bed, and in this part the salt pools occurred. First we passed a stretch of clear, brackish water, then a nearly dry reach of sand, then a trickle of fresh water lasting for a hundred yards or so; this would again disappear, and be seen lower down as another salt pool.

The creek enters the first lake in a broad estuary; this lake is some four miles long by two miles wide, lying North and South. At the southern end a narrow channel, 150 yards wide, winds its way into the large lake beyond, a fine sheet of water, eight miles in diameter. A narrow belt of open country, overgrown with succulent herbage, fringes the margin of the lake; beyond it is dense scrub, with occasional patches of grass; beyond that, sand, sandhills, and spinifex. In the distance can be seen flat-topped hills and bluffs, and rising ground which encloses the hollow of the lake. The lake has no outlet; of this Gregory satisfied himself by making a complete circuit of it. At the time of his discovery the lakes were dry, or nearly so, and doubtless had the appearance of being shallow depressions, such as the salt lakes in the southern part of the Colony; so that having followed the Sturt for so many miles — a creek which showed every appearance of occasionally flooding to a width of five or six miles — he must have been somewhat uncertain as to what happened to so great a volume of water. However, the lake is nearly thirty feet deep in the middle, and, from its area, is capable of holding a vast amount of water. The creek, below its confluence with the Wolf, is continually losing its waters, throwing off arms and billabongs, especially to the west, which form swamps, clay-pans, and lagoons. So much water is wasted in this manner that near the entrance into the lake the creek is of a most insignificant size. The fall, too, is so gradual that the water runs sluggishly and has time to soak away into the enclosing sand.

Mr. Stretch tells me that it takes eight days for the water from rain falling at the head of the Sturt to pass his homestead, which gives it a rate of one mile per hour. Heavy rains had fallen at its source about a month before our arrival, and the water was still flowing. We therefore saw the lakes as full as they are ever likely to be, except in abnormal seasons. North of the lake are numerous large clay-pans which had not been flooded, and the lakes could evidently hold more water, and had done so in time past, so that it is pretty clear that the lakes are large enough for ordinary flood waters, and, with the outlying clay-pans, can accommodate the waters of an extraordinary flood.

I feel confident, therefore, that no outlet exists, and that beyond doubt the Sturt ends at the Salt Sea, and does not "make" again further South, as some have suggested. Standing on any of the hills which surround the lake, some distance (ten miles or so) from it, one can look down upon the water, certainly five hundred feet below the level of the hills, which rise no more than eighty feet above the surrounding plain. It seems most improbable, therefore, that a creek should break its way through country of so much greater altitude without being seen by Colonel Warburton or myself, or that any connection should exist between the Salt Sea and Warburton's Salt Lakes to the South-East.

Had, however, the intervening country been of the same level as the lake, and flat instead of formed into high sand ridges and hills, there might have been a possibility of crossing a connecting creek of the same character as the Sturt without noticing it. This question has been much discussed by gentlemen interested in the geography of interior Australia, and therefore I have dealt with it at some length.

Part VI: The Journey Home

Chapter III: Our Camp on the "Salt Sea"

April 2nd to 7th we were the guests of Mr. Stretch, and whilst resting here Godfrey's eyes soon became well enough to allow him to travel. On the 7th, therefore, we set forth on our journey and bade adieu to the last outpost of civilisation in the North. Our party was further increased by a Sturt Creek boy, Tiger by name — a very smart and intelligent fellow of whom Mr. Stretch was very glad to see the last, for smart boys are nearly always the most mischievous amongst the cattle. Warri and Tiger were great friends, and the new boy's presence put Warri on his mettle, and no amount of work was too hard for him whilst he had Tiger to show off to. After I had cut his hair and shampooed his head with kerosene and soap, dressed him in trousers, shirt, and cap, he looked a most presentable youth.

Mr. Stretch accompanied us down the creek for the first few days, during which we passed some of his cattle and horses. The flies and mosquitoes worry the poor beasts terribly, and all day long the horses stand in the water in pairs, or in a line, with head to tail, each one flicking the flies from his neighbour's face with his tail. This habit of standing up to the girth in water has given rise to a horse sickness known as "swamp-cancer." The skin under the belly becomes so soft that at last a raw place is formed, and this, aggravated by the flies, spreads until it becomes a serious disease. Another horse-sickness common in the North is called the "Puffs." A horse suffering from this pants and blows after the least exertion, and in the hot weather his skin becomes puffy, and any violent exercise would be fatal. The Monk, one of our horses, suffered from this slightly; as soon, however, as we had left the Kimberley district and entered the desert he recovered entirely. Numerous small families of natives were camped along the creek, all accompanied by dogs, which gave us some annoyance at night; for salt meat, at first, should be hung out during the night to get the benefit of the fresh air, and this roused their hungry instincts. A few miles below the Wolf, Mr. Stretch left us, and we parted from our kind host with regret — he to return to his cattle, and we to the task of laying bare the richness (we hoped) or the nakedness (we expected) of the untrodden land before us.

At first we did very small stages, for the joy of travelling alongside running water was too great to be quickly passed over. The camels and horses became good chums very soon, and played about together without any signs of fear or surprise on the part of the horses, although they had never seen camels before — a different state of affairs from that in Coolgardie, where horses as a rule snort and plunge with terror on first acquaintance with an "emu-brother," as the black-fellow calls the camel. As we neared the lakes we had some difficulty in finding water fit to drink, and camped about nine miles above the lakes, whilst Godfrey and I scouted ahead to see if fresh water could be found lower down. We surprised two camps of natives, most of whom ran into the scrub as we approached — several gins and a boy remaining. One of the women had a most remarkable baby, quite a small thing, but with a tremendous growth of black hair, shiny and straight, altogether different from the ordinary coarse hair of the aboriginal. They came with us, walking beside us as we rode, jabbering and gesticulating in their usual excited manner, and inviting us to their camp, pointing to the rising smoke. Water, however, was our requirement, so we continued on our way down the creek, the boy coming with us. We shot a few ducks which our young friend retrieved, and having found a reach of fresh water just above the first and smaller lake, returned campwards, surprising a hunting-party on our way; they retired quickly, the boy following them, taking with him the ducks which we had been at such pains to stalk!

A WILD ESCORT OF NEARLY ONE HUNDRED MEN.

A wild escort of nearly 100 men

The next day we moved camp to the fresh-water reach, and had not been travelling long before a small tribe of blacks came round us, quickly followed by our friends of the day before, and presently by more, until we were marching along with a wild escort of nearly a hundred, mostly men; they were fearfully excited, though quite friendly, and with yells and shouts danced alongside, waving their spears and other weapons. I never heard such a babel, or saw such frantic excitement about nothing, or at least nothing that we could understand. Their wildness was tempered with some fear of the camels, though with the horses they were quite familiar, even going so far as to hit poor old Highlander, that I was riding, on the rump with their spears, a proceeding that he did not approve of. "Womany," "Womany," "White-fella," "Womany," "White-fella," they kept on shouting; if they meant to call our attention to the beauties of their gins they might well have spared themselves the trouble, for a more hideous lot of females I never set eyes on. Presently another wild yell heralded the approach of a large band of "womany" who waded breast deep across the creek, followed by their dogs swimming behind. These were no improvement on the first lot; all the old and ugly ladies of the neighbouring tribes must have been gathered together. Their dogs however, were worthy of notice, for they were Manx-dogs, if such a word may be coined! Closer inspection showed that they were not as nature made them. For the tails of the dingoes the Government pays five shillings apiece; as their destructive habits amongst sheep make them better liked dead than alive. A black fellow's dog is much the same as a dingo — in fact must have descended from the wild dog — and has the same value in his owner's eyes with or without a tail. A stick of tobacco is fair payment for a dog's tail. Thus all parties are satisfied except the dog; and the Government is content to pay, not dreaming that "dog-stiffeners" (i.e., men who make a living by poisoning dingoes) carry on so base a trade as bartering tobacco for live dogs' tails!

Our cavalcade still further increased by women and dogs, we proceeded on our way, until choosing a high sandy bank overlooking the estuary of the small lake on the South, the creek to the North-West, and a backwater to the North, we halted and prepared to make camp. This was attended by some difficulty, for our native friends, now in considerable numbers, evidently wished to look upon it as their camp too. They soon became so tiresome that I had to tell them through Tiger, as interpreter, that unless they retired forthwith and kept to the other side of the creek, we should take strong measures to remove them. Before long they had all done as they were bid, and made their camp about a mile away across the water — and the bulk of them we did not see again. Small parties were continually visiting us, and we were the best of friends.

Our camp was in lat. 20 degrees 11 minutes long. 127 degrees 31 minutes, and here we stayed five days to give our stock a final rest, and regale on luscious food and abundant water, before tackling the dreary country that we knew to be before us. For our own sakes we were by no means keen on leaving this delightful spot; the very thought of those sand-ridges seemed to make one's heart sink to one's boots! Our camp consisted of a bough-shade, and mosquito-nets, of course. Barring the constant torment of flies and the extreme heat, we had a most enjoyable time. The lakes and creek abounded in wild-fowl of all kinds, and fish by the hundred could be caught below our camp. Seen from our camp the estuary had so much the appearance of a low-lying arm of the sea, with the tide out, that we could easily understand why Gregory called it a "sea" rather than a lake. Numerous sandspits stand out in the middle, on which, in early morning, so dense was the crowd of shags, pelicans, snipe, small gulls, whistling duck, teal, and other birds, that to say that there was acre upon acre of wild-fowl would not be wide of the mark; but in spite of their abundance they were not easily shot; for not only did their numbers insure the watchfulness of some of the flocks, but after the first shot the whole lot rose in a cloud and settled away out in the middle of the lake, beyond reach.

Our larder was well filled here, and the natives took great interest in our shooting and fishing. I used to take Tiger as retriever when I went duck shooting, and an excellent boy he was too, simply loving the water, and able to swim like any duck; to see him after a wounded bird was most exciting; as soon as he reached it, it would dive until he would be almost exhausted. At last he hit upon a similar plan, and, diving, came up beneath the duck, seized it by the leg and brought it to shore, grinning with delight. A shot-gun would indeed be a treasure to these natives, who manage to kill pelicans and ducks only after hours of waiting, hidden in a hide of bushes until a bird comes near enough to be killed by a throwing-stick.

In some parts of Australia the natives swim out to ducks, concealing themselves under a bunch of rushes and moving very slowly; the ducks are not scared by the rushes, and fall a comparatively easy prey. From what Tiger told me the Sturt natives seem to rely solely upon waiting and stalking. They catch fish in a rather ingenious way, only practicable when the fish are in shallow water; from this they sweep them with a sort of dredge of branches, which they drag through the pools on to the banks; the water runs back through the sticks, leaving the fish high and dry on the sand. The pelican is considered a great delicacy amongst the natives, and every day deputations waited upon us, asking us to shoot the "Coyas" for them, which of course we were very glad to do. They did not repay our kindness very nicely, for they tried to inveigle Warri into their camp for the purpose of killing him, as a stranger meets with no great hospitality! I had sent Warri and Tiger out with a gun to stalk some ducks when a number of blacks tried to get possession of the gun, first by telling Tiger that they wanted to shoot an old man who had annoyed them, then by tempting him with descriptions of the beauties of their wives; but Warri was proof against all these blandishments — nor could they get the gun by force. I think Master Warri was quite glad to come quickly home, for he stood in some awe of the Kimberley natives; "Sulky fella," he called them.

One day a fresh mob of blacks came in; amongst them we recognised our old friends from Jew's Well. They as soon recognised us, and appeared tremendously pleased. The old Jew patted me, and grinned, and squirmed in a most ludicrous way; I discovered that he was thanking me for having cured his son's eyes — so the lotion had done its work well. As he and his friends sat round I made a sketch of the old man and gave it to him; it was evidently a good likeness, for his friends went into shrieks of laughter and delight. He was equally pleased, and more so still when I let him know that he could keep it.

Shortly afterwards several men came up with great mystery and secrecy, and many looks behind them to see that they were not watched, and a greybeard amongst them presented me with a flat stick carved all over into rough patterns; this was carefully wrapped between two sheets of bark, and was evidently highly treasured, and given as a mark of respect or gratitude for curing the boy's eyes. They also gave me throwing sticks, balls of hair string, a shield and tomahawk; and received numerous costly presents from us — one or two old shirts, strips of coloured handkerchief to make sporrans of, a knife or two, and so forth, and were perfectly satisfied. A curious thing about the old Jew was that he had no name. I questioned him most closely through Tiger — but no! he had never had a name. He was promptly christened "Jacob," which he repeated over and over again, and seemed pleased with his new acquisition. Godfrey soon had some of the tribe trained in the art of fishing, and this amused them immensely; the man to whom we gave the line and hooks, which we got in Hall's Creek, will be much envied by his mates. There were quantities of mussels in the creek, which the blacks devour greedily; we thought them most disgusting in taste. Larger fish were reported in the big lake, but we did not trouble them. The water of the big lake was far too salt for use, though the natives were camped near it and drink it. It makes them sick, but they use it all the same, so we were told. What happens to all the natives when the lake dries I cannot say; no doubt they scatter far and wide, and meet when the floods come down, for ceremonies, corroborees, and such-like amusements.

I collected a few words which I look upon as reliable. Nothing would be easier than to make a whole dictionary, for the natives are always ready to talk, but I have only taken words which I got from one and tested with others with good results.

English   Aboriginal Gregory's "Salt Sea." Burro. Fresh water. Nappa or Yui. Salt water. Murraba.* Creek. Gilli. Fire. Warru or Wallu.** Fish. Yagu. Mussel. Bimbirri. Pelican. Coya. Whistling duck. Chibilu.*** Moon. Yungun. Star. Gigi. Southern Cross. Wun-num.   * Hunt's Slate Well, near Lake Lefroy, Coolgardie Goldfield, which is sometimes salt, is called by the natives Murrabi.

** Same as at Empress Spring and throughout desert.

*** In imitation of the bird's cry.

Part VI: The Journey Home

Chapter IV: Desert Once More

April 20th we left our camp on the lake, steering due East to cut a creek which enters on the North-East corner; the creek was dry, and the nature of its shingly bed inclined me to think that it has its rise in auriferous country. Close by the creek we found a shallow clay-pan, and as the next day would probably see us in the desert I had every available water-carrying vessel filled. Tiger worked well, but a friend of his, who had come with us so far, watched the proceedings with suspicion. On being questioned as to waters to the South-East, he was most positive as to their non-existence, and evidently frightened Tiger so much by his dreadful account of the country that he decided on returning home — for the next morning both he and his friend had disappeared. I was very sorry, for he was a smart lad, and now we were a bit short-handed. Pursuit was of course useless, for he had too great a start, and would soon be lost amongst his tribesmen. He had worked so well that I never suspected him of wishing to go. I fear he will spear Mr. Stretch's cattle after all!

Fully loaded with water, we left the lakes, steering towards Mount Wilson (Gregory); the heat was great, and the flies worse than we had before experienced.

Riding ahead steering was most unpleasant; one hand for the compass, one for the bridle, left nothing with which to frighten the flies from the corners of my eyes, which became quite raw in consequence. Certainly riding is a great improvement on walking, and I prayed that the horses would long be spared to us. Once through the dense scrub surrounding the lake, and our old friends sand and spinifex lay before us. Crossing an open plain, we reached Mount Wilson, from which the lake was plainly visible, at a greatly lower level. This hill is the highest in a little broken range of barren sandstone hills, peaks, knobs, and cliffs of all manner of shapes and sizes. To the eastward stony tablelands can be seen, running from which I noticed what I took to be a creek.

At this point it is interesting to see what Gregory's impressions were of the country ahead. This was the furthest point he reached in 1856, having landed an expedition on the Northern coast and travelled up the Victoria River on to the head-waters of the Sturt Creek, and down that creek to its end. He says:—

"From the summit of the hill (Mount Wilson) nothing was visible but one unbounded waste of sandy ridges and low, rocky hills, which lay to the South-East of the hill. All was one impenetrable desert; . . . the vegetation on this part of the country was reduced to a few stunted gums, hakea bushes, and Triodia (spinifex), the whole extremely barren in appearance. . . The remaining portion of the horizon was one even, straight line: not a hill or break of any kind, and except the narrow line of the creek, was barren and worthless in the extreme, the red soil of the level portions of the surface being partially clothed with Triodia and a few small trees, or rather bushes, rendering the long, straight ridges of fiery-red, drifting sand more conspicuous." So Gregory retraced his tracks up the Sturt Creek, and when one remembers that he had horses, one can only say, "And a good judge too."

Leaving Mount Wilson we steered East and cut the creek that I had seen, and were glad to find feed near it for both horses and camels. I walked it up to its head, and found a little rocky pool of water, returning after dark. Breaden and Warri had been out too, but found nothing. Having watered the animals, next morning, the 22nd, I steered a course to take us through a piece of country previously traversed by Warburton, with Lake White (a dry salt-lake) as our goal, for round it I hoped to find creeks and clay-pans. I depended on none of Warburton's waters, though he had some marked on his chart, since I knew that doubts existed as to the accuracy of his positions, and I preferred to rely upon our own methods of finding water rather than to waste time in hunting for wells that we might not find. For the next few days we were crossing spinifex plains and passing distant hills and tablelands of sandstone. The days were very hot, but since rising from the hollow of the lake the nights had become very much cooler. We had come so suddenly into desert country that the animals gave us great trouble, being unable, poor things, to find any food. Late starts were the order of the day, camels having wandered miles in one direction followed by Breaden and Warri, and the horses in another followed by me.

On the 23rd we found ourselves again amongst the sand ridges, high, red, and steep; we were now in lat. 20 degrees 30 minutes, and from that date and point this awful country continued almost without a break, ridge succeeding ridge with perfect regularity and running, as before, dead across our route, until we reached lat. 24 degrees 45 minutes on June 2nd — a period of forty one days, during which we travelled 451 miles. Thus it will be seen that in the far eastern portion of the Colony the ridges of drift-sand extend over a greater length of country than in the centre; and consequently our return journey was accomplished with greater difficulties before us, and with an almost total lack of feed for our stock — less even than on the first trip but to balance these drawbacks we had cool nights, lighter equipment, and the advantage of previous experience — and the incentive of knowing that our rations would not last out unless we made all speed.

On the 24th we crossed a range of barren hills, which I named the Gordon Hills, after our friends of Flora Valley. In the neighbourhood Godfrey picked up a perfectly white egg, somewhat resembling that of an emu, which lay upon a hummock of spinifex; presumably it had been bleached by the sun. From the hills to the S.S.W., across high ridges of sand, can be seen a range apparently of some altitude, distant some twenty-five miles; this I named the Stretch Range, after our kind host of Denison Downs Station. From the Gordon Hills we continued on our course for a smoke we had sighted the day before, and before long picked up two fresh tracks, which we followed. From some stony rises a large, prominent hill came into view, as if formed of three great steps of bare rock. This I named Mount Elphinstone, after my cousin, and towards it we shaped our course, still on the tracks.

That night we were again forced to camp on a barren spot, and again our animals wandered far afield. Unless absolutely necessary, I have a great objection to tying them up at nights, for then they are sure beyond question of getting nothing to eat; whereas wandering they may find a patch of herbage or bushes. That night we saw the fire of a native camp and heard distant screams. In the morning a mob of blacks passed our camp all unaware of our presence; Breaden and Warri were hunting the camels and I the horses. As soon as I brought them in we followed and stopped some of the natives, and they returned with us to camp and presently decoyed others who were passing.

There was nothing remarkable about these savages except that they were tall and well-made and fairly friendly. One had the skin disease from which we had noticed others suffering. An old man, and a young, rather handsome, buck came with us and went ahead as guides. Their camp had been, as is the rule, on the top of a sand-ridge — chosen, no doubt, as a position suitable for watching the approach of others. A four-mile stage brought us to a nice little oasis — a small area of grass, surrounded by ti-trees, enclosed by two sand-ridges. In the centre of the grass three good soaks, in black, sandy soil, yielded sufficient for all our needs at the expenditure of but little labour. The horses appreciated the change, and unless we had given them water in instalments would have assuredly burst themselves. They drank in all sixteen gallons apiece! Seeing that they had never been in anything but good country all their lives, and that now we had suddenly come out of it into the howling waste, they showed satisfactory endurance, having been eighty hours with only six gallons of water each during that time. What English thoroughbred could have done this?

The next day Breaden and I rode up to Mount Elphinstone, which we found to be formed of three great rocky shoulders of sandstone capped with quartzite, almost bare, and stony on the top, with sheer faces one hundred feet high on the West side and a gradual slope to the East, where high sand-ridges run right up to the foot. From the summit a high tableland [Probably Musgrave Range (Warburton)] and range can be seen to the North, to the East a bluff-ended tableland, [Probably Philipson Range (Warburton)] but the horizon from South-East to South-West was a dead level.

One mile due West of the highest point we found a native well in a sandy gutter, and about 150 yards from it, to the East, a high wall of bare rock as regular as if it had been built. This wall, seen edge-on from the North-West, from which point Breaden sighted it when after the camels, appears like a chimney-stack.

As the soaks at which we were camped have the appearance of being more permanent than the usual native well, it may be useful to give directions for finding them from Mount Elphinstone. Leave hill on bearing 230 degrees, cross one sand-ridge close to hills, then spinifex plain, then another sand-ridge running East and West, from the crest of which can be seen three gaps in the next one — steer for most Westerly gap, and seven miles from the hill the soaks will be found. Having no time for further investigation, we returned to camp, and to ensure an early start tied the camels down for the night, since they had been feeding all day. Bluey again proved to be a vicious brute, and kicked me in the chest, knocking me down; but the other new camels daily improved in their manners. We had great trouble in cleaning off from their backs the clay with which they were smeared, having rolled in some shallow clay-pans near the lakes. It was most necessary to scrape it off somehow, as otherwise sore backs would have resulted; and, indeed, Stoddy's sore back started in this way by the friction of the saddle and the caked mud.

The country ahead looked so bad that I decided to take the two bucks with us for as long as they knew the waters, so secured the one to the other by the neck, with plenty of spare chain between. They marched with us apparently perfectly happy, and even anxious to point out the directions of various native wells. My object was to make as much Southing as possible whilst we could; so having two natives and one hundred gallons of water (of which the horses were given three gallons each nightly), we steered due South from the soaks, and had a long day of tremendously steep sand-ridges, up the North side of which the camels climbed with difficulty. Riding the camels was out of the question, so we took the horses in turn, Breaden and I steering hour about. Though crossing fresh tracks and though the bucks were most anxious to follow them, we did not turn from our course, for we had only left water the day before, and as our rations were calculated to just, and only just, last out, no time could be wasted. For the same reason we were travelling longer hours.

Our camp of the 28th was in lat. 21 degrees 4 minutes long. 128 degrees 33 minutes, and ahead of us to the South-West three miles distant was a range of barren sandstone hills, for which we steered; the old man, though contradicted by the young one, promising "gilli nappa," or creek water. However, he fooled us, and after much climbing we reached a small, dry well in a narrow gorge, quite inaccessible for camels.

It was now the young man's turn, who, seeing that we were not best pleased with his mate's efforts, by every sort of sign assured us that water existed in another range to the East. So turning in that direction over monstrous high ridges, crossing them obliquely, in five miles we cut a small watercourse, and following it up to its head found ourselves on the top of a range of barren sandstone hills, over which were dotted white-stemmed stunted gums — a most desolate place. The travelling was very trying to the camels, who were continually missing their footing on loose boulders and stones, in the bed of the creek. Sheer steps in the rock on either hand precluded us from marching over the hills, excepting up the watercourse.

From the summit, other similar hills could be seen to the East — hills of quite a respectable height, all bare and rocky. Numerous small gorges and glens head from the East watershed; without any hesitation our guides started down one, and before long we came to a little pool in the rocky bed. Here we watered our animals and replenished our tanks and bags; and a nice job we had to make some of the camels approach the pool; on either side were steep cliffs, and to reach the water numerous cracks and gaps in the bed-rock had to be crossed, not wide or deep, but sufficiently so to scare Bluey and some of the others. The open desert life seems to make camels, and horses too, very nervous when anything the least unusual has to be faced. The echoes amongst the rocks, and the rather gloomy gorges, seemed to make them "jumpy"; a stone rattling down behind them would be sufficient to cause a panic. Leaving the pool, we followed the gorge until it ran out as a deep, sandy channel down the valley formed by the horseshoe of the ranges. The ranges I named the Erica Ranges, after one of my sisters. All along the banks of the creek splendid green acacia and grass was growing, and a most inviting-looking plant standing some six feet high, with greenish-grey stems and leaves, and a flower not unlike wallflower. Such a place at once suggested camping, and we were proceeding to unload when Godfrey remarked that this pretty plant was very like a most deadly Queensland poison plant; he was not sure; I had never seen it before, nor had Breaden. The risk, however, was too great; it might be poison; I could see the camels eyeing its fresh charms, and it grew in such profusion that all would be devouring it in a few minutes. So we packed up again and moved further on, much to the disgust of the blacks and the animals, for all were very tired. I collected some specimens of this plant; if Godfrey had never been in Queensland we should have been in a tight corner, for the Government botanist, Perth, says,

"The plant in question is very poisonous. It is scientifically known as Gastrolobium grandiflorum*, occurs throughout the dry, tropical portion of Australia, and is commonly known as 'Desert poison,' 'Australian poison,' and 'Wallflower poison bush.'"* Near Mount Bannerman, where our camels were poisoned on the upgoing journey, this plant was not growing. The suspected plants I collected, but unfortunately the specimens were mislaid or lost. In such country as this one has one's whole mind and energies concentrated on how best to cover the ground; and what with well-digging, writing up field-books, observing, and so forth, one's time is fully occupied; I was therefore unable to collect more than a few plants worthy of notice, since they formed feed for camels, or caused their death. My companions were of course equally occupied. Besides the map I was able to make of the country, I set great store by my photographs. Of these I took over two hundred; owing, however, to defective plates, or rather films, many were failures, and nearly all that could be printed and reproduced are to be seen in this book.

On the 30th we followed down the creek until it bore too much to the West, and so far as we could see shortly ran out into the sand. From a high sandhill the next morning we got an extensive view. To the East, the main body of a long salt-lake extending as far as the eye can see to the S.S.E. Bounding the lake on the East is a high sandstone tableland, with abrupt cliffs facing the lake. Some eight miles to the North-East appears to be the extreme point of the lake, but of course from a distance it is impossible to say for certain. Except where the cliffs occur, the lake is enclosed by high red sandhills, through which it winds its way like a strip of sparkling white tinsel. Having no desire to court difficulties, I turned from this smooth-faced but treacherous bog, and, looking West, spied a fine bold range, a rugged-looking affair with peaks, bluffs, and pinnacles, suggesting gorges and water. I have no doubt that this lake is Lake White, of Warburton's, though my position for it is seventeen miles East of that assigned to it by him. It is in the same latitude, and agrees with Warburton's description as to the cliffs and sandhills.

After sighting this lake we turned West to the ranges, therefore had two lakes existed in this latitude we must have crossed the second, which we did not do. Many things go to prove that Warburton's positions are incorrect; I think I can show how, by moving his route bodily on the chart about eighteen miles to the East, a more accurate map will result. My own experience alone would not be conclusive, except that my work fits in with that of Forrest, Gregory, and Tietkens, where my route crosses theirs; but taken in conjunction with others it proves of value. In crossing the Colony, Warburton failed to connect with Gregory's traverse at the end of the Sturt as he intended, and on approaching his destination (the Oakover River) expressed surprise that he had not reached it a day or two before. Therefore he was not confident of the accuracy of his reckoning.

Two parties, one led by Mr. Buchanan, a noted bushman, another by Mr. Smith, set out from the end of the Sturt to cross the desert, made several unsuccessful attempts to locate some waters of Warburton's, though no distance away, and returned satisfied that nothing could be gained by further travelling. Mr. Smith told me that he had located "Bishop's Dell," but placed it due south of the Salt Sea instead of S.S.W, as shown by Warburton.

Mr. Wells eventually found Joanna Spring twenty miles East of Warburton's position. This correction is of greater value than any, since Mr. Wells is considered one of the best surveyors in the South Australian Service.

A combination of the above experiences shows, I think conclusively, that Colonel Warburton's route, at least on the West Australian side of the boundary, should be shifted bodily eighteen or twenty miles to the Eastward.

Considering the hard trials that Colonel Warburton and his party went through, there is small wonder that he found great difficulty in keeping any sort of reckoning.

From the journal of this traveller I take the following description of the country round the lake:

"We found good feed for the camels here, but the sandhills appear to be increasing in number and size. We have got amongst the half-dried salt lagoons, so our further progress North-West is cut off... we are quite amongst the salt-lakes, a large one lies to the West of us, sending out its arms to every point. We must round the eastern end of them, as camels and salt-bogs don't agree at all... We tried to cross but had to turn back... Country very bad, dense spinifex, high, steep sand-ridges with timber in flats. Any man attempting to cross this country with horses must perish... A strong easterly wind prevailed, blowing up clouds of sand and ashes from the burnt ground. Truly this is a desert!" This was written when I was two and a half years old. The writer little thought that an infant was growing up who would have no more sense than to revisit this ghastly region; nor as far as I remember was the infant thinking much about sand! Dear me! how easy it was to get a drink in those days — merely by yelling for it — but the strongest lungs in the world cannot dig out a native well.

Part VI: The Journey Home

Chapter V: Stansmore Range to Lake Macdonald

Shaping our course from the lake (Lake White) towards the highest point in the range, which I named Stansmore Range after poor Charlie, we had the novel and pleasant experience of travelling with, instead of across, the ridges — if only we could have turned the country round at right angles, or changed the North point of the compass, how nice it would have been! As it was, South we must go to get home, and take the ridges as they came; our Westerly course was only temporary. For twenty-seven miles we steered W.b.S., keeping along the trough of two ridges the whole time, seeing nothing on either hand but a high bank of sand covered with the usual vegetation. The trough was flat at the bottom, and about 150 yards wide. For ten miles we travelled between the same two parallel ridges, then in front the butt-end of another appeared, as the trough widened out. Deviating slightly to the South from our former course, we were again between two ridges, one of which was the same that we had followed along before. Then, again, in a few miles another ridge would start, and altering our course again, this time a little to the North, continued our march between two fresh ridges, and so on. Thus it will be seen that the ridges, though apparently parallel, are not accurately so, and that one may be continuous for more than ten miles or so, when it ends and another takes its place.

On our march our captives cleverly caught a spinifex rat and a snake (one of the very few that we saw); they greedily devoured both, and were much pleased when Godfrey refused to partake of a piece of half-raw snake which they politely offered him. We discovered that they had a great liking for our beef-water — that is, the water in which our salt beef had been cooked — and made no bones about swallowing a couple of gallons of this brine-like soup. It had one good effect, for it made them most anxious to take us to water the next morning! The hills we found to be of the usual character, barren sandstone, from which numerous rocky creeks have torn their way through the sand. Following up a little glen, terribly rough and steep for the camels, we came at length to a fine pool, hemmed in by almost sheer cliffs sixty feet high. Climbing to the top of these, I could see that the same rough country extended for a considerable distance to the westward, and that further travel up the glen was impossible; so we retraced our steps down the creek, on the banks of which we found grass and bushes in profusion, and poison plant. This drove us away into the sandhills beyond all harm, and, unfortunately, beyond all feed as well, nor had we time before night set in to cut and carry any bushes for the camels, as we might otherwise have done.

That night our camp was in lat. 21 degrees 25 minutes, long. 128 degrees 20 minutes. The following morning I ascended the highest point in the range, whilst Breaden and Warri took our animals for a final drink up the glen. The lake was just visible, lit up by the rising sun, but I doubt if during the day it could be seen. From the range numerous creeks, nine in all, run Eastwards, one of which, I think, reaches the lake, as with field-glass I could follow a serpentine line of gum trees. The rest run out a few miles from their head on to grass-flats timbered with large gums. The hills are of sandstone in layers, dipping to the West; these seem to have been forced up into three-cornered blocks, the faces of which have weathered away on the East side, forming steep slopes of stones and boulders. Between the hills low ridges of sandstone running North and South outcrop only a few feet above the surface, and are separated by strips of white sand timbered with stunted gum trees. The whole scene has a most strange and desolate appearance.

Returned to camp, I liberated the two guides, for I did not wish to inconvenience them by taking them beyond their own country. They were quite unwilling to go, and indeed waited until we were ready to start, and were most anxious for us to go to the East again. "Gilli nappa," they assured us, was to be found, making their meaning clear by tracing in the sand a winding line to represent a creek; and when at the end I drew a lake, they were highly pleased, and grunted and snapped their fingers in approval. However, when I showed them that we were going due South their faces assumed so dismal an expression, and so vehement were their exhortations to go in the other direction, that we concluded we had no picnic before us. Had they had any intentions of coming further our change of course decided them, and they made tracks for the glen, bearing with them many rich gifts. An empty meat tin and a few nails does not sound a very great reward for their enforced services, and yet they would have been far less pleased with a handful of sovereigns; they could put these to no use whatever, whereas the tins will make small "coolimans," and the nails, set in spinifex-gum on the end of a waddy, will find their way into a neighbour's head.

We had really terrible country that day, during which we made no more than nine miles. At first travelling was easy, as a flat belt of sand came between the range and the sandhills; later on, however, we were forced to climb up and down, now mountainous sandhills over one hundred feet in height, now jagged hills and breakaways of sandstone; dodging down little steep gullies, with the camels' packs almost touching each side, up steep rocks, or along their faces, until the horses and camels alike were quite exhausted. Fortunately we were rewarded by a fair camp for feed, close by a noticeable bluff. We crossed nine deep creeks, in any of which, at their heads, pools may exist.

Climbing the bluff next morning, I could see that the range curved round to the South-East for some miles, possibly a great many. To continue following round the foot would advance us but little; I therefore decided to cross the range somehow. It was evident that any great extent of this rocky country would soon place the camels HORS DE COMBAT, as every step cut their feet, and every few minutes they ran the risk of a sprained or broken limb; mules would be more suitable for such country. The further we advanced the rougher became the ground, the narrower the little glens, and the steeper the rocks. However, one final and tremendous scramble landed us all safely above the hills, and to our joy we found that a flat plain of spinifex spread before us. On it were clumps of mulga. Now we hoped we had done with the ridges. But no! more yet, in spite of hopes and prayers, and for the next two days we were crossing them at the rate of eighty-eight per eight hours. It really was most trying, and had a very bad effect on one's temper. I fancy my companions had the same difficulty, but I found it nearly impossible to restrain myself from breaking out into blind rages about nothing in particular. But the cursed sand-ridges made one half silly and inclined to shake one's fist in impotent rage at the howling desolation. Often I used to go away from camp in the evening, and sit silent and alone, and battle with the devil of evil temper within me. Breaden has told me that he had the same trouble, and Godfrey had fearful pains in his head to bear. The combination of heat, flies, sand, solitude, the sight of famished horses, spinifex, and everlasting ridges, and the knowledge that the next day would be a repetition of the day before, was enough to try the sweetest temper; and I, for one, never professed to have such a thing. Added to this we had the feeling that our work and energies could have but a negative result — that is, the proof that the country was barren and useless; and yet its very uselessness made it harder to travel through. But with all this we never had a complaint or growl from any in the camp. About this time I again became deaf, which did not tend to make me any more patient.

Another stretch of plain country, a mile or two in width, again raised our hopes and again dashed them, as more ridges confronted us on the other side. A change of any kind is welcome, therefore the gloomy desert oaks were greeted with joy; for though their sombre appearance is eminently appropriate to a funeral procession, they give some shade and relieve the eye. In due course we reached the burnt country for which we had steered, and, after hours of tracking, singled out some footsteps going straight away as if to camp. Warri and I were leading, riding Highlander in turn; on cresting a high ridge we saw before us a little clump of mulga and grass, amongst it a camp of some dozen or more natives. As soon as we advanced they all ran, except two men, who stood their ground for a short space, then, throwing a stick and boomerang in a most warlike way, they followed their tribe. It was imperative that we should have a fresh guide, so I followed on Highlander, and succeeded in stopping the last man simply by wearing him out. He was a most diminutive man, almost a dwarf, absolutely without ornament, not even a girdle of string, with a most repulsive face, and wall-eyes like a Welsh sheepdog. He was by no means afraid, and before long became friendly and returned with me to their camp.

The tribe had left behind them a number of treasures — bundles of firemaking sticks, bean-and-gum ornaments, and the usual bark "portmanteaus"* containing hair-string, feathers, red ochre, and other knick-knacks. Amongst their weapons was a curiously shaped boomerang; on one of the woommeras was a rough carving of either a spider or crab. As soon as the camels arrived we unloaded and set to work on the well, "soak-sucking" in our old style. By morning we had watered the camels and horses. The former were of course pretty fit, but the poor ponies had done a fair stage, especially so since they had had no feed except the rank dry tops of the spinifex. May 3rd sunrise, to May 8th sunrise, they had travelled on what water we could afford them from our own supply, viz., three gallons apiece nightly, and six gallons the first night. The grass around the well, though dry, was of great benefit to them. For the camels we had to cut down the mulga trees, the branches of which grew too high from the ground to permit them to browse off the leaves. A number of dingoes serenaded us as we worked at night; what they live upon is not quite clear, unless it be spinifex rats. There were other small rats in the locality, two of which the dwarf had for supper — plucked, warmed upon the ashes, torn in pieces by his long nails and eaten; an unpleasant meal to witness, and the partaker of it badly needed a finger-bowl, for his hands and beard were smeared with blood. He did not take kindly to salt beef, for his teeth were not fit for hard work, as he pointed out to us; and salt beef is not by any means easy to masticate. As a rule the blacks have such splendid teeth that the dwarf's case is remarkable, seeing that he was not at all an old man.

*Note: A native bark "portmanteau," brought back from this locality, was opened at Newstead Abbey and found to contain —

Plumes of hawks' and crows' feathers.

Neck-bands of opossum wool.

String bracelets.

Fragments of quartz, suitable for spear and chisel heads.

Fragments of sandstone, for making red paint.

Message-stick.

A stick 12 inches long, wrapped in downy feathers and greasy string; on this was wound a great length of human-hair string, forming a bobbin-shaped article, the use of which I do not know. I have now three portmanteaus still unopened.

The Dwarf Well had a better supply than any we had seen, and it is possible that there is some soakage into it from the surrounding country. It lies nearly five miles south of a low range of hills, the highest point of which bears 1 degree from it; to the North a sand-ridge, to the South a spinifex plain, six miles wide, then more ridges. I make its position to be lat. 22 degrees 19 minutes, long. 128 degrees 16 minutes. On the plain to the south are one or two small outcrops of ironstone and quartz, sticking up out of the sand, as if some hills other than sandstone had existed, and become buried by the all-spreading sand. I carved C on a tall mulga-tree close to the well.

May 9th we left the well on a Southerly course, and were soon amongst the ridges, which continued for the next two days. The night of the 11th, having skirted a line of rough cliffs, we camped about three miles North of a very prominent single hill, which I named Mount Webb, after W. F. Webb, Esq., of Newstead Abbey, Nottinghamshire. As the sun rose that morning the mirage of a lake of apparently great size was visible for 90 degrees of the horizon — that is, from East round to South. Neither from the cliffs that we skirted, nor from Mount Webb, was any lake visible, but it is more than probable that a large salt lake exists in this locality, possibly connecting, in a broken line, Lake White and Lake Macdonald. A mirage sometimes appears in exactly the opposite direction from that in which the lake lies, but I noticed when standing on the Stansmore Range that as the sun rose Lake White was clearly visible, whilst when the sun had risen a few degrees above the horizon the lake disappeared. I am of opinion, therefore, that large lakes will some day be found to lie to the North-East of Mount Webb. Had we not been so pressed for time I should have made a flying trip in this direction. Mount Webb is flat-topped, isolated, rocky-sided, innocent of all vegetation, of sandstone capped with quartzite, standing out with imposing clearness some five hundred feet above a plain of spinifex and mulga scrubs. From its summit numerous hills and bluffs can be seen; to the South spinifex plains and ridges; to the South-East a tabletop between two bluffs; to the West a low line of stony hills, beyond them a limitless sea of sandhills; to the North-West a broken range of peaks, and, far distant, a large hill swaying in the haze of heat.

From the foot of the hill a hunting-fire was seen close by. "Gabbi, gabbi," said the dwarf, greatly excited; and when we turned towards it "Yo-yo-yo" in approval. As we silently approached we saw two old hags flitting about, as nimbly as their aged limbs would allow, in the blazing spinifex — now picking up a dead lizard, and now poking about with their yam-sticks as if in search of some rat which had been roasted in his burrow. It is impossible to describe the look of terrific awe on the faces of these quaint savages. Let us imagine our own feelings on being, without warning, confronted by a caravan of strange prehistoric monsters; imagine an Easter holiday tripper surrounded by the fearful beasts at the Crystal Palace suddenly brought to life! What piercing shrieks they gave forth, as, leaving their hunting implements, they raced away, to drop, all at once, behind a low bush, where, like the ostrich, they hid their heads, and so hoped to escape detection.

It was almost impossible to gain the confidence of the gins: old ladies seem so very suspicious. The dwarf somewhat reassured them, and after much difficulty one was persuaded to show their camp — and such a camp! — perched up in the rocks on a little plot of sand, close by a miniature watercourse, and in this a small native well, so rock-bound as to preclude further opening out. And yet for this miserable affair we were glad to offer up thanks, for the sake of the ponies. What labour for a few gallons of water, not so much as we use in our baths every morning in civilised countries! But no man could stand idly by and watch the mute longing of his faithful horses. So freeing the dwarf and the old gin, a fit pair, we set to work. All that afternoon and all through the night we dug and hauled and scraped, and by morning had the horses watered and twenty gallons to boot. There had been eight or nine blacks at this camp, who, on their return from hunting in the evening, watched our proceedings with intense annoyance. They stopped about one hundred yards away, and, yelling and shrieking, brandished their spears in a most warlike manner.

That night they camped not far off, and, as on every other occasion on which we invaded their homes, I consider we owed our immunity from attack to the fact that work on the well entailed one or other of the party being up all through the night, thus acting as a watch. Had they known their power they might have made things most unpleasant by spearing our camels. Fortunately it is only those natives who have come within the civilising influence of the white man, that learn such little acts of courtesy. It is noticeable that amongst the treasures in this camp were a great quantity of "letter-sticks," which is evidence that the carvings on letter-sticks cannot be written messages, unless this camp was a desert post-office! If, however, the sticks are tokens, as I suppose, then one of this tribe may be a craftsman who carves distinctive symbols on each stick to order, and who had lately received a number of commissions for such sticks. It seems likely that one man or tribe should have a special aptitude for manufacturing message-sticks, whilst others perhaps make a speciality of hair-string or spears. Or again it may be that the number of sticks, certainly two dozen, denote orders from far-off tribes, who wish to barter such articles as pearl-shells for perhaps spinifex-gum of a superfine quality. (I have noticed that the spinifex growing on the sandstone hills, particularly on the Stansmore Range, exudes a great deal more resin than that growing on the sand.) This bartering of goods is very remarkable, and here we found pearl oyster-shells which must have passed from tribe to tribe for at least five hundred miles; pieces of glass, carefully protected by covers of woven feathers and opossum-string; the red beans which are found in Kimberley, and, as Warri tells me, in the MacDonnell Ranges of Central Australia; a stone tomahawk-head, a dark green stone (serpentine); and besides, numerous sporrans of rats' tails, feathers, nose bones, red ochre, and a piece of the top part of a human skull polished and slung on a string. Certainly for its size this was the best appointed tribe we had seen.

The position of this well, a very poor one, is lat. 22 degrees 57 minutes, long. 128 degrees 20 minutes — one mile West of Mount Webb.

Some good grass grows in the mulga scrubs which are dotted over the plain surrounding the hill. Nine miles south of the Mount, sand-ridges, East and West as usual, are again met with; from the crest of one we saw the last of Mount Webb, twenty-two miles distant. We now hourly expected to get a view of Lake Macdonald, a large dry salt lake discovered by Tietkens in 1889. Tietkens was Giles's right-hand man in all, or nearly all, his journeys — a man whose great services to his country have never been acknowledged, because, I suppose, as second in command his name seldom appeared in the accounts of his leader's travels, and yet he shared his dangers and troubles, stood by him in many tight corners, helped him no doubt with counsel and advice; and though by his work — for Tietkens was an eminent surveyor — many hundreds of miles of previously unknown regions have been mapped, a grateful country has nothing to give in return! We all know, though, how generous Governments are in such matters. Did not Ernest Giles die, only the other day, in poverty and neglect? I know he had a Government billet at 2 pounds 10 shillings a week, noble and generous reward for the best years of his life spent in toiling over the howling wilderness of the interior! Doubtless all debts will be considered paid by the erection of a statue, and nine people out of ten will not have any notion of who the man was or what he has done! Tietkens in 1889 led an expedition to determine the true extent of Lake Amadeus, the confines of which were marked as "probable." His work resulted in greatly decreasing the area of the lake, which now lies entirely in South Australia. However, this side of the border he found the lake already mentioned, and, encircling it, returned to the point on the Adelaide-Port-Darwin telegraph line from which he had started.

The lake is surrounded, at a distance, by numerous sandstone ranges and hills, the drainage from them no doubt forming it. Tietkens experienced rains in this region; no such luck fell our way, and everything was parched and drought-stricken. I was able to identify the Winnecke Hills, and one or two others, but, having only a small map of this part of the country, could not locate many points.

Close to the Winnecke Hills we again surprised two gins hunting, and, amongst their spoils of the chase, were astonished to see a common domestic black cat, evidently just killed. It must have wandered far from home! One of the women took us to their camp and small well, which was in so awkward a situation that I decided not to do any work upon it. Its position was in a very steep, narrow gorge in the sandstone, along which the camels could pass with difficulty. There was no feed for our animals, except at the mouth of the gorge a mile distant, and then there was but little. It would take three to work the well, leaving only one to look after the camp, and "tail" the horses and camels. Since the supply was problematical, the well almost inaccessible, and waste of time the only likely result, we passed on — the one and only occasion on which we left a well untried. Numerous natives must have been in this camp, for I found no less than thirteen bark "portmanteaus." As the gin had shown us the well without demur, I left all these untouched. It was a struggle between honesty and curiosity; but it seemed too mean to take things, however interesting, when they had been left so confidently unprotected. And yet birds' nests are robbed without any such scruples! I had no hesitation, though, in taking the gin with us, in spite of her unwillingness, for famished horses must be relieved. Once across the hills the sand-ridges became less high, were dotted with oaks, and even had some herbage growing on them.

Part VI: The Journey Home

Chapter VI: Lake Macdonald to the Deep Rock-Holes

On the 16th we had breakfast by moonlight, and were well on our way before daylight. From a ridge higher than the others we got the only glimpse of the lake that was permitted us by the sandhills. About two o'clock, the gin, who had been making towards the Davenport Hills (Tietkens), suddenly turned off and brought us to a little well in the trough of two ridges — the usual wretched concern, yielding no more than three bucketsful. We worked far into the night. Having to observe for latitude I stayed up last, and baled the well before going to rest, leaving about two gallons in the bottom to allow it to settle before morning. At daylight we heard loud howls and snarls coming apparently from the centre of the earth. Further investigation disclosed a lean and fierce-looking dingo down our well, which, in its frantic struggles to get out, had covered up our little pool of water and made a horrible mess of things. I never saw so savage-looking a brute, and, not feeling called upon to assist it, I ended its troubles with a bullet — a kindly act, which doubtless, on their return, gave a welcome supply of cheap meat to the tribe who had only lately retired from the well, and also added to our small store of dingo-tails, which (at 5 shillings each), so far as we could see, would be our only means of deriving any profit from our labours. I think we only got five, and they were lost!

Our position there was lat. 23 degrees 26 minutes, long. 128 degrees 42 minutes. The gin on showing us the well had been at once liberated, a step which I now rather regretted — but one cannot be unkind to ladies, even though they are black, naked savages, little better than beasts! Remembering that she had pointed towards the hills ahead, I steered on that course, and before long we came on the tracks of a man, woman, and child, walking in the same direction. Here I saw a pure white spinifex rat, leaping the tussocks in front of me, but of course had no means of stopping it.

All that day we followed the tracks, over sandhills, samphire-flats, through clumps of desert oak, past dry wells, from sunrise until sunset. Warri and I were ahead for in tracking it is better to be well in advance — riding and walking in turn until Highlander knocked up and had to be led. Breaden and Godfrey had awful work behind to get the camels along. At almost every sandhill one or other of them, usually Bluey, would drop and refuse to budge an inch until forced by blows. How the poor brutes strain, and strain again, up the steep, sandy slopes; painful sight, heart-breaking work — but work done!

We crossed the Davenport Hills shortly before sunset and waited on the other side for the main party, in case in the bad light and on the hard rocks our tracks should be missed. As they came up, we heard a distant call — a gin's — and presently the smoke from a fire was visible. The Monk had done the least work that day, and was the staunchest horse, indeed the only one capable of more than walking, so I despatched Godfrey to surprise the camp, whilst we followed. He rode right on to the tribe, and was accorded a warmish welcome, one buck casting his spear with great promptitude. Luckily his aim was poor and the spear passed by Godfrey's head.

When we arrived on the scene I found Godfrey standing sentinel beneath a tree, in the branches of which stood at bay a savage of fine proportions. He had a magnificent beard, dark brown piercing eyes, splendid teeth, a distinctly Jewish profile, and no decorations or scars on his chest or body. I shall not forget the colour of his eyes nor their fierce glitter, for I climbed the tree after him, he trying to prevent my ascent by blows from a short, heavy stick which I wrested from him, and then with broken branches of dead mulga, with which he struck my head and hands unmercifully, alternately beating me and prodding me in the face, narrowly missing my eyes. If he suffered any inconvenience by being kept captive afterwards, he well repaid himself beforehand by the unpleasant time he gave me. And if it was high-handed treatment to capture unoffending aboriginals, we did not do so without a certain amount of risk to ourselves; personally I would far sooner lie down all night chained by the ankle to a tree, than have my head and knuckles laid bare by blows from dead branches!

After a time I succeeded in securing one end of the chain round the wild man's ankle, and the other round a lower branch. Then I came down and left him, whilst we unloaded and had something to eat. We had had a long day of over ten hours continuous travel, and as the sun had long set we decided to take no steps for water-getting until morning. Being sure of soon getting a fresh supply, we gave what water we had to the horses, on whom the desert was rapidly leaving its mark. As we sat on the packs round the tree, eating our salt beef, our black friend, with evident wonder at our want of watchfulness, took the opportunity of coming quickly to the ground, only to find that he was tethered to the tree. His anger had now subsided, and, though refusing to make friends, he seemed grateful when I bound up a place on his arm, where he had been hurt in his descent from the tree. The spears of his tribe were of better manufacture than those of the ordinary desert man, having bone barbs lashed on with sinews. The next morning we moved camp, as, from our position in a hollow, we should have been at a great disadvantage had the tribe returned to rescue their mate. We found their well, a deep rock-hole, half filled in with sand, on the southern slope of a stony sandhill, situated in a small patch of grass and buck-bush. From the hill above the rock-hole, a prominent bare range of red rock can be seen to the South bearing 172 degrees to the highest point (these are probably the Warman Rocks of Tietkens). We were now within seven miles of the imaginary line forming the boundary between West and South Australia, the nearest point to that Colony our journeyings took us.

ESTABLISHING FRIENDLY RELATIONS.   Establishing friendly relations

At first we hoped the hole would prove to be a soakage, but in this we were disappointed, and had to resort to our old methods of box-sinking and clearing out the sand. Our work at first was comparatively easy, but as soon as water-level was reached a great wedge of sand fell in, and nothing remained but to clear out the whole of the cavity, scraping up the water as we went lower. From 7.30 a.m. on the 18th, until 2 a.m. on the 19th, then again from 6.30 a.m. until 4.30 p.m. on the same day, we slaved away with no more than one and a half hours' interval.

After digging out the sand and hauling it in buckets to the surface we had a rock-hole nearly conical in shape, twenty-five feet deep, twenty feet by fifteen at the mouth, narrowing in on all sides to three feet in diameter at the bottom. The first day and night we laboured until we literally could no longer move, from sheer exhaustion. Breaden was so cramped and cold, from a long spell in the wet sand below, that we had to haul him out, put him in his blankets, and pile them upon him, though the night was warm. The result of all this toil — not quite ninety gallons of far from pure water! What a country! one ceaseless battle for water, which at whatever cost one is only too thankful to get! Of the ninety gallons, sixty were distributed amongst the horses and camels, the remainder we kept for our own use and that of the horses when we continued our journey. Eight miles of sandhills on the 20th took us, under the native's guidance, to another rock-hole — full to the brim — its water protected from the sun by an overhanging ledge of rock.

Here we soon had the thirsty animals satisfied, and had time to consider the rather comical aspect of affairs from the black-fellow's point of view. How he must have laughed to himself as he watched us toiling away, coaxing out water drop by drop the days before, when all the time a plentiful supply was close at hand! Excellent grass surrounds the rock-hole, enclosed by mulga thickets, so we rested here a day, shooting a few pigeons and enjoying the first proper wash since April 25th, when we last camped at a good water. Whilst travelling, of course no water for washing could be afforded, as every pint was of some service to the horses.

This rock-hole is in lat. 23 degrees 44 minutes, long. 128 degrees 52 minutes. On May 22nd we continued our journey, marching South over irregular sandhills, forcing our way through scrubs, until, on the evening of the 23rd, we were in the latitude of the centre of Lake Amadeus, as it was formerly marked by Giles. I was anxious to see if Tietkens had perhaps passed between two lakes, leaving an unnoticed lake on his left. We now altered our course to the West, sighting a large bare hill some forty miles distant, which I take to be Mount Skene (Giles). This hill is close to the high ranges, the Petermann and others, and it would have simplified our journey to have turned to them, where good waters are known to exist, but I desired to see what secrets unknown country might hold, even though it might be only sandhills.

This proved to be the case, and during the next six days we crossed the most barren wilderness it had been our lot to see, not a bite of food for camels or horses, who, poor brutes, turned in despair to the spinifex and munched its prickly spines — not a living thing, no sign of life, except on two occasions. The first when, at the beginning of the stage, we captured a young gin, whom I soon released for several reasons, not the least important of which, was that Warri was inclined to fall a victim to her charms, for she was by no means ill-looking. The second living thing we saw was a snake, which we killed; how it came to inhabit so dry a region I cannot say. Now that our course was Westerly, we had expected to run between the ridges, but no such luck attended us. True, we marched between the SAND-ridges, but every now and again a ridge of ROCK running exactly across our course had to be negotiated. Yet further, and sandhills thrown up in any irregular order impeded us, then loose sand; everywhere spinifex, without even its accustomed top-growth, drought, and desolation! Native tracks were very scarce, even old ones; some of these we followed, only to find *dry* rock-holes and wells at the end of them.

THE TAIL-END OF A MISERABLE CARAVAN.

The tail-end of a miserable caravan

We were all walking again now, ploughing our way through the sand, men and camels alike exhausted, and the poor ponies bringing up the rear, the tail-end of a miserable caravan. And they, following behind, were a useless burden; we could not ride them, and yet for their sakes our supply of water became less and less; we denied ourselves beef (which meant at least a bucketful of water to boil out the salt) to keep them alive; poor faithful things, none but curs could desert them while life to move was left in their bodies. On the night of the 29th, for our own safety, I could allow them no water, for so great had been the drain that our tanks had but a few gallons left. The next was a day of disappointments. All day we followed the same two tracks, from rock-hole to rock-hole — all were dry as the sandstone in which Nature had placed them. We could see where the blacks had scraped out the sand at the bottom — if *they* could not find water, what chance had we? But every step took us closer — that is the great consolation in such cases. First, have perfect faith that water will eventually be found, then each forward move becomes easy, for you know that you are so much nearer relief. Every dry hole gives a greater chance that the next will be full.

Near one hole we came on a ceremonial or dancing ground — that is, a cleared space in the mulga scrub, circular in shape, with a cleanly swept floor, trodden down by many feet. In the centre stood a sort of altar of branches and twigs. It was evident that the blacks had danced round and round this, though for what purpose I cannot say.

As the sun set our faith was rewarded; before us in an outcrop surrounded by mulga lay two fine rock-holes with an ample supply. What a blessed relief! In a few minutes the horses were gorged, and hard at work on the rough grass near the holes. Hardy horses, indeed! Eight days from drink to drink (not counting what we gave them), and hardly a scrap of feed.

We took a two days' rest for the sake of the grass, and varied our daily fare of salt beef with small, tufted pigeons, which came in large numbers to drink. We shot nearly one hundred of them, and ate boiled pigeon three times a day with the voracity of black-fellows. Nor was Devil-devil forgotten in the feast; he had become an expert rider, and had a far better time than poor Val.

The curious fact of some rock-holes being full, whilst others a few miles off are empty, again exemplifies the very local character of such rain as visits these parts. The "Deep rock-holes," as we called them (in lat. 24 degrees 20 minutes, long. 127 degrees 20 minutes), are peculiar, for one is perfectly cylindrical, two feet six inches in diameter going down vertically to a depth of twenty feet; the other goes down straight for six feet, and then shelves away under the rock to a depth of at least twelve feet. It will be seen from our last few days' experience, and from that of the few days soon to follow, that in this region rock-holes are numerous. They are invariably situated on low surface outcrops of 'desert sandstone, surrounded by mulga and grass; beyond that, sand. I take it that they have been formed in the same way as the granite rock-holes in the south of the Colony — that is, by decay; that the whole country has been covered by a deposit of sand, borne by the winds, filling in former valleys and hollows, leaving only occasional patches of rock still visible. Their frequent occurrence would then be accounted for by the fact that the deposit of sand is shallower here than elsewhere. That it is so is pretty evident, for here the sand-ridges are much lower than further North, and still further South they disappear. Low cliffs are seen, and when the latitude of Forrest's route is reached, sandstone hills are numerous and rock-holes abundant. In the course of ages perhaps the sand will again be shifted until such reservoirs as the "Deep rock-holes" are filled in and hidden, or partially covered and converted by the natives into wells. Supposing a layer of sand to a depth of five or six feet could be thrown over the valley in which the Deep rock-holes are situated, the holes would at once be transformed into "Native Wells," the term "well" being a misnomer, and apt to suggest a copious supply to any unacquainted with the interior. I suppose that to the uninitiated no map is so misleading as that of West Australia, where lakes are salt-bogs without surface water, springs seldom run, and native "wells" are merely tiny holes in the rock, yielding from 0 to 200 gallons!

From our position at the rock-holes, by skirting, possibly without sighting, the end of the Rawlinson Range and steering nearly due South-West, we should hit off Woodhouse Lagoon of our upgoing journey. For simplicity in steering I chose a due South-West course, which should take us a few miles to the East of the lagoon, two hundred miles distant in a bee-line. I was anxious to see what water it held, and check my work by re-crossing our track of the previous year; and besides this, the lagoon lay on our most direct course for the nearest settlements, still 450 miles away on the chart.

Whilst resting at the rock-holes I took the opportunity of giving Bluey a lesson in manners, much to the entertainment of my companions.

Bluey was a brute of a camel, and used to give an immensity of trouble in the mornings, galloping off at full speed when he should have quietly waited to have his nose-line adjusted. Added to this, he would kick and strike with his fore-legs, so much so that none of us cared about catching him. One morning whilst Breaden was after the horses, I was helping Warri collect the camels, and tried my hand with Bluey. At the moment that I was putting the loop of his line on to the nose-peg, he reared up and struck me on the chest, his hobble-chain adding power to the blow, which sent me spinning on to my back. For this and other assaults I meant to punish him, so shortening his hobbles until his fore-legs were fastened with no more than an inch or two between, I armed myself with a stout stick. As I had expected, as soon as I started to put on his nose-line, off he went as hard as he could, jumping like a kangaroo, and I after him beating him the while. Round and round we went, the pace getting slower and slower, until, amidst shrieks of laughter and shouts of "The Leader wins!" "Bluey wins!" "Stick to it!" and so forth, from want of breath we came to a stop, and gazed at each other, unable to go further. It was a tough run, and, like a schoolmaster caning a small boy, I felt inclined to say, "Remember, my dear Bluey, it pains me as much as it does you."

The lesson had a most salutary effect, and never again did he gallop away when being caught in the morning, though he was not a well-behaved beast, and always the first to give in in the sandhills, even though carrying the lightest load. His good looks, however, were so much in his favour that subsequently a wily Afghan paid me a big price for him (comparatively), and winked to some fellow-countrymen as if he had got the best of "Eengleeshman." If he was satisfied, I am sure that I was.

Part VI: The Journey Home

Chapter VII: The Last of the Ridges of Drift Sand

On June 1st we left the rock-holes on a South-West course, crossing irregular sandhills with the usual vegetation.

On June 2nd we crossed the last sand-ridge of the great northern desert, and before us spread the rolling gravel-covered undulations of sand, treeless except for an occasional beefwood or small clump of mulga, rolling away before us like a swelling ocean. What a blessed relief it was after the awful toil of crossing Heaven knows how many sand-ridges day after day!

Taking into account the country north of lat. 24 degrees 45 minutes only — for though we had a long spell of sand-ridges between the edge of the desert and Woodhouse Lagoon, and again between that point and Lake Wells, yet these were comparatively low and less steep than those further north, and therefore their extent is not included in this reckoning — we traversed 420 miles on the upgoing journey, and 451 miles on the return journey — that is, 871 miles of actual travelling over a desert of sand blown by the wind into parallel ridges of the height and frequency already described. It will be readily understood, therefore, that we were not sorry to see the last of them! Working our way step by step, we had so husbanded the marvellous powers of endurance of our camels that, in spite of the most terrible privations and difficulties, these noble animals had silently carried their loads day by day, up and down, over the burning sand, maddened by flies, their legs worn bare by spinifex — carried them not without great sufferings and narrow escapes from death, but yet without one of their number succumbing to the horrors of the region. Accident and poison had carried off four. And now, alas! another was to meet the same fate. Poor Satan, my faithful companion in good times and bad, whose soft velvet nose had so often rubbed my cheek in friendship, was laid low by the deadly wallflower. In spite of all we could do for him, in spite of coaxing him yard by yard, Warri and I — as we had done to Misery before — for a day's march of over fifteen miles, we were forced to leave him to die. We could not afford to wait a day, always onward must it be until another water is found, so, with a bullet through his head, I left him to find his way to the Happy Hunting-grounds where there are no native wells nor spinifex, only flowing rivers and groves of quondongs! All this about a camel — "a devil and an ostrich and an orphan child in one," as we have been told — but remember that often in the solitary bush one's animals are one's only companions, that on them one's life depends. How, then, could one fail to love them as friends and comrades?

Shortly after the scene of Satan's death the mulga clumps became greater in extent, until for half the day, and more, we wound our way through dense thickets. The further South we went the thicker they became, until all day long we marched through scrub, seeing no more than forty yards ahead, with packs, saddles, and clothes torn to pieces by dead and broken branches. We saw no smokes, no spinifex rats, no natives, no tracks but old ones, and these led us only to dry rock-holes. Time after time we followed recent tracks from hole to hole, and met with no success; sometimes we were just in time to be too late, and to see that the last drops had been scraped up by the natives!

On June 6th we followed a fresh track, and found a hole containing thirty gallons. June 7th and 8th, dense scrub. June 9th, open country, lake country, gum tree flats, and magnificent green feed, the first we had seen since leaving Sturt Creek. On our right high sandhills, whose butt-ends in the distance had the appearance of a range of hills; on our left thickets of mulga, and beyond, a sandstone range. Kangaroo tracks were numerous, but none very fresh; these and the number of birds gave us hopes of water. We must find some soon, or not one horse could survive. Poor ponies! they were as thin as rakes, famished and hollow-eyed, their ribs standing out like a skeleton's, a hat would almost hang on their hip-joints — a sorry spectacle! All day we searched in vain, the animals benefiting at least by the green herbage. Ours was a dismal camp now at nights. What little water we could spare to the horses was but as a drop in the ocean. All night long they shuffled about the camp, poking their noses into every pack, overturning dishes and buckets, and, finding nothing, stood with sinking heads as if in despair. Our water-casks had to be guarded, for in their extremity the horses could smell the water, and even went so far as to pull out the wooden bung, with their teeth! Warden, the small pony, was a special offender in this respect. It is quite startling to wake suddenly in the night and find a gaunt, ghost-like horse standing over one, slowly shaking his head from side to side, mournfully clanging his bell as if tolling for his own death. Then at other times one heard the three bells sounding further and further off. This meant a hasty putting on of boots and wakening a mate to stir up the fire and make it blaze; then, following the sound through the darkness, one came up with the deserters, shuffling along in single file, with heads to the ground, turning neither to right or left, just travelling straight away in any direction as fast as their hobbles allowed. Heaven knows how far they might go in a night unless stopped in time and dragged back to camp. Indeed blankets do not mean sleep, with dry horses in the camp!

On the 10th The Monk, our best horse, fell, and was dead in a minute — run down like a clock. The other two followed slowly behind. Presently. a salt-lake [This I named Lake Breaden], enclosed by sandhills, barred our way — a cheerful sight indeed! Hung up in its treacherous bogs, with nearly empty tanks, dying horses and tired camels, what chance had we? Speculation of this kind must not be indulged in; time enough to cry out when the troubles come. Providence was with us as guide, and across the lake we dodged from sand-spit to sand-spit until we had beaten it, and not one animal was bogged.

The night of the 10th our supply was down to three gallons. None could be spared for the horses now, none could be spared for beef-boiling, only a little for bread, and a drop each to drink. Every rock-hole we had seen — but one — was dry. Alexander Spring would be dry. We should have to make for the Empress Spring, fifty miles beyond. Every thing pointed to the probability of this sequence of events, therefore the greatest care must be exercised. The horses would die within a few miles, but the camels were still staunch in spite of the weakening effect of the sand-ridges, so there was no need for anxiety. Yet we could not help feeling anxious; one's nerves get shaky from constant wear and tear, from want of food and rest. We had been in infinitely worse positions than this; in fact, with health and strength and fresh camels no thought of danger would have been entertained, but it is a very different matter after months of constant strain on body and mind. Faith — that is the great thing, to possess — faith that all is for the best, and that all will "pan out" right in the end.

The days were closing in now, the nights were cold, so we were away before sunrise, and, leaving the rolling sand, came again into mulga thickets, with here and there a grassy flat, timbered with bloodwoods — the tail end of a creek no doubt rising in the sandstone cliffs we had seen ahead of us. Shortly after one o'clock a sight, that brought more joy to us than to any Robinson Crusoe, met our eyes — a track, a fresh footprint of a gin. Whether to follow it forward or back? That was the question. On this might hang more than the lives of the horses. In nine cases out of ten it is safer to follow them forward — this was the tenth! "Which way?" said Godfrey, who was steering. "Back," said I, for what reason I cannot say. So back we followed the lady to see where she had camped, twisting and turning, now losing her tracks, and, casting, finding them again, until we were ready to stamp with impatience and shout D — n the woman! why couldn't she walk straight? Two hours brought us our reward, when an opening in the scrub disclosed a deep-banked creek, fringed with white-stemmed gums, and, beyond, a fire and natives camped. They all ran, nor did we care, for water must be there. Glorious sight! a small and green-scummed puddle, nestling beneath the bank, enclosed by a bar of rock and the bed of shingle. Before many minutes we had the shovels at work, and, clearing away the shingle and sand, found a plentiful supply. All HAD ended well, and just in time to save the horses. Considering the want of feed, and the hardships they had already suffered, they had done a remarkable stage. A stage of eleven days (from the evening of May 31st to the evening of June 11th) — a distance of 160 miles on the map, and a good many more allowing for deviations, during which they had but little water. We had brought them through safely, but at the cost of how much trouble to ourselves may be judged from previous pages and the following figures. We left the Deep rock-holes with exactly 102 gallons of water; decrease by breaking through the scrub must have been considerable, as we had nearly thirty gallons of this amount in canvas bags.

Added to this must be the 30 gallons we got from the small rock-hole — that is, 132 gallons in all. Of this supply the horses had 6 gallons each the first night, 3 gallons each subsequently until the day The Monk died and their ration was stopped. From 132, we take 90 (the horses' share). This leaves 42 gallons for four men and a dog (which drinks as much as a man) for eleven days; this supply was used for washing (an item hardly appreciable), bread-making, drinking, and beef-boiling, the last the most ruinous item; for dry-salted beef is very salt indeed, and unless boiled thoroughly (it should be boiled in two waters) makes one fearfully thirsty. What would otherwise have been an easy task was made difficult and uncomfortable by the presence of the horses, but we were well rewarded by the satisfaction of seeing them alive at the finish.

Part VI: The Journey Home

Chapter VIII: Woodhouse Lagoon Revisited

June 12th, 13th, 14th, we rested at the welcome creek and had time to examine our surroundings. I made the position of our camp to be in lat. 26 degrees 0 minutes, long. 125 degrees 22 minutes, and marked a gum tree near it with C7. Therefore I concluded that this was the Blythe Creek, of Forrest; everything pointed to my conclusion being correct, excepting the failure to find Forrest's marked tree, and to locate his Sutherland Range. However, the bark might have grown over the marking on the tree — and several trees showed places where bark had been cut out by the natives for coolimans, and subsequently closed again — or the tree might have been burned, or blown down. As to the second, I am convinced that Forrest mistook the butt-ends of the sand-ridges cut off by Lake Breaden for a range of hills, for he only saw them from a distance. The creek heads in a broken sandstone range of tabletops and cliffs; from its head I sighted a peculiar peak, about nine miles distant, which I took to be Forrest's "Remarkable Peak," marked on his map. From the sketch that I made, Sir John recognised the peak at once. From the cliffs the sandhills round Lake Breaden look exactly like a range of hills "covered," as Forrest said, "with spinifex." Another proof of the non-existence of, at all events, the northern portion of the Sutherland Range, is afforded by Breaden's experience. As I have already stated, he accompanied Mr. Carr-Boyd on a prospecting trip along this part of Forrest's Route. From his diary I see that they passed about three miles North of Forrest's peak, which Breaden identified, though by Mr. Carr-Boyd's reckoning they should have been twenty miles from it. Travelling due West across the creek on which we were camped, they found a large clay-pan, and were then hourly expecting to cross the Sutherland Range. However, no range was seen, only high sandhills. That Breaden's reckoning was correct was soon proved, for he and I walked from our camp and six miles West found the big clay-pan and their camel tracks. The lagoon was dry, though they had found it full of water. It is clear, therefore, that the range exists only as sandhills, north of lat. 26 degrees 0 minutes. Numerous other creeks rise in the broken range, and no doubt their waters, after rain, find their way into Lake Breaden.

Our camp was on the longest of them, though others that I followed down were broader. Above our camp, that is to the South-East, a ledge of rock crossed the creek forming a deep little pool which would hold plenty of water. I much regretted being unable to find Forrest's tree — but a tree unless close to some landmark is not easily come upon — as at its foot he buried a bottle holding letters and his position for that camp.

We saw no more of the natives who had been camped on the creek, but left some articles that should be of great use to them. Everything of weight that was not absolutely necessary was left here, and this included a number of horseshoes.

On, the 15th we were ready to start, and marched on a West-South-West course until we should sight Mount Worsnop, and turn West to the Woodhouse Lagoon. A mile and a half from our camp we crossed another creek, and on its banks a tree marked G.H.S., and NARROO cut in the bark. Evidently the prospectors had been pushing out in our absence, or else it was another overland party from South Australia, for Forrest's route has become quite a fashionable track, some half-dozen parties having crossed the Colony in this latitude. On the next day we sighted Mount Worsnop from eight miles (from the East it is more prominent than from the South). This was a day of miracles! It *rained* — actually *rained*! The first rain we had seen in the interior — not a hard rain, but an all-day drizzle. How cold it made us, and how wet! — not that we minded that. But the winter was approaching, we were daily getting further south, and with our blood thin and poor, our clothes of the lightest and most ragged, accustomed to scorching heat, we felt the cold rain very much indeed. Our teeth chattered, and our hands were so numbed that at night we could hardly undo the straps and ropes of our loads. A cold night, accompanied by a heavy dew, followed the rain; and for the first time on either journey we pitched a tent. During this, Devil-devil, wet and shivering, sneaked into my blankets for warmth, for, as a rule, he slept outside, in a little nest I made for him in one of the camel saddles. Such sudden changes in temperature made any "Barcoo" sores most painful; but fortunately we had suffered comparatively little from this unpleasant disease. A beautiful sun dried and warmed us in the morning, and crossing a narrow salt-lake (probably a continuation of Lake Breaden), we reached our old friend Woodhouse Lagoon on June 17th, nearly a year having elapsed since our first visit, August 19th, in 1896.

We were disappointed, but not surprised, to find the lagoon nearly dry, holding no more than six inches of water in the deepest place. But curiously enough Alexander Spring, found dry before, was now brimful, evidently filled by the recent rain, which had not been heavy enough to fill the lagoon. Here we camped for two days, which we could ill afford, as already we had to cut down our rations, and before long our meals would dwindle to one instead of two a day. Godfrey's sickness necessitated a delay — he suffered from such fearful pains in his head, poor fellow! Often after a day's march he would collapse, and lie prone with his head nearly bursting from pain. A drink of strong tea would relieve him, but when water was scarce he had just to suffer.

I had a splendid chance of replenishing our larder, and, fool that I was, I missed it. I was riding The Warden to the spring, when a kangaroo popped up on his hind legs, and sat looking at me. The Warden would not keep still; the surprised kangaroo actually waited for me to dismount and aim my rifle, but just as I fired The Warden jerked my arm and I missed, and away bounded many a good meal — and with it the pony! So I continued my way on foot, and was rewarded by finding some interesting things. A big camp of natives had been here in our absence; near the spring in the scrub was a cleared corroboree ground, twenty feet by fifty yards, cleaned of all stones and enclosed by a fallen brush-fence (this older than the other work, showing this is a favourite meeting-place). At one end was a sort of altar of bushes, and hidden beneath them a long, carved board. This I took, and afterwards gave to Sir John Forrest. In every tree surrounding the clearing a stone was lodged in the forked branches.

The pile of stones on Mount Allott had not been touched, nor had my board been removed. On it I found an addition to my directions to the lagoon — an addition made by two prospectors, Swincer and Haden, who had been in this locality two months after our first visit. I did not meet either Mr. Swincer or Mr. Haden, but I heard that my board had been of great service to them, for without it they would not have known of the lagoon, where they camped some time. G.H.S. carved on a tree near the Blythe Creek was also due to them; I believe that was about their furthest point reached, from which they returned to Lake Darlot. On their return they depended on a water which failed them, and they had in consequence a narrow squeak for their lives. On nearing camp I met Breaden and Warri, who had started to track me up, for Warden's return with an empty saddle had caused a little anxiety.

I observed for latitude that night, and was pleased to find that my two positions for the lagoon agreed almost exactly, both in latitude and longitude — a very satisfactory result considering the distance we had travelled.

On the 20th we started again, steering a course a little South of West, my intention being to round the North end of Lake Wells, and cut the Bonython Creek, with the object of seeing if another oasis, on our suggested stock route from South Australia, could be found. It need hardly be said that any idea of a stock route from Hall's Creek is absolutely impracticable. Between Woodhouse Lagoon and Lake Wells the country consists of low sand-ridges, on which grows an abundance of acacia bushes and others suitable for camels, alternating with open spinifex plains, mulga scrubs in which good grass grows, and nearer the lagoon one or two small grass plains. All through cliffs and bluffs are met with, from which small creeks ending in a grassy avenue run; and, as Lake Wells is approached, table-topped hills and low ranges occur, and occasional flats of salt-bush country. We had no longer any difficulty with regard to water, the rain having left frequent puddles where any rocky or clayey ground was crossed. In the sand no water could be seen; indeed we had a sharp shower one morning, water was running down the slopes of sand, but half an hour afterwards no sign of it could be seen on the surface. On the 23rd we sighted, and steered for, a very prominent headland in a gap in a long range of cliffs. Sandhills abut right on to them, and dense scrub surrounds their foot. The headland, which I named Point Robert, after my brother, is of sandstone, and stands squarely and steep-cliffed above a stony slope of what resembles nothing so much as a huge heap of broken crockery.

We camped at the head of a little gorge that night, having found a rocky pool; the rain cleared off, out came the stars, and a sharp frost followed, the first of the year. The character of the country was extraordinarily patchy; after crossing ridges of sand, and then an open, stony plain, on the 25th we camped on a little flat of salt-bush and grass. Our position was lat. 26 degrees 20 minutes, long. 123 degrees 23 minutes, and seven miles to the North-West a flat-topped hill, at the end of a range, stood out noticeably above the horizon of scrub; this I named Mount Lancelot, after another brother. The next day it rained again, making the ground soft and slippery. In the evening, to our surprise and disgust, further passage that day was cut off by a salt swamp. Not wishing to get fixed in a lake during rain, we camped early, pitched our tent and hoped for the rain to stop — an unholy wish in this country, but salt-lakes are bad enough without rain! The next two days were spent in trying to find a crossing, for we found ourselves confronted by a series of swamps, samphire flats, and lake channels running away to the North as far as could be seen by field-glasses — a chain of lakes, hemmed in by sandhills, an unmarked arm of Lake Wells. If we could not cross here we might have to go seventy miles out of our way, round the South of Lake Wells, and then back to the Bonython.

Part VI: The Journey Home

Chapter IX: Across Lake Wells to Lake Darlot

Four attempted crossings ended in the hopeless bogging of horses and camels, entailing the carrying of loads and saddles. At last we could not get them to face the task at all; and small wonder, for floundering about in soft, sticky mud is at least unpleasant! I am pretty confident that we could have managed to get the camels through somehow, but the horses were far too weak to struggle. Poor old Highlander sank to his belly, struggled for a minute just long enough to get further engulfed, and then threw up the sponge and lay panting until we came to his rescue. We had a job to get him to the shore, and only succeeded by digging out two legs on one side, putting a rope round them, then the same on the other, and by violent efforts dragged him on to his side. Then, one at his head and the rest on his legs, we turned him over and over until we came on firmer ground, when we put the ropes on his legs again and by main force hauled him on his flank to the margin of the lake, where he lay half dead. The others fared but little better; it was evident that a crossing could not be effected except at the cost of the horses.

From a sandhill near our camp numerous hills could be seen, the more prominent of which I named. To the West-North-West a table-top hill (Mount Courtenay, after my brother-in-law) standing in front of a prominent tableland; to the northward Mount Lancelot; to the East-South-East a line of cliffs standing above stony rises, at the southern end a bluff point (Point Katharine, after my sister); and eight miles to the South-South-West, two flat-topped hills, close together — these I named Mount Dora and Mount Elisabeth after two of my sisters. Little did I think that I was never to see again the dear face of one of them! As a last hope, I and Breaden went across the lake to these hills to look for a break in the swamps. From Mount Elisabeth an extensive view can be obtained, but no signs of the lake coming to an end. From Mount Elisabeth, which, by the way, is of quartzite, I took the following bearings: Mount Courtenay 331 degrees, Mount Lancelot 23 degrees, Point Katharine, 78 degrees. To the West numerous broken tablelands can be seen, and the same to the South. Clearly there was no chance of crossing this lake or rounding it on the North, for the white streak of salt could be seen for miles and miles in that direction. There was nothing to be done but to skirt the edge of the lake, and if connected with Lake Wells to skirt that too, until a crossing could be found. So we loaded up and steered East and then South-East to round the swamps. Due West of Point Katharine, four miles distant, we found a large freshwater lagoon surrounded by stony banks and ridges. It contained only a few inches of water, but is capable of holding it to a depth of six feet. Beyond it is a stony cotton-bush flat, and on it numerous white clay-holes of water, almost hidden by the herbage.

Water-hens were so numerous that we could not pass by so good an opportunity, and camped early in consequence, spending the rest of the day in shooting these birds. The rest was a good thing for Breaden, too, who had been hurt by Kruger as he struggled in the salt-bog. The next morning we struck South, and by night found the lake again in our way. From a high bank of rocks and stones we could see the arm that had first blocked us, running round the foot of the hills and joining a larger lake which spread before us to the South. Across it some high, broken tablelands could be seen. There was no doubt from our position that this was Lake Wells, but I had expected to find a tableland (the Van Treuer of Wells) fringing the Northern shore. However, the Van Treuer does not run nearly so far East as Wells supposed when he sighted it from the South. No crossing could be effected yet, so the next day we continued along the margin of the lake, along a narrow strip of salt-bush country hemmed in between the lake and sandhills. On July 2nd we found the narrow place where Wells had crossed in 1892; the tracks of his camels were still visible in the soft ground. The crossing being narrow, and the bog shallow — no more than a few inches above a hard bed of rock — we had no trouble whatever.

We now followed the same course as Wells had done, passing Lyell-Brown Bluff — from which Mount Elisabeth bears 339 degrees — and Parson's Bluff, eventually striking the Bonython Creek. This, as described by Wells, is a flat, shallow, and, in places, but ill-defined watercourse. In it are one or two good deep pools, of which one is probably permanent. Fringing the banks is a narrow strip of salt-bush and grass; beyond that mulga and coarse grass. This narrow belt of good country continues down to the lake, and as we saw it just after the rain looked fresh and green. There is no extent, but sufficient to form a good resting-place for travelling stock. Some cattle-tracks of recent date were visible, a small wild herd of stragglers probably from the Gascoyne. Turkeys were seen in fair numbers, but they were the shyest birds I have ever come across — so much so that we never got a shot. The late rain had left so many pools and puddles that we had no chance of waiting for them at their watering-place. One of the wild cattle beasts, amongst which must be a bull, for we saw tracks of quite young calves, would have been very acceptable, for our meat had come to an end. In consequence we wasted no time in further examining the Bonython, but made tracks for Lake Darlot. The days were getting so short now that, in order to accomplish a good stage, we had to rise long before daylight and collect the camels and horses, following their tracks by means of a fire-stick. In this way we were enabled to get a start at sunrise, having breakfasted — in imagination!

Several parties of prospectors have been to Lake Wells, and at first we followed a regular pad; however, it did not seem to be going very direct, so we left it. Between Lake Wells and Lake Darlot — a distance of about 130 miles — the country consists of open mulga thickets with a coarse undergrowth of grass, alternating with spinifex desert and sand. Occasional low cliffs and ridges occur, and nearer Lake Darlot numerous ranges, from which the Erlistoun Creek takes its rise. Amongst these hills we saw the first auriferous country since leaving the vicinity of Hall's Creek, and in the Erlistoun the first permanent water (probably) since leaving the Sturt Creek, a distance of about 800 miles. A narrow belt of grass and salt-bush fringes the Erlistoun, and in the winter looks healthy and succulent; however, a few months soon alters that, and in the summer all is parched and yellow. How pleasant it was to see such country, after the dreary desert! Tracks and roads were now numerous as we approached civilisation. The same lake lay between us and the settlement that had caused Conley, Egan, and myself so much trouble in former days. Choosing the same narrow channel where I had formerly crossed, we managed very fairly well. Most of the camels bogged, but some did not, nor did the horses, and our loads now consisted of little else but the saddles, and were therefore no great weight to carry. The weather was lovely now, bright warm days and frosty nights; unfortunately this tends to sharpen the appetite, which we had small means of satisfying. For the last ten days we had had nothing but damper, and not much of that, on which we spread tinned milk which had previously been discarded as unfit for use, being dark brown instead of white, and almost solid. Nevertheless it was better than nothing; a ten hours' march, begun on an empty stomach, and finished on a slice of bread, cannot be indulged in for many days before it leaves its mark. We were not sorry, therefore, to reach Lake Darlot township on July 15th, and, choosing a nice spot, made camp. This day we saw the first white face since April 9th, and our journey was practically over.

The excellent feed growing all over the flats near Lake Darlot gave us a good opportunity of recruiting our animals' strength. For nearly a month we moved slowly about between Lake Darlot and Lawlers prospecting in a desultory sort of way. Our departure from the former place was deeply regretted — by the butcher, whose trade had increased by leaps and bounds during our stay. "I never see'd coves as could stack mutton like you chaps," he said, in satisfied wonder; "why, a whole blooming sheep don't seem to last you a day; can't ye stop until I get some bullocks up the track?" Certainly that was the best fresh mutton I have ever tasted, and no doubt we DID do our duty by it.

By degrees the camels fattened and fattened, until the combination of flesh and the hard muscles their work had formed, made it difficult to believe how great the trials were they had been through. The horses were also getting less like skeletons, though they take far longer than camels to regain their strength; as a rule, if they have been through great hardships they never do regain it and are, practically, useless afterwards. Stoddy, whose back had been bad, was also recovering — this the only sore back amongst them after so many miles of country well calculated to knock both packs and backs to pieces.

Part VI: The Journey Home

Chapter X: The End of the Expedition

By easy stages and frequent halts we eventually reached Coolgardie, after an absence of thirteen months. Of these, ten and a half months were occupied in travelling, during which we traversed a little over three thousand miles. Of this, 550 miles was traversed by roads and tracks, whilst the remainder was through country beyond the limits of any settlements.

Sources of Water Supply. Found on upgoing and return journeys between the limits of settlement. **Holding water. Nearly Dry. Quite Dry. Springs** 2 1 Helena, Empress and Alexander (Forrest). **Creeks** 9 * Including Christmas, Janet, Mary, Margaret, and Sturt in Kimberley; Blythe,+ Bonython,+ Erlistoun. **Clay-pans** 2 4 **Rocky pools in gorges** 8 ** **Rock-holes** 3 3 21 Of these 4 were completely drained, and 2 left with water. **Native Wells** 8 3 22 Of these 6 were completely drained, and 5 left with water.   *Numerous small dry watercourses were seen.

**Numerous dry pools in rocky gorges were seen.

+The only two in the desert area.

Table showing character and extent of country traversed. **Upgoing Journey   Return Journey   Total in Miles.   From edge of desert to Woodhouse Lagoon** 220 *Mixed country* including low sandhills, spinifex plain. Desert Gum flats with occasional scrubs and patches of grass **From Woodhouse Lagoon to edge of desert** 260 **From end of Sturt Creek to Gordon Hills** 50 530 **From Woodhouse Lagoon to Family Well** 370 *Undulating desert* of spinifex, stones, and gravel, with occasional scrubs. **From Deep Rock-holes to Woodhouse Lagoon** 210 580 **From Family Well to Mount Bannerman** 420 *Sand-ridges*. Desert of sand blown into parallel ridges running on an average course of East and West, varying in height from 20–100 feet. **From Gordon Hills to Deep Rock-holes** 450 870 **From Cutmore's Well to edge of desert** 100 *Country other than desert*, including open scrubs with grass, open grass plains, belts of grass fringing river banks, small oases, and hilly country. **From Mount Bannerman to Hall's Creek** 150 **From Hall's Creek to end of Sturt Creek** 160 **From edge of desert to Lake Darlot** 50 **Oases (Helena Spring, Woodhouse Lagoon, Lake Wells, &c.)** 10 470 2,450 * 550 By roads and tracks 3,000 **   * Of which 2,210 were through country unmapped except where routes of previous explorers were crossed. ** Total mileage in round numbers, taking into account all deviations.

From the above table it will be seen that the greater part of the interior of the Colony seen by us is absolutely useless to man or beast. It is possible that between the Lake Darlot goldfield and the 25th parallel of latitude isolated areas of auriferous country may be found, though nothing that we saw proves this to be likely; and I base my opinion only on the facts that quartz and ironstone are known to occur in the vicinity of Lake Augusta and the Warburton Range. It is also possible (and this I have already discussed) that a travelling route for stock may be formed from South Australia along the 26th parallel as far as Mounts Allott and Worsnop, and thence VIA Lake Wells and the Bonython Creek. to the Erlistoun Creek and Lake Darlot.

Failing either the finding of gold, or the formation of a stock route from oasis to oasis, I can see no use whatever to which this part of the interior can be put.

North of the 25th parallel the country is absolutely useless until the confines of the Kimberley district (about lat. 19 degrees) are reached. That a stock route through the desert is quite impracticable we have clearly demonstrated. Even supposing that there was any water supply, there is no feed; nothing but spinifex grows in more than wee patches at very long intervals. As any one who has followed me through this book can see, our water supply was most precarious, depending as we did upon rock-holes and native wells (which at any time may be found dry), and these yielded an only just sufficient quantity to keep no more than nine camels from dying for want of a drink — every well that we found, with the exception of one or two, was drained and left empty. Indeed on our two journeys there are only two watering-places on which I should care to depend, viz., the Empress Spring and Helena Spring. Throughout our journey we never once found water by chance — though chance took us to more than one dry hole — but found it only by systematic and patient work, involving many scores of miles of tracking, the capture of the wild aboriginals, and endless hours of manual labour. Without having resorted to these expedients I have no hesitation in saying that neither we nor the camels would be living today, for though without having done so, other parties have crossed as great an extent of arid country, it must be remembered that our journey was accomplished through infinitely worse country, and with a party exactly half as large as the smallest of the previous expeditions across the interior. Where, with a large number of camels, it would be possible to carry a great quantity of water and do long stages, using the water for camels as well as men, with a small number such tactics as going straight ahead, and trusting to luck, could only end in disaster.

It has been my fate, in all my exploration work, to find none but useless country, though when merely prospecting on the goldfields I have been more fortunate. So far, therefore, as being of benefit to mankind, my work has had no better result than to demonstrate to others, that part of the interior that may best be avoided. No mountain ranges, no rivers, no lakes, no pastoral lands, nor mineral districts has it brought to light; where the country was previously unknown it has proved only its nakedness; nevertheless I do not regret one penny of the cost or one minute of the troubles and labours entailed by it. Nor, I am confident, do my companions repine because they wasted so many months of their lives in such a howling wilderness. May good fortune attend them wherever they go; for they were brave and true men, and to them I once more express my feelings of thanks and gratitude for their untiring energy and help through all our journeyings. I verily believe that so large an extent of country, good or bad, has never been travelled through by a more cheerful party, or by one, the members of which were more in accord; and to the unanimity, and ready co-operation that prevailed throughout the camp, the successful issue of the expedition must in a large degree be ascribed.

Before leaving Coolgardie I had to perform the melancholy task of selling off my camels and all belongings. I have seldom felt anything so deeply as the breaking up of our little band, and the sale of my faithful animals. However, it was a matter of necessity, for much as I wished to pension off my favourites I was not in a position to do so, and eventually made my exit from the Colony in much the same state as that in which I arrived.

Before leaving for home I spent some time in Perth, where the Surveyor-General, Mr. Johnston, did all in his power to assist me in the preparation of plans and maps. These, together with all information I had gathered, I placed at the disposal of the Government, for which they were pleased to express many thanks. At a gathering in the Perth Town Hall, at which I was present on the day of my departure, Sir John Forrest, the Premier, proposed the toast of the guest and said many kind things, to which I replied:

"... I regret that I am only able to give such a bad report of the far interior of this Colony; but even so, and even though it has not been our fortune to discover any country useful either to the pastoralist or miner, yet I hope we have done good service in proving the nature of a large tract of country

previously unknown. Our late journey will, I think, give an answer to the oft-repeated question, "Does the gold-belt extend in a direct line from Coolgardie to Kimberley?" and the answer is in the negative. At least we have demonstrated the uselessness of any persons wasting their time and money in farther investigation of that desolate region. Such an expedition might be undertaken for pleasure, but this I should not recommend, for few countries present such difficulties of travel or such monotony of scenery or occupation. Although I am leaving this country, probably for good, I would not wish it to be thought that I have no faith in it, for the late developments and marvellous returns from the goldfields should convert the most sceptical. Nor have the other sources of wealth to the Colony failed to impress their importance on me... Every one is glad to return to his home, and I am no exception; but however happy I am at the prospect of again seeing my native land, yet I cannot say goodbye to the numerous friends I have been fortunate in making in this Colony without sincere feelings of regret. Every day the Old Country, which we are all proud to call Home, and the New are learning to understand each other better, and the bond of friendship between them is ever strengthening. If I have been able to promote these feelings in however small a degree, and have been able to show that the Home-born is still able, and willing, to take his share in the pioneer work of this continent of Australia, as his fathers were before him, then I have not worked in vain."

Appendix

The foregoing pages would, I fear, give the reader a very bad impression of the Colony of West Australia, until it was fully understood that my experiences relate solely to the interior and to that part of the interior the borders of which can only be reached by a journey of some four hundred miles by train from the coast — that part of the Colony, in fact, which lies to the East of longitude 121 degrees.

Now West Australia is so large that, despite the desert nature of so much of it, there still remain many thousand square miles of country suitable for settlement and rich in mineral wealth.

The settled portions show a picture the reverse of that I have been compelled to exhibit in the course of my travels.

The Colony altogether covers no less an area than 975,920 square miles, a little over eight times the area of Great Britain and Ireland. It occupies the whole of the continent West of the he 129th east meridian. In 1826 a party of soldiers and convicts formed the first settlement at King George's Sound. Three years later a settlement was established on the banks of the Swan River. From this modest beginning the progress of the settlement, which at first was slow in the extreme, came with a rush on the discovery of gold. The population of the Colony now exceeds 150,000 souls, and there can be no doubt that this population will be substantially added to annually, when the advantages which the country possesses, over and beyond its auriferous districts, come to be more generally known and recognised.

The progress of prosperity and civilisation undoubtedly runs parallel with railway progress, and since the Government of the Colony became autonomous that progress has been rapid. Seven years ago the total mileage was 193. There is now, as I write, a total length of 1,200 miles, 1,000 of which have been constructed during the past six years. Of these 1,200 miles, 923 belong to the State and the balance to a private company, whose line runs from Perth, along the coast northward, to the port of Geraldton. But though lines have been laid from Perth to Coolgardie, Kalgoorlie, and Cue, settlers are breaking ground farther afield, and further extensions both in the direction of the agricultural districts and of the goldfields are contemplated. The State railways, which may be looked upon as completely efficient, have paid, according to a statement in the West Australia year-book, a dividend of 11 1/2 per cent.

Although I have elsewhere described the primitive nature of the postal arrangements on the goldfields, it must be borne in mind that this relates to early days; now, the number of letters passing through the offices reaches 26,000,000; of newspapers, 17,000,000; while parcels to the extent of 5,000,000, and over a quarter of a million of postcards, and 1,000,000 telegrams were dispatched in one year, although the Postal Department all over the Colony is shockingly managed. There are no less than 5,429 miles of telegraph line open. The rapid increase displayed in these figures is the outcome, undoubtedly, of the gold discovery. The first official record of gold production was in 1886, when the yield for the six months ending that year was 302 oz., valued at 1,148 pounds. The yield for 1897 was over 700,000 oz., representing rather more than 2 1/4 millions sterling.

Owing to the "sporadic and pockety" nature of the finds it was at first supposed that gold would only be found in superficial deposits. This supposition has now been completely upset by the result of sinking operations at Kalgoorlie and elsewhere.

The richness of the Western Australian goldfields is established beyond the possibility of a doubt, and though over-capitalisation and want of proper management have had their customary ill-effects upon the industry, yet the undoubted and immense value of the auriferous yield should make the ultimate prosperity of the Colony a matter of certainty.

But the Colony does not rely alone upon its gold for prosperity. It has other and substantial sources of revenue in lead, copper, tin, coal, and timber, to say nothing of the excellence of the agricultural outlook.

The mineral district of Northampton, connected with the port of Geraldton by railway, is rich in lead and copper. Tin has been found in great quantity at Greenbushes in the South-West. Thirty years ago these districts were worked for their ores, but a great scarcity of labour, combined with a sudden fall in the prices of the metals, led to the abandonment of the mines. Since, however, the discovery of telluride ores at Kalgoorlie the abandoned lead and copper mines have recovered their old value, and many mining leases have quite recently been taken out in the Northampton district for the purpose of working them, and after the preliminary work of emptying the old shafts of the water which has accumulated, has been accomplished, there is every probability that smelting operations will yield a handsome profit. Coal has been found on the Collie River district and, tested by the Government, has been proved to be of good quality and to exist in seams varying from two to four feet in thickness.

The Government, by way of trial, raised 1,000 tons of coal at a cost of about 16 shillings per ton. The field is open to private enterprise, and as the land may be leased on the lowest possible terms there seems to be a good opening for the capitalist.

In considering other sources of revenue in the Colony I should be inclined to put that of the timber industry at the head, and this the more so that steps have been taken by the West Australian Government for the proper conservation, systematic working, and efficient replanting of the forest-lands. Hitherto in young colonies the disafforesting of districts has been for agricultural and other purposes recklessly proceeded with. Warned by example, the West Australian Government have taken steps for the preservation and utilisation of their valuable forest-lands. In 1895 Mr. J. Ednie-Brown was engaged by the Bureau of Agriculture to make a tour of inspection in the Colony. This gentleman having had experience as Conservator of Forests both in South Australia and New South Wales, was eminently fitted for his position as Conservator in West Australia. Having made his tour in 1896 he issued his report. It is to this report I am indebted for the information contained in this brief notice.

The principal commercial forests lie in the South-Western districts of the Colony.

Mr. Ednie-Brown gives a list of thirty-five varieties of indigenous forest-trees, but as only a certain number of them are known to be of real commercial value, I shall confine my remarks to the better known and more widely used species. These are: Jarrah (*Eucalyptus marginata*), Karri (*Eucalyptus diversicolor*), Tuart (*Eucalyptus gomphocephala*), Sandalwood (*Santalum cygnorum*).

In addition to these are many important but secondary forest-trees, as the Wattle (*Acacia saligna*), Raspberry Jam (*Acacia acuminata*), Badjong (*Acacia microbotrya*), Peppermint Tree (*Agonis flexuosa*), Banksias of all sorts — the Sheoaks (*Casuarina fraseriana, glauca* and *decaisneana*), the Red Gum (*Eucalyptus calophylla*), Wandoo (*Eucalyptus redunea*), Mallee (*Eucalyptus oleosa*).

There are many other trees of some value, but the foregoing represent the chief.

The total area of the principal forest regions of Western Australia covers no less than 20,400,000 acres, made up of: —

Jarrah 8,000,000 acres. Karri 1,200,000 Tuart 200,000 Wandoo 7,000,000 York Gum, Yate Sandalwood, and Jam 4,000,000 20,400,000 Jarrah is, without doubt, the principal forest-tree of Western Australia. This tree is dark grey in colour, with the bark strongly marked in deeply indented furrows. It grows on an average to a height of 90 to 120 feet, with stems 3 feet to 5 feet in diameter, running 50 to 60 feet to the first branch. There are, of course, very many larger individual specimens. The wood is red in colour, polishes well and works easily, and weighs when seasoned about 63 lbs. to the cubic foot. It is extensively used for wood-paving, piles, jetties, bridges, boat-building, furniture, and railway sleepers. It makes splendid charcoal, and when cut at the proper season exhibits remarkable durability both in the ground as fence-posts and in water.

Karri is the giant tree of West Australia. It is extremely graceful in appearance, with a yellowish-white smooth bark, which flakes off each year like that of our planes. The trees grow to a height of 200 feet, with a diameter of 4 feet at a height of 3 or 4 feet from the ground, and the first branch generally occurs at a height of 120 to 150 feet from the base. This tree does not occur in such numbers as the Jarrah, its field of growth being limited. Its timber resembles that of the Jarrah, but cannot be wrought so easily, though for purposes of street-paving it is superior. It is this wood which is so extensively used in London. It is also of value for bridge planking, shafts, spokes, felloes, waggon work, and beams.

File:Spinifex and Sand Illustration 46.jpg A karri timber train [Missing image]

Tuart is also comparatively limited in extent. It attains to a height of 100 to 150 feet, having a diameter of 7 to 9 feet at the base and about 40 feet to the first branch. Its timber is extraordinarily hard and tough and difficult to split. It is of great value as bridge supports, dock gates, stern posts, engine supports, &c., and it is also extensively used in the making of railway wagons and wheelwright's work generally.

Sandalwood, which is more of a bush than a tree, runs small as a rule. It is fairly distributed over the Colony. Formerly there was a greater trade in sandalwood than now; but the overstocked Chinese markets being sold out, the West Australia trade is rapidly reviving.

Raspberry Jam is a handsomely shaped rounded acacia, and gets its name from the scent of its wood, which is exactly that of the raspberry. An oil is extracted from the wood, which is highly perfumed. The wood is impervious to the attacks of the white ant.

In addition to these the Red Gum, the Wandoo, and York Gum are timber trees of value.

The total output of the saw-mills for 1895 was 130,000 loads, representing a gross value of 400,000 pounds.

It will thus be seen that the forests of the Colony form no inconsiderable portion of its wealth, and afford employment to large numbers of workers both in the forests themselves and in the saw-mills and wharves.

The culture of the vine and various fruits is carried on in the South-Western districts to a great extent — the soil, the climate, and the elevation all tending to give the best results.

The chief fruits grown are apples, pears, peaches, nectarines, plums, cherries, apricots, quinces, oranges, and lemons.

Viticulture forms a marked industry, though as yet largely undeveloped. There are 1,450 acres under cultivation, and this area is rapidly increasing. The slopes of the coastal ranges are admirably adapted for the culture of the vine, and the chief varieties grown are those most suitable for wine-making and for the table. Chasselas Doradillo, White Rice, Black Alicante, and Muscat of Alexandria are largely cultivated. There is, I conjecture, a good field open for the capitalist in the direction of the wine manufacture.

Pastoral and agricultural pursuits are carried on with success in many districts; agriculture is chiefly confined to the South-West corner of the Colony. Cattle, sheep, and horses are raised all along the coast-line from Albany to the De Grey, and in the far north, the Kimberley district.

The Nor'-West, however, labours under the disadvantage of drought on the one hand and floods on the other. There are several regulations governing land tenure, and when the emigrant has made a selection of the land suitable for his purpose (and in this he should exercise great care), he can get his land either as a free grant, or on lease, or by conditional purchase. On these points emigrants will be fully informed at the office of the Agent-General (Sir Malcolm Fraser, K.C.M.G.), 15 Victoria Street, Westminster, S.W.

There is no doubt that the soil of the S.W. district is fertile to a degree, and capable of supporting a large pastoral and agricultural population; and, as prices rule high, doubtless an emigrant suitable for either pursuit would find good remuneration for his capital and labour.

In addition to the foregoing industries, there is another of almost equal importance — that of the pearl and pearl-oyster fishery. Reports have been issued by piscicultural experts, proving the suitability of the coasts for the culture of the fish, and the matter has "come into official consideration"; and it is to be hoped that Government will take steps to foster this lucrative pursuit, the centres of which are at Shark's Bay, about two hundred miles North of Geraldton, and at Broome, yet further North. In 1896, twenty-one tons of mother-o'-pearl were exported at a net profit of about 40 pounds per ton. However, there is every reason to suppose that, properly and scientifically nurtured, pearl fishing should prove well worthy of attention.
 File:Spinifex and Sand Illustration 47.jpg A pearl shell station, Broome, N.W. Australia [Missing image]

Though I have come to the conclusion that, unless Spinifex and Sand can be conjured into valuable marketable products, the far interior of the Colony is worthless for any purpose, yet I have also shown that beyond the borders of the desert Nature smiles her brightest; and, given population, West Australia may well vie in wealth and usefulness with any of her sister colonies.

THE END